THE ROSECROSS

THE ROSECROSS

FRANCIS X. CAIAZZA

gatekeeper press™

Columbus, Ohio

The Rosecross
Published by Gatekeeper Press
2167 Stringtown Rd, Suite 109
Columbus, OH 43123-2989
www.GatekeeperPress.com

Library of Congress Control Number: 2021931038

ISBN (paperback): 9781662909733
eISBN: 9781662909740

FOR FELICIA

*His daughter captures his whole being.
Gently he holds her like the petal of a
precious flower. He's consumed by her
perfection.
A gentleness finds its way into his life that
only his daughter can find.*

I SHOULD HAVE KNOWN

I had never experienced a real tragedy until recently, until my mother was murdered. For more than a year, my father trapped me in the epilogue of his life. It was a twisted journey and along the way, he put me in touch with a menagerie of characters, some savory and some not, who were somehow connected to my mother's killing. For some reason, he picked me, his rebellious son, to solve a mystery the police had blundered badly. Indeed, it was a strange bequest, but, then again, my father was a peculiar man. My assigned task was to follow a path he had charted, to bring closure, and even provide a taste of retribution for our family, bitter as it may be. As I plotted along, I analyzed all the characters—except one. It was a lax omission. So, I stand here now, on a crowded sidewalk, bewildered, ready to pay the price for my carelessness.

The sirens silenced, the flashing lights dimmed, I stare blankly into the eyes of a man sitting in the passenger's seat of a nondescript car parked at the curb. He stares back before turning away, the stoic just sitting there, gazing blindly out the car's windshield. Passersby stop and gawk. I lower my head and sit in the back seat, listening to the vehicle's whine, its engine idling, then engaged as the driver shifts into first gear; he merges into traffic and then weaves through a Washington traffic snarl, slow and calculating, like a thoroughbred angling to break from the pack. We're off to a new adventure, the story's end as foggy as the one I'm about to tell.

CHAPTER 1

ROSALINA BARTOLACCI

M y mother—Rosalina Bartolacci—was born in Abruzzi, a region in Southern Italy blessed with beechwood forests and vast sandy beaches along the Adriatic Sea. Her family migrated to the United States when she was eight years old. She spoke fluent Italian, and her Abruzzi dialect lent a Mediterranean accent to her flawless English. Whether she was engaging in casual conversation, healing a wound, or teaching, her love and compassion filtered to the depths of my soul, Francesco, the first of her three children, the calculating, inquisitive son.

Grazia, my sister, the middle child, brought peace to our family, a welcoming prelude to the arrival of Giancarlo, my obstinate, stubborn brother. It was a diverse menagerie for Rosalina to manage alone, mainly because our father, Giovanni, was continually tending to his law practice, both day and night—a ritual that Grazia and Giancarlo chose to ignore and a devotion I abhorred. But with Rosalina's unyielding guidance, her steady hand nurtured us through puberty, adolescence and beyond. Fortunately, she had been able to revel in her children's good fortunes before her untimely passing. Grazia had graduated from Brown, Giancarlo had graduated from Catholic University, and I was a third-year law student at Georgetown. Unfortunately, her husband lost the most cherished lesson she left to her children—a devotion to *la famiglia*.

———————

My parents met in the fall of 1958 during a dance at Catholic University in Washington where my mother was a student. She majored in Italian Studies. My father— Giovanni Micco—was in his first year of law school at Georgetown. I recently read once again the first chapter of an unfinished novel he was writing before he died. It was a roman-a-clef and the heroine was a thinly disguised Rosalina Bartolacci:

> She was standing alone in a corner across the room. I squeezed through the crowd and made my way to her side.
>
> "Not enjoying yourself?" I asked.
>
> She stared at me blankly, unsure whether to answer. I took a chance and pressed on.
>
> "Me neither," I said, raising my eyebrows. "I'm John Cozza"
>
> Her glance returned to the dance floor, uninterested.
>
> "I'm Roselee Patti."
>
> "You're a student here?"

"I am."

An awkward silence followed, but her indifference only drew me in closer.

"May I get you something to drink?" I asked. "I hear the punch is delicious."

She grimaced. "No. I'm fine."

"Would you like to go somewhere else?"

A mischievous smile crossed her face.

"Trying to pick me up?"

"At a Catholic school dance. Perish the thought."

Surprisingly she reached for my hand. "Let's get out of here. There's a cool piano bar in Georgetown."

A cab took us to M Street. A blinking neon sign—Swing Lobby—lit the entrance. I paid the driver and helped Roselee from the cab. It was a small club. Ten tables at most. A piano player sat at an upright playing a song I recognized as 'My Favorite Things.' We sat next to the bar. Our server immediately recognized her.

"Welcome back, Miss Patti. So nice to see you again."

He pulled out her chair.

"Thank you, Sam," she said.

As they chatted, I sensed a shyness to her, a softness when she spoke. Her eyes were fixed on the server as he complimented the jazz artist performing later in the evening.

"Do you like jazz?" she asked me.

"John Coltrane, Herbie Hancock, Charlie Parker, Billie Holiday," I answered.

She turned toward me, another mischievous smile, inviting eyes, her elbows resting on the table, hands steepled.

"I like you, John Cozza."

"The usual, Miss Patti?" the server asked.

She nodded.

"And you, sir?"

"What's her usual?"

"A perfect martini."

"I'll have the same."

Roselee leaned forward, the strains of *My Favorite Things* setting the mood. The room slowly filled, a young gathering, mostly college-age, some older, probably jazz aficionados. The servers scurried about taking drink orders before the Miles Davis Quintet began playing. Clouds of smoke curled toward the ceiling, the chatter a cacophony drowning our conversation. When the music started, the crowd's murmur turned soft. Quietly our server brought us our second perfect martini. During the first set—*Milestones*—at her nudging, I confessed my life's plan to practice law and eventually become a judge. An Italian

Studies major, she hoped to teach after her children had abandoned the nest.

"Hope?" I said. "I'm sure you'll make it happen."

She only smiled while scribbling a note on a napkin and motioning to Sam.

"Give this to Mr. Davis, please."

"Of course."

When the set ended, Sam handed the note to him. Davis nodded to Roselee and mouthed, "Be glad to." After giving the downbeat, the quintet played, *'Autumn Leaves.'*

"My favorite," she said.

She hummed the melody and then quietly sang the lyrics last words, *"But I miss you most of all, my darling, when autumn leaves start to fall."*

Time passed quickly. After intermission, we ordered our third perfect martini, listened to Miles Davis, and then sipped black coffee in the empty club as he packed his trumpet into its case at three in the morning.

A year later, my father proposed to his soulmate before dinner at Hogate's, a restaurant on Washington's Southwest waterfront. More than once I've read the words he wrote in his unfinished manuscript, the novel he couldn't finish— his words describing the woman he was about to ask to be his wife:

She was wearing a black dress. Thin straps drew my eyes to her angular, bare shoulders, a sharp contrast to her soft presence. Black hair, classically Italian, merged seamlessly into her olive-toned complexion. Short bangs partially hid a diving widow's peak—foretelling her dominant personality. An Emerald necklace with shades of black plunged teasingly into her dress. The glisten of her diamond earrings paled to the sparkle of her eyes, hazel and penetrating. Roselee Patti was a beautiful, sensuous woman. It was time to ask her to be my wife.

One week after he graduated from law school, Rosalina Bartolacci and Giovanni Micco were married at St. Matthew the Apostle Cathedral in Washington. Two months later, his local board drafted him into the army. Rosalina remained with her family in Washington. It was 1962. After basic training, Giovanni was shipped to Vietnam.

CHAPTER 2

Giovanni Micco

A fter returning from Vietnam in 1963, Giovanni and Rosalina moved to the city where he was born and raised—New Castle, a small town in Western Pennsylvania. With many Italian immigrants, New Castle offered him an opportunity to build a lucrative law practice. He rented one room in the Lawrence Savings and Trust building two blocks from the local courthouse. Giovanni furnished his office with a used desk along with two chairs for clients, one for himself, and an armchair. Conserving costs, he shared a reception room and a secretary with a small law firm across the hallway. When his practice grew, he moved to a more opulent suite.

Bored or tired of trudging up the steep hill to the courthouse, Giovanni mused how the seat of power rested almost comically close to his own, his ratty armchair now worn after a decade of use. Although wary of politics, he shunned his colleagues' advice and decided to run for judge. With Rosalina's unyielding help and an army of friends and townspeople, Giovanni narrowly won the election. He became Judge Giovanni Micco.

Giovanni's position as a state trial judge did not escape his father-in-law's calculating eye. Gaspare Bartolacci was a tailor who migrated from Italy to the United States with his family in 1948, ultimately settling in Washington, D.C. For a few years, he worked at Hecht's Department store but later opened a small tailor shop in the Northeast section of Washington, not far from Capitol Hill.

He was a tall, slender man dressed in suits with a continental flair accentuated with a heavily starched white shirt and a matching tie, complemented by a perfectly tied Windsor knot. Grandpa Gaspare's clientele expanded beyond his wildest dreams, mostly because of his entrepreneurial bent, and the salesmanship skills to go along with it. Soon, lawyers, lobbyists, and Congress members became his customers, primarily because of his dedication to detail and his haberdashery's European flavor.

By the time Giovanni met Rosalina, Gaspare Bartolacci was a rich man. He was also a generous contributor to the Republican National Party. As time passed, his political influence, buoyed by his wealth, reached into Congress and eventually into the White House. Finally, in 1987, after years of social hobnobbing, his connection to the Washington power brokers paid a considerable dividend. Through Gaspare's influence, President Ronald Reagan appointed a Common Pleas judge from a small town in Western Pennsylvania to the United States Court of Appeals for the District of Columbia Circuit. Giovanni Micco was now a federal appeals court judge.

My sister and brother, and perhaps even my mother, resented being uprooted from family and friends in New Castle and transplanted to Virginia. But as one year rolled into another, Grazia and Giancarlo accepted their destiny. Washington became their surrogate home.

The years treated me differently. As childhood slipped away, my father's loyalties became unevenly divided. His cameo appearances at little league games, soccer matches, concerts, and recitals, disappointments I had stored, took an emotional toll on me. Like an officer barking commands, Giovanni demanded discipline and academic excellence. The enforcer? It was always my mother. From the narrow perspective of Giovanni Micco, his role as a father was a dutiful obligation satisfied by delegation and void of emotion. The daily homilies, delivered mostly at the dinner table before he hurried back to the office, stressed the importance of family. From my perspective, he shunned us all, his wife and children, and chose instead to scurry off each night, catering to the whims of his jealous mistress—the law.

CHAPTER 3

APRIL 2001

It was my last day of law school at Georgetown. After my final class, I headed home. As I drove along the narrow winding road that led to our house on Days Farm Road, I was refreshed by the signs of spring. For a moment, I took my eyes off the road and glanced at a cluster of flowering dogwoods and ribbons of daffodils lining the annual renaissance of grass. A blue canopy covered the cloudless, sunny day; soon, the cool spring would sneak into a hot summer.

Usually, I spent the weekends with my parents at our Vienna, Virginia house. I arrived each Friday in the early afternoon, shouldered the side door open, deposited my duffle bag full of dirty clothes on the laundry room floor, and walked down the narrow hallway leading to the kitchen. *La Cucina*, the sanctuary for *nostra famiglia*, was the place where we met each morning and exchanged greetings before we scurried off in different directions. For Mom and me, it was our haven, the refuge where we rendezvoused each Friday afternoon. She always set the table—two cups for our *bella tazza di caffe* and plates for my favorite Italian dessert, lemon ricotta cake.

When I arrived home, I noticed that the side door was slightly ajar. In keeping with my weekly custom, I deposited my duffle bag on the laundry room floor and walked into the kitchen. The demitasse and dessert plates were placed, as usual, on the kitchen table. A ricotta cake, its tempting aroma filling the air, sat on the stove.

"Hey, Mom, I'm home."

She didn't answer. I walked around the kitchen island and glanced down. Stunned, I stood there, numbed, thoughtless, helpless, trying to will reality away—but soon shaken from a trace that had paralyzed me. I gasped for air. My eyes bulged. I stared at my mother. She was sprawled on the kitchen floor, face off to the side, arms spread, eyes wide open, blood trickling from her neck. I knelt beside her, sobbing, blinded by tears, drawing deep breaths, one after the other, the next more extended than the last. I placed my hand under her head, pulled it close to my chest, closed her eyes, and caressed her body, the feel of warm blood still oozing from her neck, validating her death.

CHAPTER 4

A Confrontation

I notified the Virginia police and waited in our driveway on Days Farm Road. Two cruisers arrived within minutes. One parked in the driveway with lights flashing and sirens muted; the other parked on the street. A containment barrier soon cordoned off entry to our house. The lead homicide detective identified himself as Rocco King. Moderately tall, he appeared dapper in a striped gray suit, solid black tie, glossed tan shoes, and an open tan trench coat. We spoke in the driveway as another detective, burly and wearing a tweed sports coat with khaki pants, entered the house. He was rolling a black luggage case. Walking beside him was a tall African–American lady, stylish in a black pants suit and spiked heels, stride long, obviously anxious to begin her work.

"That's Doctor Carlotta Cox. She's our chief forensic officer," King said as I glanced her way. "And that's detective Joe Deck," he added, nodding.

After a few questions, he closed his spiral notebook.

"Would you rather stay outside?" he suggested.

"No. I can handle it."

We walked through the garage entrance and into the hallway leading into the kitchen. Deck was dusting for fingerprints while Cox, crouching next to my mother, examined the body. Hearing a car door slam, I glanced out the window. A nondescript Chevrolet was parked at the curb. Two men were escorted to the front door and led into the kitchen by the uniformed officer stationed outside. One man approached King.

"I'm FBI agent Timothy Healey," he said, flashing his badge. "And this is my partner, agent Bill O'Donnell."

Although he was trespassing on state turf, Healey's gruff introduction told me that he was reluctant to respect Virginia's jurisdiction.

"Do you have anything yet?" he asked.

"Nothing," King said.

Healey took out his iPhone camera and was about to take my mother's picture while Cox was examining her body.

"Put that away. No pictures," King snapped.

"Our boss wants a photo of the victim," Healey snapped back.

"Tell your boss to keep his nose out of our business," King said gruffly.

Taken aback, Healey slid his iPhone into its belt case.

"Mind copying me with your findings?" he asked sheepishly. "Our boss wants us to keep current with your investigation. Her husband is a federal appeals court judge."

King eyed Healey, his glance turning into a suspicious stare.

"Leave me your card. I'll ask my boss."

Along with King, the two FBI agents waited while Cox conducted her examination. The crime scene investigation would not begin in earnest until King asked the Feds to leave.

"Find anything interesting?" O'Connell pried as Cox removed her gloves after giving Deck the last of five evidence envelopes.

"Nothing," Cox replied, grimacing.

O'Donnell tested his limits.

"We have a state-of-the-art forensic lab. You can use it."

Cox eyed O'Donnell furiously, towering over him by at least three inches in her spiked heels, her voice intimidating.

"Shove your lab," she said, smirking.

King intervened.

"As a matter of professional courtesy, I allowed you onto a crime scene. You have now tested my patience. Please leave, or I'll call the Virginia police and have you evicted," his comment directed at both Healey and O'Donnell.

"Don't be so testy, King," Healey said arrogantly.

"Allow me," Deck said, as he nudged Healey and O'Donnell toward the vestibule. When he reached the door, Healey stared at King, his face smug.

"Don't you think it's odd? Murder in the morning and no signs of a struggle."

"It crossed my mind, Healey," King said as he slammed the door shut.

King's phone rang as he watched the two FBI agents walk across the grass to their nondescript Chevrolet.

"King here."

A lull.

"Be there in three hours."

He glanced at me. I was kneeling beside my mother.

"That was the coroner. Do you want an autopsy?" he asked softly.

"That's my father's decision."

"Have you notified him?"

It was odd. I hadn't even thought about my father. It was her children's loss—not his. Giovanni Micco could now devote full time to his jealous mistress.

"Not yet," I answered. "My father's attending a judicial seminar in the Virgin Islands. He's scheduled to return today."

CHAPTER 5

MY MOTHER'S FUNERAL

O ur family and close friends formed a circle around my mother's casket at the Micco family plot in New Castle. The priest immersed the aspergillum in a bucket held by the altar boy and then sprinkled the black shroud covering Rosalina's coffin with holy water. As he circled the casket again, blessing it this time with incense, I turned slightly to the side and stared at my father. His head was bowed, his eyes closed. He then whispered three words.

"God, forgive me."

After a few seconds, he turned toward me. Our eyes met. He placed his hand in mine. His stare told me he wanted to say something, perhaps a plea for mercy, but the time and place dictated otherwise. It would be useless for him to ask, anyway. Forgiveness was far beyond my reach. Then, just as the priest began the committal prayers, my father lunged forward and draped himself over Rosalina's casket before falling on his knees.

My sister, Grazia, elbowed me and whispered sternly, "Francesco, go to your father, comfort him. He needs you. This is not the time to be unforgiving."

I couldn't move. I stood motionless. Annoyed, Giancarlo hurried past me, knelt beside our father, and helped him to his feet. Giovanni stood, humped over. Grazia rushed to his side and whispered something in his ear. His youngest son and only daughter escorted him back to the mourners as the priest continued with the committal prayers. When the graveside service ended, Grazia and Giancarlo accompanied our father back to the limousine. I lagged, waiting for Grandpa Tony and Grandma Grazia, my paternal grandparents. As they walked toward me, I reminisced.

They were the founders of the Micco Candy Company. Grandpa Tony started the business in the family homestead's basement. He eventually moved it into the Phillips Mansion, a vacant building adjacent to their home. Gramps expected me to be at the candy shop no later than four o'clock. Each day after school, the nuns marched us, paired two by two, to the first intersection, led us safely across the street, and then, with a backhand waving freely through the wind, released us as we all scattered in different directions. My route was always the same—up Jefferson Street, across to Grant, and then up the steep hill to Phillips Place. The pay was meager, one dollar a week. I would have worked for nothing. That's because Gramps was my best friend.

When my grandparents reached me, I stood between them and offered each an arm. We began walking toward the limousine when Gram tugged at my suit sleeve, suggesting she wanted to talk. Before she uttered a syllable, I knew her words would have one purpose—to forge peace between father and son before she died. Gram always said that after God, only family mattered. From her perspective, everything else was meaningless. But viewed from my perspective, peace with Giovanni Micco came with a steep price. And with my mother's body about to be interred in the cold earth, it was a price I vowed never to pay.

"Do you love me, Francesco?" she asked.

"Very much, Gram," I answered, with no hesitation.

"Well, my son, it's the same love I have for your father."

She paused and looked up at me, her eyes welling with tears, pleading for a reconciliation between the prodigal son and his aging father.

"When you hurt him, you hurt me," she said, her words a gentle plea.

Gram said nothing more. She snuggled close to me and tightly grasped my hand. I looked down and studied her face. Her puffy eyes, misty with tears, gave everything and asked only for peace in return, nothing more. I felt Gram's pain as she stared through the limousine windows, searching for her son. My father was sitting in the back seat of the stretch limo with my sister. His head was bowed. Grazia wrapped her arms around his shoulder. When we reached the limousine, the chauffeur opened a door and helped seat Gram. With his arm hanging on the opened door, Gramps took up her plea.

"Give us the peace we both want, son. That's it, nothing more."

He then offered a sobering thought.

"When you're young, Francesco, everything is in front of you. But when you grow old…"

Pausing, he riveted his eyes to mine and then continued.

"…all you have left is an occasional memory."

I helped Gramps into the limousine. After closing the door, I asked the chauffeur to wait for a moment. I returned to my mother's casket now draped with flowers. The caretakers had begun to dismantle the tent and were placing the folding chairs into a cart. I stood motionless, bowed my head, and then whispered a poem form "Canzoniere", the work of Francesco Pettraca, my namesake and my mother's favorite lyric poet:

> *Alone and deep in thought, I*
> *measure out the most deserted*
> *fields, with slow, dark steps, with*
> *eyes intent to flee whatever sign of*
> *human footprints left within the*
> *sand.*

I returned to the limousine, opened the door, and sat beside my father. I grasped his hands as our glassy eyes met. Then we hugged. Gram turned and slowly a smile spread across her face as the limousine moved toward the wrought iron gates. I will never again recount the details of her murder and the days that followed. Those memories are buried with my mother. And there they will remain interred forever.

CHAPTER 6

A Federal Case

The day following my mother's funeral, I returned to Washington. I had registered for a review class before sitting for the D.C. bar examination. The course was taught at Howard University's law school, not far from my apartment. At eight o'clock in the morning, I dressed, poured milk over a bowl of Rice Krispies, gobbled it down, grabbed my bar review materials, and hurried out the door. As I walked down the front stoop, a car with the words 'U.S. Marshal' displayed on its side panel stopped at the curb on Georgia Avenue. The door opened and was slammed shut. A man, tall and wearing black pants and shirt, approached me.

"Are you Francesco Micco?"

"I am."

He showed me his badge and identified himself as a deputy U.S. Marshall.

"I'm serving you with notice."

He then handed me an envelope and continued.

"There's an emergency hearing this morning in the U.S. District Court on Constitution Avenue."

"About what?' I asked, startled.

"The U.S. Attorney is asking the district court to issue an order preempting your mother's murder case," he said soberly.

"The government wants jurisdiction of the case transferred from Virginia to the Feds?" I commented curiously.

"Yes. As an interested party, you have a right to receive notice of the hearing."

"Can I make any statement to the court?"

"No. But will you attend the hearing?" he asked.

"Of course."

"Jump in. We'll drive you there. The hearing begins at nine o'clock."

The flashing lights and an occasional siren made it a short ten-minute ride to the federal courthouse on Constitution Avenue. I passed through security, took the elevator to the third floor, and entered the courtroom of the Honorable D.H. Ziegler. I immediately recognized five people—Rocco King, Joe Deck, and Carlotta Cox sitting at one counsel time across from Bill O'Donnell and Timothy Healey at the other table. The room was otherwise empty, except for me, the assistant U.S. Attorney arguing the case, Scott Beatty, and a woman I assumed to be the attorney representing the state of Virginia. My father remained in New Castle. He hadn't returned to Washington yet.

"What's the basis of your jurisdictional claim, Mr. Beatty?" Judge Ziegler asked Beatty.

"We are basing our claim on the federal murder-for-hire statute," Beatty answered, standing. "It defines a federal crime as 'the use of interstate commerce facilities in the commission of a murder-for-hire.'"

"What are the interstate commerce facilities used in this case?"

"The relevant cases hold that the use of a telephone represents interstate commerce."

While the questions were being asked by Judge Ziegler and answered by Scott Beatty, I had one of my own. How did the FBI learn so soon that my mother had been murdered? Healey and O'Donnell arrived almost simultaneously with the Virginia police.

"Have you focused on any telephone calls that are related to the murder of Rosalina Micco?" Judge Ziegler asked Beatty, a pointed question that aroused my curiosity.

"Yes," Beatty answered. "We centered on a call a broker made in the early morning hours of the day Mrs. Micco was murdered."

"How did you learn about the call?"

"Fortuitously. The broker was under active surveillance because of an ongoing investigation. We had a tap on his phone."

"Do you know who the broker hired?"

"Yes."

I leaned forward, surprised but pleased to learn that the government could identify both the broker and the assassin, two pieces of crucial evidence that should lead to an early arrest. Still, the government's push to preempt the case was an anomaly. The Feds could have easily turned the evidence over to the Virginia police, two law enforcement agencies cooperating.

"Can you disclose their names?" Judge Ziegler asked.

"Not at this time, Your Honor. It will impede our investigation."

"Do you wish to make an offer of proof, Mr. Beatty?" the Judge asked.

"Yes, Your Honor," Beatty answered, approaching the bench. "The government will present evidence verifying the call. Our agents will testify that a known broker made the call. That evidence should be sufficient to satisfy the jurisdictional requirements of the federal murder-for-hire statute."

"Do you know who retained the broker, Mr. Beatty?" Judge Ziegler asked.

"Not yet."

After Beatty had presented the Government's evidence, the attorney representing Virginia argued that the crime of murder still fell within the state's bailiwick. Judge Ziegler disagreed. My mother's murder investigation was preempted. It was now a federal case.

CHAPTER 7

SEVEN MONTHS LATER

Following Rosalina's murder, my father returned to Vienna only to collect his clothes. He rented an apartment near the federal courthouse and never returned to our family home. Within a month, he purchased a condominium at the Watergate South in Washington. Whenever I took time from my law practice to visit him in Washington, I stayed at the adjoining Watergate Hotel.

Each night, I walked through the promenade on my way to his condo and sat with him on his balcony. He had a sweeping, panoramic view across the Potomac into Northern Virginia, a sight that ferried him back to our Vienna home on Days Farm Road. After a couple of visits, we cosmetically reconciled some of the differences that separated us. Time passed, and our conversations always extended into the early morning hours and sometimes reached into the dawn. But we never talked about Rosalina. She was an icon adorned in reverence, and we each kept a silent watch over her memory.

It was late fall. Thanksgiving had just passed, and it was my last visit before Christmas. We sat on the balcony, father and son, each reminiscing but saying little as we stared across the Potomac into Northern Virginia in the late hours of a chilly night, silencing the frosty air with blankets and hot toddies. Occasionally, I turned toward him, each time seeing only the silhouette of Giovanni Micco sitting erect and still—his eyes fixed on Northern Virginia, his thoughts, I suspect, centered on our Vienna home's kitchen.

My father was not a man given to spontaneity, always introspective and cautious to a fault. So, with meticulous care, weighing each word, each thought, he asked me a question on that brisk evening designed judiciously, I now realize, to initiate a dialogue that would affect a more meaningful reckoning between father and son. In retrospect, I know now that the Judge's question was paradoxical. There was no correct answer; simply put, it was an invitation to open a dialogue between a demanding father and a rebellious son.

The question?

"Have I been a good father?"

I didn't answer, but my deafening silence made the implication clear. The Judge's words echoed, each ricocheting against the last. Time slowly slipped away, the passing seconds offering me a chance to make peace with my father. Courtesy, respect, whatever lesson I had learned from my mother required that I say something allowing my father to purge his guilt. But as the clock wound down, my father heard only a haunting stillness, shouting that forgiveness was far beyond my reach. Finally, he lowered his head. The tormenting silence had taken its toll. He rose from his chair and walked toward the balcony rail. His gaze cut through the glistening streetlights across the Potomac and into Northern Virginia. The pendulum clock tolled two times. He asked that I turn off the vestibule light when I left. Saying nothing more, he walked toward his bedroom, blanket and an empty glass in hand. The door clicked shut.

For one hour, I sat on the balcony alone, suppressing a kinetic power nudging me towards my father's bedroom. It was my mother's touch. When the pendulum clock tolled three times, I walked from the balcony, paused at his bedroom, moved into the vestibule, and flipped the light switch. It was pitch dark. Before leaving, I glanced back and saw a strip of light escaping into the darkness from the threshold beneath my father's bedroom door. First, a sigh and then a step toward his bedroom—just as darkness doused the light. He died the next day in his chambers at the federal courthouse.

CHAPTER 8

THE CAST OF MOURNERS

With Grazia and Giancarlo, our hands tightly joined, we listened as the priest read the traditional committal prayers at the Judge's graveside service. After, aspergillum in hand, he sprinkled the black shroud spread on his casket with holy water and blessed it with incense. When the service ended, an honor guard folded the American flag, their white gloves blurred by a strict cadence as they tucked in its corners. One of the guards then presented the flag to my sister Grazia.

Meanwhile, I surveyed the cast of mourners through a cloud of smoke oozing from the holes in the sensor cover, colleagues and others who had traveled to New Castle for my father's Mass at St. Vitus and the committal service: my father's former colleague, Supreme Court Justice Salvatore Sacco; Leonardo Mendici, my father's lawyer, and the founding partner of Mendici Melrose, a mammoth Washington law firm; Luther Ashe, the Attorney General of the United States; and Claudio Armondi, my father's most trusted friend. Two older men, both strangers, intrigued me. One, a tall, gangling thin man with drooping posture, hid behind at least two days of stubble. He was dressed in a wrinkled gray suit. A black tie, the knot loose, dangled from his neck. A wide brim Fedora shadowed his pallor face. Leaning forward, his long, knobbed, yellow fingers pressed against the chair in front of him. The other man was much shorter with a slight build. His white hair, combed straight back, was complemented by thick, fluffy eyebrows. A pair of square, wire-rimmed glasses rested on his nose. A tan, unbuttoned trench coat, with its belt hanging, partially hid a shiny sharkskin suit, complemented by a white, starched shirt and a blue tie patterned with narrow red horizontal stripes.

As the crowd dispersed, my sister, brother, and I placed a white rose on the black shroud and walked away. Glancing back, I saw a lady dressed in black approach the casket. She, too, laid a rose on the Judge's shroud—but hers was red. As she stepped back from the casket, she dabbed at her eyes with a tissue and then walked toward a waiting limousine parked on the side of a narrow cemetery passageway. A chauffeur opened its door. She entered, and the car moved slowly toward the wrought-iron cemetery gate. My curiosity was aroused by the lady in black—but I was more intrigued by the other cast of mourners and the thoughts they buried as my father was laid to rest beside my mother.

CHAPTER 9

CLAUDIO ARMONDI

The intercom in my office rang. My secretary said that Claudio Armondi was in the reception room. Having just returned from Italy to attend my father's funeral, his red-stained eyes and yawns were evidence of jet lag. Uncle Claudio was my godfather, and his frequent visits to our home were welcomed and encouraged. Without fail, he always came bearing expensive gifts. His visits, however, were not without controversy. He worked in New York City for a healthcare company and maintained a residence in Sicily. My mother speculated that Uncle Claudio was a member of the Mafia. Although she had never offered her reasons, I can only surmise that she had formed her conclusions because Claudio Armondi had the usual Mafioso trappings—a black Lincoln Continental, hand-tailored clothes, a familial connection to the Gotti family, and, most importantly, lots of money.

My secretary ushered Uncle Claudio into my office. I moved from my desk and walked hastily toward him. His pace was also brisk, his arms outstretched. We met. First, a hug, and then we exchanged the traditional Italian greeting—a kiss on one cheek and then one on the other.

"Ciao, Uncle Claudio."

"Ciao, Francesco."

I positioned two chairs in front of my desk. Gesturing, I offered one to Uncle Claudio and I sat in the other. Leaning back, he first sighed and then reached into his pocket.

"It's so nice to see you, Francesco."

He handed me a small box.

"A gift for you. I got it in Messina before I left Sicily last week. Nothing big. Just a pair of cufflinks. I hope you like them."

I opened the box. Reminiscing, I thought back to the days when Uncle Claudio visited us in New Castle. He always came bearing gifts. Along with Grazia and Giancarlo, we carried our treasures from his car into the house. Keeping with tradition, my father and Uncle Claudio exchanged hugs, first, one on the right side and then one on the left. Even as a young child, I felt the energy of an ethereal force that bound them together. Their Vietnam experience connected Giovanni and Claudio's souls—fighting side-by-side in the battle of Binh Gia. Rosalina, always the gracious hostess, waited until they had exchanged their salutations before she broke the silence.

"Molte grazie, Zio Claudio."

I now echo her words.

"Grazie, Zio Claudio."

"Prego, Francesco."

Claudio had arrived in New Castle the day before my father's funeral. We had spoken briefly with each other, mostly at the calling hours, the Mass, the graveside service, and mercy dinner. I suspected the purpose of his visit was to engage in a personal conversation and then be on his way. I was wrong. His demeanor somber, he segued into the real reason for his visit.

"Francesco, about a month before your father died, he entrusted me with a manila envelope," Claudio began cautiously. "He gave me explicit instructions to deliver it to you immediately if he died."

He reached for an envelope tucked in his attaché case and handed it to me.

"In this envelope is a message from your father," he said, his eyes riveted to mine. "Please read it carefully."

He handed me the envelope.

"If you ever need my help, contact me. Advice, money, whatever you want, just ask," he said resolutely.

Although my father and I had cosmetically healed the breach in our relationship before he died, I was intrigued by his decision to communicate posthumously with his rebellious son.

"Why me?" I asked curiously.

Uncle Claudio leaned forward, choosing his words cautiously.

"Maybe you have inherited a gift that will start you on a journey he couldn't finish," he suggested, shrugging.

Forcing a smile, Uncle Claudio moved to the edge of his chair, signaling that he must leave. His chartered flight was due to depart the Greater Pittsburgh Airport in two hours. He was the major shareholder of an Italian health care company— *Santia per la Famiglia*—and its directors had scheduled him to chair a meeting in Sicily. It was an abrupt end to a telling visit. We stood and embraced. He pulled back, arms extended, hands grasping my forearms. Our eyes met. He left without another word.

The yellow manila envelope rested on my desk. Uncle Claudio had performed his errand. I leaned back in my swivel chair, unsealed the envelope, and removed a single sheet of manuscript paper. It was monogrammed with a gold cross. My eyes focused on the red rose etched into the intersecting bars. The message read:

Dear Francesco,

I hesitate to communicate with you in this manner. But it is the only way. May I start by saying that my selfish ambitions and errors in judgment have smothered me. My family eventually suffered the most dreadful consequence. Unfortunately, in trying to resolve Rosalina's murder, I have been exposed to a draconian plot that even I could not have imagined. Although the final steps are uncharted, you may need to follow a path that I have mapped. If so, I will guide you along the way. But for now, do nothing. Remember, our family has paid part of the price for my mistake, and it may have to pay the balance. If more harm comes, only you can decide what to do. Use your best judgment.

CHAPTER 10

AN INVITATION

It came as a surprise, one I hardly expected. Laying prominently on top of the mail my secretary laid on my desk was an envelope embossed with the Supreme Court's seal. It was obviously from Justice Salvatore Sacco. Once close friends, the relationship between Giovanni Micco and Salvatore Sacco had recently waned for some reason, a breakup I didn't inquire about nor did I care to explore. Frankly, I was surprised that he took time from his busy schedule to attend my father's New Castle services. After my mother was murdered, Sacco only penned a note to my father and sent a flower bouquet. I opened the envelope and read his letter:

Francesco,

> *When I learned of the sudden passing of your father, I was deeply saddened. Judge Micco was a respected jurist, and he was one of my most cherished friends. It was an honor to attend his funeral. Again, please accept my sympathy. I have personally communicated with the Clerk of The Court of Appeals for the District of Columbia Circuit to arrange for*

your late father's memorial service. He will
contact you soon and ask that you visit him
personally in Washington to make whatever
arrangements you consider suitable for the
Micco family, including your travel and
lodging. Please advise my secretary when you
will be in Washington, and we will have lunch
in my chambers. I am looking forward to our
visit.

Your Friend,
Salvatore

Following a career in government service, mostly as a member of the Equal Employment Opportunity Commission, Salvatore Sacco was appointed to the Court of Appeals for the District of Columbia Circuit by the President a year after my father received his appointment. Because they each latched onto an unyielding conservative bent, Judges Micco and Sacco instantly aligned themselves and, together, anchored a wing of the court, championing a belief that the judiciary should assume a limited role in the three-branch system of government. My father often mused that judges should not write laws but rather interpret them. The wedding of Giovanni Micco and Salvatore Sacco was a union the President had in mind when he appointed them to the Court of Appeals. He envisioned that a professional and personal relationship would develop because of their intellectual and cultural similarities. Together, they would rein in activist judges who interpreted the Constitution too liberally. As a law student, I studied their opinions. These two conservative bastions did not disappoint their benefactor.

As it played out, the President's plan was prophetic. Their uncompromising romance with conservatism meshed with their similar ethnic heritage. Soon, Judges Micco and Sacco's relationship extended beyond their judicial duties; they became close friends. Frequently, our families exchanged visits. Whenever it was our turn, my mother would prepare dinner. First came the antipasto and then the wedding soup which she always cooked in a big pan. Next, she served pasta, always gnocchi, complimented by a basic tomato sauce. The meat course was usually Justice Sacco's favorite—chicken with prosciutto and fontina cheese. For dessert, Mom usually baked a pine nut tart—again, Sacco's favorite. Next, espresso was served with Italian almond cookies. Finally, and gratefully, a glass of *Amaretto di Saronno* aided our digestion.

After dinner, my mother placed two carafes on the table and these two conservative stalwarts of the federal judiciary dwelled endlessly on their ideology. No verbal jousting, no provocative discussion, no lively exchanges between these two pals, just ad nauseam rants which were as bold and challenging to swallow as the Montepulciano wine they were drinking. Giovanni Micco and Salvatore Sacco were marching in sync to the United States Supreme Court.

CHAPTER 11

A LUNCHEON DATE

O ne week later, the clerk for the Court of Appeals for the District of Columbia Circuit invited me to Washington to help plan the Judge's memorial service. Also, as promised, Justice Sacco invited me to lunch in his chambers. My flight landed at Dulles International at noon. Because time was tight, I hired a cab and arrived early at the Supreme Court Building, the neoclassical shrine where seven men and two women crank out their opinions for nine months each year before taking the summer off. After I entered the anteroom, I was escorted into the Justice's chambers by one of his law clerks.

A Christmas tree was set in a corner adjacent to Sacco's desk, and its evergreens lent a festive scent to his chambers—the lights, the decorations, the manger all breathing life into the holiday season. The room's cherry wood walls were lined with bookshelves, stocked with a set of the Supreme Court Reporters and the Federal Reporters latest volumes. A crystal chandelier hung from the sculptured ceiling. A kaleidoscope of subdued colors filtered through stained glass windows. The wide-planked hardwood floor, probably oak, was partially covered by an ornate rug splattered with a blend of strikingly bright colors, intricate designs, and uneven hand-woven lines. When I entered, Justice Sacco moved from behind his desk and came toward me, both hands extended as we offered each other our salutations.

"Francesco, come stai?"

"Molto bene, grazie. E lei, Justice Sacco?"

"Bene."

Pleasantries exchanged, he placed his arm around my shoulder as we walked toward a furniture grouping. Respecting judicial protocol, I glanced around his chambers, waiting for Justice Sacco to sit. His cherry desk, shiny and void of any papers, was positioned at one end of the rectangular room. A double-monitor display screen sat on a credenza placed behind a high-back black leather chair decorated with brass nails. At the opposite end of the room, a leather couch was placed between two casual chairs. Off in a corner were two ornate Chippendales separated by a reading lamp that sat on a marble-topped table. Sacco chose one of the casual chairs; I sat on the leather couch.

"Francesco, I'm truly sorry about your father's passing. We were not only colleagues but, more importantly, we were friends," he said solemnly. "Giovanni was a legal icon, respected by both the bench and the bar."

As he spoke, my eyes turned from Justice Sacco and once again circled the room, chambers once promised to my father but snatched from him by the Senate Judiciary

Committee. My distraction did not escape the perception of Supreme Court Justice Salvatore Sacco.

"It *is* a beautiful chamber, Francesco," Sacco added, nodding as his glance roamed the room.

I forced a smile. He continued.

"I'm in constant awe of the legal giants who have served this court—Felix Frankfurter, Benjamin Cardozo, Oliver Wendell Holmes. I am honored that this has happened to me," he added. A braggart's boastful words, I thought.

Sacco paused, his eyes once again surveying the opulent chambers.

"America. What a country," he said, his eyes fastened on the American flag hanging limp on the right side of his desk. "The son of Italian immigrants, the son of a shoemaker, the son of a domestic—appointed to the United States Supreme Court."

Reveling in his good fortune, Salvatore Sacco had shrugged off the torrent of events that surrounded his appointment. In 1999, my father's nomination to the Supreme Court had been derailed by the Senate Judiciary Committee because of Giovanni Micco's purported association with a member of the Carlo Gambino family. The link between my father and the Mafia? Claudio Armondi. Because of a mounting political maelstrom, the President quietly asked my father to withdraw his nomination voluntarily. He obliged. And who was waiting in the wings to replace Giovanni Micco? Salvatore Sacco.

"The Micco family is proud of you, Justice Sacco," I remarked begrudgingly. "And it's thoughtful for you to take an interest in my father's memorial service. He would have been grateful. The law was his life."

"Giovanni Micco was special, Francesco. He was brilliant. But above all, he was honest. Unfortunately, he was loyal to a friendship that aborted his appointment to the Supreme Court," Sacco observed, a snide remark I brushed away. Out of respect for Uncle Claudio, I thought it best to let the subject rest.

Our attention turned to my father's memorial service. I provided him with family member names that my father would have wanted at his service. I had also jotted down the names and addresses of state court judges that my father befriended through the years and handed the list to Justice Sacco. He glanced at it and then assured me that the ceremony would be both solemn and joyful—"a celebration" to use his words.

———————

Lunch, ordered by Justice Sacco from Tosca, a nearby restaurant, was served in the Italian tradition. First, soup and then a serving of linguine with fresh tomato sauce.

"Probably cooked in a copper kettle, just like the big pan your mother used when we enjoyed our Sunday dinners together. I can still see her stirring the sauce with her special wooden spoon," Sacco said, reminiscing. "You remember, the one your father gave her years ago as a gift."

I remembered it well—the words 'For Rosalina. You are a magical chef' were engraved on the silver-plated wooden spoon.

The entrée was outstanding—Milanese-style breaded chicken cutlet with arugula and Parmesan cheese salad over oven sun-dried tomatoes. I enjoyed the lemon ricotta cake; he sipped his cappuccino and then raised an innocuous subject seemingly meant only to engage in conversation.

"I recently learned that your father was writing a novel," Sacco said curiously, a statement I interpreted as a question. My father's literary effort was a surprise to me. I waited for Sacco's next question.

"Did he share the manuscript with you, Francesco?" Sacco inquired sheepishly. "I'd like to read it."

Justice Sacco was prying. I doubted that he had the time or interest to read a debut novel—even if the author was his judicial colleague.

"I know nothing about the novel," I answered, shrugging. "How did you learn about it.?"

"Fortuitously. Your father and I hadn't spoken to each other for some time. About a week before he died, I called him and mentioned that we should have lunch together," Sacco explained, a meeting he conveniently arranged, I thought. "Giovanni suggested his chambers. I agreed, and we met the next day. That's when he told me."

I knew Giovanni Micco better than anyone. My father had a fetish for privacy. He would have told Justice Sacco about the unfinished manuscript only if he had good reason. It was my turn to pry.

"Did he reveal anything to you about the plot?" I asked, my curiosity aroused.

"No. Your father said he was pressed for time. I took the cue," Sacco explained. "We shook hands and agreed to meet again soon for lunch in my chambers."

"That ended your luncheon date with my father?"

"It did. But as I was leaving, something odd happened. Judge Micco's secretary ushered two gentlemen into his chambers."

"Did you know them?"

"No. But I was curious. When your father's secretary returned to the reception room, I asked her for their names. She's an old friend. I knew her since your father and I served on the court of appeals together."

"Did she identify the two men?"

"She did. One was Shawn O'Leary—the agent-in-charge of the Washington FBI bureau, and the other was Terrance Brady—the assistant U.S. Attorney in charge of white-collar crime."

CHAPTER 12

GRAZIA

T he day after returning to New Castle, I visited my sister, Grazia. Her resemblance to our mother was haunting. With painstaking care, the genetic gods had reincarnated Rosalina Bartolacci in the form of Grazia Micco. The raven black hair, the Mediterranean complexion, the penetrating, brown eyes—and the widow's peak. Grazia had the same patrician elegance as our mother.

Like me, Grazia loathed Washington, and, wanting to avoid the din of a metropolitan city, she had returned to New Castle after college and rescued the family chocolate business. Anxious to retire, my grandparents sold the Micco Candy Company two years after we moved to Washington. My sister, however, reclaimed its ancestral lineage. With some of the money inherited from Grandpa Gaspare, Grazia purchased the company. She was now transforming the Micco Candy Company into a successful manufacturing enterprise. Christmas was only weeks away. It was a busy time for her. Knowing she was scurrying around trying to fill orders, I dropped in on her at the factory anyway to inquire about the Judge's literary effort.

"Did you know the Judge was writing a novel?" I asked innocently.

She fired back, scolding me, the prodigal son who refused to respect his father.

"You tell me something, Francesco," she said sarcastically. "Did you ever try referring to your father as someone other than 'the Judge'? It's a matter of simple respect."

I gave her a remorseful glance.

"You're right. I should be more respectful."

Unsatisfied by my contrition, her demeanor nevertheless changed. One of my father's qualities reflected in Grazia was her ability to quickly shift from one emotion to the next, as though instantly forgetting her initial frustration. She ran her hands across the tablecloth, brushing away the anger like crumbs to the floor, her voice still gruff.

"But, for the record," she said, eyes cast down, "I did know he was writing a novel."

"You did?" I said, the excluded sibling.

"Yes. He told me," she said, still at a distance.

My sister must have loathed our father's devotion to his jealous mistress, but, in contrast to me, she was careful not to expose her displeasure, becoming complicit in his unequal delegation of family responsibilities. Strangely, I admired her. She was a master at maintaining her close relationship with him, appearing indifferent to his relentless demands but inwardly despising his treatment of our mother.

"What did he tell you about his literary venture?" I asked cautiously.

Grazia frowned.

"Are you being cynical, Francesco?" she snarled.

"No. Just wondering what you know about the book?"

"I don't know anything," she answered.

"Where's the manuscript?"

"That's a good question, Mr. Lawyer," she said cynically. "I knew nothing about the book until a month before he died. He called me from Sicily."

"What did he say?"

"Just that he was writing a novel and asked that I edit the manuscript."

It made sense for my father to ask Grazia to edit his book. While he discouraged my dream to be a writer, he encouraged her to earn a Master of Fine Arts degree from Brown University. His rationale for allowing her to pursue a writing career was simple. Grazia would marry a lawyer, and the money flowing from the billable hours charged to his affluent clients would enable her to spend endless days sitting in front of a MacBook cranking out a series of best sellers. Poking fun at my resentment, she frequently sent me the final drafts of her writings for my reading enjoyment. But I couldn't resist the temptation to edit them and ship the manuscripts back to her—with a copy to the Judge. I became impatient.

"Grazia, where's the manuscript?" I asked sternly.

"I'm getting there, Francesco," she said sharply. "Don't be so testy. That's the trouble with lawyers. You want answers too fast."

"Sorry," I said with a tinge of sarcasm.

"I told Dad that I was going to Sicily in about three weeks. He said he would leave the manuscript there for me—in our secret hiding place."

I could sense that she was attempting to hide behind a veneer of stoicism but could also see the lines of grief crack across her face.

"But due to his passing," she said sharply, "I never made it to Sicily."

When we were young, our grandfather Gaspare purchased a house in Taormina, a charming seaside village situated on the side of a mountain in Sicily. The embers of Mount Etna appear as a faint star in the evenings. The town sits at least two hundred meters above the sea, with crests of houses snugly tucked into the mountainside topped by a small church. A statue of the Virgin Mary is shadowed inside.

Our home is in such a location. Two roof patios on the house provide a panoramic view of the Ionian Sea and the Bay of Taormina, a luxury even among the century's old inhabitants of the town. Pedestrian steps cross like veins down the slopes, leading to the narrow medieval streets that create the daily grid through which the village people move. Many high-priced specialty shops, secluded bistros featuring lush gelatos, and hotels with a new kind of decadence cater to the tourist trade.

The locals, for the most part, live in a series of terraced houses at the far end of the village, each equipped with a complete view into the homes of their adjacent neighbors who might be seen hanging laundry or laying out a slatted chair to sit and enjoy the day. We try to vacation there each year during the Easter season so that our family can attend the religious services and enjoy the traditional festivals —a mandatory vacation.

"Where is your secret hiding place?" I asked, half-amused, half-repulsed.

"Sorry, Francesco, that's between Dad and me. A father-daughter thing."

"Did he tell you anything else?"

"No, not much. Dad seemed exhausted."

"Working too hard, as usual?"

"I suppose—he had just finished a controversial case."

"How do you know?"

"Read about it in the Washington Post."

"Do you recall any details?"

"Not really. Just that it involved a man charged with espionage. Unfortunately, somebody murdered him before his case went to trial," she paused, trying to recollect.

"I realize how difficult it was for him to digest legal arguments, decide cases, deal with lawyers—how muddled his feelings were," Grazia explained, holding back tears. "It was around the same time as Mom's death."

She looked wistfully away again.

"A strange and difficult few months," she added, staring blindly at me.

I returned her stare with a rigid placidity, trying to obscure my concern.

"Strange indeed," I said.

CHAPTER 13

GIANNA

When I returned to New Castle following my graduation from Georgetown, I joined our family's former parish, St. Vitus. Before Giovanni's appointment to the federal bench, we attended the eight o'clock Mass each Sunday. Grazia, Giancarlo, and I were always sandwiched between our parents—Giovanni, rigid and tall in his conservative suit, Rosalina, proud and smiling, in her classical attire on the other.

To maintain tradition, I attended the same Mass. Each Sunday, I arrived early, lit five candles, returned to my pew, my eyes fixed on the flickering lights lined in a row, reveling in memories that somehow saddened me. After Mass, the Micco family always visited the PO Lunch, appropriately named because it was across the street from the local post office, a large neoclassical structure built during the administration of Franklin Roosevelt. The PO Lunch was owned by my father's Greek friend, Mike Theodorou. The fare was always the same—eggs, bacon, sausage, toast, pancakes, coffee for Giovanni and Rosalina, orange juice for their three children. Then off we went to our home. It was time for Rosalina to prepare the Sunday feast while Giovanni hurried off to his law office.

On a Sunday, about six months after I returned to New Castle, I paid particular attention to an attractive young lady who always attended the same Mass and always sat in the fourth pew. As was the case on each preceding Sunday, I didn't fix my eyes on the priest throughout the liturgy but rather on her striking figure. Each week, my chance to speak with her idly slipped by. But on this celebrated Sunday, I was rescued by fate. During the sign of peace, she turned and offered me her hand. We touched, and a thrill shot through my body from head to foot. My eyes locked on hers. I refused to uncouple our fastened hands. Simply put, I was mesmerized. She pulled back. I held on, obsessed, perhaps paralyzed, by the ecstasy of the moment. She was offended. I was embarrassed. After Mass, I followed her to the parking lot. Somehow, I had gathered enough courage to explain my bizarre behavior.

"Excuse me," I said apologetically as she unlocked her car door, "but I didn't mean to hold your hand so long."

Her quizzical stare blossomed into a smile just as the morning sun reflected off the diamond pendant pinned on her lapel. Its luster was dimmed only by the radiant glow of her eyes.

"It *was* a rather tight squeeze," she said brazenly.

"Sorry about that. Let me try again," I said, holding out my hand.

"I'm Francisco Micco."

"Nice to meet you, Francisco Micco. I'm Gianna DiFusco."

She smiled and began to turn away. Desperately, I plotted on.

"Do you always attend the 8 o'clock Mass?" I asked.

"I do," she said, reaching for her car's handle.

"If I promise to loosen the grip of my handshake next Sunday, will you agree to join me for breakfast on this beautiful morning?"

She laughed.

"This beautiful morning…" she repeated while looking around the parking lot as the other parishioners loaded up their cars. She allowed the mood to sway her.

"Trying to pick me up?"

"In the church parking lot?" I asked.

She smiled.

"Where do you have in mind?" she asked.

We went to the PO Lunch. On the way, I asked all the questions. She lived in New Castle. Gianna's father had invited her to work in his auto wrecking business, but she declined. Against his wishes, she went off to college. A recent graduate of Duquesne University, she worked in the administrative office of a utility company, Pennsylvania Power.

I held the door open as we entered the restaurant. Mike, the owner, led us to a booth. I introduced him to Gianna. We chatted for a while, reminiscing. It was another tradition the Judge stole from his family when he dragged us to Washington. After Mike took our order, I turned to Gianna.

"Do you like your work?" I asked.

"Love it. Someone has to keep the lights on. Where do you spend your days?"

"I'm a lawyer."

"Oh. One of those?"

"Is that a compliment?"

She laughed.

"I'm sorry."

"No need to apologize."

After the bacon and eggs, home fried potatoes, an order of pancakes, which we shared, and a sticky bun, the waitress refilled our coffee cups.

"Are you from New Castle?" she asked.

"I am. My father was a judge here when I was younger. Our family moved to Washington after the President appointed him to the federal bench."

She leaned back in her chair, embarrassed, surprised.

"You're Judge Micco's son?" she asked rhetorically.

"I am."

"He recently died?"

"Yes. How did you know?"

"I read about it in the New Castle News. And your mother was murdered?"

"Yes."

She reached across the table to take my hand.

"I am so sorry, Francisco. I should have recognized your name," she said apologetically.

I closed my eyes. Tears slid down my cheeks. Her hold tightened.

"Do you want to talk about it?" she asked quietly.

"Not now. Perhaps another time."

Our hands uncoupled. Gianna gave me a tissue. I wiped my eyes. One hour stretched into two. We talked, smiled, laughed, a good beginning, I thought. It was a short ride back to the church. On the way, we said nothing, our eyes dead ahead, her hand resting on the car seat. I covered it with mine—a soft touch, a glance.

"I'm late. Got to get home and help Mom with Sunday dinner," she said when we reached the parking lot.

"The usual Italian fare?"

"Of course. Wedding soup, pasta, chicken, salad, biscotti, and my father's homemade vino, straight from a barrel in our basement."

I pulled my car next to hers and began to open the driver's door. She stopped me. The stubborn, independent side of Gianna DiFusco emerged.

"Stay put, Francisco. I'm not helpless."

She opened the passenger door. It clicked shut. She walked toward her car, hesitated, turned, and came back. I leaned over and rolled down the window.

"Do you have plans today?" she asked.

"No."

"Would you like to join my family for dinner?"

"I would."

"You may regret it, Francisco. It's a raucous bunch. At least fifteen people."

"No different than my family."

"Don't be so sure."

Breakfast at the Post Office Lunch after Sunday Masses became a ritual for us. I also had a standing invitation for Sunday dinners at the DiFusco home, which I accepted. Saturday was always date night—dinners, movies. And then there was the weekend visit to Washington when I introduced her to my family—or what was left of it. It was a whirlwind romance. Three months later, I proposed to Gianna DiFusco. She accepted. The following month we were married in the same church that introduced me to my soulmate. Through a kind twist of fate, I learned that the owners of our family home on Sumner Avenue had passed on, and, with the help of a gracious financial gift from Grandpa Gaspare's trust, we were able to purchase it. Eleven months later, our son was born. We named him Michele.

CHAPTER 14

LEONARDO MENDICI

Leonardo Mendici was the founding partner of Mendici Melrose. His Washington law firm employs more than four hundred lawyers. Politicians and lobbyists who patrol the corridors of Congress consider it the most influential legal emporium in the city. Mr. Mendici rarely becomes involved in the firm's daily business, mostly because of its size. He's the rainmaker. And a good one.

Only because of my father's constant urging, I interviewed at Mendici Melrose during my third year of law school at Georgetown. Ranked second in my class, I had the credentials to land a job there. Plus, my father was a judge on the Court of Appeals for the District of Columbia Circuit. That fact never appeared on my resume, but it was a silent perk. The firm's business manager asked me to return for a third interview with Leonardo Mendici himself. Much to my father's chagrin, I canceled the interview because I knew I would be offered a position with the firm—an offer I would decline. With my mother's blessing, I had decided to return to New Castle to open my practice.

It was a Friday, the day after I had met with Grazia. After work, I returned home. Holding Michele, Gianna greeted me at the door. She handed me our son. I raised him high in the air; his giggle refreshed my soul. He was waiting anxiously for Santa Clause's visit. Holding Michele with one arm, I leaned over and kissed Gianna. She smiled and walked into the kitchen. With Michele perched on my shoulders, I followed her.

"An attorney from Washington called you about ten minutes ago. He said he represents your father's estate. He asked that you return his call. His number is on the fridge."

"Was it Leonardo Mendici?"

"Yes."

I handed Michele to Gianna and returned Mendici's call. We exchanged the usual salutations, and, after some casual comments, he suggested that I make an appointment with the attorney who would be working on my father's estate. I agreed and said I would make arrangements to meet with her when I traveled to Washington for my father's memorial service. After disposing of the amenities, he segued into the reason for his call.

"Francesco, yesterday Justice Salvatore Sacco telephoned me."

Being contacted by Washington's most influential lawyer informing me that he had just spoken with a Supreme Court justice puzzled me.

"I assume his call to you involved me?" I inquired, surprised.

"Indirectly."

"How?"

"He said your father was writing a novel, and he asked if I had the manuscript."

Like Sacco, Mendici was prying.

"Why did he call *you*?" I asked.

"Because I represent your father's estate."

"He assumed you had the manuscript?"

"Apparently. Justice Sacco also said that he asked you for the manuscript."

"He did," I responded. "We met in his chambers to plan my father's memorial service. I told him I knew nothing about the book."

"Justice Sacco seems extremely anxious to read the manuscript," Mendici commented.

"Appears that way. Do you know the reason?" I asked suspiciously.

It was a question meant to draw Mendici out.

"I have no clue."

His elusive answer aroused my curiosity. Two of the mourners who paid their respects at my father's grave-side service were now searching for the Judge's manuscript. Obviously, Sacco and Mendici were prodding me— the managing partner of a mammoth law firm and a Supreme Court Justice passing off my father's novel as nothing more than a literally venture by an unpublished author. I wasn't the naive country lawyer they thought me to be. There had to be more.

"But I will say this," Mendici added. "If you do find the manuscript in your father's personal belongings, get it to me. It may be an asset to his estate."

"Does it have any value?" I asked, coaxing him for more detail, drawing him out, expecting an answer that would confirm my suspicion.

"It might," he said cautiously. "Mendici Melrose represents Random House. But timing is everything. I'll get the manuscript to one of their editors, and we'll see what happens."

His offer might have been convincing to the untrained ear, but I had heard enough of my father's lame excuses to know when a promise had a hidden motive. When the call ended, I looked out the kitchen window. Gianna and Michele were playing. Interesting, I thought, as I watched them frolicking in the yard. The Judge's manuscript now had two suitors—but were they competitors or partners?

CHAPTER 15

GIANCARLO

Of the three Micco children, my brother Giancarlo was the most contentious. Although blessed with a keen intellect, he had little inclination to develop his gifts. He survived through wit and charm. But with patience and prompting, at times gentle but usually firm, Rosalina counseled him through his fragile teen and college years. A year before our mother was murdered, Giancarlo graduated from Catholic University with a degree in information systems management. Following graduation, he moved to Italy and took up residence at our family retreat in Sicily. He was employed by StarGazer, an American computer company with an office there. Fortunately, Giancarlo was in Taormina when the Judge called Grazia and asked that she edit his novel. It was about nine in the morning in Italy when I spoke with Giancarlo. As usual, he was grumpy but otherwise happy to hear my voice. He was also alarmed.

"Why are you up so late, Francesco? Something wrong?"

"Not really. I just want to ask you a question about Dad."

"Go ahead, ask," he offered suspiciously.

"While he was in Taormina, did Dad do any writing?"

For a moment, there was only a silence filled by the static of our transatlantic call.

"As a matter of fact, yes," Giancarlo said, finally answering. "He powered-up his computer before dawn and wrote until he went to bed. Seven days a week. It was like a marathon. I thought he was writing one of his boring legal opinions."

I continued to press.

"Did anything unusual occur while he was there?"

A short pause as static once again filled the silence.

"There is one thing that caused me some concern," Giancarlo said. "One night at about eight he received a call. Dad kept saying rather loudly, 'I don't think you're truthful with me.' The conversation went on and on for about an hour."

"Did you overhear anything else?"

"Just one thing. Dad said rather sharply, 'The professor won't return my calls.'"

"Do you know the professor's name?"

"No."

"Did Dad appear to be angry?"

"Angry and loud."

I was conflicted. Being 'angry' and 'loud' was contrary to the mild-mannered Giovanni Micco, a trait he guarded closely on and off the bench.

"Did you talk to Dad later?"

"No, I went to bed. The next morning, I peeked into his den," Giancarlo added hurriedly. "He was pecking away at his computer with two fingers. I told him I was leaving for work. He still seemed distraught."

"Do you know who he was talking to the night before?"

"Yeah, I asked him."

"Who was it?"

"His friend, Salvatore Sacco."

"Did Dad appear calm when you left for work?"

"Yeah. He mellowed. He even called Grazia and ordered some chocolate boxes. I guess it was a peace offering for Sacco."

CHAPTER 16

A CLOSE CALL

"**I** reviewed your father's medical records, and it's unlikely that he died of a cardiac arrest, especially if he recently passed a thallium stress test."

These were the words of the pathologist I had retained to testify as an expert witness. As the executor of my father's estate, I had presented a petition to the motions court judge in New Castle, requesting an order allowing me to exhume my father's body. I cited the cause of his death stated on the death certificate and the pathologist's opinion as the reason for my motion. When viewed in juxtaposition with my mother's murder, his sudden passing was too suspicious. But my curiosity was mostly aroused because after eight months, the U.S. Attorney's office had made no arrests in my mother's murder investigation although the government knew the identity of the broker and the hitman. Also, the U.S. Attorney had transferred Scott Beatty to Tulsa. He was the prosecutor who represented the Government in the preemption hearing. Oddly, no one had replaced him, and my mother's investigation remained in limbo.

———————

It was just past midnight. The court administrator scheduled the hearing for nine o'clock in the morning. After my legal research was finished, I locked my office door, walked toward the freight elevator, pushed the down button, opened the scissor gate, and rode to the ground floor. The back exit led to an alley. I opened the door and began walking to my car. As I headed to the parking lot, I heard the idle of a car's engine behind me. The driver had dimmed its parking lamps. As I hastened my pace, the car's headlights brightened the alley. I turned. With its engine revving, its tires screeching, its headlights bulging, the driver's aim was fixed on me. I ran, long strides, arms pumping, glancing back at the car, its headlights blinding, the distance narrowing, my escape almost futile. Just then, a force shoved me hard against the building. The car whizzed by. I turned. The frightening stare of a man looked down at me. Tall and burly, he wore a suit, an opened-collar shirt, and an unbuttoned trench coat. The remnants of his fedora rested in the middle of the alley.

"Who are you?" I asked, astonished, grateful, confused. "Why are you here?"

"Doesn't matter."

He retrieved the briefcase I had discarded and then walked me to my car. I opened the door and sat. He hovered over me, his hand hanging on the car's roof.

"Be extremely careful," he commanded sternly. "Take no chances. Pay attention to your father's message."

His warning was telling, my father's message clear—'It may be necessary for you to follow a path I have charted. But for now, do nothing,' the advice I didn't heed. I started my car's engine and drove from the parking lot, the glare of my protector's headlights glaring in my rearview mirror until I reached my home on Sumner Avenue.

CHAPTER 17

ROOSEVELT WARD

The court dismissed my motion for exhumation because the pathologist I had hired failed to appear. I called his office to inquire into his whereabouts, but the receptionist only said that he decided not to testify and that he would return the fee I had paid him. She gave me no reason for his decision, and I didn't ask. Recognizing my plight, the judge agreed to provide me with a continuance. I politely refused. The attempt to run me down last night, the subtle warning by the stranger, and his advice to 'take no chances' were sufficient to end my excursion into the plot my father had discovered. It would be useless for me to try again, anyway. Regardless, any other expert I retained would likely find it inconvenient to testify. Someone wanted my father to rest in peace.

When I returned to my office, a tall, slender African-American was sitting in the reception room. He was dressed conservatively in a gray, three-button suit, a muted tie, and shiny wingtips. Erect and confident, he identified himself.

"Good morning Mr. Micco. I'm Roosevelt Ward," he said, standing.

He flashed his identification badge and said he was an FBI agent. I glanced casually at his credentials.

"Can we speak privately? It won't take long. I've been assigned to your mother's murder investigation." It was an announcement I welcomed.

"Of course," I said.

Ward followed me into my office. Finally, I had a chance to ask someone why my mother's case was placed on hold by the government. He sat and forced a smile.

"May I offer you a coffee?" I asked.

"No. I'm fine."

Fidgeting with his briefcase, he removed a small note pad and asked innocuous questions about my mother. I suspected he already knew the answers. The charade over, he slid to the edge of his chair and asked a question.

"There's one more thing, Mr. Micco," Ward said as he reached into his briefcase and removed a folded paper.

"Will you consent to a search of your father's Watergate apartment?" he asked calmly.

Ward had finally raised the subject which prompted his visit to my office—a trip to New Castle to get my signature on a document that would allow the FBI to search the Judge's condominium. He was on a fool's errand. I ignored his offhand question, a query meant to disarm me.

"Has the broker been arrested yet?" I asked bluntly.

My question jarred Ward. He jerked back, the dazed boxer fooled by a sucker punch.

"No," he answered.

"Why?"

"He's the subject of a continuing investigation."

It was the same lame excuse.

"And the assassin?"

"He'll be arrested soon."

Ward was hedging. He was on a mission, and it wasn't to gather evidence against the broker and assassin who slit my mother's throat. I thought it useless to explore her case with Ward any further. He was only the government's emissary, sent to entrap me, the unsuspecting country lawyer who would happily surrender to the federal government's whims.

"I'll be happy to cooperate with you, Mr. Ward, but before I give the FBI the right to a consensual search, I'll confer with my attorney."

"You *are* an attorney, Mr. Micco," Ward shot back.

"True, sir, but you know what they say about a lawyer who represents himself."

Ward let out a short, forgiving laugh as I gave him a wry smile. He returned to business.

"You understand that the U.S. Attorney can apply for a search warrant?"

"I do. But can the government satisfy its probable cause requirement?"

Ward grinned and said nothing more. As we walked to the door, I assured him I'd contact my attorney within the next day or so, and I would be in touch with him before the end of the week. After wishing each other a Merry Christmas, he left my office. As a lawyer and an FBI agent, we each knew there would be no consensual search of the Judge's residence at the Watergate—at least not until I had the opportunity to sift through my father's belongings.

CHAPTER 18

THE ROSEN CASE

The day following my meeting with Roosevelt Ward, Gianna and I sat in the kitchen that chilly winter morning, enjoying our cappuccinos. I had already told her that I would be spending the Saturday after New Year's Day at my father's Watergate condo in Washington to take inventory of his personal belongings. At least for now, she didn't need to know about the message Uncle Claudio delivered to me the day following the Judge's funeral. I began innocently by soliciting a female perspective on the lady dressed in black who attended the Judge's graveside service.

"Yes, I saw her, Francesco. Who could miss her? I thought nothing of it. Like it or not, she was probably your father's friend. She came to pay her last respects. What's the big deal? Your mother died more than a year ago. Life goes on. Our parents…" she looked at me closely, "…are only human."

I imagined, with dark amusement, an elderly Gianna standing by my graveside, whipping off her mourner's black trench coat to reveal a tight cocktail dress as she stepped into the limousine after the wake. As selfish and as silly as it might be, I honestly dreaded the thought of her being with another man.

"I guess my definition of a soulmate is too Pollyannaish," I remarked.

She turned and focused her eyes on mine. A silly smirk crossed her face.

"Yes, my dear husband," she said with a Transatlantic flair, resting her face in her hand like a classic starlet staring at the moon. "I can see it all now. I pass on first, and you spend the rest of your life dressed in black. Each day, rain or shine, you'll religiously place a rose on my grave, praying for the day to come when you're laid to rest beside me."

"You know me well, my dear wife."

We stood. I took her arm in mine.

"Fasten your chastity belt!"

She laughed and put her arm around my waist.

"Yes," I said, putting my hands together in prayer, "and to seal my covenant, I now agree to live a monastic life if you visit the great beyond before me."

Next came the question I should not have asked.

"And you, my dear wife, will you make the same promise to me?"

After a derisive smile, she scoffed.

"Don't lie, dear husband. You'll follow the first set of legs that invites you in for 'further review,' as lawyers often say."

"Never in a million years, my dear Gianna."

"Well, then I promise to spend the rest of my life in a cell doing nothing more than praying for you."

As we looked out the kitchen window, each of us stared into the marrow of a beautiful winter morning, the threat of snow and a white Christmas a hopeful sign. After Gianna went upstairs to wake Michele, I brewed another cappuccino, sat, and spread the *New York Times* on the table. Above the fold on the first page was a story that attracted my interest:

> WASHINGTON —The Justice Department announced today that it was reopening its investigation into the murder of Saul Rosen. Rosen, a lobbyist for the American Israel Public Affairs Committee, was murdered in his Georgetown apartment in late April 2001. At the time of his death, he was under federal indictment for violating the Espionage Act. Rosen allegedly disclosed state secrets to Israeli diplomats with strong connections to AIPAC.

My interest deepened when I read the last part of the news story:

At the time of the murder, Rosen's case was on appeal in the United States Court of Appeals for The District of Columbia Circuit. The issue was whether the court should order the government to provide the defense team with evidence that the prosecution had labeled "highly sensitive." That issue was never decided because of Rosen's murder. The case was pending before Federal Appeals Court Judge Giovanni Micco, now deceased.

CHAPTER 19

ANNA ANGELISANTI

Christmas passed, the annual celebration of Christ's birth somewhat somber without Rosalina and Giovanni. Gianna cooked sauerkraut and pork for New Year's Day—hopefully, a remedy that would bring us 'good luck' in 2002. First on my list was a trip to my father's Watergate apartment. It would be a sentimental journey, one I was reluctant to take, but time was of the essence because I expected Roosevelt Ward to convince a federal judge to issue a search warrant.

I decided to travel to Washington by rail. The rhythmic sound of the train wheels rolling over the tracks put me to sleep. Being a sole practitioner, I rationed my time. I decided to leave on a Friday night, stay in Washington on Saturday, and then return late in the evening. According to Amtrak's schedule, the Capitol Limited would leave Pittsburgh at nine twenty-eight in the evening and arrive at Union Station at seven the following morning. Reclining in the seat, I rested my head on the folded pillow given to me by the attendant. I fell asleep instantly.

The Capitol Limited arrived in Washington one-half hour early. It was nearly six-thirty on a Saturday morning and most people in the city were still sleeping. Thankfully, it was unseasonably warm for January. A drizzle dampened the deserted streets, but it didn't discourage a few loyal runners from taking their early morning jog. The cab headed down Virginia Avenue toward the Watergate, its windshield wipers slowly moving back and forth as the rain dripped down the passenger window. Still apprehensive about my search of the Judge's apartment, I mused about the secrets I'd uncover as I rummaged through his belongings. I was about to trespass upon a part of his life I would rather leave undisturbed. But I had no choice. Like it or not, I was being dragged into the secret life of Judge Giovanni Micco.

Through the past two years, I'd become acquainted with the personnel at Watergate South. I waved to the doorman. He extended his sympathies with a glance. I proceeded through the lobby and rode the elevator to the ninth floor. As I stepped into the hallway, I smiled at the familiar staid decor that greeted me—a long gold-framed mirror behind a tall vase of dried eucalyptus leaves. I took a moment to assess my visit's boundaries, recognizing that the logistics of Giovanni Micco's mystery were taking their toll.

My father's inclination toward orderly appearances was a fetish. I knew what to expect when I began to pry into his private life. His suits, designed and tailored by Gaspare Bartolacci, would be hung neatly on racks with coordinating ties and belts draped over the hangers. In a separate compartment, his casual trousers would ride next to matching monogrammed polo jerseys. His dress shirts, white, along with a few blues and stripes, would be stored inside a chest of drawers. Shoes, one pair for each suit, shined and buffed, would sit neatly on a rack. On his desk, I expected to find a stack of cards, notes, and letters that Grazia and Giancarlo had sent to him over the past year, all expressing love and hope. A few came from me. If the Judge could ever reclaim a meaningful connection to his family following Rosalina's death, it had to come from us.

I inserted the key, shouldered the door open, and entered his apartment. A soft noise drew my attention to the bedroom. I crept down the narrow, dark hallway. The bedroom door was ajar. Slowly pushing it open, I stuck my head inside. I saw nothing suspicious and heard only the splash of raindrops trickling down the frosted-glass pane. I walked into the bedroom. The adjoining bathroom door was partially open. I drew my eyes to an array of memorabilia displayed on my father's chest of drawers— Giancarlo's college graduation picture, a rendering of Grazia commissioned by our mother when she was a child, Rosalina's photo helping him slip into his robe when the chief judge swore him in as a federal jurist. There was no picture of me.

As I entered my father's walk-in closet, I was startled by its contents. There were seven long formal dresses— three black, two red, and two white, all with thin straps and plunging necklines. Off to one side of the closet was a low shelf with seven pairs of matching shoes, one for each dress. I shook my head in disbelief. While my conversation with Gianna had prepared me for such a revelation, and I knew that I was there to uncover secrets, seeing my father's private life laid out so plainly reached beyond embarrassment and into shock. I stepped back from the closet, left the bedroom, walked down the hallway into the living room, and opened the door to his balcony. Hunching over the railing, I stared into Northern Virginia, reminiscing—Sunday morning Mass, breakfast before the traditional Italian Festa in the late afternoon, the Friday mother-son talks with Rosalina as we sipped a cappuccino while enjoying her lemon ricotta cake.

My nostalgic musings over, I left the balcony and walked again toward my father's bedroom. In an instant, comfort turned to panic. Standing in the bedroom doorway was the lady in black—the mystery mourner who had laid a red rose on the black shroud covering my father's casket following his graveside service. Trying to coax words from me, she stood motionless, arms folded, the stern stare of a sentry guarding the bedroom. Hearing nothing from me, she broke the silence.

"I know you think I shouldn't be in your father's apartment, but Francesco, I'm a guest," she proudly announced.

"What's your name?" I asked, stunned.

"Anna Angelisanti."

"Why are you here?"

"For the past year, your father has been writing a story. He retained me as his agent. I'm looking for his most recent manuscript," the daunting words of yet another suitor for the Judge's debut novel.

"How long have you been here?"

"For about an hour. I was hiding in the bathroom when you came in."

"Why were you hiding?"

"Because you surprised me," she said with a shaky, uncertain laugh.

Another awkward pause followed. Anna gestured to the twin armchairs that sat opposite each other in the corner of the room. Her hands tightly clasped, she perched on the edge of her seat and leaned forward, about to raise a delicate topic. Before she spoke, she lowered her head. A moment passed. I stared at her. Anna Angelisanti was an alluring woman. Her hair, blonde and highlighted with dark caramel-colored strands, was pulled straight back into a ponytail and secured by a black bow. She was wearing casual Saturday attire: jeans and a black crew-neck sweater, white sneakers with white ankle socks.

"First, Francesco, I want you to understand one thing. My relationship with your father was purely platonic. Not that I wanted it that way," she said pensively, her eyes glassy, struggling to find words.

"You wanted a commitment from him?" I asked.

"Not really, nothing permanent, just…"

Her voice trailed off.

"A more loving relationship?" I suggested.

She gazed blindly past me.

"Your mother was the only love of his life," she said quietly. "He made that crystal clear in his relationship with me. She was, is, and always will be his soulmate."

Anna wiped her eyes with a tissue.

"And don't be misled by the clothes you found in his bedroom," she said candidly. "I accompanied your father to bench-bar functions, literary events, and an occasional dinner. Because we were on such a tight schedule, it was easier for me to dress here instead of my place."

"How did you get in here so easily, Anna?" I asked, switching the subject. "This place is as secure as the White House."

"I have a key," she explained. "When your father was at work, I came during the day to read the manuscript. We were on a rather tight schedule because I had a publisher interested in the book."

"And you never printed a copy of the manuscript?"

"Never."

"And you never copied it onto a hard drive?"

"No. I religiously followed your father's instructions."

My initial assessment was that Anna Angelisanti was telling the truth. If she had a copy of my father's latest manuscript, she wouldn't have been rummaging through his belongings on a rainy Saturday morning. To put her at ease, I turned our conversation to more generic things.

"Where did you go to school, Anna?"

"I have a bachelor's degree from Bard and an MFA from Brown."

"Where do you work?"

"H.V. Babcock. It's a small Washington publishing firm."

I decided to test the boundaries of our conversation.

"Where did you meet my father?"

"At a party a few months ago in Georgetown."

"When did he hire you as his agent?"

"The next day. We met for lunch."

She fidgeted, uncomfortable with the question. I pressed on.

"As his agent, I assumed you read the manuscript?"

"I did."

"Can you tell me anything about the plot?"

She opened the drawer of an end table and reached for a pack of cigarettes.

"Do you mind?" she asked.

"No."

She reached for a lighter in her jeans pocket and lit a cigarette, her hand unsteady.

"I paid little attention to the plot. To be honest, Giovanni's writing was horrible," she said after taking a drag as swirls of smoke circled to the ceiling. "Deleting text and making suggestions consumed my time. The story read like one of his legal opinions."

She was hedging the truth, I thought—finding a publisher for a debut novel, written horribly I suspect, and with a plot she conveniently hid from me.

"But you were his agent, not his editor," I asked, testing her.

"Correct. Someone else was your father's editor."

Anna didn't give me a chance to explore any further. She stood up, doused her cigarette, and asked permission to return later and remove her clothes. We exchanged telephone numbers, and after a gentle hug, the lady in black walked toward the door, removed a hooded jacket from the vestibule closet, and left the apartment.

After making a cappuccino, I started my private search of the Judge's condominium in the bathroom that adjoined his bedroom. I opened the door and immediately noticed that Anna had left her iPhone on the sink. My first inclination was to chase after her, but I decided to begin my work as an investigator. I searched her recently dialed numbers and noticed that she made several phone calls to a Luca Botti. I decided to call him. A recorded voice left a message: "Please enter your access code."

CHAPTER 20

A Confrontation

I t was about two in the afternoon. A couple hours had passed since I began my search of the Judge's Watergate apartment. I emptied drawers, turned coat pockets inside-out, looked under rugs, removed each pillow from every piece of furniture, and inspected the back panels of the Judge's reproductions of Andy Warhol floral lithographs, a nod to his childhood in Western Pennsylvania. I turned to his laptop. Before she left, Anna had given me his password. I pulled out a small chair tucked under his desk, opened the computer, and logged on.

Unfortunately, someone had emptied the computer's store. Disgruntled, I shut it down. The screen quickly faded to black. I placed the computer into its carrying case and flipped the strap over my shoulder. I decided to take it to New Castle. Maybe a wizard could feed the computer a magical potion and access any information the Judge might have secreted in a hidden file. I glanced at my watch. In about two hours, my train to Pittsburgh was scheduled to leave Union Station. After calling for a cab, I adjusted the shoulder strap on the computer's carrying case. But, as

I walked toward the door, I was stunned by a loud knock followed by a stern formal announcement.

"This is FBI agent Roosevelt Ward. I have a search warrant issued by a federal judge," he shouted, his bark startling me. "Open the door immediately, or we will break it down."

He bellowed the warning three times. I wanted to ignore Ward's threat and then witness the daunting force of the federal government as its agents smashed the door down and barged into the apartment. But I had more respect for peace through negotiated compromise. I opened the door, knowing their search would be futile, just like mine. Along with two other men, Ward faced me. One was a uniformed Watergate South security officer. He dangled a passkey. A startled Ward spoke first.

"Francesco, what are you doing here?" he asked, surprised to see me.

"Do you have an objection?" I responded sarcastically. "It's my father's apartment."

"No," Ward said, embarrassed, "of course not."

He regained his composure, reminding himself of his rank.

"Now, if you'll stand aside, we'll begin our search."

"Just a second, Mr. Ward," I said, interrupting his advance. "I need some identification from your friend."

Ward was visibly frustrated. He nodded to his comrade who flashed a photo identification card. His name was Carlton Frisk, an officer with the Defense Intelligence

Agency. Strange, I thought. The DIA and Justice must be joining forces. My campaign to irritate Ward forged onward.

"I want to see a copy of the search warrant and the affidavit," I demanded.

"You have no right to either," he answered curtly. "We're searching your father's residence, not yours."

"True, my friend," I responded, shrugging, "but he's dead, and I'm the executor of his estate. Shall I call my attorney, Leonardo Mendici?"

"No need to," Ward answered gruffly. He gave me an affidavit. I read it:

> A confidential informant, who
> has provided credible information
> in the past, has told FBI agent
> Roosevelt Ward that Judge
> Giovanni Micco has classified
> intelligence stored on his computer
> connected to the murder of
> his wife, Rosalina Micco. The
> Government requests that a search
> warrant be issued and that Judge
> Micco's computer be seized, along
> with any other relevant evidence.

"Have a good search, Agent Ward, and don't forget to give a copy of the inventory to Leonardo Mendici," I said, about to leave, my hand on the doorknob.

"Where do you think you're going?" he shot back.

"To Union Station—unless you have a warrant for my arrest."

He eyed the case hanging from my shoulder.

"If that's your father's computer, you can't take it with you."

"It's mine."

"You're lying," Ward shot back. "Give it to me."

"Shall I call my attorney?"

"You're smart *and* stupid, aren't you?" Ward said arrogantly.

A burst of anger shot through me. I slid the strap from my shoulder. The computer fell to the floor. With outstretched arms and beaded eyes, I pushed hard against Ward's chest as he backed away.

"Stop, Francesco. Don't do anything foolish," he cautioned sternly, retreating further down the hallway.

I ignored his caveat and moved closer as Ward stood his ground, his steely stare, lifted palms, warnings to harness my anger.

"Let's talk," Ward pleaded as I moved even closer.

We now stood face-to- face.

"Don't he foolish," Ward advised, head cocked, his threatening stare a final warning I foolishly ignored. Lunging, I pushed Ward against a wall. He easily turned me around in one fluid motion, pinned my arms behind my back, and slammed me down. My face crashed against the floor. Immediately, I sensed the flow of warm blood gushing from my nose. I was lethargic but conscious.

"Call 911!" Ward shouted to Frisk.

After placing the call, Frisk applied an ice pack to my nose once Ward had placed a pillow under my head. The bleeding soon subsided, but by the time the ambulance arrived, I was confused and disoriented. Two paramedics lifted me onto a gurney and wheeled me out of the Judge's Watergate apartment. Its siren bellowing, the ambulance weaved through traffic. While a paramedic monitored my blood pressure, Ward sat beside me, now questioning his decision to smash my face into the apartment floor. I shared his sentiment.

"Francesco, I'm sorry. But why did you come at me that way?" he asked, apologizing.

I turned my head away. How had I arrived at this moment? All I wanted was to practice law in a small town, marry my soulmate, and raise our family. It was a simple dream. But here I was, riding in an ambulance, a sack hanging from an IV pole feeding fluid into one of my arms through a catheter while a cuff, strapped tightly around my other arm, measured my faltering blood pressure. Staring through the small ambulance window, I answered Agent Ward's question.

"You don't have time to hear the story, Roosevelt. Let's just drop it. It was a dumb thing to do."

CHAPTER 21

A SURPRISE VISITOR

I was treated at the emergency room of the Washington Hospital Center. The doctor admitted me because she suspected a concussion and thought it best to observe me for twenty-four hours. It was late Saturday evening; I had no other engagements, so I accepted her invitation. Agent Ward was indulgent. He forgave my trespass and remained with me until an orderly transferred me to my hospital room. Before leaving, he gave me his cell phone number "in the event I needed anything." His parting words were brotherly advice.

"Cooperate with Attorney General Ash, Francesco. He's determined to solve your mother's murder."

Opting not to tell Gianna about my incident with Roosevelt Ward, I called her from the hospital. I explained that my inventory of the Judge's apartment took longer than expected. Cataloging his condo furnishings would delay me in Washington for a day.

"Did you find anything interesting?" she asked.

"Not really. How's Michele?" I asked quickly, changing subjects.

"He misses you."

"Is he sleeping?"

"I put him to bed about an hour ago."

Hearing her voice calmed me, something I badly needed.

"Love 'ya."

"Love 'ya more," she answered.

After our conversation ended, I couldn't sleep. I laid awake, my thoughts drifting to the judge's message that Uncle Claudio delivered to me the day after my father's funeral. I called him in New York from my hospital room late Saturday night. I described the surreal events that interrupted my visit to the Judge's Watergate South apartment and asked to see him as soon as possible. While we talked, he purchased a plane ticket and made reservations at the Helmsley Park Lane Hotel at Central Park South. His office was located just around the corner in the Trump Tower on Fifth Avenue. We made arrangements to meet there at nine Monday morning.

My flight arrived at LaGuardia late Sunday afternoon. I took an airport shuttle to the Helmsley. When I registered, the desk clerk handed me an envelope marked "Courtesy of Uncle Claudio." I opened it and found five hundred dollars, along with a ticket to a Broadway show, *Mamma Mia*. I looked at the ticket with some confusion—a bizarre joke.

Because I intended to be in Washington just one day, I carried no luggage on the Capitol Limited from Pittsburgh.

Uncle Claudio, as he did so often, had anticipated my dilemma. In my room, I found a pile of Saks Fifth Avenue bags filled with new clothes. An Italian suit, designed by Fabio Inchirami, hung on the closet pole, again with a note reading "Courtesy of Uncle Claudio" as if I didn't know. A Gucci suitcase rested on the luggage rack. Before going to the show, I showered, dressed, and then took the elevator to the lobby. While walking through the reception area, the night clerk motioned me over to the front desk. He spoke softly, almost in a whisper.

"About ten minutes ago, a man asked me if Francesco Micco was registered here."

"Did you tell him?"

"No. I said that hotel protocol didn't permit me to reveal that information."

"What did he look like?"

"He was tall. Dressed in a suit and tie."

"Did he say anything else?"

"No. He thanked me and left."

I gave the clerk a twenty and pushed my way through the revolving doors. I glanced up and down the sidewalk and then blended in with the crowd, staying close to the buildings, walking against the flow. I slipped into a dark cubbyhole about a block down and watched the crowd hurrying in both directions. Then I saw him, pushing and shoving his way through the public—Carlton Fisk, the DIA agent who accompanied Roosevelt Ward when they searched the Judge's Watergate apartment yesterday. For some reason, the Government's sight was now centered on me, while Rosalina Micco's murder investigation simmered on the back burner.

———————

On Monday, I arrived at the Trump Tower lobby promptly at nine in the morning. After passing through security, I took an elevator to the fifth floor. Immediately across the hallway, an unpretentious sign identified the office suite occupied by Uncle Claudio's company. It read: *Marymount HealthCare.* I entered and introduced myself to his receptionist. Within a second or two, Uncle Claudio appeared. A smile stretched across his face. I clasped his arms and kissed him once on each cheek. He then placed his arm around my shoulder and escorted me into his office. We sat in front of his desk.

"Francesco, ti e piaciuto l'albergo?"

I told him that the accommodations were more than satisfactory and that he didn't need to smother me with gifts.

"Hey, you're my godson," he said. "I can do whatever I please. How have you been?"

"Frustrated." An honest answer that led to a sensitive subject.

"Why?" he asked slyly.

"Too much going on," I answered, avoiding his question.

Uncle Claudio leaned back, his stare penetrating, the stern face of a headmaster about to conduct an inquiry into a rule violation.

"Why did you file the exhumation motion in court?" His tone was grave, a rebuke that sent me a message.

"Because I believe that my father's death was a homicide," I answered bluntly.

I couldn't tell if Uncle Claudio shared my feelings, but his question and disapproving stare kept me from exploring the subject.

"If someone murdered Giovanni," he answered sternly, "I have the means to retaliate."

His cold comment was a reminder of my mother's suspicion that Uncle Claudio was a Mafioso. It was also an edict commanding that I follow my father's directions and play by the rules.

"Didn't Giovanni tell you in the note I delivered to do nothing?" Claudio asked rhetorically.

"He did."

"Then follow his instructions." Another sharp command. "If anyone contacts you or asks you to do anything whatsoever, contact me immediately. Do you understand?"

"You're referring to Roosevelt Ward?"

"I am. And anyone else who contacts you."

"Does that include Salvatore Sacco and Leonardo Mendici?"

"It does."

I paused while refreshing my recollection.

"I have an appointment with Mendici soon," I recalled. "An attorney with his firm represents my father's estate."

His nod gave me tacit approval. It was apparent that Uncle Claudio was protecting me. Still, I remained curious about my father's manuscript and its role in the 'draconian plot' he had discovered. My next question was a segue into a welcome change of subjects.

"Did you know that my father was writing a novel?" I asked.

"Yes."

"Have you read it?"

"No."

His short answers suggested a reluctance to explore the Judge's literary effort further, but I prodded.

"Where's the manuscript?"

"It's in Sicily."

"At our home in Taormina?"

"Your father left it there for Grazia to edit."

"Why was he writing a novel?"

"Let's just say that he had a story to tell and leave it at that."

It was becoming apparent. Somehow my father connected his story to the plot he had discovered. Perhaps he was writing about real events overlaid with a facade of fiction, the characters thinly disguised—a possibility that presented a risk to my sister.

"Will Grazia be safe in Sicily," I asked anxiously.

"She will be well protected," he answered assuredly.

Uncle Claudio stared at me, my concern apparent.

"You should relax, Francesco. Return to New Castle, enjoy your family, build your practice," he advised loudly, his words sending me to the bench, the yell of a coach barking orders to the third-string quarterback. I planned to take his advice—at least most of it. But before I left Marymount, I was determined to learn more about the monogrammed parchment paper on which my father had penned the message Uncle Claudio delivered the day after the Judge's funeral.

"The Rosecross? What does it represent?" I asked.

He answered my question with a stare. I persisted.

"Is it a symbol of a secret society?"

His gaze turned to a smile.

"Since the time of the ancient Greeks, Francesco, roses have been painted on ceilings, and societies conducted meetings sub rosa, or under the rose, meaning they were secret gatherings," he explained, smiling broadly. "Even today, the Freemasons hold closed meetings. So do the Knights of Columbus. That doesn't make them sorcerers."

Abruptly ending any further talk about the monogram, he invited me to meet his business manager in the United States, Guido Borgese. We walked down a short corridor.

Uncle Claudio tapped on his door, stood aside, and motioned me into a small office decorated sparsely.

"Francesco, meet Guido Borgese. He's the brain trust behind Marymount." Borgese moved from behind his desk and extended his hand.

"Francesco, I feel I already know you," he said warmly. "Claudio always speaks so well of the Micco family."

He invited us to sit. With guarded eyes, he listened attentively as Uncle Claudio paced through the series of events that had controlled my life since the Judge's death. When he finished, Uncle Claudio turned toward me.

"Francesco, listen carefully. If, for some reason, I'm not available to help you, please call Guido. He's been my trusted confidant for many, many years."

When our meeting concluded, Uncle Claudio accompanied me into the reception area. He asked his secretary to print the boarding pass for my trip to Pittsburgh. Before returning to his office, he excused himself.

"Please, Francesco, stay in touch."

As I exited the elevator on the ground floor of Trump Tower, I spotted a Starbucks on the mezzanine level overlooking the lobby. I was exhausted and needed an espresso. I took a seat that overlooked the lobby entrance. I watched the crowds of people move across the floor— haggard young assistants with dry cleaning and coffee trays, maintenance workers laughing while pulling heavy carts, not to mention the professionalized men and women, stoic in their business suits.

I called Gianna and assured her I'd be home soon; she told me that Michele was asking about me. I said everything I could to ease her mind without disclosing too much of this incredible affair, the many lines of which I could barely follow. In the last few days, new people had entered into my life—Anna, Roosevelt, Guido—each reflecting a new turn in my father's afterlife. I also thought of how Giovanni Micco's death had finally allowed me to see him as a mutable man, far from the bullish, stubborn person I had known. As I spoke to Gianna, I felt strength in our shared understanding of one another, comfortable in the knowledge that we saw each other with almost total clarity. I hoped that my father's new character would not darken the waters, as I wished Gianna a good afternoon.

But before I left Trump Tower, another complication emerged. From the mezzanine, I saw a familiar face approach the security officers in the lobby below. Without showing any identification to the guards, he was allowed to enter the elevator. He was obviously a frequent visitor. It was my brother Giancarlo.

CHAPTER 22

Elisha Forde

The Judge's memorial ceremony was scheduled in the Court of Appeals for the last Friday in January. Wanting to move along the administration of his estate, I flew to Washington the day after I returned to New Castle. I had made arrangements to meet with Leonardo Mendici two days before the service. My wife and son, along with my brother Giancarlo, would join me the following day. I was unable to meet with Grazia because she was attending a confectioner's show in Chicago. She booked an early morning flight and would arrive in Washington on the day of the memorial. I planned to meet with Grazia sometime after the service and explain to her—detail by detail—the events that had invaded my life since our father's funeral. Irrespective of Uncle Claudio's advice, I'd ask her to allow me to read the manuscript.

Just as I recalled, the offices of Mendici Melrose were opulent, the spoils of a legal system that generated mighty fees from mighty clients who wielded their drunken power through the halls of government. It was a life my father wanted me to embrace, one I would have loathed. The receptionist offered me coffee and a danish. Politely, I refused. Within minutes Leonardo Mendici emerged from his inner sanctuary. With his arm draped around my shoulder, he ushered me back to the firm's boardroom.

"It's nice to see you again, Francesco," he said, patting my back.

"It's good to see you, Mr. Mendici," I answered, forcing a smile.

"I think it best to start by introducing you to the attorney who will be representing your father's estate," he began. "After you finish, we'll have a private lunch, just you and I."

Mendici used one of the telephones scattered around the boardroom. He dialed an intercom number.

"Elisha, Francesco Micco is here," he said.

Within a minute, there was a soft knock on the door. As she entered the room, our eyes met. I nodded before she turned her attention to Mendici. She was alluring. Her straight, frosted, blonde hair hung straight to her shoulders. Crystal blue eyes complimented her smile. She was dressed in a striped, navy-blue business suit and a white blouse with a ruffled bow. Her tailored jacket was unbuttoned, and a sheath skirt hemmed slightly above the knees clung closely to her hips. Navy pumps matched her suit.

"Francesco, this is Elisha Scott."

Elisha Scott. The former Elisha Forde. I haven't seen her for nearly two years.

CHAPTER 23

MEMORIES

During my second year in law school, Elisha Forde sat behind me in our constitutional law class. She was a Smith graduate and drove a red Mercedes convertible. My initial thought was that Elisha was distant and aloof. I concluded she was the spoiled daughter of a privileged family. Halfway through the semester, she joined my study group. Reality rescued me.

She was engaging, not distant, gracious, not aloof. And she was beautiful. Her blonde hair, much longer and lighter then, hung freely over her shoulders. Whenever we spoke, her eyes never strayed but remained focused. Her smile, permanently fixed, conveyed an elegance that extended well beyond her attractive physical features. The impetuous opinion I had initially formed of Elisha Forde was dead wrong.

As the school year progressed, she seemed impressed with how I grasped the professors' law concepts. She asked that I tutor her. "A paid position," she assured me. I jumped at the chance. Although my financial statement was colored red, I refused to accept any money. Instead, she promised to invite me to her apartment for dinner. It was a fair exchange, tilted slightly in my favor, I thought. Together, we read and briefed cases, researched legal issues, and challenged each other's analysis of the law.

The arrangement also included a social side. Sometimes we ordered a pizza, sometimes Elisha prepared her favorite dish, baked chicken cordon bleu, and sometimes, usually on weekends, we cut short the work sessions and went off to Luigi's, a small, intimate Italian restaurant, for lasagna and a late movie. But through it all, our relationship remained platonic.

Besides holding her hand, I was reluctant to make even the most obscure move that would suggest I wanted a more intimate relationship. At times, she tempted me—a lingering stare, a tight squeeze when we held hands, resting her head on my shoulder after a long nights study session. But I always resisted, afraid that accidental differences determined our destiny. She was the daughter of an investment banker whose wealth was measured by the stock market's barometer. I was the son of a federal judge, whose income was limited by the whims of Congress. A meaningful relationship just wouldn't work. When the school year ended in June, Elisha went home to Massachusetts. I made a short trip to Northern Virginia. In August, it would all change.

A small law firm in Vienna, Virginia hired me to do legal research. Although I had received an offer to intern with Mendici Melrose, I explored the idea of returning to my roots in New Castle. Perhaps during my final year of law school, I would intern at Mendici Melrose if they would have me. Then I could compare the two experiences. At least that was my plan, which was endorsed by my mother, Rosalina, and opposed by my father, Giovanni.

For extra money, I worked nights in a coffee shop as a barista. On a Friday evening in early August, an unfortunate circumstance would cause my relationship with Elisha to strike an amorous chord. It was just before ten in the evening when I returned home from work. My mother and father were in the family room. She was reading a book, and he, as usual, was editing the draft of a legal opinion he had authored, along with the assistance of one of his three law clerks. My mother had a message for me.

"Francesco, Elisha called you about an hour ago."

During the school year, I had occasionally invited Elisha to our home on Sundays to enjoy a typical Italian dinner. At first, Rosalina was overly observant, cautiously evaluating this young, beautiful girl who, she thought, might someday become her daughter-in-law. She was reserved but courteous, quiet but curious, acting as the mother of a son who was about to choose his mate. Elisha was equally cautious, and she, too, was inquisitive. Was Rosalina a mother who meddled in her children's lives? Would she allow them to spread their wings and fly away? Did she have veto power over their choice of mates?

As for me, I considered their sparring match to be meaningless because the privileges Elisha enjoyed would certainly doom our relationship. From my perspective, even before the competition began, her family's wealth eliminated me from the list of suitors who someday would win her hand. Nevertheless, as time crept by, Rosalina and Elisha became friends, each having passed their respective litmus tests.

"What did she want?" I asked.

My mother placed her book on an end table and removed her reading glasses. A somber expression covered her face, causing me to suspect the news she was about to pass on was not good.

"Her mother passed away this morning. It was sudden. Something about an aneurism. Her phone number is on the fridge. She asked that you call her."

Apprehensive, I dialed her number. The phone rang only once.

"I'm so glad you called, Francesco," she said, her voice quivering. "Did your mother tell you?"

"Yes, she did."

"It was so sudden."

Her voice trailed off.

"Much too sudden," she added.

I could almost feel her grief, her pain.

"Had she been ill?" I asked, searching for words.

"No. Dad found her on the bathroom floor. He called the paramedics. By the time they arrived, she had passed."

"You were at home when it happened?"

"Yes. It was a drenching experience."

"When are the calling hours?"

"In four days. The church service will be in The Old South Church."

I glanced at my mother rocking in her chair, reading glasses perched on her nose, turning a page of her novel, eavesdropping on my conversation. Like counsel doled out in a lovelorn column, I almost heard her advice: 'Ask her!'

"If you like, I could come to Boston?"

"I'd love that."

———————

Two days later, my flight arrived at Logan International Airport at eight in the morning. Elisha was unable to meet me because her father and she had a meeting with the church pastor and the funeral director. She made arrangements with a limousine service to take me from the airport to the Charlesmark Hotel. Elisha, an only child, lived with her parents in Boston's Back Bay district. It was her neighborhood, and I was happy to be there. I changed my clothes and waited. At about eleven she called.

"Francesco, I'm happy you're here. I'll come as soon as possible. Sorry I couldn't be at the airport. Meet me in the lobby in fifteen minutes."

I took the elevator to the first floor and sat in a high-back chair, watching as guests left and visitors arrived through a revolving door. Then, a face in the crowd caught my stare. It was Elisha. I saw her smile and outstretched arms as we raced towards each other. We hugged. I could feel her heartbeat in sync with mine. For nearly a year, I had used her father's wealth to keep my feelings at bay. Now I found myself walking, hand in hand, down Newbury street with Elisha Forde. The sidewalks bustled with shoppers. We passed sidewalk cafés, browsed through flower shops and art galleries as well as upscale stores that offered expensive wines. It was, however, an uneasy time for her. Elisha's mother's death had left a void in her life; I wondered whether she had pulled me here only to help her recover from an emotional trauma. As we sat in a sidewalk café sipping cappuccinos, she sensed my apprehension. When our conversation waned, Elisha Forde became the aggressor.

"Francesco, sometimes you're close to me, and other times you're distant," she said softly, her eyes glassy. "You're trying to scale a wall to reach me on the other side, but when you get to the top, you can't climb over."

Regrettably, by waiting to express my feelings, I had relinquished the chance to speak first. She didn't let the moment pass.

"I know the problem you perceive, but you should know that perception isn't reality," she said soberly. "All I want, Francesco, is a life with you. Nothing more."

We locked our hands. Tears trickled onto her blushed cheeks. She leaned toward me and then came words I longed to hear.

"Francesco, I love you."

There was no pause because I had no doubt.

"And I love you, Elisha."

We left the café, walked hand-in-hand back to the Charlesmark, through the lobby, into the elevator, down the hall, and into my room.

CHAPTER 24

A Rude Awakening

It was our last year at Georgetown. Elisha had invited me to visit Boston during our Christmas vacation. Earlier in the semester, her father, Franklin Forde, was in Washington on a business trip. He took us to dinner and during the evening I concluded that he was an insatiable workaholic with an equally voracious appetite to stockpile money. His professional accomplishments consumed the table talk. Occasionally, he would take a respite from his favorite topic and ask me a question about my career. Elisha propped me up against her egomaniacal father, making sure he knew that I was ranked second in my class and that I was the Georgetown Law Review editor.

"A very distinct honor," she remarked.

However, the table talk eventually drifted back to his accomplishments as a savvy investment banker, although he sporadically slid in a snide remark, voicing his disapproval of my plans to practice law in a small town.

"Can't make much money there," was his curt opinion.

Elisha assured him that my plans were not 'carved in stone'—to use her words—and perhaps I would accept one of the many lucrative offers being made to me from prestigious law firms both in Washington and New York.

"They would start him off at six figures, Dad," she boasted on my behalf.

I didn't appreciate her patronizing endorsement. At Elisha's prodding, I had submitted applications to several metropolitan law firms, and I was impressed by the responses they generated. I'm sure they were prompted just as much by my father's position as a federal appeals court judge as my academic record.

Throughout the interview process, my plans to return to New Castle became more definite. Elisha assured me, however, that she would accept my decision. She also suggested, transparently, that I should juxtapose the financial benefits of eventually becoming a partner in a large law firm with the limited potential offered by a general practice in a small town. Her thoughts seemed condescending, but her plan made sense. However, I wanted to believe in her love and brushed aside my class sensibility in favor of her humanity. If I decided to return to New Castle, Elisha assured me that she would join me there "as a partner, both in marriage and in law." As I looked across the table at her father, dunking his steak with great gusto into a pool of ruddy sauce, I began to have my doubts.

We drove to Boston the day after our Christmas break began. The plan was for me to stay there for two days and then fly home to Virginia. She would remain in Boston and celebrate Christmas with her father. I needed to celebrate Christmas with my family, a Micco tradition that no guilt could displace.

Late the same day, we arrived at her family's brownstone in Back Bay. I had not told her yet, but I decided to decline the offers of employment I received from law firms in New York and Washington. I was already in contact with friends and family members in New Castle, looking for an office. I planned to make a full disclosure before I gave her the engagement ring, knowing already that my choice would undoubtedly be a part of her calculations. She was, beyond everything else, a discerning lawyer.

Franklin Forde had planned an intimate dinner party in their home on my last night in Boston. The guest list included Randolph Scott, a wealthy industrialist, Mr. Scott's wife, and their son, Randolph Scott, Jr. I was pleasantly surprised by the cordial mood that permeated the evening. Mr. Forde was gracious and pleasant. Not once did he mention his accomplishments as an investment banker. Instead, he made sure everyone seated at the dinner table became acquainted with my academic achievements, as well as the offers of employment I had received "from some of the biggest and most prestigious law firms in this country." He also acknowledged, surprisingly, that I might decline the offers.

"He's even thinking about returning to his hometown to build a law practice, and that would be fine, too," he said, slanting his wine glass in my direction then taking a sip before he continued with his ringing endorsement.

"Entrepreneurs like Francesco are exactly what this country needs. Young, energetic people who are willing to take risks, who want to build businesses, who are willing to expose themselves to failure before they eventually succeed."

His homily paused, Franklin Forde's stare shifted to his contemporary, Randolph Scott, CEO of Scott Enterprises.

"As Randolph knows better than anyone at this table, it takes time and lots of hard work."

He was also careful not to exclude his best client's son's credentials and stroke his ego. It was a sound business practice. At least, that was my naive conclusion. I later learned that Franklin Forde was a cunning sort. By rote memory, he rattled off the staid history of Scott Enterprises and, raising his glass of wine to offer a toast, concluded that someday Randolph Scott, Jr. would assume the company's reins.

The evening was elegant and with a few glasses of wine, I felt completely at ease amongst my intimidating and unfamiliar fellow guests. I joked with Randolph Sr. about a neurotic professor of mine known around Washington for his bizarre mannerisms, pivoting to an intense conversation surrounding labor law and business practice. As he leaned in, as he laughed, I felt as if I could belong to Elisha's world, that it wasn't so difficult, the rewards, financial and social, very alluring.Looking at Elisha while wallowing in her endorsement of me, I could acknowledge that all of the talks about my accomplishments were not meaningless. I *was* the dynamic and brilliant young man she had described. For a moment, I questioned my choice.

Elisha and I thanked her father for a delightful dinner party and, after the guests had left, we sat for a short while in a cozy den, a small cherry-paneled room furnished with leather chairs facing a fireplace. It was drizzling rain, and Mr. Forde started a fire saying that he was "taking the chill out of the room." After a short while, sensing it was a good time for the two men in her life to engage in a private conversation, Elisha excused herself and went off to her bedroom. Waiting just long enough to assure himself that she had tucked herself in bed for the night, Franklin Forde quietly closed the door and sat in the chair beside me, his eyes fixed on the fire.

"So, you want to ask my daughter to marry you?"

"Yes, I do."

Franklyn Forde was a discerning man, and his observation didn't surprise me. But his even, quiet tone left me confused.

"Please understand, I'm not an intruder," he said calmly, his eyes riveted to mine. "I won't interfere with your plans."

He paused for a moment and turned his stare to the flames crackling in the fireplace. I sensed his next words would caution me about the fragility of a relationship based on love alone.

"I guess the protocol has changed. Before I asked for Mrs. Forde's hand in marriage, I had to get her plutocrat father's permission, and I didn't come into the marriage empty-handed," he said softly as the flames flare lit his face. "He was a cranky miser who wanted his accountant to analyze my financial statement before he gave me his blessing."

He glanced at me before returning his stare to the fire.

"But I loved his daughter very much," he said, reminiscing. "I assured him I had considered not only my emotions but also my ability to provide her with the affluent trappings she was accustomed to."

His concerns were real, not a pretext. As Elisha's father, he was determined to protect his daughter from entering into a world that was foreign to her. Saying little, I assured him I recognized the differences from a social perspective that separated us. His next comment bluntly told me that Franklin Ford's dinner guests were invited for a purpose.

"Take a long, hard look at young Randolph Scott and his family. Mind you now, I'm not saying Elisha would be better off with Randy than you," he cautioned. "But someone like him will best satisfy her lifestyle, her expectations. Elisha and Randy have common backgrounds."

Laying aside his rude observation, hearing their names in the same sentence offended me. I wanted to say something, anything that would somehow refute the opinion of Franklin Forde, but his thoughts were not without merit. He was only echoing my reservations about our relationship.

"Please, believe me, Francesco, I honestly like you, and if you and Elisha decide to get married, I'll welcome you into our family," he remarked, a patronizing gesture. "But there is one thing you must promise me."

Franklin Forde leaned to the edge of his chair and focused his eyes directly on mine.

"You know you've decided to return to your roots and start your law practice. Tell Elisha that before you ask her to marry you."

His plea deserved no response. It was an easy promise to make.

———————

Early the next morning, Elisha drove me to the airport. We arrived at Logan International about two hours before my flight left for Washington. During the short drive, we made plans for her to visit with my family sometime during the week following Christmas. She seemed inordinately happy, and I was reluctant to tell her that I had decided to return to New Castle to practice law. Simply put, I refused to suffocate while laboring in the billable hours' department of a mammoth legal emporium. I allowed myself a moment of casual conversation before stumbling into the delicate topic that could signal an abrupt end to our relationship. Doggedly, I continued to search for a wedge in our discussion where the news of my decision would best fit. Finally, Elisha asked a question, and an opening emerged, one I fumbled with.

"How did your conversation with my father go last night?" she asked curiously.

"It went well."

I said nothing else. Elisha looked confused because I didn't take the bait, forcing her to ask another question.

"Did you talk about *me*?" she asked, flicking a glance at herself in the rearview mirror.

"Of course we did, Elisha," I said nervously. "You were the focus of our conversation."

I placed my hand on her lap.

"I told your father we loved each other," I said softly, a precursor to the news I was about to deliver.

Her eyes remained focused on the road. Elisha smiled but said nothing, pushing me to speak. My heart palpitated. Trapped by silence, the moment of reckoning had finally arrived. Words began flowing out of my mouth like water splashing from a wide-open faucet.

"I've decided to return to New Castle to practice law," I blurted out.

My decision stung Elisha. Her grip on the steering wheel tightened. Her face was flush with disappointment. As she swallowed hard, I explained that the assignments of demanding law partners would entrap me in a career that I would loathe.

"It doesn't surprise me, Francesco," Elisha said, sighing before she brushed away a tear. "To be honest, I had hoped you would stay in Washington with your family. But your decision has been made," she continued, shrugging. "You'll have to stick with it. It's that simple."

Barely feigning lightness, she looked at me with a pained smile and fell quiet. Punched hard by Elisha's silence, I searched for words that would draw her close to me. But the only words I found were hers. The ones she spoke as we sat in the café on Newbury Street. *"All I want is a life with you, nothing more."*

Before I boarded my flight, we set a date for her visit to Virginia. She planned to come the day after Christmas and remain until New Year's Day. I had purchased a diamond ring with the money I had saved and a "loan" from my mother. She had invaded a trust fund established by her father.

On Christmas night, Elisha called and said she had changed her plans. A client, probably Randolph Scott, invited her father to vacation three days at an Aspen ski lodge. He asked her to accompany him.

"He's lonely, Francesco. He misses my mother. It's the first Christmas he'll be without her. I couldn't say no to him," she said, shrugging off her promise to me. "I'm very sorry. As soon as I get back, I'll call you, and we'll set another date."

An empty apology.

She never called.

During my last semester at Georgetown, I worked as an intern at the Department of Justice. I received four credits, all that I needed to graduate. I had no classes at the Law Center. I stayed away from the school on E Street—and from Elisha Forde. I had not seen her since the day she drove me to Logan International Airport.

CHAPTER 25

FINALLY—AN APOLOGY

After introducing me to Elisha Scott, Leonardo Mendici excused himself and said he would meet with me later in his office. Elisha and I stared at each other for a moment. She spoke first.

"It's been a long time, Francesco."

"Yes, it has been, Elisha."

Though worn a little from work, her face still held within it the vibrant energy of her focused and alert mind.

"I see time has treated you well. How have you been?" I asked.

She didn't answer my question. I meant it as an impolite segue into a mystery that had stumped me for over a year. Elisha was a paragon of manners, but yet she didn't have the courtesy to tell me she had decided to remain safely sheltered in a mammoth law firm. Her explanation mellowed my attitude.

"Francesco, I'm truly sorry. I should have told you. But I was afraid."

"Of what?"

"I was afraid of you—if I would have seen you, even if I had just talked to you…"

Her voice trailed off. Elisha's glassy eyes and fragmented explanation mellowed me. The rational side of the love conundrum won out. Her tone turned somber.

"Let's be honest with each other, Francesco," she said, her glassy eyes staring me down. "It would not have worked out. That's the bottom line. You know that."

"So, instead, you married Randolph Scott."

Saying nothing, she closed her eyes and turned away.

"And how is Randy?" I asked, trying to ignore an emotion that suddenly appeared—one I tried to smother but couldn't.

Elisha lowered her head and again faced me. Her eyes narrowed to hide the pangs of sorrow.

"Don't be rude, Francesco," she said, "Our marriage was over before it began. We just divorced."

Despite my feelings, I was embarrassed at upsetting her and apologized. I had already extracted my ounce of retribution. From the outset, our fragile relationship, built on insecurities and refusals to live simply, had been destined for failure. In the end, Elisha alone suffered from the fate that saved us from each other. She offered to ask Mendici to assign another attorney to represent my father's estate. Not wanting to insult her further, I assured Elisha we could work through it together. We stood and, for a short moment, looked at each other, smiled, and then gently hugged—bound by the separate lives we each had chosen.

CHAPTER 26

An Empty Chair

Adhering to a stately display of protocol, the memorial service honoring Judge Giovanni Micco was formal. The members of the United States Court of Appeals for the District of Columbia Circuit gathered in the chief judge's chambers to robe. In the courtroom, a sextet played selections by Tommaso Alboni, the Judge's favorite Italian composer. Two movements from the San Marco Trumpet Concerto and an allegro movement from a Concerto for Two Trumpets in C entertained the subdued gathering. When the ceremony began, the bailiff asked the audience to stand and announced in a loud, firm voice:

> *Hear ye, hear ye. All persons having business before the United States Court of Appeals for the District of Columbia Circuit approach and be heard. God save this Honorable Court and the United States of America.*

As her words resonated, the judges, in black robes, ascended onto the bench and sat as the music faded to a pianissimo. Along with the full complement of circuit court judges, Justice Sacco had decided to pay homage to his departed friend. He sat tall next to the chief judge, brimming with pride. His black robe was accentuated with four gold bars on each sleeve, a decoration displayed for all to see as he rested his folded hands on the bench. I was surprised to see him there, having expected him to offer some lame excuse explaining his absence. Not wanting to tarnish his pristine reputation, Justice Sacco had limited his association with my father after his appointment to the Supreme Court. I assume it was due to my father's friendship with Uncle Claudio. The memorial service began.

Gianna and Michele, along with my brother Giancarlo, sat to my right. To my left was an empty chair reserved for Grazia. I asked the bailiff to delay the ceremony until she arrived. Her flight from Chicago had been late, but the judges' schedules, including Justice Sacco's commitments, permitted only a brief stay. When she arrived at Dulles International at about eight in morning, I talked to her on my cell phone. She had just disembarked from the plane and was about to take a cab to the federal courthouse. A Washington traffic snarl had probably delayed Grazia's arrival. At least she'd be able to attend the reception that would follow the ceremony.

While the chief judge expounded on the first speaker's credentials, Justice Sacco, a bailiff handed me a sealed envelope and whispered that a man standing in the back of the courtroom asked that it be delivered to me immediately. With the platitudes of Justice Sacco echoing in the background, I opened the envelope and read the message:

> *Francesco:*
>
> *I stand in the back of the courtroom and stare at the empty chair beside you. The one reserved for your sister, Grazia. Unfortunately, Grazia will not be attending this impressive ceremony, which honors the distinguished jurist, Judge Giovanni Micco. She is with us, safe and sound—at least for the moment. But that, my dear friend, could soon change. We have no monetary interests. However, we do have another interest—the manuscript of your father's novel and the disc that only you can deliver. Give the manuscript and disc to us, and we will return Grazia to you. There is one caveat: DO NOT MAKE A COPY OF THE MANUSCRIPT OR DISC. If you do, just look to your right—your wife and son are at risk of being empty chairs. We will follow you as you search for Grazia's ransom.*

Anxiety gripped me. Panicked and paralyzed, I folded the program sheet and began to feel dizzy. Too riled to reason and beaded with sweat, I fidgeted in my chair. The words of every speaker, high flown, dragged out, syllable by syllable. The jargon, the pomp, the note clutched in my hands made everything feel false, slow, too cinematic to be a reality. Almost hysterical, I wheeled around to find Uncle Claudio in the audience. Now hunched forward, he was sitting two rows behind me. As our eyes connected, a stark reality numbed me. The Judge's prediction had taken root. "My family has already paid part of the price, and it may be subjected to pay the balance." I assumed Grazia had been kidnapped by a cabal connected to the plot my father discovered, and her ransom was the Judge's manuscript along with a mysterious disc. As the eulogies continued, I stared at the empty chair beside me. The cunning ploy of Grazia's abductors struck me hard. The rigidity of the ceremony was impenetrable: there was no way for me to leave, no way for me to interrupt.

Mercifully, the tributes finally concluded. The chief judge declared that the court "is now in recess." As the jurists filed from the bench and the guests dispersed, I motioned for Uncle Claudio to meet me. Realizing that something was wrong, he hurriedly wove his way through the crowd as I held high the message the bailiff had given me. Thankfully, Gianna and Michele were distracted by Justice Sacco who spoke with them in the courtroom's well.

"What did the note say?" Uncle Claudio asked nervously.

"Grazia's been kidnapped."

Uncle Claudio turned pale. I asked a deputy if there was a vacant room available. Sensing my alarm, he quickly ushered us into a room used by attorneys to confer with their clients privately. My hands clammy, I gave the note to Uncle Claudio. His mouth opened wide as he read the words demanding the Judge's manuscript and a disc as Grazia's ransom.

"I let your family down, Francesco," Uncle Claudio said, his remorse bordering panic. He paused, put his hand to his temples, eyes glassy, struggling to find something else to say.

"We'll get the manuscript," he finally uttered, determined to find and surrender at least part of the ransom demand. "That's all that matters, nothing else."

"What about the disc?" I inquired, befuddled by the mystifying ransom piece demanded by Grazia's kidnappers. "Did my father ever mention it to you?"

"He did," Uncle Claudio drawled, pursing his lips. "Giovanni said that he came upon the disc fortuitously."

"What did he mean by that?" I asked, puzzled.

"He wouldn't tell me," Uncle Claudio explained vaguely, causing me to wonder whether he was hiding something. "But he did say that the information stored in the disc was direct evidence of the plot he had uncovered."

"Did he have the disc?" I asked sharply.

"No," Claudio said glumly, lifting his face, eyes wide and still. "But Giovanni said that he was in negotiations and would have it in seven days."

"In negotiations with who?" I asked, my eyes squinted, brow furrowed, bewildered by Giovanni Micco's strange deal.

"I asked, but he said secrecy bound him."

"He never got the disc?" I responded, disgruntled.

"That's right," Claudio answered tightly. "Your father died five days after our last conversation."

Grazia's kidnapping drew me into the vortex of the plot the Judge had discovered. I was now a player in a game blindfolded by its rules. Uncle Claudio and I decided to make only a brief appearance at the reception. Before we left the room, I asked Uncle Claudio a question.

"Should we notify the FBI?"

"No," he answered quickly.

"Why?"

"Just a hunch."

Knowing something was amiss, Gianna and Giancarlo halted Uncle Claudio and me in the hallway as we were headed to the reception. I led them back into the conference room and explained in detail the events that had consumed my life since our father's funeral, leaving nothing unrevealed.

"Where do you go from here, Francesco?" Gianna asked.

I was conflicted. Because Grazia's kidnapping was a federal offense, my first inclination was to turn to Roosevelt Ward and the FBI for help. But Uncle Claudio thought otherwise. I agreed. It was nothing but blind trust. Nevertheless, I couldn't sit idly by and wait for the manuscript and disc to appear suddenly. As I saw it, Uncle Claudio can chase after the disc. The manuscript? My father had stowed it away in Grazia's secret hiding place in Sicily. I looked out the conference room window into a dark, dreary day, knowing I'd soon board a flight to Italy.

CHAPTER 27

Taormina

Two days later my flight arrived at Rome's Fiumicino's airport at eight in the morning. From Rome, I boarded an Air Sicilia flight to Catania. After arriving at Fontanarossa International, I rented a car. In about an hour, I arrived in Taormina. The weather was calm, but that would soon change. I could make out the word for "rain" in the rapid crescendo of voices on the car's radio.

I drove to our Sicilian retreat and deposited the few belongings I had brought with me. Storm clouds began to gather. The wind increased, but only traces of rain fell. I decided to venture outside. Using the pedestrian walkway, I headed down the mountainside toward the Bay of Taormina. Once there, I gazed beyond the storm clouds, marveling at the white sun as it sank into the surging water. Shivering, I tightly folded my arms and fixed my eyes on the towering waves splashing against a cluster of boulders before spraying the rocky shore.

Soon the wind gathered force, warning me to leave before the gust turned into a gale. When I reached home, the house was dark, the remote location making it an easy target for outages that frequently burdened the fragile cliffside electrical grid. I lit a kerosene lamp, a dusty, rusty relic of a long-gone generation of the Micco family, and placed it on the kitchen table. Reminiscing, I sat and stared at my shadow, flickering against the wall of the house. My lonely silhouette leaned over the table with both elbows propped, hands steepled, yearning for the shadows of family to join.

I sat with Giancarlo, Grazia, and my father in this exact pose while Rosalina roasted a ham. It was Holy Saturday. At noon Lent would be over, ending our forty days of fasting. As a family, we knelt in the room where I now sit, and each of us kissed the floor. We then feasted on the ham following our long fast. After an espresso, the Judge always excused himself and left for an unknown destination with Grazia.

One year I followed them. Hand-in-hand, father and daughter walked along the pedestrian stairs, zigzagging down the mountainside to the narrow, medieval streets below before finally reaching the Corso Umberto, the main strada in Taormina. Their destination was Geletomania, a quaint gelato shop in Piazza IX Aprile. They sat together at a small table near the front window and enjoyed a decadent treat—a crown of cream on top of colorful shaved ice. I laid back, not wanting to intrude on their secret rendezvous. Sometime after that Holy Saturday afternoon, Gelatomania became my second home in Taormina. Each morning, I skipped down the pedestrian stairs that led to the Corso Umberto, sprinting to Gelatomania. I watched as the shop's proprietor, Gaetano Curinga, mixed milk, eggs, sugar, and an assortment of pistachios, hazelnuts, almonds, lemons, and crushed fruits. After smudging his shop window for a week, he asked me if I wanted to work at Gelatomania. I happily accepted his offer of employment.

Even the sounds of Easter echoed while I sat alone in the kitchen. The bellowing Alleluia at Mass, the Judge accompanying Grazia on the piano after dinner while she sang Peter Cottontail, Giancarlo pounding on his drum. And the most endearing sound—the clang of Mom's copper kettle as she reached into the cabinet and pulled it out.

"You must always have a big pan and a stirring spoon," she lectured as I reminisced, the advice she passed on to me after Elisha had canceled her Christmas visit.

"Your grandmother once told me that there's magic in whatever is simmering inside, be it chicken soup or a pot of marinara sauce. It will heal you—whether it's the flu or an ailing heart."

Her words still echo as I squeezed my teary eyes, the image crystal clear—Rosalina reaching into a utensil drawer and pulling out the stirring spoon my father had given to her as a gift many years ago.

CHAPTER 28

A TRADITION

The storm had subsided. At mid-morning, I walked down the pedestrian stairs that led to the Corso Umberto and headed to Gelatomania. Now older, I appreciated the Bay of Taormina's panoramic view, marveling at the contrasting colors of spring flowers cascading down the steep mountainside. When I finally reached the gelato shop, Gaetano had just finished filling the stainless-steel bins with the gelato that would delight the parade of customers, locals, and tourists who patronized his store throughout the day and late into the evening. Gaetano was elated to see me. A broad smile covered his face as he opened his arms. We exchanged kisses and embraced. Mostly it was a happy visit—lasting until I told Gaetano that the Judge had died.

Not surprisingly, he reacted with shock and apologized for the recent Micco family tragedies, each one of us kin to the shop owner we adopted as our Uncle Guy. A bachelor with a brother who lived in Florence, his only relative, Gaetano was our guest during the Easter festivities. Each year, his gelato treats graced our dinner table; Torrone, Menta, Canella, and Rosalina's favorite, Stracciatella.

When the assassin murdered my mother, I notified Gaetano immediately. This man of meager means crossed an ocean to pay his respects to a friend. I hesitated to tell Gaetano that Grazia had been kidnapped, at least for now. There was no need to burden him with more sad news. But I had to know whether the Judge came to Gelatomania when he was in Sicily during the summer.

"Quando e stata l'ultima volta che hai visto mio padre?"

His answer was just as I had expected. Each day, the Judge visited Gelatomania and sat alone in the shop, working on the novel that has brought havoc to our family. Suddenly, this small gelato shop in Taormina had become the focal point in my search for the Judge's manuscript. The place where Grazia and my father often rendezvoused might hold the ransom that would save her life. Not wanting to alarm him, I proceeded cautiously and asked whether Grazia and my father visited his shop frequently.

"Mi dica, signor Curinga, mio padre trascorreva molte ore qui con Grazia?"

Recognizing I was searching for information relating to a father and daughter's annual custom, Gaetano detailed the tradition that bonded my father, sister, and the Gelatomania. Each year, on Good Friday afternoon following church services, the Judge delivered a package to Gaetano. The next day, on Holy Saturday, Grazia and my father made their annual visit to the gelato shop. As they sat together enjoying their treats, Gaetano, playing his scripted part in the Judge's drama, gave Grazia the package, saying, with a wink of the eye, that her "secret admirer" had left it there.

"Questo e un regalo del tuo ammiratore segreto."

As the years passed, the tradition endured. But adolescence faded into womanhood, and, somewhere along the way, Grazia learned her anonymous friend's identity. It was the Judge's annual Easter gift to his only daughter.

"Era il regalo di Pasqua annuale dei Giudice a Grazia."

Hopefully, Giovanni had continued the tradition by giving Gaetano a gift for Grazia during his last visit to Taormina. Although I wanted to spare him the details of Grazia's kidnapping, my search for clues, underscored by my anxious demeanor, signaled to Gaetano that my trip to Taormina, more particularly his shop, was more than a friendly visit. Forced to reveal the events that had unfolded since my father's funeral, I meticulously recounted the bizarre circumstances that had brought me back to Taormina.

Telling him that I must find the manuscript, Gaetano dropped his eyes, said nothing, and then walked behind the gelato case. He removed a small package, handed it to me, and sat across the table. Proceeding deliberately, I loosened the knot, untied the brown twine, and folded back the wrapping paper, knowing that the manuscript could not have been wrapped in a small package—unless the Judge had stored his novel on a disc. However, at this juncture in my search, I'd be satisfied to uncover any clue that would help me find my sister's ransom. Nervously pressing the wrapping paper flat against the table, I gazed at Grazia's gift—a small hardback book. I held it in my hands and glanced at its title: "A Father and His Daughter."

I flipped through the pages. It was a compilation of stories by fathers and daughters paying tribute to each other. I gently laid the book on the table and, with disappointment, stared at Gaetano. The book lying on the table was the last gift the Judge would deliver to Grazia through his Sicilian agent, Gaetano Curinga. And it offered me no clue to the whereabouts of the Judge's manuscript. I opened the book and hurriedly glanced through a few stories. My father had folded the edge of one page into a triangle. A handwritten inscription by the Judge read: *"Grazia, this is my message to you."* From all the selections in the book, he had chosen one that best expressed his affection for his daughter:

> His whole being is captured by his
> daughter. Gently, he holds her like
> the petal of a precious flower. He's
> totally consumed by her perfection.
> A gentleness finds its way into his
> life that only his daughter can find.

I decided to return the book to Gaetano. But suddenly, guided by fate's hand, I opened the book and fixed my sight on the inside hardcover. My eyes bulged and a wide grin slowly spread across my face as I read an inscription scrawled by the Judge and addressed to Grazia. I read it once, quickly. I reread it, carefully.

> *Grazia,*
>
> *Please accept this book of tributes as a gift from me. Throughout the years, we have met here every Holy Saturday since you were a little girl. And I have watched as you have grown into a beautiful woman—mostly because of your mother. You will find no personal praise from me in this book, but each of the tributes describes my love for you.*

I looked up, staring at Gaetano, somewhat guilty for infringing on my father's sentiments meant only for the eyes of his daughter. I read on:

> *Now, concerning my novel, I have found it necessary to hide it from everyone. You will find it in the small attic area of our home here in Taormina. Your mother kept a box in the attic for each of our children. You will find a box with your name on it. In the box, you will find part of my unfinished manuscript. More pages will follow. Discuss it with no one. When you have finished editing my manuscript, please offer me your criticism. Be objective.*

Although I was anxious to read the manuscript, Gaetano insisted on taking me to dinner at a small restaurant, a Zammara. It was tucked away in a narrow medieval lane, Fratelli Bandiera, off the main road. After dinner, we returned to Gelatomania for an espresso. It was early in the evening when I finally left the gelateria. Rain clouds were again forming, and the weather forecasters predicted another round of severe storms. I walked down the Corso in the direction of the Porta Catania and began hiking up the winding pedestrian stairs that led to our home, constantly glancing over my shoulder, fearful that Carlton Fisk was still shadowing me. It was a long climb, but I needed time to plan. I was elated that I had found part of the ransom demanded by Grazia's kidnappers, a payment I would gladly surrender for her safe return. But I was exhausted. I had one objective for the night, and the weather would not be a deterrent—I planned to read the Judge's novel.

CHAPTER 29

A VISITOR

Holding a kerosene lamp in one hand, I climbed to the second floor of the house, pulled down the portable stairs and climbed into the dark attic. Clusters of thunder rumbled, and a torrent of rain pounded on the shingled roof as sparks of lightning threw zigzagging volleys of flashing light through the small windows at each end of the room. The wind encircled the house, threatening to separate it into pieces. I laid the lamp aside. I saw a pile of boxes stacked in a corner through a scattering of exiled tables and chairs. They had remained untouched since Rosalina filled each box with memorabilia, hoping that someday the stored treasures would rekindle the memories of her three children.

Maneuvering in the attic's close quarters, I rummaged through the discarded furniture. In a corner, I eyed a bicycle we had used as children. Bending over to avoid hitting my head on the low-pitched ceiling, I made my way to the stack of boxes piled by Rosalina many years ago, one on top of the other. There was a box marked with Grazia's name.

I opened it, found a package, and lifted it out of the box. It was no more than a half-inch thick—less than a hundred pages—and covered with brown wrapping paper, secured by heavy twine. Tucking the package under my arm, I carefully climbed down the stairs, returned to the kitchen, set the manuscript on the table, and stood motionless—the faint sound of even breaths feeding my senses. I wasn't alone.

"Hello, Francesco."

Startled, I turned around and saw a familiar face. Anna Angelisanti was standing in the kitchen with a revolver aimed at my head.

CHAPTER 30

A CASUALTY

I couldn't look away from the revolver's muzzle staring me in the face.

"Make it easy for both of us, Francesco," Anna suggested.

Brandishing her gun, she pointed to the package lying on the table.

"Step back. I'll take the manuscript." A stern command I ignored.

"Why the gun, Anna?"

"Let's just say I need the chapters of your father's manuscript he wrote while he was here in Sicily," she explained, forging her lips into a tight smile, almost a smirk.

I didn't move from the table's edge, realizing I had few options and little time. Perhaps I could appeal to Anna's compassionate side, assuming she had one.

"Grazia's been kidnapped," I blurted out.

Anna stiffened. She raised her eyebrows, and then a sigh, a faint sign of empathy.

"I'm truly sorry—but I need the manuscript," she said, quickly brushing away the news of Grazia's abduction. "Please stand aside."

"I need the manuscript, too, Anna," I pleaded, staring at her with wide, warm eyes, trying to sway her. "It's the ransom demanded by Grazia's kidnappers."

She retreated a few steps, lowering the gun, saying nothing, her beaded eyes showing little remorse.

"How did you get here from the airport?" I inquired, a frivolous question asked only to buy time.

"I rented a car."

"Where is it parked?"

"On the Corso Umberto."

She moved closer, the gun in one hand steadied by the other, still aimed at me.

"Stop the stupid questions," she ordered sternly, determined to fulfill her mission.

"Let's be reasonable," I suggested, holding my ground. "If I give you the manuscript, what will you do with it? Like it or not, we're both marooned here for the night."

She continued to wield the gun at my head. My options nearly exhausted, I raised a dilemma she faced, my last chance to borrow time.

"Do you intend to hold me captive here until the storm passes?" I asked slyly. "What if I refuse to surrender the manuscript? Will you kill me and invite a murder investigation by the Italian carabinieri with Anna Angelisanti as the main suspect?"

She stepped back and dangled the gun at her side. The flame in the kerosene lamp flickered, signaling that its fuel supply would soon be spent, enveloping the room in darkness—my ally.

"Think of your wife and son, Francesco," she countered. "This is your chance to live. Put some wood in the fireplace. You can then throw the manuscript in the fire, and we'll both watch it pass into eternity."

I gathered the manuscript from the table and retreated. Anna moved closer.

"The pages will burn to a crisp," she drawled as a cunning smile crossed her face. "The flames will cremate the cast of characters who played a part in your father's story."

Anna moved toward me, backing me against the wall, the manuscript pressed close to my chest.

"Then," she continued after sighing, "my assignment will have been completed."

Her role as my father's agent was a disguise, but this wasn't the time to question her. She wouldn't reveal her secrets anyway, her ruse a distraction. My sole mission now was only to salvage Grazia's ransom.

"I won't be able to rescue my sister if I burn the manuscript," I pleaded, a last, futile effort that fell on deaf ears.

"Make a choice, Francesco. Between life and death."

Once again, she brandished the gun.

"Start the fire."

I placed the manuscript on the fireplace mantel and then stacked logs on slivers of kindling and loosely folded paper. Striking a match, I lit the paper. First, a streaking flame shot upwards. Next, fed by the kindling wood, the logs began to burn. The pointed flames crackled as sparks shot from a fire that would soon devour the manuscript. I removed the package from the mantel and untied the twine that secured the brown wrapping paper. First, I threw the string into the fire and then the wrapping paper. Instantly, a draught swept up their remains through the chimney.

"It's time, Francesco," she said, wielding her revolver, the executioner standing ready to lower the guillotine's blade.

I crumbled the title page in my fist and tossed it into the fire. The flames quickly reduced it to ashes. I then turned to the second page. Inscribed in the middle were words surrounded by a sea of white space:

> *I dedicate this book to my wife and*
> *soul mate. The girl who will be my*
> *dance partner into eternity and*
> *back again. Rosalina Bartolacci*
> *Micco*

"That's enough, Francesco."

The reprieve ended. Anna delivered an edict.

"You've had a glimpse of your father's manuscript. Now burn it."

Ignoring her demand, I turned to the first chapter and began reading Giovanni's words describing the evening he first met Rosalina at a Catholic University dance:

> She was standing alone in a
> corner across the room;
> I sensed a shyness to her,
> a softness when she spoke.

"My final warning," she drawled. "Burn the book." A stern command.

Reading nothing more, I blindly fed the manuscript to the fire's flames. Chapter after chapter, the charred remains faded to brown and then crispy black as each page of the manuscript was sucked up through the chimney chute, scattering the Judge's manuscript into the swirling winds of a stormy night in Taormina. When I fed the last page to the fire, Anna rested the gun at her side and walked to the table.

"Now, let's talk," she said.

Suddenly, I heard the staccato pop of a gunshot and the shatter of glass. Blood gushed from Anna's neck near her carotid artery. I rushed toward her. She fell listlessly into my arms. Gently, I placed her on the floor and, keeping low, crawled toward the window. Crouched down, I saw the taillights of a car disappear over the crest of the winding road leading to our home. I returned to Anna and fell to my knees. I could do nothing to stop the flow of blood that spilled freely. Leaning over Anna, I gently placed her hand in mine, her glazed eyes staring eerily into the endless bounds of eternity. Grimacing with pain, she fought to squeeze another moment into her life. But her slow breathing, forced and frightening, suggested that soon she would succumb to her mortality. Gripping energy from some mystical force, her eyes pierced through mine as she tried to raise herself from the floor. I placed my hand under her head, gently lifted it, and turned my ear toward her mouth. Laboring, she struggled to say something. I could barely hear her faint whisper.

"Francesco, look under…"

Unable to finish her sentence, Anna's head fell to one side. Gently, I removed my hand from the back of her head and rested her limp body on the floor. I tried to find a pulse. There was none. The lady in black was dead.

CHAPTER 31

GUERINO REGANTINI

I dialed the emergency 113 number to report Anna's murder to the carabinieri—the Italian police— but the telephone lines were dead. My only choice was to venture outside and make my way to the police station. But because the storm continued to ravish Taormina, I decided not to drive. Before leaving on foot, I discarded my blood-stained shirt and tossed it in a hamper. I rummaged through the clothes I kept in Taormina and found a flannel shirt. I then covered myself with a cape and zigzagged down the pedestrian pathway, fighting the wind and rain along the way. The police station—the questura—was located in the Piazza S. Domenico, a short distance away. Hopefully, someone would be on duty. When I finally reached the station, I looked in the window but saw no movement inside. It was dark. I tried to open the door, but the janitor had probably locked it before leaving the station.

Occasional flashes of thunderbolts continued to cast spurts of light on a stormy night. The daunting thought of spending the remainder of the night with Anna was uninviting. The kerosene lamp had probably spent its fuel, and the house was now pitch-black inside. Recognizing I

had no option, soaked and exhausted, I decided to head
back down the Corso Umberto toward the Porta Messina.
But before I began to make the long trek toward the steep
pedestrian pathway, a voice, intimidating but welcome,
rescued me.

"Venga! Entri! Posso aiutarla? Sono Guerino
Regantini."

I was invited into the police station by an officer
who identified himself as Guerino Regantini. He was the
poliziotto on duty. Explaining that the storm had disrupted
the electricity, he extended an invitation for shelter, which
I happily accepted.

"Come mai lei e uscito con questo tempaccio?"

He asked why I had ventured out on such a stormy
night.

"Sono venuto ad informarvi di un omicidio."

After I told him I was there to report a murder,
Guerino, surprisingly unmoved, said nothing. He fiddled
around in his pants pocket, found a match, lit a kerosene
lamp, and invited me to sit at a table. While dousing the
match, he sat across from me. I now saw him better. He
had loosened his tie and unfastened his top shirt button.
His age was difficult to estimate, but he was probably in his
late middle years, approaching fifty, I suspected. His head
was balding on top, but he had a crop of hair on each side,
full and combed straight back. All in all, he was somewhat
messy, probably because the weather had caused him to
serve an extended tour of duty.

"Come si chiama?"

"Francesco Micco."

"Quale e nome della vittima?"

I identified myself, and he asked for the victim's name. With a little forethought, the fabrication began. I told Guerino that the victim was a stranger and she came to my house seeking shelter from the storm. Suspicious, Guerino shrugged, his face sporting a quirky smile.

"Come e stata uccisa?"

He asked how the assailant had killed her. I explained that her assailer fired a shot through a window, and it struck my visitor in the neck. At least that part of the story was real.

"Forse sarebbe meglio se adesso andiamo a casa."

He suggested that we go to the house immediately. He locked the questura and led me to his car. Because of the ravaging storm, Guerino drove cautiously along the narrow, winding road that led up the hill. The wind continued to howl, but its intensity had relented somewhat. With the windshield wipers whopping back and forth, Guerino kept his eyes fixed on the winding road, saying nothing, while I questioned my decision to hide the truth. But it was now too late to make a full disclosure. Judging from his stoic reaction to my story and his staid, quiet demeanor, Guerino Regantini wouldn't believe me anyway. Who could blame him?

When we arrived, Guerino and I stepped out of the car and walked down the brick pathway toward the house. Guerino proceeded ahead of me, lighting the way with a flashlight. Side by side, we stood on the front stoop. I unlocked the door. We entered the house and walked through the dark living room and headed toward the kitchen. The wind was still blowing through the shattered window. When we reached the kitchen, Guerino flashed the light along the floor—back and forth, up and down, one side to the other. Again and again, he shined the light across the pristine floor. With the light pointed directly in my face, Guerino stared quizzically at me.

He was confused.

I was baffled.

Anna's body was gone.

CHAPTER 32

AN ITALIAN CONNECTION

I found a small stash of kerosene stored against the kitchen cabinet's back wall. After lighting the lamp, it flickered, providing only a glimmer of light. I placed it on the kitchen table. Guerino sat while I stood at the stove, brewing una bella tazza di caffe. While the water boiled, we chatted awkwardly about the weather and his job. He spoke fluent English, explaining that he dealt daily with tourists from the United States as a police officer. When the bubbling sound ended, I tipped the pot and poured the espresso into a demitasse cup. He drank it with a quick swallow and then made what lawyers term 'a full disclosure.'

"Before you decide whether to speak with me about the murder, you should know something," Guerino said, hunched forward, his elbows resting on the table with one hand covering the other and his eyes fixed on mine.

"Your grandfather, Gaspare, was my uncle," he announced warmly as his eyes circled the room. "I often visited him in this home with my parents, especially when Uncle Gaspare traveled from the United States to celebrate the traditional Easter festivals."

A warm, friendly smile lit his face.

"And I remember you," he recalled, reminiscing, "much younger, bicycling on the Corso Umberto on your way to Gelatomania. And I remember Grazia and Giancarlo."

"So, you are my cousin?" I inquired, stunned.

"Yes. Your older cousin," he mused.

"My parents—do you remember them?" I asked hurriedly.

"Of course. Your father and I shared many good times. We were like brothers. And your mother, Rosalina…"

Guerino paused as his eyes, glassy once again, circled the kitchen.

"…she was beautiful and kind."

Because Guerino was my cugina—my cousin—I decided to tell him the entire story. Through the waning hours of the night and into the early morning, I related to him the events that have plagued my life since my father's death. While I talked, he listened, saying nothing. I spared no detail—factual, personal, or emotional. It was a matter of innate trust. Guerino was a magnet that attracted my confidence.

———

After Guerino left, I dozed through the following morning. At noon, the ring of my telephone woke me.

"Pronto," I said.

It was Guerino.

"Buon Giorno, Francesco."

"Buon Giorno, Guerino."

Before leaving, Guerino assured me he would gather whatever information about Anna Angilsanti that was available from the Director-General of the Italian National Police. He also had connections at The Agencia Informazioni e Sicurezza Esterna—the External Intelligence and Security Agency, Italy's version of the CIA. He began by saying that Anna's dossier was short but telling. Then a pause. I suspected he was reluctant to pass on information that the Italian government may have labeled as classified. But I imagined that he had decided to help me, moved, I'm sure, by the strange events that have invaded my life since my mother's murder—and because of our family connection.

"Ho scoperto che il nome di Anna Angelisanti era solo una copertura. Il suo vero nome e Lucia Lazzerini," he informed me.

Anna Angelisanti had duped the Judge. Her real name was Lucia Lazzerini. I suspected that there was more, but I sensed that Guerino was torn between two loyalties— his position as a carabinieri and his bond with the Micco family. I heard him shuffling through papers, either searching for details or deciding whether to pass on more classified intelligence. I suspected the latter. In the end, after struggling between allegiance to work or family, he opted for the latter.

"It's more complicated than I had suspected," Guerino said, hesitating before passing on information that would add another layer of intrigue to the mission bequeathed to me by my father.

"Lucia Lazzerini was a federal undercover agent," he related stoically. "She worked for the Defense Intelligence Agency at the Pentagon."

CHAPTER 33

A MURDER SUSPECT

W ithin two hours, Guerino arrived at my Taormina home. Judging from his disheveled appearance, I suspected he had not slept but spent the night trying to shuffle through the mess that was suffocating my life. My flight did not leave from the Catania Airport for Rome until about nine in the evening. I again brewed una bella tazza di caffe, and we sat together at the kitchen table. It was my final chance to quiz Guerino. My initial query related to Claudio Armondi. His membership in the Mafia has been a mystery for years.

"Guerino, mi dica, Lei sa se e di Cosa Nostra?"

Our eyes locked. Guerino's contemplative stare, coupled with a lingering silence, suggested that he was reluctant to tell me if Uncle Claudio was a Mafioso. After some thought, he relented.

"Si, lui e di Cosa Nostra."

Rosalina's assessment voiced many years ago proved to be true. Claudio Armondi was a member of the Cosa Nostra, and his dossier with the Italian National Police was extensive. After Claudio was discharged from the

Army following his Vietnam tour, he returned to live with his family in New York City.

"Where did he work?" I inquired.

"He sold insurance for a Hartford Insurance Company."

"That didn't satisfy his business appetite?" I asked rhetorically.

"Hardly. While working for Hartford, he contrived a business plan designed to provide medical assistance to people who didn't have immediate access to health care facilities," Guerino explained, a nod to Uncle Claudio's entrepreneurial skills as well as his penchant to help the less-privileged. "There was just one glitch. He had no money. He was, however, the nephew of John Gotti."

"The boss of the Gambino crime family in New York City?" I asked, stunned.

"Yes."

"Gotti funded Marymount HealthCare?"

"He did. But Claudio had bigger ideas," Guerino said, grinning. "He expanded the business internationally to southern Italy. He named the Italian company Sanita per la Famiglia—Family HealthCare."

"The business grew, I assume?"

"It did. By leaps and bounds," Guerino explained as his grin widened. "The Italian government, through the Servizio Sanitario Nazionale, bought into his idea."

"Gotti was still in the picture?" I asked, a senseless question given the Mafia's proclivity to launder ill-gotten gains.

"Of course." Guerino answered, chuckling "He was Claudio's Italian Mafioso connection. Sanita per la Familgia built medical facilities in Puglia, Campania, Calabria, and Sicily."

Guerino's expression faded grim.

"Interestingly, each of the facilities were located in areas with a significant Mafia presence—in Puglia, la Sacra Corona Unita; in Campania, la Camorra; in Calabria, la n'Drangheta; and in Sicily, Cosa Nostra."

It was sheer genius, I thought—the wedding of good and evil. Claudio Armondi provided healthcare to the people in southern Italy while laundering Mafia money at the same time.

"The business continued to grow?" I asked, impressed by Uncle Claudio's ingenuity.

"Dramatically," Guerino answered, citing both the good and the evil. "With the influx of government money, as well as the endless flow of cash filtered through the company by la Mafia, Sanita per la Famiglia flourished."

Guerino paused, smiling comically.

"Claudio was indeed clever," he admitted. "His facilities became recognized as the most advanced medical providers in Italy."

Recalling my brother Giancarlo's visit to the Marymount's office at Trump Tower, I decided to raise a delicate subject. Something peculiar joined Giancarlo and Uncle Claudio in a relationship shrouded in secrecy. Giancarlo lived in Sicily, near the four facilities operated by Sanita per la Famiglia, and he had free access to Marymount's office in New York. Is Giancarlo connected to the Mafia? I wondered. Guerino satisfied my curiosity.

"Francesco, Giancarlo lavora per la Sanita per la Famiglia. Per quanto ne sappia, lui ha 'amici' nella Mafia."

Once again, the prodigal son had strayed—but not too far. Santa per la Famiglia employed Giancarlo. He was the administrator of the medical facilities in Puglia, Campana, Calabria, and Catania. Thankfully, Uncle Claudio vetoed his application for membership in the Mafia.

While we talked, Guerino's cell phone rang. Excusing himself, he moved to a corner of the room and answered it. As the caller talked, he listened, occasionally nodding his head. Whispering, he tried to mask the calls urgency. When the call ended, he related to me the information passed on to him by one of his colleagues.

"The carabinieri have found Lazzerini's body," he informed me somberly.

"Where?"

"Near Mazzaro Bay."

"Have they identified her?"

"Not yet. But the body meets your description. Tall, blond, caramel strands of hair. A gunshot wound that punctured her carotid artery."

"Why wasn't her body thrown into the bay?"

"Because the assassin wanted the carabinieri to find her."

"That's odd."

"Not really," he said, pausing. "The assassin planted evidence."

"Connecting me to the murder?" I guessed.

His fixed stare was enough to answer my question.

"Her assailant scribbled your name and address on a sheet of paper found in her blouse pocket."

Not only did the carabinieri want to question me. I was the prime murder suspect.

CHAPTER 34

A TRAIN RIDE

My relationship with Guerino stood at a pivotal juncture. Wedged between two loyalties, he held my fate in his hands, but Guerino's next words—a warning—told me that he had decided to help.

"Non può partire da un aeroporto! Deve prendere il treno fino a Roma e poi l'aereo."

I couldn't leave Sicily from the airport in Catania. The government had ordered the police to seize my passport and to detain me for questioning. My escape had to be through an alternate route.

"Travel by rail to Rome," he suggested.

Guerino offered no other advice or help, nor did I expect any. We hugged. He moved back and grasped my arms, his hold tight, his eyes welded to mine.

"Buon viaggio," he said—have a safe journey.

He walked to the door, opened it, and, without glancing back, Guerino was gone. I gathered a few belongings and hurriedly climbed down the pedestrian walkway leading to the Corso Umberto. My destination was the bus terminal located on Via Luigi Pirandello, below the center of town.

Before entering the terminal, I carefully surveyed the ticket office and the surrounding area. Thankfully, I was not confronted by la polizia. Their stakeout, hopefully, was restricted to the Catania Airport. From there I took a bus. It slowly snaked down the narrow road carved into the mountainside. In about five minutes, I reached the Taormina-Giardini rail station. I exited the bus and slowly walked toward the train station. As I approached the railroad agent to purchase a ticket, I observed Guerino standing alongside a poliziotto—a policeman— dressed in full regalia. His name tag read: "Caporale Rossi."

I quickly turned away and mingled under the arrival-departure board with the crowd waiting for the next train. Hoping Guerino would direct Rossi's attention to another part of the station, allowing me to purchase a ticket, I turned to one side, observing Guerino and his colleague. Their conversation was animated. Voicing an objection, Guerino raised his arms into the air while Rossi pointed in the direction of the passengers who were awaiting the arrival of the next train. The train station's venue belonged to Caporale Rossi, and he would not voluntarily surrender his jurisdiction to Guerino. Together, they slowly walked toward me as I blended in with the other passengers huddled beside the train tracks.

As Guerino and Rossi approached the passengers, I worked my way onto a platform, searching for cover. A railway attendant gathered most passengers under an elongated canopy that straddled the tracks. The powerful sound of its diesel engine signaled the approach of the Eurostar. It began to stop, and its piercing whistle muffled the screech of its steel wheels scratching the steel tracks. With its horn bellowing, the train got closer. The crowd moved toward a gate marked "Roma & Napoli." The public address announcer blared the arrival of the train. With its bells loudly clanging and with steam spilling from its undercarriage, the Eurostar chugged to a stop.

The first onboard, I climbed the steps and stood on the deck. The conductor requested my ticket. Because I could not purchase one at the purser's window, I asked to buy one from him. Reluctantly, he agreed. I didn't have the exact fare.

"Mantenere il resto dei soldi," I said.

I suggested he keep the change. He smirked but offered no objection. With a small bag swinging from my shoulder, I entered the carriage and searched for a seat. There was a sparse selection. I sat next to an elderly lady who was sleeping in an aisle seat. Being careful not to disturb my traveling partner, I carefully climbed over her and sat next to the window. Outside, a few straggling passengers were boarding. Guerino and Rossi anchored the end of the line.

The chug of the train engine signaled that it was slowly moving out of the Taormina-Giardini station. Slouching in my seat, I noticed Guerino speaking with the conductor. His colleague, Caporale Rossi, was standing nearby. The train soon gained momentum as the melodic roll of its wheels signaled we were now on our way to Roma. It promised to be a bumpy ride.

Seat by seat, Guerino and Rossi requested identification from each male passenger. As a foreigner, either Guerino or Rossi would request my passport. Mine bore the name of Francesco Micco, the suspect wanted by the police in Taormina for the murder of an unidentified woman found near Mazzaro Bay. Guerino maneuvered himself to my side of the aisle. I produced my passport when he reached my seat. He looked at it, then at me, handed it back, face stern, and moved on. For the moment, I was safe. Tired, I sat back and dozed off to sleep as the train rolled toward the Messina Strait.

The screeching sounds of wheels—steel scratching steel—woke me as the engineer braked the train's speed. The seat beside me was empty. My snoring had probably chased my seat partner to another carriage. Before I drifted off, I noticed that there were only two extra seats— one directly across the aisle next to the window and the other immediately behind me. Guerino now sat across the aisle, and Rossi occupied the seat behind me. I glanced out the window. The train had reached the ferry that would carry it across the Strait of Messina to mainland Italy. The Eurostar's gliding rhythm gradually slowed as it approached the ferry. Its clanging bells were silenced as the engineer continued to engage the brakes. I leaned forward and looked at Guerino. He was sleeping. Needing to stretch following my short nap, I stood, turned around, and glanced at Caporale Rossi. It was not a good move.

I tried to focus my attention elsewhere, but suspicion settled his eyes on me. His instincts as an investigator had kicked in. He moved and sat in the empty seat beside me. Guerino continued to sleep. I could expect no help from him. Rossi's first question was a cursory inquiry, but he was just beginning to feed his suspicion—was the passenger seated next to him the murder suspect?

"Dove va?" he asked—where are you going?

"A Roma," I answered calmly.

A more immediate crisis soon trumped my attempt to remain anonymous. Walking down the aisle toward me was my friend from Gelatomania, Gaetano Curinga, probably traveling to Roma for a holiday. Trying to hide without being conspicuous, I slumped down in my seat and dropped my head between my hands. Hopefully, he would pass by without noticing me. He didn't.

"Amico, Francesco, dove vai?"

Hearing my name, Rossi abruptly turned toward me, knowing that fate had handed him a clue that might trip the fleeing murder suspect. Guerino, who had not slept for two days, remained in a deep slumber, oblivious to the events that were unfolding around him. Rossi hovered over me. For the first time, I appreciated his imposing stature. He was burly and barrel-chested, at least six feet tall, with square, broad shoulders, a strong jaw, and a handlebar mustache that complimented his chiseled face. His reptilian eyes—fixed on mine—were buried in deep, shadowy sockets. As his stare bore into me, he asked a question meant to stop a fleeing murder suspect.

"Mi fa vedere la sua carta d'identità?"

He wanted my identification. Trying to remain calm, I reached for my passport and glanced past Rossi, fixing my eyes on Guerino. Exhausted, he continued to doze. Holding my passport, I smiled grimly at Gaetano who continued to stand in the aisle adjacent to Rossi, my trembling, clammy fingers signaling that my liberty was at stake. Suddenly, the train jerked forward. Having failed to secure himself, the joggling, staccato movement of the train, coupled with a gentle shove from Gaetano, caused Rossi to fall backward into the aisle just as the Eurostar trundled into the dark hold of the ferry that would carry us across the Strait of Messina to mainland Italy.

Seizing the opportunity, I shoved my way through the crowd of passengers and moved toward the exit. As I glanced back, I saw Rossi stretched on the floor and Gaetano standing over him, blocking his way through the narrow aisle. The commotion woke Guerino; he sat erect and instantly saw that Rossi had somehow identified me. I continued to weave my way through the aisle as the rush of passengers collectively escorted me from the carriage into the hold of the ferry. Rossi, his gun drawn and sight fixed on my head, chased after me. As I separated from the crowd, I heard the pop of a gunshot. My arms and legs remained intact. I continued to sprint toward the stairs that would take me from the ferry's hold onto the deck. Before reaching the stairs, I turned and saw a crowd of people gathering in a circle. I had escaped, but a gunshot may have felled Caporale Rossi.

I climbed the stairs and forced my way through a crowd gathered on the deck. Merging into the crowd,

I walked toward the rail and mingled with a group of passengers assembled near the ferry's stern. Looking down onto the port, I saw two people dressed in white uniforms—probably paramedics—slide a stretcher into an ambulance. With its siren bellowing, the ambulance sped away, probably carrying Caporale Rossi to one of Uncle Claudio's emergency care hospitals. I turned, walked from the stern toward the bow, and looked over the side of the ferry. Standing below, I saw Gaetano and Guerino. They looked up. I waved.

"Arrivederci, amici."

CHAPTER 35

ANOTHER MESSAGE

The Taormina police's order to detain a fleeing murder suspect did not timely reach Rome's carabinieri. I was able to pass through customs at Fiumicino without incident. Exhausted, I slept through most of the flight from Italy to New York. After a brief delay at Kennedy International, I boarded a commuter flight home. Gianna met me at the Pittsburgh International Airport in the late afternoon. During the short ride to New Castle, I related each event that had taken place during my visit to Sicily, including Lucia Lazzerini's killing— but I was reluctant to tell her that I was a suspect in the murder investigation. As she drove, Gianna's eyes, fixed on the road, never strayed, even to sneak a glance at me. For ten minutes, she listened, her hands squeezing the steering wheel, a peek in the mirror, her head nodding, saying nothing. The growing tension would worsen when I told her that I was a murder suspect—a reality I couldn't wash away like dirt scrubbed from my hands. When we approached the tollgate, I decided to tell her.

"There's something else," I said cautiously.

Her fingers drummed on the steering wheel, eyes dead ahead, each tap the countdown of the executioner waiting for the guillotine to drop. There was no easy way to tell her, so I blurted it out.

"I'm a suspect in the Lucia Lazzerini murder investigation."

She didn't react, immune from shock, the cascading events a vaccine that immunized her from emotion.

"Did you do it?" she asked stoically.

"Do what?"

"Kill her."

"Of course not."

"Why are you a suspect?"

"The police found my name on a sheet of paper in her blouse pocket."

She sighed, a deep breath, and said nothing more. Before passing through the turnstile, she pulled to the road's berm and idled the car's engine. Her tears flowed freely. The maddening events consuming our lives since the Judge's death, piled one on top of the other, had become too heavy a burden for her to carry. I moved toward Gianna and placed my arm around her shoulder. We caressed until she regained her composure. Before moving back, I wiped the tears trickling down her blushed cheeks as I stared into her puffy eyes, red and glassy.

"This must stop, Francesco," she insisted, her words firm but tinged with fear. "You can't be running off to Italy, Washington, risking your life, leaving Michele and me alone. Are you blind? Can't you see our lives are in danger?"

Gianna's concerns were real. I've tried to balance the competing interests facing me—mostly my family's safety and Grazia's kidnapping. But I felt entrapped. Somehow, I had to strike a balance, realizing that my priority rested with Gianna and Michele. But, then again, I couldn't ignore Grazia. Unfortunately, her safe return was in serious jeopardy. I had burned the Judge's manuscript and the disc demanded as her ransom was in the possession of an unknown associate who had a secret pact with my father. Adding to my dilemma, Grazia's abductors had failed to contact me since her kidnapping.

"I'm afraid, Francesco, terrified," Gianna confessed, her words bordering panic. "Three days ago, Uncle Claudio had an alarm system installed in our house, and he assigned six men to guard us. They work in shifts."

Her fear cried out to me, louder than the watchman who proclaims the daybreak. Gianna opened her purse, removed a tissue, and dabbed at her glassy eyes. Her voice quivered as she related to me news that would add yet another layer to the juggernaut bequeathed to me by Judge Giovanni Micco.

"Giancarlo called me this morning," Gianna said softly, staring through the car's windshield. "He couldn't reach you."

She loosened her tight grip on the steering wheel and passed on Giancarlo's message.

"Uncle Claudio died last night."

Early in the evening, I reached Giancarlo on his cell phone. Claudio Armondi maintained an apartment in New York's Upper West Side near Lincoln Center. For the past month, my brother stayed there while working on plans for a new medical facility that Sanita per la Famiglia was building in Lampedusa, a small island off the western Sicily coast with little access to emergency care. When he answered the phone, I went directly to the purpose of my call.

"What happened to Uncle Claudio?"

"It's too early to tell, Francesco," he said grimly, his words drawled. "A pathologist is performing an autopsy as we speak. All I can tell you is that I came home at about seven last night and found him lying on the kitchen floor. I felt no pulse. He was dead."

As we talked, I realized that Giancarlo assumed I knew that he worked for Uncle Claudio and Sanita per la Famiglia—rather than StarGazer, the mythical computer company with a satellite office in Italy. His employment with StarGazer was a façade designed to hide Giancarlo's relationship with Uncle Claudio from our mother. I thought it best not to inquire about their surreptitious relationship. At least for now.

"Was he feeling ill?"

"No. But oddly, about five days ago, Uncle Claudio gave me an envelope and asked that I read the note inside if he died."

"Did you read it?"

"Of course."

"What did it say?"

"It concerns you. Hold on. I'll get it."

After a few seconds had passed, he returned and read the message:

> *Giancarlo,*
>
> *Unfortunately, it has become necessary for you to read this message, but life is full of strange twists and turns. I accept my fate. Read this note and pay strict attention. There will be a memorial service for me in Washington at St. Stephen's Church. You will be informed of the date and time. Without fail, make sure that your brother, Francesco, attends. Farewell Giancarlo. Always remain faithful to the lessons of your parents. You have been a true friend.*
>
> *With love,*
> *Uncle Claudio.*

CHAPTER 36

STAY SAFE

Gianna and I talked in the living room for a short while after tucking Michele in bed. I told her about the note Uncle Claudio had left for Giancarlo and that he had asked that I attend his memorial service, an invitation that would drag me back to Washington. Exhausted, we turned the lights out and walked up the stairs to our bedroom without discussing the note, each silently knowing that I couldn't ignore Uncle Claudio's message. The six Mafioso guards, the alarm system, and the trap lights that lit our yard brighter than the lamps illuminating Fenway Park gave me some comfort. Even from the great beyond, Uncle Claudio's 'Italian Army' was watching over my family—Grazia's kidnapping a lesson learned.

I now had to find my way in the dark, my father and Uncle Claudio leaving me alone, no one to turn to, despondency making my eyes heavy, despair, the final emotion that drained my energy before a sleep that didn't last long. As I laid in bed listening to Gianna's breaths, I realized that my family's safety, Rosalina's murder, Grazia's kidnapping, and the plot my father had uncovered are all connected. They stand together, my task being to unravel the common thread.

I woke before seven the following morning, brewed a pot of coffee, and stood on the front porch. Cup in hand, I admired the twin Japanese Red Maples that adorned each side of the walkway leading to our home, smiling as a Cardinal rested on a branch, his red crest contrasted against the white remnants of an early morning snowfall.

"Hey. You're up early." Gianna's cheerful voice, who, unlike me, didn't need a dose of caffeine to start the day. She stood beside me wrapped in a blanket. I placed my arm around her waist and drew her close.

"You're up early, too," I said, relieved that the new day had brightened her attitude, yesterday's storm hopefully blown away by the breeze of a soft March wind.

"I'll get you a coffee. Just brewed," I offered.

"Let's talk first," she suggested.

"Shall we sit inside?" I asked, anticipating that Gianna wanted to discuss my invitation to Uncle Claudio's memorial service.

"I'd rather stand here," she said, my arm still wrapped around her waist.

"We can't ignore reality," Gianna began. "Grazia's been kidnapped, the Italian police suspect you of a murder, an assassin killed your mother, and your father discovered a plot that may have cost him his life."

As I listened to her words, my eyes remained fixed on the red maples as muted rays of sun snuck through the branches—the Cardinal's rest now over, taking flight, his wings flapping, fueling his ascent high into the blue morning sky.

"This isn't the perfect day it appears to be, Francesco," Gianna said softly. "We're walking through a storm and you're the only one who can tame the wind," poetic words with one thinly veiled message.

"What are you saying?" I asked.

"Do what you must—but stay safe."

CHAPTER 37

NINO VIOLA

O nce again, I traveled to Washington by rail. Uncle Claudio's memorial service was held in a small Roman Catholic Church on Pennsylvania Avenue in Washington's Foggy Bottom—St. Stephen's. As a mixed choir sang a Gregorian chant, I walked into the church and sat alone in a middle pew admiring St. Stephen Martyr Church. Cones lining the walls funneled light onto the beige-colored arched ceiling. The Virgin Mary's statue was nestled in a cove off to my left. Votive candles encased in red jars burned at her feet. A crucifix hung behind the altar. A round, stained-glass window high above the cross was divided into four parts by two leaded bars forming a cross. A red rose was etched into the intersection.

The turnout was sparse. The only person I recognized was Guido Borgese, Uncle Claudio's business associate and the gentleman I had met when I visited the offices of Marymount HealthCare in Trump Tower. We exchanged glances, mutual salutatory gestures appropriate for the sanctity of a church. I was present. The ceremony began. It was a brief memorial. First, there were two speakers. Both offered only superficial remarks. Although short on

eloquence, their messages had one redeeming attribute—
they were mercifully short. Finally, the priest, dressed in an
Alb for the informal service, gave a brief sermon. Before
concluding, he paused, turned to one side and pointed to
the stained-glass window.

"I would be remiss if I didn't thank Claudio Armondi
for his generosity," he said loudly, his voice bellowing,
echoing throughout the church. "It was his gracious
gift that allowed us to install the beautiful stained-glass
window that now graces our church."

He turned around, his back facing the congregation,
his head raised upward, his arms stretched out toward the
stained-glass window, his words meant only for Francesco
Micco.

"Please pay particular attention to the red rose that
casts light on our grateful community of worshipers at St.
Stephen's—a light that commands us to spread the truth."

The service concluded. The priest headed for the
sacristy as Guido thanked the gathering for paying
its respects to "a true visionary." With that remark, we
were excused. I remained in my pew for a moment,
contemplating Uncle Claudio's request that I attend
his memorial. Confused but wanting to leave, I joined
the mourners filing out of St. Stephen's. My exit was
interrupted.

"Psst . . . Francesco," a whisper that respected the
church's sanctity.

I turned to the side of the church. All I could see was
a silhouette standing in the shadows near a confessional. I

walked closer. It was Nino Viola. For the past three years, he had been my father's senior law clerk. As I approached him, he turned away and slipped into the compartment of the confessional reserved for the priest—a strange place for a rendezvous, I thought. Taking the cue, I entered the side stall of the confessional used by the penitent.

"Can you hear me, Francesco?" he asked softly.

I looked through the small, square screened opening in the dark confessional and saw Nino's silhouette.

"Yeah, I can hear you well. Why are you here?" I inquired, baffled by his presence at the service.

"Because your father gave me an envelope and asked that I deliver it to you if there was ever a memorial service for Claudio Armondi at St Stephen's."

"Who made you aware of the service?"

"I received an invitation by courier yesterday."

"Who sent it?"

"Don't know. It was unsigned."

The venue of our meeting was rather odd, I thought; perhaps it was a subtle message from my father—the penitent son's sins forgiven, his penance about to be doled out.

"Why the confessional?" I asked.

"Because your father thought it best that we not be seen together."

"Why St. Stephen's?"

"He said that after you read the message, you should look closely at the stained-glass window above the crucifix."

As he spoke, Nino slid a white envelope through a narrow opening under the screen separating priest and penitent.

"Here it is."

I slipped it into my pants pocket.

"You may want to meet me after you read the message," he said anxiously. "Give me a little time after I leave the church. My apartment is not far from here. The address is on the envelope."

I knelt in the confessional a short while, giving Nino time to leave St. Stephen's. Except for a priest kneeling in the sanctuary, rosary in hand, the church was empty. I genuflected, sat in the last row of pews, broke the seal of the white envelope, removed the note, and read the message:

> *Francesco:*
>
> *I am genuinely sorry that I must now involve you in the conspiracy that's gripped me since I began searching for Rosalina's killer. If you are reading this note, it means that Claudio Armondi has died. Because of his passing, I need your help. The option to assist me, however, will rest with you. Either discard this note and return to your family or ask Nino to give you a sealed brown envelope I have placed in his possession. I have instructed him to keep the envelope for three days following*

Claudio's memorial service. If he does not hear from you, he'll destroy the envelope. Remember, the decision rests with you.

CHAPTER 38

ANOTHER CASUALTY

It was a short cab ride to Nino's apartment. He stayed in a brownstone on M Street in Georgetown, not too far from St. Stephen's. When I arrived, I paid the cab fare, punched in the code Nino had given me, and walked into the three-story apartment building. Nino's walk-up was on the third floor. I climbed the stairs, reached the top, took a moment to catch my breath, and then knocked on his door. There was no response. I knocked louder. Again, no answer. I reached for the knob and turned it slowly. The door was unlocked. I entered the apartment. Nino won't mind, I thought.

"Hey, Nino, are you here?" I shouted.

He didn't answer. Perhaps Nino ran an errand after Uncle Claudio's memorial service. Or maybe he was just enjoying a leisurely walk home on a beautiful, late winter day. Looking for the most inviting seat, I chose a cushioned chair and placed my feet on an ottoman. Before I settled in for a short nap, a groan from another room startled me. Moving cautiously and quietly, I removed my feet from the ottoman, slid out of the chair, and made my way into a bedroom. There, beside the bed, I found Nino lying on the floor, drifting in and out of consciousness with blood trickling down the side of his head. I placed my finger on his carotid artery and searched for a pulse. Thankfully, it was strong and steady.

His bedroom had been ransacked. Dresser drawers hung open. Clothes—underwear, socks, shirts, ties—were strewn on the floor along with pillowcases and sheets stripped from the mattress. The walk-in closet was in disarray. Nino's suits and shoes were scattered in piles on the floor. An open phone book laid on the bed. The room was a mess. I ran into the kitchen, wrapped ice cubes in a dish towel, tied a knot, and applied the cold compress to Nino's wound before dialing for an ambulance. Within a few minutes, and before the paramedics arrived, Nino's eyes opened. Through dazed eyes he stared up at me, groggy but conscious.

"Nino, what happened?" I asked excitedly.

"After I left you at St. Stephen's, Francesco, I hurried back to my apartment. I thought that you would be coming here," he said as I tucked a pillow under his head. "I came into the bedroom, and that's all I remember."

"Where did you keep the envelope my father gave you?" I asked quickly, suspecting that it had been stolen.

"I hid it in the phone book," he drawled, still muddled but coherent.

I stared at the open directory lying on Nino's bed. His assailant had stolen the envelope my father entrusted to him—rousing my curiosity because the circle of confidants who knew about the message was small.

"Besides my father and you, did anyone else know about the envelope?" I asked suspiciously.

"I assume Mr. Borgese?" he mumbled.

"Why?"

"He called me early this morning."

"What did he want?"

He asked if I planned to attend the memorial service.

───────────

With its siren bellowing, the ambulance rushed Nino to Georgetown University Hospital. I rode with him. After we completed the paperwork, Nino was placed on a gurney and wheeled into a treatment room. I explained to the doctor that I was Nino's friend and had found him lying on the floor in his apartment's bedroom, probably the victim of a burglary attempt. Although I was stretching the truth, that was all the information that needed to find its way into Nino's hospital records. After a detailed examination and a series of tests, the emergency room physician informed Nino that he had a slight concussion. Before hurrying to his next patient, the doctor scribbled a prescription, tore it off the pad, gave it to Nino, and told him to return home and rest for a day or two. I was reluctant to accept his suggestion. Nino's assailants probably followed us to the hospital, and, like bloodhounds, eagerly awaited our departure. A hospital aide transported Nino in a wheelchair to the ER exit.

"Hospital policy," she explained.

I hailed a cab.

"Where to?" the driver asked.

"Union Station," I responded.

Nino, stunned, looked at me, puzzled.

"Why Union Station, Francesco?"

Although I accepted my role in the Judge's twisted plan, the resentment I had harbored against my father surfaced again. I was the lone survivor in the epilogue of his life, but I was disturbed by the Judge's decision to give Nino a part in his unfinished story.

"Allow me to say this, Nino," I said frankly. "My father has placed us both in a dangerous situation. I've been hospitalized, you've been assaulted, and I'm being led blindly through a maze by messages such as the ones my father left with you."

Nino's eyes met mine.

"I understand, Francesco, but where do we go from here?" he answered innocently, not knowing the details of his commitment.

"I'm caught up in this, Nino," I warned. "And I must see it through to the end, wherever that might take me."

"And I'll take the ride with you," he offered blindly.

I gave him an option.

"Perhaps you should return home and open a law practice," a hallow suggestion.

"Save your breath, Francesco," he said adamantly. "I'm staying with you."

I knew that full disclosure was a requirement in a relationship that had unforeseen consequences. But, in making his offer, Nino had failed to perform his due diligence. With detailed precision, I related each circumstance that led to our rendezvous at St. Stephen's Church, including Grazia's kidnapping—her whereabouts, her safety, her survival, thoughts that haunted me every moment of every day.

"All the more reason for me to help you, my friend," Nino answered, shrugging, his words nothing more than blind trust.

CHAPTER 39

THE FOUR SEASONS

B ecause Washington was the setting of the Judge's unfinished novel, we needed a place to stay. Nino's apartment was too insecure. Unfortunately, my cash was low, and I had maxed out my credit cards. Only one option remained. I decided to call Elisha after we reached Union Station.

"I think your assailant is following us, Nino," I cautioned as the cab headed down Massachusetts Avenue toward Union Station. "Once we get there, I'll make a telephone call. We'll meet at a designated place. You go one way, and I'll go another—weave in and out of the crowd. Do anything you must to shake his tail. I'll do the same."

Crowds of people—shoppers, travelers, tourists— were patronizing the boutique stores and restaurants at Union Station. Some browsed in the food court while others paraded up and down the mezzanine level. Nino ordered a sandwich at Au Bon Pain while I slipped into a Starbucks and ordered a cappuccino before calling Elisha. Apologetically, I told her very little, just that I needed some cash and a place to stay for a couple of days. She promised to deposit five hundred dollars into my checking account—her money. Elisha also told me that Mendici Melrose maintained a suite at the Four Seasons Hotel on Pennsylvania Avenue.

"No one is using it. Francesco," she said after a brief pause, confirming its availability with her secretary. "I'll call and reserve the suite in your name."

She didn't want to pry, but I'm sure my strange request aroused Elisha's curiosity. Just as our call ended, Nino met me at Starbucks. As he ate his sandwich, I revealed our meeting place to him. After finishing his sandwich, Nino crumbled the wrapping paper, placed it into a bag, and shoved his chair back. He then deposited the bag into a trash container and hurriedly merged into the crowd. I waited a few minutes and then raced off in another direction, weaving in and out of traffic, blending into the shoppers and travelers as the public address announcer bellowed the arrival and departure of trains to and from Union Station.

About an hour later, Nino and I met at the Four Seasons Hotel on Pennsylvania Avenue in Georgetown. The lobby was elegant. Authentic Persian area rugs were spread over black Italian marble floors and cherry-stained paneled walls extended from baseboard to ceiling. A bronze medallion surrounded the canopy of a crystal chandelier; the sculptural ceilings were painted in earth tones. Black leather sofas decorated with bronze nail heads furnished the seating area. A beveled mirror hanging on the far wall expanded the spacious lobby. Surprisingly, the concierge approached me and asked if I was Francesco Micco.

"Yes," I responded.

Softly ringing a bell, he summoned a porter.

"Take Mr. Micco directly to the Mendici Melrose suite in the west wing," he ordered quietly.

The suite was elegant. A mauve floral couch with two purple pillows was placed beneath a Will Moses lithograph print in the sitting room. Twin occasional chairs complimented the sofa; a coffee table separated the two chairs. A twenty-seven-inch plasma television hung on the far wall. I opened the twin paneled doors leading into the bedroom and found more opulence: two queen-sized beds, two purple chairs that matched the patterned mauve rug, and a large pedestal desk. Fancy digs for the high rollers who patronized Mendici Melrose. God save the billable hour. After the porter left, I collapsed onto the bed, but my attempt to find rest was interrupted by Nino.

"Francesco, I have something to tell you," he said contritely.

I hunched my back against a pillow and leaned against the bed's headboard. Nino sat on the edge of his bed. He hung his head and clasped his hands. His eyes rose to meet mine.

"When the Judge gave me the envelopes, he left specific directions," he began, the plotting lawyer orderly arranging his thoughts. "First, your father instructed me never to open them. Second, he told me to deliver the first envelope to you whenever I received word that there would be a memorial service for Claudio Armondi at St. Stephen's."

Sensing Nino's discomfort, I lifted my head off the pillow and sat on the edge of the bed, folded my arms, and faced him. He had my full attention.

"The Judge also told me to give you the second envelope," he continued sheepishly, his eyes drilled on mine, "but only if you contacted me within three days after Claudio Armondi's memorial service. Otherwise, he instructed me to destroy the second envelope."

"You attempted to carry out the Judge's instructions," I remarked, shrugging. "But, unfortunately, someone stole the second envelope. Not your fault."

"Francesco…"

Nino's voice trailed off, his expression the somber look of a penitent about to confess an egregious sin.

"…I opened the second envelope and read the message."

CHAPTER 40

QUESTIONS AND ANSWERS

Nino's confession was good news—mostly because he was an Oxford Scholar with the uncanny knack of recalling whatever he had read. Fortunately, Nino Viola was blessed with a photographic memory. My father often relied on his gift, especially during oral arguments whenever the lawyers spewed legal principles that put a strange twist to cases they were citing. A quick correction scribbled by Nino on a yellow legal pad and placed on the bench signaled that Judge Micco would soon ask a pointed question—the lawyer's forlorn stare that of a schoolboy watching as his father read the message sent home by his teacher.

"You haven't betrayed the Judge, Nino," I remarked, reassuring him. "Things happen. Just tell me what you remember about the message?"

"Essentially, it was a cryptic code—a series of generic questions only you could answer."

"Did he give you any instructions for me?" I asked hopefully.

"Just one," he responded guilefully as a smile crossed his face. "The Judge said you should 'answer the questions and pay a visit.'"

"Nothing more?"

"That's it. We were both tired. It was well past midnight when your father gave me the envelopes."

"Why so late?"

"We were working on the Rosen opinion."

"Rosen—as in Saul Rosen?" I asked anxiously. "The guy murdered a short time after my mother was killed?"

"That's the man, Francesco. As you probably know, the Judge was adamant about resolving cases expediently. Rosen was on a fast track."

"What charges were pending against Rosen at the time he was murdered?" I inquired.

"He was indicted on two espionage counts," Nino answered. "The Justice Department charged that he had obtained classified information from the United States government and disclosed it to think-tank personnel and the Israeli government."

"What was the issue before the court?"

"It was an epic battle over the disclosure of information. The trial judge ruled in favor of the defense and ordered the Justice Department to disclose a boatload of information."

"The government appealed to the circuit court?" I asked.

"Yes. The case was assigned to your father."

"Who did Rosen work for?"

"The American Israel Public Affairs Committee."

"AIPAC?"

"That's the acronym."

"He was a lobbyist?"

"Yes."

"By chance, Nino, did one of the issues before the court involve a disc?" I asked suspiciously.

"Yes," he answered, after pausing. "The Rosen case *did* involve a disc." His squinted eyes told me we both held the same thought—it was the same disc demanded as Grazia's ransom.

"I was in court during the oral argument," he said slowly while giving me a pensive stare. "The lawyers quibbled incessantly about the transcript of a private conversation between three Pentagon officials that was stored on a computer disc."

"The defense team wanted access to the disc?" I asked rhetorically.

"Of course. But the Government argued that the three officials were discussing highly classified information that related to the Administration's Middle East policy."

"Executive privilege?"

"That was the Government's argument."

"So, my father had to decide whether the prejudice to the government outweighed defense council's right to listen to the information stored on the disc?"

"Exactly."

Giovanni Micco was not an impetuous man, calculating to a fault, and the message given to Nino—the one his law clerk read—was perhaps related to the Rosen case and the disc Grazia's kidnappers demanded as her ransom.

"Did you memorize the questions?" I asked.

"Didn't have to."

The fruits of a photographic memory, I thought.

"The first question?"

"He asked you to identify his favorite card game."

"That's an easy one," I responded. "My father loved playing blackjack."

"Isn't there another name for the game?" Nino asked.

"Yes. Some players refer to it as 21."

"That's what I thought," he said, nodding.

We rolled on, a game that frankly amused me.

"What was the second question?"

"He asked you to name your mother's favorite artist and painting."

"Leonardo da Vinci. His painting of 'The Last Supper' was one of her passions," I recalled warmly. "At least three times we visited the Piazza Delle Grazie in Milan to see it."

We were now chugging along on all cylinders.

"The number of people at the Last Supper?" he asked.

I stared curiously at Nino. He knew the answer.

"The twelve apostles and Christ," I responded. "A total of thirteen."

"And the next question?" I inquired hurriedly.

"He asks you to identify his favorite actress."

The question caused me to pause, a momentary lapse while I mused retrospectively. Perhaps I had judged my father too harshly. The simple questions, so easy to answer, opened my eyes to a gentler, caring, more loving Giovanni Micco. The card games, our trips to Milano, the movies we enjoyed at the Cinema Theater Olimpia while in Taormina, the question and answer games we often played together—such as I'm doing now with Nino.

"Think, Francesco," Nino ordered starkly, shaking me from my trance. "You should have these answers on the tip of your tongue."

I blurted out her name.

"My father's favorite actress? Catherine Gloria Balatta."

Nino frowned.

"I'm a serious movie buff, Francesco. Never heard of her."

"That's her real name, Nino," I explained. "The Judge was her biggest fan. Her father was an Italian immigrant."

His impatience grew.

"What's her stage name?" he snapped.

"Kaye Ballard," I answered.

"Her first name is Kaye?"

"That's what I said, Nino. Kaye."

Now we had another answer and another clue.

"And the last question?" I asked.

"What was your father's favorite movie?"

This time I was ready with an answer.

"North By Northwest, an Alfred Hitchcock thriller. We must have watched that movie a thousand times," I said, reminiscing. "The Judge loved Cary Grant and Eva Marie Saint."

A smile brightened Nino's face. The Oxford Scholar had deciphered the cryptic message.

"What's the Judge telling me, Nino?" I asked bewildered, my eyes squinted.

"Think about your father's instructions, Francesco," Nino answered calmly. "'Answer the questions and pay a visit.'"

I stared quizzically at Nino.

"Pay a visit?"

"Yes, Francesco, pay a visit."

"To where?"

"To 2113 K Street, Northwest."

CHAPTER 41

H. VICTOR VONBRONSTRUP

The cab ride to the K Street address was only about five minutes from the Four Seasons. The building was a two-story brick structure with a basement apartment. Nino and I walked up a set of stairs to a front stoop. A familiar symbol was painted on the front door—a cross with a red rose etched into the intersecting bars. Signage appeared underneath:

Office of The Rosecross
Second Floor

I opened the door and we walked into a dingy, dark vestibule with a faded white tile floor. A lamp with a lopsided shade sat on a small, three-legged table. It shed little light. To our right were three buzzers. White paper tabs secured by scotch tape identified the tenants: Hudson D'Priest, Editor Emeritus, occupied the basement apartment. Two law students lived on the first floor, one from Georgetown and the other from George Washington. The second floor was the office of a society that intrigued me—The Rosecross. We walked up the stairs, reached a landing, and walked up more stairs that led to a dimly-lit hall. The faded, pale-green walls clashed with the bright red door. I glanced at Nino. He returned my stare. I knocked. We waited a few seconds. The door opened partially.

A gangly, thin man with drooping posture and gray stubble stared at us.

"Wait—just one second?" he requested quietly.

Gray strands of hair, needing a comb, lay scattered unevenly on his head. His attire was somewhat unusual—pajamas in mid-afternoon. Slowly, with his long, knobbed fingers hanging onto the door's edge, he unlatched the safety lock and opened it wider, the loud squeaks evidence that the hinges badly needed a spray of lubricant.

"Can I help you?" he asked politely.

His raspy voice was coarse, but it had the paternal, pristine quality of a kind man. Although his ragged appearance added years to his age, I would estimate he was as old as my father given his penchant to avoid the use of combs and razor blades.

"My name is Francesco Micco," I said, hoping my introduction would ease an otherwise awkward moment.

My name meant something to him. A smile crossed his face as he stood aside and invited us into his apartment. It was a mess. Slivers of paper were strewn over the floor. Placed high against one wall were stacks of cabinets, commonly used to store index cards. The room, which was at the front of the building, was his office. A pile of magazines and old newspapers was scattered on a round oak table. Lined against a wall were four mismatched chairs, the fabric worn and frayed. Adding to the disarray, antiquated lamps and worthless pieces of furniture cluttered the room. A bay window overlooked K Street. Muffled rays of sunlight, funneled through the partially drawn drapes, lent a subtle touch of warmth to the room. Four cats cordially greeted us, none of whom could brag about its ancestral heritage.

"So, you're Giovanni Micco's boy," he said, cuddling one of the cats in his arms, gently scratching the cat's head as he spoke.

Being called a "boy" was usually offensive, but his reference was made within a father and son's familial context. Besides, his welcoming smile told me he was a gentleman. It put me at ease.

"Yes, I'm the Judge's son."

He said nothing, hunched, still gently scratching the cat's head, towering over us by at least three inches. Nino and I exchanged glances. To break the silence, I found a question to ask.

"Do you know the Judge recently passed away?"

Just as soon as the words slipped from my mouth, I thought back to my father's graveside service. One of the mystery mourners—the tall, gangly, thin man, with a drooping posture dressed in a wrinkled tan suit and wearing a wide-brimmed Fedora, was standing before me. I stared at him, and, like an epiphany, it all came back. When I was a young boy, the Judge often spoke about H. Victor VonBronstrup. He had graduated from law school with the Judge, first in his class "by many furlongs," as my father said. Following law school, he earned seventeen academic degrees—quite a feat, even when viewed through the critical eyes of Giovanni Micco. I can't recall the precise time, but for some unexplained reason, the Judge stopped talking to us about H. Victor VonBronstrup. I hurriedly followed my question with an apology.

"First, allow me to recognize you properly," I said regretfully. "I should refer to you as Dr. VonBronstrup."

"There's no need for that, Francesco," he remarked, smiling gently. "Victor will do fine."

I felt comfortable being more formal. The Judge would have expected as much. Somewhat embarrassed, I continued.

"And I also must apologize for not recognizing you at my father's funeral. I'm truly embarrassed," I said contritely.

Dr. VonBronstrup didn't respond, but his mellow smile warmed the moment. What was an uneasy conversation instantly became more relaxed.

"You're being far too kind, Francesco," he remarked cordially. "I should have introduced myself to you."

Now, more at ease, Nino and I exchanged glances.

"I'm honored to finally meet you, Dr. VonBronstrup," I remarked briskly. "My father described you as the 'ultimate academician.'"

Pausing for a moment, he acknowledged his classmate.

"Judge Micco also was much too kind."

I introduced Nino to Dr. VonBronstrup and then struggled to find a segue into the reason that prompted our visit to his home. Recognizing my dilemma, Dr. VonBronstrup rescued me.

"I assume your father put you in touch with me?" he asked guilefully, eyes wide, his stare pleasant but intense, knowing the answer to his question.

"Yes, Sir, he did," I responded quizzically.

"And you are wondering why you're here?" he asked, staring at me.

"I am."

"Do you enjoy cooking, Francesco?" he asked casually.

"At times, Doctor," I responded uneasily, shrugging, my eyes squinted, unable to connect his question with my father's request that I visit 2113 K Street. "But I'm a sole practitioner. Unfortunately, I have little time to hone my culinary skills."

"That's unfortunate," he said, stroking his chin, digesting my reaction to his odd question. With his head he gestured to the stack of index cabinets that lined the apartment wall.

"I have accumulated an assemblage of recipes that would satisfy the cravings of the most discerning palates," he announced proudly.

I searched for words but found only a generic comment.

"It must have been a gargantuan task, Doctor," I commented respectfully, although I suspected senility was settling in. "Why have you done it?"

"Think about it, Francesco," he answered sternly, his eyes prodding me. "Do you ever read the weekend supplements in the newspapers?"

"Occasionally."

"Allow me to tell you this, son. All of them have one thing in common. Do you know what that is?"

I could only speculate, but I had a more fundamental question: why would a multi-lettered man devote his energies to a project that had so little redeeming value?

"No, Doctor, can't say I do," I answered, shrugging.

He looked at Nino and repeated the question. He got the same answer.

"Well, gentlemen, I've decided to engage in an entrepreneurial pursuit that will surely result in a deluge of cash. Here's the plan," he explained excitedly.

Still cuddling a cat, he walked toward the cabinets and stood before his collection of recipes.

"Each weekend newspaper supplement has an article devoted entirely to food. In the article, a chef, a matronly grandmother, or some other connoisseur of fine foods, suggests a recipe."

He laid the cat down and watched as it scampered toward the litter box.

"And the demand for recipes renews itself each week," he continued. "I plan to provide the recipes. What do you think?" he asked, cocking his head, smirking—suspecting that Nino and I were questioning his senility.

"You might be onto something, Doctor," I remarked enthusiastically, applauding his venture,

He smiled brightly at my feigned endorsement as Nino and I exchanged welcome glances. Dr. VonBronstrup was jiving us.

"What's your favorite food, Francesco?" he asked, laughing hardily.

"Nothing special, Doctor. Other than a dish of pasta with marinara sauce, I'm a meat and potatoes guy," I answered, relieved.

Dr. VonBronstrup paused while glancing at his index cabinets.

"Well, maybe I have something for you." he said artfully. "Take a look at the recipes under 'U.'"

I walked over to the cabinets, located the drawer marked "U," opened it, and turned to the only card. I read it once, turned toward Nino, and reread it:

United States of America

v.

Saul Rosen

312 F.3d. 821

Dr. VonBronstrup leaned back, arms folded, as a smile crept across his face.

"You should read the case," he suggested eagerly. "GW's law library is just up the street."

CHAPTER 42

GIUSEPPE SABINO

It was a short walk from Dr. VonBronstrup's apartment to George Washington University's School of Law on H Street. After getting directions from a law student, Nino and I entered the library on 20th Street and proceeded to the section storing the Federal Reporters. The librarian had stacked the volume we needed high on a shelf. Nino found a ladder, climbed up three or four steps, reached for Volume 312 F.3d, and handed it to me. Flipping through the book, I turned to page 821. My eyes bulged. Stepping off the ladder, Nino whispered, "What's wrong?" I passed him the book.

"The Rosen opinion. Someone ripped it out," I said surprisingly.

With his face buried in the book, Nino removed a folded sheet of note-sized stationery tucked between the pages I had failed to see. He closed the book, placed it on a shelf, and handed me the paper. We stood aside as two students squeezed through the narrow aisle. Nino waited impatiently. I unfolded the paper. My eyes were drawn to the stationery's monogram: a red rose etched into the intersection of a gold cross. Printed directly beneath the monogram was the name of my father: **GIOVANNI MICCO**. Nino stepped behind me and, together, we read the message—penned in the Judge's hand:

> *Francesco,*
>
> *Your search for truth has brought you to the library of The George Washington University School of Law. I ask that you contact Giuseppe Sabino. He is a member of the GW faculty who teaches criminal law. I believe he has one piece of evidence that would connect the dots leading to Rosalina's murder. Unfortunately, I told your mother about a disc the government refused to give me in the Rosen case. Ask Professor Sabino about it. He has been on an extended sabbatical, and I have been unable to contact him.*

Puzzled, I stared at Nino.

"Do you know Professor Sabino?" I asked.

"No, but I recognize his name. Before he was hired at GW, Sabino was an assistant U.S. Attorney at Justice," Nino explained. "He worked in the Intellectual Property Section of the Criminal Division."

"Did my father know him well?"

"Mostly on a professional basis. Sabino argued many cases before your father, and when he later applied for the faculty position at GW, Judge Micco gave him a glowing recommendation."

"Did their relationship change after he left Justice?"

"It did—now that Sabino no longer was a prosecutor. There were more frequent social contacts."

A law student approached. Nino cleared his throat and stood aside. She smiled and passed by. The aisle again clear, he continued.

"Sabino wrote a book on federal criminal procedure," he explained. "Your father authored the foreword. Judge Micco's name appeared in the acknowledgment section."

"Anything else?" I inquired.

Nino shrugged.

"The usual. Sabino and your father went to lunch several times. As I recall, Judge Micco even gave guest lectures to Professor Sabino's criminal procedure class at GW."

"So, they became friends?"

"You could say that. Not beer-drinking buds. Just two pals exploring common interests."

"Did my father ever ask his advice about cases pending before him?"

"Yes. Occasionally the Judge asked for the perspective of an academic," Nino said as he climbed the ladder. Stretching from the top rung, he replaced the book and stepped down. We walked from the aisle and approached the reference desk. A young lady sat behind a stack of books waiting for a librarian's aid to shelve them. She looked up.

"May I help you, gentlemen?"

"Can you please give us directions to Professor Sabino's office?" Nino asked. She stood, removed her glasses, held them by a stem, and approached the counter.

"I'm sorry, but the Professor is on sabbatical. I believe he's already left. Shall I ring his office for you?"

Nino and I exchanged glances.

"Please," Nino said. "We appreciate your help."

Just as she reached for the phone, she glanced over her shoulder.

"Well, gentlemen, this is your lucky day," she said briskly.

She pointed to a man hurriedly approaching the exit. He was wheeling a piece of carry-on luggage; a tan trench coat was slung over his shoulders.

"That's Professor Sabino," she said, nodding.

As he approached the turnstile, Nino shouted his name.

"Professor Sabino!"

He stopped abruptly and turned toward us. We quickly approached him.

"Professor Sabino, I'm Francesco Micco," I said warmly.

Perplexed, his brow furrowed, eyes squinted, he stared at me.

"Francesco Micco?" he answered, hesitating, unfamiliar with my name, a pause and pretense that baffled me. For a moment, there was silence as our eyes met. Then an apparent awakening.

"Oh. I am so sorry. You're Judge Micco's son," he remarked cautiously.

Sabino extended his hand, exposing sleeves with angled French cuffs closed with silver links. The buttonholes on his black tweed sports coat were accentuated with red stretching, complementing ash gray trousers, an open-collared white shirt, and buffed crocodile loafers. Stocky, with broad shoulders, a trimmed beard and goatee, he fixed his wary eyes on me through round, rimmed glasses as he shook my hand, his touch unsettling.

"It's a pleasure. I should have recognized you," he apologized haltingly. "I recall seeing you at your father's memorial service. For some reason, we missed each other at the reception."

I nodded and then introduced Nino.

"This is Nino Viola, Professor. He was my father's senior law clerk."

"Yes. It's nice to meet you, Nino," he said hurriedly, offering his hand.

I asked to speak with him in a private study room or perhaps in his office. I received only a blank stare, prompting my next question.

"Did you speak with my father before he died?" I asked, sensing he was troubled by my visit.

"Unfortunately, no," he answered as his eyes canvassed the library.

"*Please* give me a moment, Sir? My father suggested I speak with you."

Nervously, he adjusted the trench coat hanging over his shoulder. He reached for the handle of his luggage.

"No, not now," he responded abruptly. "You must excuse me. I'll miss my plane."

He headed toward the door. Without looking back, Professor Sabino struggled with his luggage as he maneuvered through a turnstile and rushed toward the door, startling a student who was blocking his escape route.

"Wait!" I shouted. "If you change your mind, I'm staying at the Four Seasons on Pennsylvania Avenue."

Nino and I stared at each other as Professor Sabino wheeled his luggage onto 20th Street.

"Something scared him off," I remarked.

"Surely seems that way."

CHAPTER 43

RUN

For some reason, our mission at the GW Law School had gone awry. Confused by Professor Sabino's reluctance to speak with us, we pushed through a turnstile and walked into the library's vestibule. But before we reached the door, our exit was interrupted by a whisper coming from behind us. The tone was soft, and the voice firm.

"Both of you—don't turn around, walk out quietly, and get into the back seat of the black car parked at the curb. I can help you."

Nino and I exchanged excited glances. Our eyes widened. We ignored the order, bolted out the library door, sprinted up 20th Street, and headed toward Pennsylvania Avenue. Our pursuer followed close behind, and the chase began. Hampered by age and lack of exercise, I tried to keep pace with my running partner. I suspected that Nino's stride had purposely slackened out of deference to me.

"Run hard, man, go!" I said loudly.

Our pursuer followed closely.

"You're being foolish," he shouted. "I can help you with Professor Sabino! Stop running."

Wanting to measure our lead, I turned and glanced at the man chasing us. He was gaining ground, but we kept moving, side-by-side, Nino encouraging me to run hard, my spirit willing, my body protesting as I sucked in the air trying to keep pace. Exhausted, our steps lessened when we reached Pennsylvania Avenue. The traffic signal blinked, 'Do Not Walk.' For a second or two, we hesitated to catch our breath. I glanced back. Our pursuer was losing ground as he wedged his way through a crowd of children frolicking on the sidewalk, forcing him to continue his pursuit on the street. Recognizing we had no option, discarding caution, we ventured boldly across Pennsylvania Avenue. The scene was tumultuous. Horns honked, cars swerved and came to sudden stops as Nino and I wove in, around, and through traffic.

Miraculously, we reached the sidewalk on the far side of Pennsylvania Avenue, tired but otherwise unscathed. I turned to see if our pursuer, too, was testing the hazards of Pennsylvania Avenue. He was nowhere in sight. Somewhat relieved, Nino and I paused to catch our collective breath, but almost instantaneously, we were startled by the sharp pop of a gunshot. Someone was shadowing our pursuer.

Cautiously, we walked toward the curb. Across the street, a crowd was beginning to gather. Traffic snarled. Sirens bellowed. Horns honked. Our curiosity was headed in one direction, and our sense of survival in another. The crowd began to swell. Should we join them and risk further involvement with our pursuer? Or should we detach ourselves and seek asylum in Dr. VonBronstrup's apartment? We waited for a few minutes before deciding to throw caution aside and mingle with the crowd.

Shoving and weaving, we worked our way through and reached a vantage point close enough to see the motionless body of a man lying face-up on the sidewalk in a pool of blood. Leaving Nino behind, I maneuvered myself forward until I was restrained by a police officer cordoning off the scene. I had now reached the front row of spectators standing behind the yellow security tape cording off the crime scene. My line of vision was unrestricted. The victim's head rested on the cold, concrete sidewalk, positioned off to one side, eyes open, buried in shallow sockets. Along with the swarm of other curious bystanders, I hovered near the body, but the dead man's eyes were fixed only on me. It was Carlton Frisk—the DIA agent who helped Roosevelt Ward search my father's Watergate apartment and the gumshoe who followed me the night before I visited Marymount HealthCare in New York.

CHAPTER 44

HUDSON D'PRIEST

Nino and I returned to Dr. VonBronstrup's apartment after leaving Carlton Frisk's body lying on the sidewalk off 21st Street. I knocked on the door. There was no answer. We walked down the staircase. Maybe the law students were in their apartment. I tapped lightly on their door, but again there was no response. It was midday. They were probably at school, buried deep in jurisprudential thought. Next, we went outside and walked down the steps leading to the basement apartment. The paper tab taped on the wall in the vestibule identified the tenant as Hudson D'Priest. Nino rang the buzzer. There was no answer. He tried again. After a brief wait, a short, older gentleman with a slight build opened the door.

He stood erect. His piercing green eyes, lying in shallow orbits, suggested he was suspicious. Thick, fluffy eyebrows complemented his stark white hair, neatly parted to one side. Although he had probably been in his apartment the entire day, he was aptly dressed for a corporate board conference, or perhaps an editors meeting at the local newspaper.

"How can I help you?" he asked suspiciously.

A pair of square, wire-rimmed glasses rested halfway down his nose. Bifocals, I suspected. He was wearing a white shirt, a blue tie patterned with horizontal stripes, and an unbuttoned gray vest. A pair of wide, black suspenders held up his tan trousers. His age was well into the seventies or maybe beyond. I recognized him. He was the other mystery mourner who stood beside Dr. VonBronstrup at my father's graveside service.

"Are you Mr. D'Priest?" I inquired.

"Yes, I'm Hudson D'Priest."

I explained that we met with Dr. VonBronstrup earlier in the day and wanted to speak with him again. Perceiving some urgency in our visit, he reluctantly set aside his suspicion and opened the door wider, standing off to one side.

"Come in. Vic left a few minutes ago," D'Priest explained. "He does accounting work for a restaurant on K Street. I expect him back in about an hour."

As soon as we entered the apartment, Nino and I were struck by a stench. I suspected the source to be an old Maxwell House coffee can conveniently set near a cot with a pillow and blanket that rested flush against one wall, convenient to a nearby sink. Next to the sink was a small countertop. Pushed to the back was a two-burner hot plate. D'Priest had cluttered the room with stacks of newspapers piled high on tables scattered throughout the small efficiency apartment. After we entered, Mr. D'Priest closed the door behind us.

"You must have an affinity for reading newspapers, Mr. D'Priest," I remarked. "Not really. I crop articles from three newspapers," he answered starkly.

I had expected him to be reticent, but he surprised me. D'Priest continued.

"On these tables, you'll find copies of *The New York Times, The Washington Post,* and *The Wall Street Journal.*"

"For any special reason?" I asked.

"Depends."

"On what?" I said, prying.

"On whatever Vic asks for."

"Any particular subject?"

"Not that I care to talk about."

There were no overhead lights, just two floor lamps. A small, rectangular window positioned high on the front wall facing K Street allowed a glimmer of natural sunlight to sneak into the basement apartment. On the back wall, there was a closed door. I suspected it led to the bathroom. Almost hidden by the mound of newspapers was a desk snuggled into one corner. On it rested a small lamp and a vintage Smith-Corona typewriter. All of the amenities of home squeezed into one room.

"How long have you lived here, Mr. D'Priest?" I asked, only to make conversation.

"Too long to remember," he responded, annoyed by my meddling.

His brusque comment caused me to appreciate the delicacy of the moment. Trying not to compromise D'Priest's hospitality, I retreated and chose to pass the time by engaging in meaningless small talk. Perhaps Dr. VonBronstrup would return soon. Meanwhile, Nino, with both hands in his pants pockets and careful not to touch anything, moved inconspicuously around the room. As I continued to talk, Nino slyly maneuvered himself toward the back wall, slowly turned the knob on the door, opened it, and snuck into the adjoining room. I continued to distract Hudson D'Priest. Moments passed. After what seemed to be an eternity, Nino reappeared, quietly closed the door, and joined our conversation. From his ashen complexion, I suspected Nino had stumbled onto something unsettling. Hurriedly, we excused ourselves, assuring Hudson D'Priest that we would return later to speak with Dr. VonBronstrup.

We walked down K Street, up to 20th, and headed toward Pennsylvania Avenue. The D.C. Police had cordoned off the area where an anonymous assassin had just shot Carlton Fisk. The crowd had dwindled. Police cruisers, their lights flashing red, blocked off access to 20th Street. As we passed the scene, I told Nino that I had confronted our pursuer twice—when he appeared with Roosevelt Ward to search my father's Watergate apartment and the next day in New York when I spotted him following me. We turned the corner onto Pennsylvania Avenue and passed the Capitol Grounds Coffee. I asked no questions about his detour during our visit with Hudson D'Priest. Perhaps Nino could better describe his backroom encounter if we talked in a coffee shop's informal sanctuary. We ordered two cappuccinos and listened to the bubbling hisses as a barista prepared our frothy drinks.

"This is the non-fat one," she announced while placing the two cappuccinos on the counter. I reached for a cup sleeve and took the non-fat. Nino claimed the other. After grabbing napkins, we sat at a table near a window.

"Now, tell me what you saw in Hudson's backroom," I asked.

After folding the froth into the espresso, he raised his head, fixed his eyes on mine, and described a scene riddled with contrasting symbols.

"The door in the rear of Mr. D'Priest's apartment leads into a vestibule—probably ten by ten," he said. "As I walked through the first door, I saw another door, bright red, with a brass knocker. A chair was positioned off to one side. When I opened the red door and entered the room, I was amazed by its size."

"How big was it?"

"I'd say twelve by fifteen. The walls are dark blue and stars are painted on the ceiling. The floor is covered with a checkerboard carpet—black and white squares. Two pillars stand in the middle of the room."

He sipped his cappuccino, wiped the froth from his mouth, and continued.

"The first thing I saw was a compass. It was painted on the far wall."

"And the needle pointed to the East?" I presumed.

"Precisely. And it also pointed to three ornate seats, decorated in purple velvet."

As Nino talked, I recalled visiting the Scottish Rite Cathedral in New Castle when I was a child. It was the home of the Freemasons. While frolicking in the building with a friend one summer day, we stumbled into a meeting room. Mesmerized, I studied the room, taken in by its decor, and then hurried off—knowing we had trespassed into forbidden quarters. The room now being described by Nino was markedly similar.

"Anything else?" I asked.

"Yes. There was an altar. It faced three ornate seats, and a white linen cloth covered it."

"Anything on the altar?"

He responded by asking me a question.

"Were you an altar boy, Francesco?"

"Yes."

"So, you prepared the altar for Mass?"

"Of course. Why do you ask?"

"Because every item I saw on the altar is used during the liturgy of the Mass."

A strange union, I thought, a Catholic presence in a Freemason's meeting room. It was an anomaly, given the history of the divide between the two—Catholics excommunicated from the Church if they became Masons; the Freemasonry belief that its Masonic principles are irreconcilable with Catholic doctrine.

Confused, I urged Nino on.

"So, what else did you see?" I asked.

"There were two carafes—one filled with water and the other wine."

"You mean two cruets—not two carafes?"

"From a Catholic perspective, you are correct," he said. "As an altar server, I always filled two cruets with water and wine before Mass—not two carafes."

"And when the water and wine are poured into the priest's chalice at Mass, the mixture becomes the blood of Christ," I remarked.

"Almost," Nino said, lecturing me. "The transformation occurs at the Consecration of the Mass."

I was again puzzled, this time over the contrasting dogma—the Catholics belief that the wine represents the actual blood of Christ, the Masonic doctrine that it is nothing but symbolism.

"There's more," he said anxiously. "A chalice was placed in front of a seven-sided tabernacle with a purificator draped over it."

"A purificator?" I asked.

"It's the linen cloth used to purify a chalice. And a paten was laid on top of the chalice and purificator."

"A paten," I said, smartly, "is the plate used for communion."

Nino smiled.

"About time you woke up," he snickered.

A blaring siren interrupted our conversation. I walked toward the coffee shop's window and saw an ambulance parked at the curb, its rotating red light flashing, the hatch door open, about to cart away the body of Carlton Frisk. I returned to our table.

"Anything else?" I asked.

Nino continued.

"Yes. A large host was placed on the paten."

"The symbol for the body of Christ?"

"You're right, Francesco, the *symbol* for the body of Christ—until the Consecration of the Mass. Then it becomes the body of Christ."

The Consecration was another conflict in dogma between the Masons and Catholics. But besides being confused, I was now suspicious—mainly because of my father's apparent association with a sect somehow connected with a society known as The Rosecross that was headquartered at 2113 K Street NW.

"The paten was covered with a pall," Nino said, continuing.

"What color?"

"White. And it was embroidered with a red rose. A strange equation was painted on the wall behind the altar."

"Strange?"

"Yes—it was a symbolic sign."

Nino scribbled the symbols on a napkin: $X + \Delta = O$.

"What does it mean?"

"I don't know."

The conflict in dogma aside, I was now more perplexed by Giovanni Micco and his apparent partnership with Dr. VonBronstrup, one a conservative jurist and the other the head of a mysterious society—both men teaming up for a reason I couldn't comprehend.

"That's it? Nothing more?" I asked.

"There was one more symbol, Francesco—the most perplexing."

"What was it?"

"A cross was painted on the wall below the equation."

"With a red rose etched into the intersecting bars?" I presumed, venturing a guess. Nino pursed his lips.

"No," he remarked excitedly. "The body of Christ was painted on the crucifix—but His arms were not nailed to the cross."

Nino hesitated.

"Instead, He was holding something."

"What?"

"A red rose."

Indeed, a strange union. For some reason, Catholic doctrine had been reconciled with Freemasonry at 2113 K Street Northwest.

CHAPTER 45

A WARNING

When Nino and I returned to the Four Seasons Hotel, the desk clerk handed me a message written on a yellow memo sheet. Leonardo Mendici wanted me to contact him. The clerk had scribbled his phone number on the pad. I used a house phone in the lobby while Nino returned to our suite.

"Thanks for calling me," Mendici said after I had worked my way through two secretaries.

"Sorry for the late return call. I just returned to the hotel."

"Not a problem," he responded." Do you like the accommodations at the Four Seasons?"

I was embarrassed. It was an opulent suite, and I should have made an effort to thank Mendici for the firm's generosity. Besides being a friend, Leonardo Mendici was my father's attorney, and I'm sure that the firm's founding partner reduced Mendici Melrose's services at a bargain hourly rate.

"The suite is exceptional," I said gratefully. "And I'd like to thank you for allowing me to stay here."

"It's my pleasure, Francesco," he responded. "Anything for Judge Micco's son."

Leonardo Mendici was a busy man. He wasted no time on pleasantries.

"Early this morning, I received a call from the Attorney General," Mendici began. "He wants to meet with you."

"Luther Ash?" I asked, astonished, taken aback by the strange invitation.

"Yes," Mendici answered calmly.

I wasn't accustomed to receiving invitations from the power mongers who patrol the government halls, the Attorney General of the United States being one of them.

"Why does he want to see *me*?" I asked, wide-eyed, thinking our nation's chief law enforcement officer had more pressing needs to address than meet with Francesco Micco.

"I thought it best not to ask," Mendici responded.

"Could it be about my mother's murder investigation?" I suggested—the lone proceeding connecting the Micco family with the Justice Department, given that I had decided not to report Grazia's kidnapping to the FBI.

"Perhaps," he said, indifferently shoving aside my thought. "But I highly doubt that Ash is personally involved with criminal investigations."

He paused, apparently contemplating.

"Unless it involves national security," he added somberly.

I was reluctant to confer with Ash. As a lawyer, I recognized the trap I'd be walking into. I was a suspect in Italy for the murder of a DIA undercover agent, Lucia Lazzerini. Being familiar with the Attorney General's propensity to enforce the law strictly, I hesitated to voluntarily surrender myself to a zealot who would gladly sponsor my immediate extradition to Italy. But I decided to take a chance. I needed to establish a dialogue with the competitors who wanted the Judge's manuscript and the disc, suspecting they were the force that sponsored Grazia's kidnapping. Luther Ash might be one of them.

"When does he want to see me?"

"Tomorrow at eleven. In Ash's office."

"Shall I meet you there?"

"No. I'll stop by the hotel. Say nine. We'll talk before the meeting."

The following day, Leonardo Mendici met me in the lobby of the Four Seasons Hotel. We took a leisurely ten-minute walk on that chilly spring morning up Pennsylvania Avenue to a Starbucks Coffee shop. Along the way, we engaged in meaningless chatter. When we arrived, Mendici ordered a double espresso. I ordered a tall cappuccino. We sat at a secluded table toward the back of the coffee shop. Both Nino and I surmised he would be a disinterested, neutral third party during the meeting— the Washington power broker acting as the intermediary between Luther Ash and Francesco Micco. He sipped his espresso, placed the demitasse on the table, and then asked a question that surprised me.

"Did your father ever speak about H. Victor VonBronstrup?" he asked curiously, his beaded eyes riveted to mine.

"Yes, frequently," my words careful, given that the Judge recently made an effort to code a message that directed me to 2113 K Street—the home of Dr. VonBronstrup. "Why do you ask?" I inquired suspiciously.

"Just hear me out. Consider what I am about to tell you a warning," the stately words of a mentor offering me counsel. With a long swallow, he gulped down his double espresso.

"Years ago, VonBronstrup was convicted of sedition in the Federal District Court here in Washington," Mendici began, after brushing a finger across his mouth, wiping it dry. "He filed an appeal to the District of Columbia Circuit and lost. The Supreme Court denied certiorari."

"What was he accused of doing?"

"He was a member of an organization—the Order of The Rose Cross—that encouraged an insurrection against the government. I can't recall the specific details of the case, but the Judge sentenced him to five years in federal prison and placed him on five years supervised release."

From what I could tell, my father recently partnered with Dr. VonBronstrup, and, strangely, Leonardo Mendici was about to issue me a warning that was somehow related to the Judge's law school friend. I listened intently, making only an innocuous remark.

"A rather light sentence for such a serious crime," I noted casually.

Mendici nodded.

"A few months after his supervised release period had expired, VonBronstrup formed a society he named 'The Order of the Rosecross,'" Mendici explained. "But this time, he was more discreet. He based his new society on the fatherhood of God. It's nothing more than a rogue Freemason Lodge that encourages violent public protests."

"Why didn't the government shut him down?" I asked, shrugging.

"Because his society's religious status deterred the U.S. Attorney from seeking to dissolve the Order of the Rosecross as being a subversive organization."

Mendici rested his elbows on the table and steepled his hands. He gave me a sad stare, a tease that aroused my curiosity, a harbinger of bad news perhaps?

"Francesco…"

Mendici fiddled with his empty demitasse.

"…when your father passed, he was under investigation for unlawfully disclosing classified information stored on a computer disc."

My surprise didn't morph into shock. I've been immunized by the strange events that have consumed my life since my mother's murder. I took a calculated guess.

"The Government suspected he made a copy of the disc and then passed the intelligence on to VonBronstrup?" I surmised.

Mendici grinned and then sighed as his eyes widened.

"Yes," he answered, pursuing his lips. "Our office represented him."

"Was the classified information related to the Rosen case?" I guessed wildly.

"It was," Mendici answered, nodding. "The disc was given to him by the U.S. Attorney so that he could resolve a discovery dispute raised by Rosen's lawyers."

"I'm certain you asked my father if he conspired with Dr. VonBronstrup?" I asked, recognizing that Mendici was bound by the attorney-client privilege, but knowing it died with my father.

"I visited Judge Micco in his Watergate condo a week before he died," Mendici answered quickly, anxious to answer my question. "As always, Giovanni denied any wrongdoing."

I expected his warning to come next.

"If you do happen to find a disc rummaging through your father's belongings," he said suspiciously, "under no circumstances should you give it to VonBronstrup."

He set his eyes to mine, a fatherly look.

"If you do, Francesco Micco most assuredly will become the target of a federal grand jury investigation."

I couldn't tell if his comment was a warning—or a threat.

CHAPTER 46

AN IMPOSTER

Luther Ash's digs were opulent. His desk, dwarfed by the intimidating size of the massive room, was cluttered with memorabilia leaving little space for the pile of documents awaiting his signature. Under patriotic etiquette, an American flag was placed to the right of his desk. An engraved seal designating his cabinet-level position hung imposingly from the wall behind his high-backed leather chair. A row of paneled windows lined the white walls, each dressed in tied-back, red-velvet drapes that softly touched the carpeted floor. Positioned off to one side was a large conference table with sixteen black leather chairs decorated with shiny brass buttons and polished cherry arms. A plush scarlet red rug covered the floor of his chamber.

"It's nice to meet you, Francesco," Ash said, extending his hand as I entered the room. "I knew your father for years," he added quickly. "He was a respected member of the Court of Appeals."

"It's an honor to meet you, General Ash," I responded nervously, recognizing that Ash's complimentary comment about Judge Giovanni Micco conveniently ignored the FBI's investigation.

The Attorney General invited us to sit in a more casual setting—an intimate corner of his sprawling office reserved for meetings with friends and foes who were not part of his official family. I was the invitee, whose role in Ash's plan was still a mystery. Six overstuffed chairs faced a fireplace. A marble-topped coffee table sat in the center of the furniture arrangement. The setting was a paragon of comfort—the spoils of government. As soon as we entered his office, the Attorney General asked his secretary to "Tell Roosevelt Ward that Mr. Micco and Mr. Mendici have arrived." Luther Ash had invited my friend to join us.

"Nice to see you, Leonardo," Ash said, smiling gleefully, shaking Mendici's hand. "Thanks for arranging this meeting," he added, grateful for his friend's intervention.

"My pleasure, General Ash," Mendici responded, nodding.

Mendici and Luther Ash were political allies, at least for as long as the present administration held sway. To survive in the political environment that fed his lucrative law practice, Mendici swung freely with the changing political landscape. He was color-blind. To him, red and blue were just two of the three colors decorating the American flag. After Ash and Ward had exchanged pleasantries, there was a soft knock on the door. Ash's secretary entered the room.

"Agent Ward is here," she said softly.

"Show him in."

Ward entered, nodded at me, and sat. After clearing his throat, Ash began.

"Before we go any further, Francesco, there is one matter we need to clear up. The lawyers call it 'full disclosure.'"

Ash glanced at Ward, inviting him to join the conversation. Ward moved to the edge of his chair while his eyes surveyed the audience. But before making his 'full disclosure,' Ward shifted his attention solely to me.

"Late in the day that the court issued a warrant to search your father's apartment, I received a telephone call from a person at the Pentagon who identified himself as Carlton Frisk," Ward began. "He said he worked for the Defense Intelligence Agency. He wanted to speak with me about your father and the pending search of his apartment."

"Was the warrant sealed, Mr. Ward?" Mendici injected, interrupting Ward.

"Yes, sir, it was."

"Then how did Mr. Frisk know a federal judge had issued a search warrant for Judge Micco's apartment?" he asked, frowning, his eyes drilled on Ward. Suddenly, I felt more secure in the company of Leonardo Mendici.

"When he called me, Mr. Mendici, I asked him that precise question," Ward explained. "We made arrangements to meet in my office later the same day. When he arrived, he showed me his credentials and said that Defense was interested in the case. I just glanced at them. They seemed to be in order. According to Frisk, he learned that a warrant had been issued 'through a confidential source.'"

Leonardo Mendici remained puzzled.

"Are you telling us, Mr. Ward, that you allowed Frisk to assist you in the search of Judge Micco's apartment because he had access to information from a 'confidential source' that Frisk obtained in violation of a court order?" Mendici asked sharply.

"I acted too fast," Ward answered candidly. "The search was scheduled to be effectuated the next day, a Saturday. We were short-staffed. I perceived no harm in allowing him to accompany me to Judge Micco's apartment."

"Well, Mr. Ward, no harm, no foul," Mendici injected, shrugging.

Eased somewhat by Mendici's forgiving words, Ward eyed the Attorney General. Ash returned the stare.

"Better tell them, Roosevelt," Ash suggested dolefully.

Ward dropped his glance to Luther Ash's scarlet red carpet.

"I've since learned that Carlton Frisk doesn't work for the Defense Intelligence Agency," he revealed glumly.

I was stunned, a snafu reminiscent of the bungling Keystone Cops.

"Then, who is this Frisk guy?" Mendici asked excitedly

"We don't know," Ash said, shrugging, addressing Mendici's question, "but we're working on it as we speak."

Perhaps I should tell our nation's chief law enforcement officer that a man was recently killed on Pennsylvania Avenue near the campus of George Washington University.

If he contacted the D.C. police, he might discover the occupation of the man who masqueraded as Carlton Frisk. I chose to remain silent and let the G-Men play their game.

CHAPTER 47

A CONNECTION

After making his full disclosure and sensing that Mendici wanted to move the meeting along, Ash turned to the topic that prompted his invitation.

"This may be a difficult discussion for you, Francesco," he began cautiously. "But please understand, our interest here at Justice is to solve your mother's murder." A hollow promise, I thought.

More than a year had passed since an assassin had killed my mother. Now, under the guise of the federal murder-for-hire statute, the Justice Department had decided to breathe life into its stalled investigation after arm-wrestling it from the state of Virginia—the site of the killing. Before beginning, Ash glanced at Ward and then turned to me. I was skeptical. Was Ash interested in pursuing my mother's murder case, or was the renewed investigation merely a subterfuge somehow related to Grazia's kidnapping.

"We have a theory, Francesco," he began. "There are two parts to our investigation. Both are tied together— your mother's murder and the killing of Saul Rosen."

"What's the connection, Luther?" Mendici asked, a question that aroused my curiosity. Was Mendici only the broker who arranged this meeting—or was he also acting as my attorney?

Leaning forward, hands clasped, Ash began.

"As we all know, Mrs. Micco attended a seminar at the National Enterprise Federation the night before she was murdered," Ash began, glancing first at Mendici and then me.

"NEF, the conservative think tank on 17th Street?" Mendici inquired.

"Yes, Leonardo," Ash answered.

"And Judge Micco was not with her?"

"That's right, Leonardo. He was attending a judicial conference in The Virgin Islands. It was a commitment he had made months earlier."

"Why was my mother there?" I asked curiously, her presence there long a mystery to me.

"The President was sifting through a list of nominations to a possible Supreme Court vacancy," Ash explained. "Judge Micco was on the shortlist and had the NEF's support, who had the President's ear. Giovanni wanted representation at the seminar."

"So, he asked his wife to attend?" Mendici asked, his comment more a statement than a question.

"Who better?" Ashe quipped.

"But what's the connection between Rosalina Micco's murder and the killing of Saul Rosen?" Mendici inquired again.

I remained puzzled. The FBI knew the broker and the assassin's identity for more than a year yet chose to shield them from prosecution and instead focus on connecting the murders of Rosen and my mother.

"As you all may recall, Rosen had been indicted by a federal grand jury under the Espionage Act," Ash said, his eyes circling from Ward to Mendici and then resting on me, the mentor instructing his class. "It's also important to note that Rosen was an employee of the American Israel Public Affairs Committee."

"Also known as AIPAC," Mendici added rhetorically, anxious to move the conversation along.

"That's the acronym, Leonardo," Ash said. "According to the indictment, Rosen allegedly divulged a state secret to Israel and a Washington think tank."

Mendici already knew the history Ash was reciting. He bunched his hands into fists, squirming, eyes squinted, the impatient parishioner listening during the priest's homily, praying that it would soon end. Finally, he couldn't wait any longer.

"I'll ask the question again, Luther—what links the two murders?" Mendici asked anxiously, pushing Ash for an answer

"Roosevelt will explain our theory, gentlemen," Ash responded, bowing to Mendici's impatience. Ward moved to the edge of his chair and bent forward—glancing momentarily at Mendici and then me.

"The issue in the Rosen case was extremely sensitive," Ward began. "Whether the government should surrender information stored on two computer discs to the defense team."

"There were *two* discs?" I asked, stunned, totally surprised. Mendici had intimate knowledge of the Rosen case—given its press coverage, his role as the Judge's attorney, and his political connections. Yet when we met at Starbucks, he failed to tell me about the second disc.

"Yes, two discs," Ward answered quickly. "And the defense argued it had the right to access information stored on *both* discs to show that the allegations cited in the indictment proved nothing more than the time-honored Washington practice of 'back channeling.'"

"Back channeling?" I questioned. "It's a term I'm not familiar with."

"Back channeling," Ward explained, "is the leak of information by unidentified sources within the administration to either the media or non-governmental agencies—sort of a preview of coming attractions."

"So, the defense argued that the Administration used Rosen to back-channel intelligence to AIPAC?" I presumed.

"That was the defense team's strategy," Ward answered. "The Government voluntarily turned over the first disc to the defense team—but not the second disc."

Ward glanced at Ash. Ash nodded, approval granted.

"And Judge Micco ordered the Government to provide him with the second disc sought by Rosen's defense lawyers so that he could properly decide the case," Ward explained.

"Allowing him to review the contents of the disc en camera?" Mendici asked.

"Right, Mr. Mendici," Ward answered, nodding. "Judge Micco wanted to review the information stored on the second disc himself, in the privacy of his chambers, to determine whether the probative value of the information sought by the defense outweighed the prejudice to the government."

"I thought it was the trial judge's responsibility to review the second disc?" Mendici asked suspiciously, his eyes squinted.

"Usually is," Ash answered, frowning. "But for some reason, Judge Micco decided to review the second disc himself. Remember, most cases are heard by three-judge panels. But this was an emergency appeal. Judge Micco was next on the wheel, and the case was automatically assigned to him."

How odd, I thought. Our family's fate was determined by chance, the roulette wheel turning 'round-and-round,' finally stopping at Judge Giovanni Micco's name.

"What information was stored on the two discs?" I prodded.

"The first disc was a wiretapped conversation between Rosen and a mole at the Pentagon who passed on classified information to Rosen, disclosing intelligence that had the potential to jump-start the administration's new aggressive policy in the Middle East."

"Who was the mole?" Mendici asked.

"His identity is classified," Ash answered.

"Can you at least tell us the details of their conversation on the first disc?" Mendici inquired, prodding, his interest intriguing to me.

"All I'm at liberty to say is that it involved the purchase of pure uranium by a country in the Middle East that could result in a military strike by the United States."

Ash's plan was becoming increasingly clear to me. He was connecting the two killings with a dark side of the administration's new aggressive policy in the Middle East, a probe that reached far beyond the murders of Rosalina Micco and Saul Rosen—as well as Grazia's kidnapping.

"Was the information stored on the first disc the same intelligence that Rosen leaked to AIPAC and NEF?" I inquired.

"Yes," Ward responded, "and it was the main piece of evidence in the Government's case against Rosen."

"And the information stored on the second disc?" I asked.

"We don't know. The Pentagon refused to give us the second disc," Ward said contritely.

The pieces were beginning to fit. The *second* disc was the ransom demanded by Grazia's kidnappers. And it was not only the lynchpin of Ash's theory but probably the reason the government had launched an investigation into the private life of Judge Giovanni Micco.

"Do I understand this?" I asked. "You, our nation's chief law enforcement officer, refused to comply with the order of a federal judge?" I asked sternly, my daring question challenging the Attorney General of the United States, an out-of-character moment surprising even myself.

"We did our best," Ash answered contritely. "After I was advised of the problem by both the U.S. Attorney and the prosecutor assigned to the case, I contacted the DIA agents at the Pentagon and informed them of the Judge's decision."

Ash paused as he pursed his lips.

"A day or two later," he continued, frowning, "we received a call from an Under Secretary of Defense who suggested we drop the charges against Rosen because the content of the second disc was too sensitive."

"Too sensitive?" Mendici quipped. "Not classified?" he added.

"Sensitive—that's the word they used," Ward said, nodding. "The prosecutor never got a chance to review the second disc. The Under Secretary of Defense General Ash spoke with refused to surrender it."

Whether the information stored on the second disc was classified or sensitive was meaningless. Whatever its content, the disc has caused the murders of Rosalina Micco, Saul Rosen, and Grazia's kidnapping.

"So, you had no option but to eventually ask the trial court for permission to withdraw your prosecution of Rosen?" Mendici concluded.

"That's right, Leonardo," Ash said. "We asked the trial judge to dismiss the case because the information stored on the second disc was too sensitive for even a judge to review."

"You must have been in a quandary," Mendici remarked sympathetically. "Trying to end Rosen's prosecution, but rebuked by a federal judge," he added, summarizing Ash's conundrum.

"Exactly, Leonardo. We argued strongly that its disclosure would be a threat to national security," Ash said, nodding. "But the trial judge denied our motion. She threatened to hold the Secretary of Defense and everyone under him in contempt of court unless the government produced the second disc for Judge Micco's review."

"And the legal wrangling became meaningless after Rosen was murdered?" I interjected, a veiled accusation that wasn't lost on Ash.

"Can't prosecute a dead man," Ash said again, turning to Mendici, anxiously moving on to another subject.

———————

"You ask, Leonardo, why I wanted to meet with Francesco," Ash said after laying the groundwork which led to his request to meet with me. I leaned forward. Ash stared at me, the fuddled look of a recruiter trying to sway the star quarterback to attend his school.

"As you may know," Ash continued, shifting his stare to Mendici. "Judge Micco had asked one of his friends, Giuseppe Sabino, to accompany Mrs. Micco to the NEF seminar because he was in the Virgin Islands. During the reception, I saw Sabino standing at the bar next to the mole and Richard Stone."

"You attended the seminar?" I asked curiously, his appearance there seemingly contrived.

Ash nodded before Mendici interrupted.

"Stone? The director of the Office of Strategic Plans?" he asked.

"Yes. That's the guy. Do you know him, Leonardo?"

"Not personally. But I do know that Stone advises the President on Middle Eastern affairs," Mendici answered.

It was becoming increasingly apparent to me. There was a connection between the NEF seminar, the two murders, Grazia's kidnapping, and the plot my father discovered—Stone, Sabino, and the mole perhaps being antagonists in the story the Judge was writing.

"Stone appeared tipsy," Ash said. "When he drinks too much, he talks too much."

"Was Stone talking to Sabino?" I asked.

"No, he was talking to the mole," Ash answered. "During their conversation, Sabino appeared to be leaning into their conversation as if he was eavesdropping," he continued haltingly. "When the bartender gave him the drink he had ordered, Sabino took it to Mrs. Micco. And then something strange happened."

Ash was doing his best to recruit me as his ally, teasing my curiosity, edging me closer and closer to his side, connecting the murders of Rosalina Micco and Saul Rosen—and, unbeknownst to him, tying their killings to Grazia's kidnapping.

"Sabino laid the drink on the table and sat," Ash said, continuing to spew out his theory. "He was whispering to Mrs. Micco. They talked for a long while—or I should say, Professor Sabino was talking while she listened, occasionally nodding her head. He then pulled her chair back, and together they left the reception."

"Did you ever question Professor Sabino?" Mendici asked.

"Roosevelt did," Ash answered. "Sabino claims that Mrs. Micco wasn't feeling well, and he took her home."

Ash turned to Ward and then focused his attention on me. I glanced at Mendici, a subtle request for counsel. He nodded. Ash continued.

"As you know, we confiscated your father's laptop computer during the search of his Watergate Apartment," Ash said—an event I could hardly forget. "Roosevelt gave it to our technicians. They were able to retrieve a series of emails authored by Judge Micco that he recently deleted. One was most revealing."

"An email to whom?" Mendici asked Ward.

"To Guido Borgese, Claudio Armondi's business associate," Ash answered.

"What did my father say in the email?" I asked curiously as Ash moved closer to the reason for our meeting.

Ward reached for his laptop and opened it. I read the message and then showed it to Mendici:

> *Guido,*
>
> *Thank you for speaking with me today. As I told you, I did not connect the Rosen case to Rosalina's murder until recently. An assassin killed her because of my selfish ambitions. Under our conversation, I am forwarding a disc to you via a private courier. The disc's information will help expose the plot that caused the death of my dear soul mate. Remember, share the information with Francesco only if Claudio and I cannot continue searching for the assassins who killed Rosalina.*

Mendici glanced quizzically at Ash.

"What do you want Francesco to do, Luther?"

Ash turned toward me— somehow knowing that Borgese hadn't shared the information stored on the disc with me.

"I know you don't trust the government, Francesco, and you have a good reason," he said, sighing. "After your mother was killed, the FBI did little to nothing to resolve her murder."

Impatient, Mendici repeated his question.

"What do you want Francesco to do?" Mendici insisted starkly.

"We contacted Borgese," Ash said, glancing at me. "He denied receiving the disc. Frankly, we don't believe him. Perhaps you could convince him to cooperate with us."

Ash was either naive or disingenuous. Or perhaps I was his only option. I suspected the latter. As he spoke, his secretary walked into the room and patiently waited until he finished his sentence.

"You have an urgent call on your secure line, General Ash," she said quietly.

Ash excused himself and followed his secretary out of the room.

"Must be a national security issue," Mendici surmised quietly.

Within five minutes, Ash returned.

"Well, gentlemen, we've found Carlton Frisk. His body is cooling in the D.C. Morgue. Frisk was murdered."

"Have you gathered any background information about him?" Mendici asked.

"Yes, we have, Leonardo."

"What did he do?"

"You mean—what was his line of work?"

"Yes."

"He's a hitman. He kills people for a living."

CHAPTER 48

A SECRET BROTHERHOOD

Later in the day, I returned to the Four Seasons. Nino's eyes were focused on a computer screen. A book entitled *The Rosicrucians,* along with stacks of papers with scribbled notes, lay scattered over his desk.

"Where did you get the computer, Nino?"

"Mendici Melrose. I called your friend Elisha. A courier delivered it."

I walked toward Nino and peeked over his shoulder.

"What's so fascinating?" I asked.

He turned and glanced up at me. I pulled a chair next to him and sat.

"When we first went to Dr. VonBronstrup's apartment on K Street, the cross with a red rose etched into the intersecting bars aroused my interest," he said, pondering for a moment. "And when I went into the room behind Hudson D'Priest's apartment, my curiosity exploded."

According to the Judge, Nino's intellectual curiosities extended well beyond the law and centered mostly on history disciplines and Catholic theology. He spent a year in the seminary before opting out and attending law school instead. Perhaps I was mired too deeply in the sparse collection of clues left by my father. But I could conceive of no connection between the Judge's manuscript, the second disc, my mother's murder, Grazia's kidnapping— and an ancient sect known as The Rosicrucians. Nino disagreed.

"Just a hunch, Francesco," he acknowledged. "But I think we need to learn everything we can about your father's friend, H. Victor VonBronstrup."

Glancing at the Rosicrucian book sitting next to the computer, I asked a question, already knowing the answer.

"Where did you get the book?" I asked, giving Nino an accusing stare.

"Elisha. I called her again, and within two hours, I had it," he answered, returning my look, forcing a wry smile.

"By courier?"

For a moment he looked at me with squinted eyes, turned away, and glanced blankly at the computer before answering my question.

"No. Elisha bought it at Barnes & Noble and delivered it. She said she'd call you later," he said curtly.

When we met at Mendici Melrose, I knew I could not isolate myself from Elisha. She offered to assign my father's estate to another associate in the firm. I refused her offer but vowed our dealings would remain on a professional level. My relationship with Elisha Forde Scott was one part of my life I was able to control. It was the maniacal part—my father's request—that was spinning wildly out of control.

"So how do the Rosicrucians factor into our search, Nino?" I asked reluctantly, appeasing Nino. Purposely, he avoided my question and focused his attention on my father's law school friend.

"First, Francesco, you should know something about H. Victor VonBronstrup," he said briskly. "He's the author of many articles I've read on the internet. Most of them deal with occult societies."

"Did you learn anything?" I asked, feigning interest.

Nino thought for a second, a retrospective moment while he stroked his chin.

"I did. From one article," he answered, pondering. "It was entitled *Confessio Secretium Fraternitatis RC.*"

While I mused over the Latin title of a book I couldn't pronounce, let alone read, Nino flipped through the pile of papers scattered on his desk but found little, saying that he found only a few stray comments on the article.

"What was it about?" I asked, just to be polite, recognizing that the article had generated little or no interest among readers.

"It was mostly about a select few Rosicrucians who could foresee the future," Nino explained.

"A visionary who anticipates the state of the world for centuries to come?" I asked, somewhat cynically, offending Nino. He only shrugged. Since we met at his apartment on K Street, I was intrigued by the eccentric Dr. VonBronstrup. Nino shared my feelings. But judging by the papers stacked high on his desk, his interest went well beyond fascination.

"First, Francesco, Dr. VonBronstrup believes in reincarnation."

"Who was he in his prior life?" I asked just to keep a flow in our conversation.

"Johann Valentin Andreae," Nino answered.

"I'm not familiar with the man," I said brashly.

"Nor should you be," he said, brushing aside by cynicism, "unless you're a sixteenth-century scholar. Johann Valentin Andreae was a devout Lutheran pastor who was born in 1586."

Nino, a history major at Yale and an Oxford Scholar, searched for words that best described a forgotten period in European thought dominated by spiritual enlightenment and intellectual knowledge. He called it 'The Rosicrucian Era.'

"The Rosicrucians first surfaced in a manifesto written anonymously in 1616 in Germany," he explained, continuing his lecture. "It was entitled *The Chemical Wedding of Christian Rosencreutz,* an allegorical romance tale that spans seven days. Its symbol is a Calvary cross with a rose in its center."

"Who wrote the manifesto?" I asked, Nino's mention of a Rose Cross arousing my interest.

"Johann Valentin Andreae later claimed to be its author, known four centuries later as your father's law school buddy, H. Victor VonBronstrup."

"The protagonist was Christian Rosencreutz?" I questioned, amused by H. Victor VonBronstrup's persona in his prior life.

"Yes. He was a legendary German doctor and mystic philosopher known as Brother C.R.C. or Brother Rose-Cross."

Mysticism bored me, but I was beginning to follow Nino's logic. Andreae, one of the few Rosicrucians who could foretell the future, gazed into the twenty-first century and wrote a manifesto sending a message through Brother C.R.C. that traveled through centuries.

"What's the cliff notes version of Andreae's story?" I asked, showing some interest in a manifesto written 500 years ago that somehow effected the life of Giovanni Micco centuries later—at least according to Nino.

"Through Brother C.R.C., Andreae explained Rosicrucianism in his Manifesto as a spiritual and cultural movement built on truths hidden from the average man."

"What truths?" I asked, musing, my thoughts centering on the words stored on the second disc—the one the Government refused to surrender to Rosen's lawyers.

"Andreae used 'truth' as an allegory," Nino explained, drawing on his expertise as a history scholar. "He was referring to the secret truths of alchemists who were preparing to transform the political and intellectual landscapes of Europe."

"Why were the truths concealed?" I inquired.

"Because the political power mongers of the day wanted it that way," Nino explained.

Nino's attempt to draw similarities between Andreae's story and our mission began to fascinate me. I recalled General Ash's words when asked to reveal the information stored on the first disc. *"All I'm at liberty to say is that it involved the purchase of pure uranium by a country in the Middle East that could result in a military strike by the United States."* And then there was Grazia's ransom demand, the information stored on the second disc, the truth concealed, Ash's words again revealing. *"We received a call from an Under Secretary of Defense who suggested we drop the charges against Rosen because the content of the second disc was too sensitive."*

Searching for hidden clues in a story written centuries ago offered me little insight into Grazia's kidnapping, two murders, and the plot my father had discovered. Yet, I felt an urge to hear Nino out, mostly after he had devoted much time and effort into his Rosicrucian research—but also because he might be on to something.

"How does the story end?" I asked, wanting to move on to a more earthly subject—the eccentric H. Victor VonBronstrup.

"It was a time of great turmoil," Nino explained. "In the story, Brother C.R.C. traveled to the Middle East because he could not garner any interest from European scientists and philosophers."

The excursion of Brother C.R.C. to the Middle East also intrigued me, but I remained confused by Nino's foray into the past. Clearing the fog somewhat, I again revisited my meeting with General Ash—and Leonardo Mendici's mention of Richard Stone.

"Stone? The Director of the Office of Strategic Plans?" Mendici asked.

"Yes. That's the guy. Do you know him Leonardo?"

"Not personally. But I do know that Stone advises the President on Middle Eastern affairs."

"What did Brother C.R.C do in the Middle East?" I asked.

"He formed a small circle of intellectuals—a secret brotherhood— and founded the Rosicrucian Order. It had no more than twelve members, and their mission was to reveal the hidden truth."

"Why twelve?"

"Probably in deference to Christ's twelve apostles. They then paired off in teams of two."

"They traveled together?"

"Yes. The couple's mission was to spread the truth. To quote Andreae, 'if any household refuses to listen to your message, shake its dust from your feet as you leave.'"

Like any competent lawyer, Nino was laying a foundation, connecting the past with the future. I played along, knowing it best that I follow the path he was mapping and ask questions that followed Brother C.R.C.'s life and death.

"I assume Brother C.R.C. died when the story ended."

"He did, at age 106. And when his disciples visited the mausoleum where Brother C.R.C. was buried, they found inside a seven-sided cylindrical vault," Nino said, pondering. "It had the same configuration as the tabernacle I saw in the room behind Hudson D'Priest's apartment—a vault with seven sides."

"What was inside the tabernacle?"

"Andreae described it as a 'fireball carved into the vault's ceiling,' something akin to the sun. In his words, it was 'a beacon casting light into eternity.'"

"Did Brother C.R.C. leave any messages for his disciples?"

"Just an inscription carved into the wall sealing his crypt."

"What did it say?"

"'Thou Shall Find the Hidden Treasure.'"

The similarity of the two tabernacles intrigued me, but I was growing impatient.

"That was then, Nino. This is now. What connects the past with the future?"

"Think about it. Andreae's novel was a *roman a clef*—a story about real events within a facade of fiction—and it was built on truths hidden from the average man."

"And my father's novel is *a roman a clef*—a story about thinly disguised real people acting within a fictional tale?" I surmised.

"Exactly. And Judge Micco probably centered his story around 'truths hidden from the average man.'"

I remained baffled by Nino's comparison—two novels written centuries apart with little in common— only the author's design to fuse reality with fiction.

"So, what's the significance of all this?" I asked, my impatience exhausted.

A chuckle crossed Nino's face as he spun around in his chair, his amusement apparent, the calculating detective about to unravel a mystery.

"Use your imagination, Francesco. Andreae's manifesto centers around a hidden truth, a secret brotherhood, and disciples who set out in pairs of two 'to spread the truth.'"

The imagery suggested by Nino struck me, their union absurd—one a dedicated Rosicrucian, the other a devout Catholic.

"Your theory is that in my father's novel, a thinly disguised Giovanni Micco and H. Victor VonBronstrup joined forces to form a secret brotherhood?"

"Yes."

"And it's a relationship we should focus on?"

"It is."

"Are you suggesting that my father was a Rosicrucian?"

"I am."

"That's absurd."

"Don't be so sure."

CHAPTER 49

E. McWade Williams

Nino wheeled his chair back and faced me, the trial lawyer marshaling evidence, about to make his final argument to a jury of one, determined to prove that H. Victor VonBronstrup and Judge Giovanni Micco had formed a secret brotherhood.

"I checked the records at the federal courthouse," he began. "VonBronstrup was indicted by a federal grand jury on a sedition charge, pled guilty, and was sentenced to five years in federal prison. He was also placed on supervised release for another five years."

"Did you learn anything else?" I asked.

"No," Nino responded. "The criminal dockets didn't tell me much. Knowing VonBronstrup was an eccentric old guy, I felt the real story was written between the lines."

"Was it?"

"It was."

"What did you do?"

"I tracked down his trial attorney—E. McWade Williams."

"The prominent defense attorney back in the sixties?"

"That's the guy."

Williams was a legend, a brilliant trial strategist. Like Giovanni, and me after him, he was a Georgetown graduate. Unfortunately, Williams was living in a nursing home in Silver Spring, Maryland.

"Was he willing to speak with you about the case?" I asked.

"He was elated."

"Why?"

"Because I was resurrecting the story of the *United States v. H. Victor VonBronstrup*."

Leonardo Mendici had forewarned me about Dr. VonBronstrup, saying that he was a convicted felon, now an uncontroverted fact, part of the record, as the lawyers say. But Nino's search went beyond the record, gathering facts that supported a secret union between a federal appeals court judge and a convicted felon. According to Nino, when VonBronstrup graduated from Georgetown Law Center, he was recruited by the biggest and best law firms in Washington and New York, but he accepted an offer by the Department of Justice because he wanted a career in government service. He was assigned to a group of attorneys who prosecuted cases dealing with subversive organizations.

"Did Dr. VonBronstrup belong to a Mason lodge?" I asked.

"Not until he began working at Justice," Nino answered. "There was a Lodge in Washington on Massachusetts Avenue."

"Was it a Freemasonry Lodge?"

"It was."

"I assume the Lodge approved Dr. VonBronstrup's application?"

Nino learned from Williams that it took some time for Dr. VonBronstrup to gain membership in the lodge because the Chapter's by-laws limited membership to twelve people—oddly enough, similar to what John Valentin Andreae wrote about in the Chemical Wedding of Christian Rosencreutz. When a slot opened, the Lodge's secretary approved his application.

"What eventually led to VonBronstrup's prosecution?" I asked.

"As any competent trial lawyer would do, E. McWade Williams wanted to be precise," Nino answered, wheeling around, his eyes peeled on me. "When I asked him that question, he reached in his pants pocket and pulled out the key to his storage bin. He gave it to a nurse's aide and asked him to pull the VonBronstrup file."

"E. McWade Williams has a law office in the nursing home?" I asked comically.

"Just about. Dr. VonBronstrup was a celebrity there—a famous trial lawyer who had an ownership stake in the old Washington Senators baseball team," Nino said, chuckling.

"All the nursing home personnel—the nurses, the janitors, the aides—made up his staff."

I chuckled, too. It was a hearty laugh I badly needed. But there was a crucial side to Nino's Rosicrucian research and his effort to delve into the facts behind Dr. VonBronstrup's conviction. The story 'between the lines' might provide me with insight into the reason behind Leonardo Mendici's warning. Nino said that when the aide returned, Williams fiddled through the file and pulled out a paper showing the lesson plan the Grand Imperator of the Potomac Lodge wrote on a chalkboard at VonBronstrup's first meeting.

"Did Williams allow you to keep the paper?" I asked.

"He did," Nino responded. "After I told Mr. Williams the reason for my visit. He then said I could keep it."

Turning toward his computer, Nino shuffled through the Rosicrucian materials stacked on his desk, found the paper, and gave it to me. It read:

> Chapter Seven: Our Fraternity is open to
> all who sincerely seek the truth;

> Chapter Eight: The world must sleep
> away the intoxication of the Catholic
> Church's poisoned chalice;

> Chapter Nine: We accuse the Catholic
> Church of the great sin of possessing
> power and using it unwisely;

Chapter Thirteen: We disavow the
Papacy;

Chapter Fourteen: We vow to publicly
reveal the truth.

From my perspective, the lesson plan clearly showed
that Giovanni Micco and H. Victor VonBronstrup could
not have formed a secret brotherhood, their spiritual
divides an impediment. I pointed that out to Nino— a
conflict he clearly recognized.

"You're right," he admitted hesitantly. "While studying
dogma in the seminary, I learned that the Church was a
persistent critic of Freemasonry ever since *In Eminenti
Aposolatus* was published by Pope Clement XII in the
seventeenth century."

Nino also revealed—according to Williams—that Dr.
VonBronstrup recognized the lesson plan as the teachings
of a seventeenth-century Dominican Friar—Giordano
Bruno. The chapters the Grand Imperator wrote on the
chalkboard were taken from Bruno's *Confessio Fraternitatis*.

"A Catholic Friar fueling the Protestant revolt?" I
asked.

"Exactly. And Dr. VonBronstrup argued to the lodge
members that the seventeenth-century teachings of
Giordano Bruno were obsolete. He thought it was time to
effect a reconciliation between Catholics and Protestants."

Nino was on a roll, bent on showing that a secret brotherhood was forged between H. Victor VonBronstrup and Giovanni Micco.

"I suspect the other eleven members opposed him?"

"They did."

"As far as I can tell, at this point in the story, Dr. VonBronstrup had committed no crime?" I commented.

Nino agreed, nodding, and then explained that during Dr. VonBronstrup's last meeting at the Potomac Lodge, its members conspired to scatter leaflets on the campuses of Georgetown and Catholic University, encouraging a demonstration against the war in Vietnam. By no means would it be peaceful. The lodge planned to supply the protesters with baseball bats, tear gas canisters, billy clubs, and stun guns. The goal of the conspiracy was to embarrass the Catholic Church. Despite it all, VonBronstrup maintained his membership in the Massachusetts Avenue Lodge. Apparently, he was a masochist—or he had another plan.

"Did Dr. VonBronstrup convince anyone to veto the demonstration?" I asked, baffled by his inaction.

"No. But the D.C. police squashed the demonstration soon after it began. The U.S. Attorney then ordered that Dr. VonBronstrup be placed on unpaid leave from his job. He was now a target in a federal grand jury investigation."

Soon after, according to Nino, VonBronstrup and the other eleven members of the lodge were indicted. After retaining Williams, Dr. VonBronstrup pled guilty when

Williams bargained for a five-year prison term because of his brief membership in the Potomac Lodge.

"I assume he lost his credentials to practice law because he was a convicted felon?"

"He did."

Nino related that before their meeting ended, Williams showed him a copy of an article that Dr. VonBronstrup wrote while he was in jail. It was entitled *Confession Secretium Fraternitatis RC*—the Confession of the Secret Brotherhood of the Rose Cross. It was the same article Nino found little about when he began his Rosicrucian research.

"Do you know the reason Dr. VonBronstrup wrote the article?" I asked.

"According to Williams, Dr. VonBronstrup's purpose was to fulfill a prophecy."

"Did Williams allow you to keep the article?"

Nino wheeled his chair back to the desk and opened the drawer. He reached in, pulled out the article, thin, no more than ten pages, a paperback. He handed it to me. I read the title, turned to the first page, and read the epigraph:

> For what we do presage is not in Grosse,
>
> For we are brethren of the Rosie Crosse
>
> We have the Mason Word and second sight
>
> Things for to come we can foretell aright

—*Henry Adamson, The Muses' Threnodie.*

There it was, Nino's proof of a secret brotherhood. *For what we do is not in Grosse*—something not small, the revelation of a hidden truth stored on the second disc. *For we are brethren*—the union of H. Victor VonBronstrup and Giovanni Micco. *We have the Mason Word*—the chambers of The Rosecross on K Street. *A second sight, things we can foretell*—Dr. VonBronstrup's gift of prophecy.

CHAPTER 50

THE KLINGLE MANSION

At half-past midnight, the telephone rang in my hotel suite. It was the night clerk in the hotel lobby. A courier had just delivered an envelope. The messenger said that it should be delivered immediately. I was alone. Nino had returned to his apartment in Georgetown, still intrigued by the Rosicrucians. He went there to retrieve a small collection of European history books he had stored in a bin at his apartment building. Because there was a shortage of staff on duty early in the morning, I threw a robe over my sweats and stumbled down the hallway to the elevator and then to the front desk in the hotel lobby.

"You have an envelope for me? I'm Francesco Micco."

"Yes, Mr. Micco."

The desk clerk reached under the counter and handed me a yellow manila envelope. I opened it. There was a smaller white envelope tucked inside with instructions printed boldly in black ink:

TO BE OPENED ONLY BY FRANCESCO MICCO—IMMEDIATELY!

I returned to my room. Reaching into the envelope, I removed the single sheet of paper, unfolded it, and read the short message:

> *Meet me in the parking lot in front of the*
> *Klingle Mansion in Rock Creek Park at 3 a.m.*
> *I have information that may save your life.*
> *Come alone.*

The note was unsigned. Having lived in the Washington area for several years, I was familiar with Rock Creek Park. Christened a historic district and blessed with green meadows and natural woods, it was an oasis tucked away within Washington's boundaries. The Klingle Mansion was situated in a secluded area of the park, on Williamsburg Lane, above the west bank of Rock Creek.

Thankfully, I knew that part of the Park well. During the fall term of our final year at Georgetown, Elisha and I had visited the Park frequently. We often studied in the area of the Klingle Mansion and Pierce Mill. I called the concierge, who assured me that Enterprise would deliver a rental car to the hotel no later than 2:15 a.m. Given that the traffic would be light this early in the morning, I had sufficient time to meet the phantom host who had invited me to the Klingle Mansion.

As promised, the rental car was waiting for me at the hotel's entrance. Other than an occasional taxicab, the streets were deserted as I traveled down Pennsylvania Avenue. Aware of the trap that might greet me at the Klingle Mansion, I chose to adhere strictly to the directions set out in the message: "Come alone."

I reached 29th Street and turned onto Q Street. Hopefully, my host had information about Grazia's abductors, but the note suggested otherwise, saying I would gain information that could save *my* life. From Q Street, I turned onto Connecticut Avenue. A thought intrigued me. Maybe I was about to meet an agent who operated from the Virginia side of the Potomac, a whistleblower perhaps who would shed some light on the plot my father had discovered. From Connecticut Avenue, I turned onto Porter Street. The Park was deserted. Fear began to set in, but I found some consultation in a strange but twisted thought. I was worth nothing to the rivals chasing after the Judge's manuscript—and the disc— if I was dead.

From Porter Street, I turned onto Williamsburg Lane. I was now in Rock Creek Park. My destination was the Klingle Mansion, a two-story stone and wood frame barn. Because it set back far from the road, I couldn't see it from Williamsburg Lane. I drove my car into the empty asphalt lot. The light from two mercury vapor lamps attached to poles at both ends of the lot cut through the darkness. It was a quiet night except for the mating calls of a few crickets and the hum of an occasional car passing through the Park below on Williamsburg Lane.

The sound of a car door clicking shut attracted my attention to a dark area somewhere in the back of the lot between the barn and the mansion. Glancing in my rearview mirror, I saw a silhouette walk out from under the cover of darkness and merge into the hazy pall cast by the flickering mercury vapor lights. I turned and looked through the rear window. I couldn't discern much—a misty face, a ball cap, a trench coat, hands tucked in pockets. The phantom specter approached the car, walked toward the front passenger door, and stood erect. Only the trench coat and a twisted belt were visible through the window. I leaned across the seat and unlocked the door. It opened. He slid into the passenger's seat and turned toward me.

"Hello, Francesco."

It was Supreme Court Justice Salvatore Sacco.

"Sorry to meet with you this way, Francesco, but I had no option," he began, staring out through the car's windshield.

"Why the secret meeting?" I asked, puzzled.

"It's best we not be seen together," Sacco explained.

He removed his cap. I couldn't see his face; his head's silhouette was shadowed against the passenger window.

"Earlier today, an FBI agent visited me in my chambers," he said somberly, still gazing into the night. "He asked to interview me because he was investigating your mother's murder. Of course, I was pleased to meet with him."

"What's his name?" I asked, puzzled by the FBI's involvement of Sacco into my mother's murder investigation.

"Roosevelt Ward," he answered, a name I anticipated.

General Ash had begun his renewed investigation. But it was difficult for me to comprehend what Justice Sacco could add to a case that by now should have resulted in an indictment. But Ash was dealing with a much broader plot, one that centered on the motive behind two murders—a conspiracy probe that focused on a web of actors now circling for cover.

"Why did Ward want to question *you*?" I inquired.

"He asked if I attended the NEF seminar the night before your mother was murdered," a relevant question— and a connection I hadn't thought about. Mostly because of his telephone conversation with my father while he was in Taormina, I had become leery of Salvatore Sacco, the Judge's words feeding my suspicion.

"I don't think you're being truthful with me."

"The professor won't return my calls."

And our clandestine meeting at Rock Creek Park in the early morning hours added to my suspicion. Also, I couldn't associate Ward's visit with Sacco's message that I should meet him at the Klingle Mansion because he had information that could save my life.

"What did Ward want to know?"

"He asked if I spoke with your mother or Professor Sabino during the reception," Sacco said, shrugging. "I told him no. But before the reception ended, we all walked out the door together, rode the elevator, and said 'good night' in the parking garage. Rosalina and the Professor went to their car, and I went to mine."

Sacco continued, saying that Ward asked only a few more question, mostly innocuous queries about my mother that had little significance to the murder investigation.

Pausing, he turned his stare into the night, the lingering silence interrupted only by the crickets mating calls and an occasional cars hum down below on Williamsburg Lane—an interlude signaling that Sacco had more on his mind than Roosevelt Ward's visit. Breaking the stillness, he turned his head and stared at me, his beady eyes cutting through the darkness.

"Are you a suspect for a murder in Sicily?" he asked sternly, the scolding father searching for the truth.

I pondered, thoughts swirling, calculating what part of the story I could reveal and what past was best left untold, playing my role close to the vest just in case Sacco was prying for information.

"How do you know I'm a murder suspect?" My question was a tacit admission.

"Ward told me," he answered sharply before delivering a perilous message. "He said that the Italian government is preparing an extradition warrant and that the Justice Department will cooperate."

It was odd that General Ash would seek my help and then support my extradition to Italy. But there was another possibility—the clash of converging interests at Justice and the Pentagon. Or perhaps Ash would use my extradition as a bargaining tool. I related little to Sacco about the homicide, saying only that a lady was killed while seeking shelter from a storm in our Taormina home. I volunteered nothing more, and Sacco didn't press me.

"Why did Ward tell you?" I asked, puzzled.

"You have a friend in Ward, Francesco," he answered tactfully. "I suspect he knew I'd warn you."

I thanked Justice Sacco for alerting me, anticipating his next words—the surrogate father advising his wayward son.

"I suggest you seek counsel immediately."

"Who should I retain?"

"Leonardo Mendici."

CHAPTER 51

A LIMERICK

I was reluctant to accept her invitation, but Elisha assured me our dinner engagement would be a business meeting. For a few days, I had been cloistered at the Four Seasons, dining there three times a day at the expense of Mendici Melrose. This evening's dinner, however, promised to be a culinary treat. Elisha had made reservations at Primi Piatti, an Italian restaurant on I Street, Northwest.

"If you arrive first, tell the maitre d' the table is reserved under Forde. It's for seven o'clock," she said.

When I arrived, Elisha had already been seated. It was a comfortable early May evening so she decided that we would dine al fresco—at a table in the open air near the bar. The restaurant was filled with politicians and their guests, all attired in tuxedos and dinner dresses. Later, they'd be attending a black-tie event at the Kennedy Center. Before approaching our table, I stood back and observed the vain environment that surrounded me. It was Elisha's world: by night, mingling with her influential clientele and, by day, advising the egocentric power barons who patrolled the halls of government. Our worlds were galaxies apart. Having juxtaposed our lives, I maneuvered my way through the crowd toward the Forde table.

"Hello, Elisha."

A smile lit her face.

"Francesco, it's so nice to see you."

"Sorry I'm late. Taxicab issues."

"No problem. I've only been here a few minutes."

Her dress, simple and black with thin straps clinging tightly over her bare, tanned shoulders, suggested a social engagement rather than a business meeting. A necklace, embellished with opals in shades of green on gold, hung sensuously. Her frosted blonde hair, straight and barely touching her shoulders, partially hid the small opal earrings that matched her necklace. As I sat down, her crystal-blue eyes, highlighted by a hint of mascara, became fixed on mine.

"Would you care for a drink, Francesco?" she asked softly.

"Wine would be fine."

"May I order?"

"Please."

She chose a bottle of Chianti Riserva. For an appetizer, she ordered steamed shrimp.

"This is one of my favorite D.C. haunts, Francesco," she said brightly, her eyes glistening and fixed on mine

"Your favorite dish?" I asked, returning her smile.

"The lamb chops."

"Sounds delicious," I said, closing the menu.

After sipping the wine and finishing the steamed shrimp, our server approached the table, a college student, uncomfortable in his starched shirt and slanted black bow tie.

"Are you ready to order?" he asked nervously.

"We'll make it simple tonight," she said, easing his anxiety.

The meal *was* simple—and elegant: asparagus soup followed by roasted lamb chops covered in a black olive crust and served with a red pepper sauce. By the time we began eating, most of the guests had already left the restaurant because of the Kennedy Center's eight o'clock event. Almost instantaneously, the bustling restaurant was more intimate. Elisha told me that tonight the National Sympathy Orchestra played Wagner's "Prelude" and "Liebestod" from Tristan and Isolde.

"Perhaps when you are in D.C. again you will allow me to take you to the symphony, Francesco," she said, her eyes inviting as she cradled a wine glass, her elbows propped on the linen table cloth. "Two old friends enjoying the music we both love," she suggested quietly.

"Perhaps," I answered, trying to smother a feeling I couldn't suppress.

While eating, we engaged mostly in meaningless chatter—my practice, her work at Mendici Melrose, and the professors we liked and avoided at Georgetown. I hesitated to talk about Gianna and Michele, but Elisha inquired about them and I gladly answered her questions.

Her warm smile and glistening eyes conveyed a genuine interest in my family. I shied from asking about her personal life, and she volunteered little, except to say she was avoiding serious relationships since her divorce from Randolph Scott. I nodded and said, "I understand."

We ordered coffee but skipped dessert. As our server swept the crumbs from the white linen tablecloth, Elisha slid the check away from me and segued into the reason that had prompted her dinner invitation. She reached into her purse, removed an envelope, and placed it on the table. Her eyes bore into mine.

"A few days before your father died, he came into my office," she said haltingly. "I thought he wanted to make changes in his will."

Elisha eyed the envelope and nudged it toward me.

"Instead, he asked that I deliver this envelope to you—but only if he and Claudio Armondi had died," she continued, her beaded eyes drawing me down.

Elisha explained further that she didn't know how to respond to my father and asked him if she should file the envelope with his estate papers in the firm's safe. He only said "no" and asked her to keep the envelope in a place where it couldn't be found by anyone, except her.

"Why didn't you give it to me when we met in your office?" I asked, puzzled.

She pulled back. Her pause suggested that she was searching for words to describe another eccentricity of Judge Giovanni Micco.

"The day your father died, I was taking a deposition," she explained. "My secretary interrupted me and said that I had an urgent call from your father."

"Did you take it?"

"Of course."

"What did he want?"

"He told me to burn the envelope."

"Why?"

"I asked. Your father told me he'd call and explain later in the evening," she said softly throughs glassy eyes. "Unfortunately, when evening came, he was lying in the morgue of the Washington Hospital Center."

"Why didn't you burn the envelope?"

"I don't know. Just a hunch."

"Why are you giving me the envelope now?" I asked, puzzled.

"Because something strange is going on in your life," she said indignantly, the mood changing quickly. "You stayed in Washington after the memorial service; you have no money; you're holed up in the Mendici suite at the Four Seasons with your father's law clerk who is researching some arcane sixteenth-century cult."

Her stare bored into me.

"Add to that, your father's odd behavior," she said briskly. "Does that answer your question?" Her words were a stern rebuke.

"It does," I said apologetically.

"Then tell me. What's going on?" Elisha said softly, her tone calmed.

A slow, deep breath, a moment's reflection, and then I told her part of the story, a revelation to someone I could trust.

"Grazia's been kidnapped."

Her eyes bulged. Searching for words, Elisha reached for my hand—a lifeline extended to her drowning dinner partner.

"I'm so sorry," she said warmly.

My eyes teared, pausing our conversation. I looked away, struggling to stifle my emotion as Elisha handed me a tissue.

"I'm afraid she's been harmed, Elisha," I said, sighing after regaining my composure, thinking the worst. "Her kidnappers haven't contacted me. Too much time has slipped away."

"When was she kidnapped?"

"The day of my father's memorial service."

"Did you contact the FBI?"

"No."

"Why"

Although it was a rash decision, it was time to tell her the rest of the story. I caught our server's attention.

"Two glasses of Amaro, please," an Italian liqueur, our usual after-dinner drink when we were a couple.

We sipped our drinks as I told her the story, beginning with the note Uncle Claudio delivered to me the day after my father's funeral and ending with my recent meeting with Justice Sacco. There was one omission. I didn't tell her about the pending extradition proceeding. It would needlessly worry her. While I spoke, her eyes teared, regrets perhaps, a sip of Amaro, an occasional smile, forced but warm, two wayfarers traveling in opposite directions, imagining what might have been. By the time I had finished, her glance had grown to a sad stare.

"Perhaps this will help you," she said, sliding the envelope closer to me. I removed the seal, opened it, and read the message inscribed on stationery engraved with the symbol of The Rosecross:

> *Look to the past, and you will find,*
> *an answer hidden in your mind.*
> *The feast suspended,*
> *her time now ended,*
> *the alchemist's equation,*
> *the key to the rhyme.*

A limerick. A lousy limerick. I handed it back to Elisha; she read it, folded the stationery, and slid it into the envelope. Grimacing, she passed it back to me.

We left the restaurant at about eleven o'clock and stood outside under a canopy. It was drizzling rain. I placed my suit coat over Elisha's bare shoulders to keep her dry. For a few seconds, we stared at each other, saying nothing. Elisha broke the silence, asking whether we should share a ride. I motioned for a valet to hail a cab.

"Yes, sir. It'll be only a moment."

As we waited at the curb, a soft wind mussed Elisha's hair. Shielding ourselves from the chilly breeze, we snuggled close together as she wrapped her arm around my waist. We faced each other and shared glances.

"Your cab, sir," the valet said as he opened the door.

Elisha sat in the back seat and slid to the middle. I tipped the valet and stood on the curb.

"U Street—the Ellington Apartments," she told the driver.

Our eyes met. Elisha handed me back my suit coat. I closed the door and stepped back onto the sidewalk, watching from the curb as the cab's taillights disappeared into the night.

CHAPTER 52

A DECEPTION

As Nino pointed out, it was devious for me to accept the first-class ticket to New York paid for by the United States Treasury with no intention of cooperating with Attorney General Luther Ash. But we both agreed that it was essential I speak with Guido Borgese, my father's email to him saying that the disc he had sent to him by private courier had information relating to the plot that led to my mother's murder. Because the disc was to be delivered to me after my father and Uncle Claudio had died, I was baffled by Borgese's failure to follow the Judge's instructions. Uncle Claudio—the last survivor— had died more than three months ago.

It was the day after my dinner with Elisha at Primi Piatti. My flight arrived at LaGuardia in Queens in the late morning, and by noon I was at the office of Marymount HealthCare at Trump Plaza in New York.

"It's good to see you, Francesco," the welcoming words of Guido Borgese, spoken in the company's reception room. His secretary was on her lunch break. He led me down a long hall and then into a small conference room. Along the way, I glanced into Uncle Claudio's empty office.

Although I appeared as the Attorney General's special envoy, I came to New York to test Claudio Armondi's bond with my father. I recalled his words when we met in his office following my altercation with Roosevelt Ward: *If for some reason I'm not available to help you, please contact Guido.* As we sat across from each other at the conference table, I related to him the details of my meeting with Attorney General Luther Ashe. Borgese listened intently but was amused at the task General Ash had assigned to me.

"Ash told you that Giovanni sent me a disc?" he asked, smirking.

"He did."

"And that I denied receiving it?"

"That's what he told me."

"And, your assignment is to convince me to turn it over to you?"

"It is."

"A rather presumptive assignment, wouldn't you say?" he remarked pompously.

I nodded.

"Did Ash tell you that his agents searched Marymount's office three days before you met with him?" Guido inquired.

"A federal judge had issued a search warrant?" I asked with little surprise.

"Yes."

"But they didn't find the disc?" I remarked smugly.

Guido's smirk answered my question. He stood and led me into Uncle Claudio's office. A Salvatore Dali lithograph hung on the wall behind his desk. Guido removed the print, revealing a vault carved into the wall. Dialing the combination, he turned the knob on the safe one way, then another, then back, pulled on the handle, and opened the door. Kneeling, Guido loosened a wooden plank from the floor and removed a magnet. He pressed it hard against the safe's back wall and slowly maneuvered it out. Reaching far back into the safe's cavity, Guido removed a disc. He then inserted it into his computer and invited me to sit beside him, giving me a view of the monitor screen. Guido selected the proper drive, and, after a series of left clicks, the screen revealed a message stored on the disc:

The Office of Strategic Plans

Antidote

Alexandria Arnold

Jefferson St. N.W.

Washington, D.C.

Guido,

As I told you earlier, please pass this information on to Francesco. I regret to involve him in our plan, but I have no other option. We must expose the conspiracy, and Rosalina's murder must

be solved. Hopefully, he can be my alter
ego and acquire the disc that I was unable
to secure. Remember to tell Francesco
that the only antidote to the conspiracy
planned by the Office of Strategic Plans
is Alexandria Arnold. Unfortunately, the
lone memory my son will have of me is
that I have been an unloving, demanding
father who continued to control his life
beyond the grave. I accept my fate and
will carry it with me into eternity.

I was too invested in my search for the manuscript and disc to be distracted by my father's addendum to his message. Instead, I focused on the newest character in my father's novel, Alexandria Arnold, as well as a mysterious entity—The Office of Strategic Plans. But I remained puzzled by Borgese's failure to follow my father's instructions. He gave me the disc three months after Uncle Claudio had died—and only because Luther Ash had sent me on a fool's errand. I approached the subject delicately.

"I find myself in a delicate position, Mr. Borgese," I began cautiously. "My father's demands didn't stop after he died. Instead, they became more intense."

Guido turned his chair and faced me. Leaning forward, he listened as I continued my rant.

"He expected me to find his manuscript, have his novel published, expose a conspiracy, and to either reveal a truth I know nothing about—or protect the Micco family. My choice."

Guido offered no comment, the silence and his introspective stare unsettling.

"Do you remember your father's first message?" he finally said. "The one delivered by Claudio after your father's funeral. He told you to do nothing."

"But only if he and Uncle Claudio had lived," I recalled. "Unfortunately, neither survived."

Guido paused, his look again uneasy.

"Giovanni called me the morning he died," Guido related somberly, words drawled. "Claudio was in Sicily, but the Judge couldn't reach him." Next came a sheepish stare, a harbinger of bad news, Guido's eyes riveted to mine.

"Your father asked me to tell Claudio that you were no longer part of the plan," he said meekly, his head lowered.

"Did you call Uncle Claudio?" I asked excitedly, bewildered at first, startled that my father had dismantled a plan he had so carefully designed. Then, like a knockout punch, reality struck me hard. My father's last order was ignored by his best friend.

"Yes, I called Claudio," Guido responded contritely.

"Then why did he deliver the message to me?" I asked boldly, baffled by Uncle Claudio's betrayal.

Guido's remorseful stare settled me.

"It was Claudio's decision," he explained ruefully.

I was confused by Uncle Claudio's decision not to honor my father's last wish, especially after he had scolded me when we met at Marymount HealthCare following my altercation with Roosevelt Ward, ordering me to return home and 'do nothing.' Somebody had convinced Claudio Armondi that it was imperative I remain a player in my father's plan. My suspicion centered on Armondi's Mafioso connections.

"I assume you ignored my father's request today by showing me the message on the disc?" I asked presumptively.

"I did," Guido admitted. "And I was also instructed by Claudio not to cancel his memorial service."

And then there was the message Elisha delivered at Primi Piatti—the limerick my father told her to burn. The pieces now fit. My father's decision to exclude me from his plan was made because of the question he asked at the Watergate the night before he died.

"Have I been a good father?"

My silence answered his question.

Nevertheless, I remained embedded in the Judge's plot because Uncle Claudio had disregarded my father's last wish. Perhaps Claudio Armondi's relationship with La Cosa Nostra trumped his friendship with Giovanni Micco.

CHAPTER 53

ANOTHER MURDER?

My return flight from New York arrived at Reagan National at noon the following day. Elisha met me there because I had left my cell phone on the table at Primi Piatti. She had retrieved it from the maitre d' and planned to return the phone when we met at the luggage carousel. She appeared unsettled as I wheeled my bag in her direction.

"Your wife called about an hour ago," Elisha said as she handed me the phone.

"Did you answer the call?" I asked.

"No. I thought it best."

"Do you mind?" I asked, pointing to the phone.

"Of course not."

I moved away from the crowd as Elisha took her place in line at a Starbucks. After leaning my luggage against a wall, I called Gianna.

"I tried to reach you earlier," she explained excitedly, "but the call went to voicemail. Your mailbox is full." She was frustrated because she couldn't reach me. Rather than tell her that Elisha had my phone, I explained that I didn't switch the airplane mode off until after my flight from New York had landed at Reagan. Sooner or later, I'd tell her about Elisha, but this wasn't the time.

"Someone else is also trying to contact you," she said calmly.

"Who?"

"An FBI agent. Roosevelt Ward."

"What does he want?"

"He said that the U.S. Attorney in Pittsburgh had filed a motion in court asking permission to exhume your father's body."

"When is the hearing?" I asked, elated that someone else suspected foul play.

"Tomorrow afternoon at one-thirty in the County Government Center here in New Castle."

Elisha drove me back to the Four Seasons. At six the following morning, I rented a car and returned to New Castle. It was an uneventful five-hour trip. I enjoyed my time alone. Just before noon, I arrived and parked my car at the curb on Sumner Avenue. Michele, his short, chubby legs chugging along, ran to greet me. Lagging, Gianna watched. I took Michele in my arms, raised him high, and then gently brought him close to my chest. Holding my son in one arm, I approached Gianna.

"I'm happy you're home," she whispered as we hugged.

Gianna and I arrived at the courthouse a half hour before the hearing. We met Roosevelt Ward in front of Courtroom One on the second floor of the Government Center. He introduced me to an assistant United States Attorney from the Western District of Pennsylvania, Paul Williamson, who represented the government. Citing his theory when we met at his Washington office, General Ash had intensified the government's investigation into the murders of Rosalina Micco and Saul Rosen. But I was surprised to learn that Luther Ash was now investigating my father's death.

"Sorry, I couldn't give you more notice, Francesco," Ward said. "When the court administrator realized that the hearing involved your father, she scheduled the hearing immediately."

"Why do you want my father's body exhumed?" I asked, searching for clues he may have found.

"Trust me, Francesco, all three deaths are linked together," he teased, saying nothing more.

I, too, wanted to learn if my father was murdered, my attempt to exhume the Judge's body thwarted by someone who scared off the expert I had retained to testify at the hearing. Maybe the government's fortune will be better. Ward continued.

"Time is short," he said, ushering us toward a set of paneled doors. "Come into the courtroom and listen to the testimony. If you have an objection, place it on the record. The judge can then decide whether to grant or deny the motion."

"Fair enough."

We all snapped to attention as the bailiff's voice bellowed.

"All rise, this court is now in session. The Honorable Howard White Lyon presiding."

The Judge, his robe unzipped and flowing freely, walked through the door leading from his chambers, gingerly climbed a set of steps, and took his seat. The clerk banged her gavel, and we all sat as she called the case.

"In the Matter of Giovanni Micco. Motion for Exhumation."

Assistant U.S. Attorney Paul Williamson approached the bench and addressed the court.

"Good afternoon, Your Honor," he said respectfully. "I have before the court a motion to exhume the body of Judge Giovanni Micco. As you probably know, he was recently buried here in Lawrence County."

Having appeared before him countless times, I was acquainted with the Judge, Howard White Lyon. He was a student of the law, and neither Roosevelt Ward nor Paul Williamson was dealing with a provincial county court judge who would bend to the whims of the Attorney General of the United States of America.

"What's your burden of proof?" Judge Lyon asked, testing Williamson.

"The Government must show that the exhumation would be useful to obtain facts in support of litigation, your Honor," Williamson responded without hesitation.

"Let me hear what you have," Judge Lyon said as he leaned back in his chair.

Williamson nodded to the lone person sitting at the counsel table.

"As its only witness, the government will call Roosevelt Ward."

Ward approached the witness stand. He was administered an oath, unbuttoned his suit coat, and sat.

"State your name, please," Williamson asked starkly.

"Roosevelt Ward."

"By whom are you employed, Mr. Ward?"

"The United States government. I'm an FBI agent on special assignment."

"And what is that assignment, Mr. Ward?"

"The FBI is investigating the murders of Rosalina Micco and Saul Rosen, a lobbyist for AIPAC—the American Israel Public Affairs Committee," Ward began, providing Judge Lyon with some relevant history. "We now have evidence that points to a possible third murder— Judge Giovanni Micco."

A scowl covered Judge Lyon's face as he interrupted Williamson's questioning.

"Murder, counselor?" he asked curiously, hesitating. "Isn't murder a crime that the feds leave to the state courts? Are you poking your nose into our business?"

Judge Lyon was expressing my sentiment. If the Feds hadn't preempted my mother's murder case, the broker and assassin responsible for her killing would be behind bars by now. Instead, her case was stalled, bogged down by a much broader investigation.

"No, Your Honor," Williamson answered artfully, "the federal government has jurisdiction in this case, under the murder-for-hire statute."

"What's the citation, Mr. Williamson?"

Williamson was sharp. Flashing a maroon volume of the United States Code, he was ready with an answer.

"Eighteen, United States Code, section nineteen fifty-eight."

"Thank you, Mr. Williamson. You may continue," Judge Lyon said, giving Williamson a complimentary glance.

"Tell the Judge, Mr. Ward, why you are requesting an order from this court that will allow the government to exhume the body of Judge Giovanni Micco."

Leaning forward, Ward adjusted the microphone. Armed with the federal government's resources, I assumed Williamson based his motion on more than idle speculation. Someone had to be feeding information to Luther Ash.

"First, we know that Judge Micco died because of an apparent cardiac arrest," Ward began. "His son, Francesco, was kind enough to provide us with an authorization to obtain the Judge's medical records from the Washington Hospital Center in D.C."

Williamson approached counsel table and retrieved a stack of papers.

"These are the records, Your Honor," Williamson said, handing them to Judge Lyon's clerk. "I authenticated them before the hearing and had them marked as Government's Exhibit A. I offer them into evidence."

"Admitted," Judge Lyon said without inspecting the records.

"When you reviewed Judge Micco's hospital records, did you find anything suspicious?" Williamson asked.

"No, but we knew that six months before his death, he had a complete physical examination."

"Was he given any tests relating to his cardiac health?"

"Yes. Judge Micco underwent a thallium stress test and an EKG. His preliminary diagnosis was arrhythmia."

"Arrhythmia?" Williamson asked, glancing at Judge Lyon, testing his bounds, knowing that he was treading too far with questions usually directed to an expert witness.

"Simply stated, it's an abnormal heart rhythm," Ward answered, Williamson relieved by Judge Lyon's patience.

"Does Judge Micco's death certificate state the cause of his passing?"

"Yes."

"And what was the cause?"

"ASCD, Mr. Williamson. A sudden and non-resuscitated cardiac arrest."

As I listened to the testimony unfold, I realized that I owed a debt of gratitude to whoever had convinced the pathologist I had retained not to appear at the hearing on my motion to exhume the Judge's body. I wasn't as prepared as the government, nor did I have its resources. Williamson's questions were pointed and direct; Ward's answers crisp and clear. They had a plan.

"So, Mr. Ward, Judge Micco died of a heart attack?" Williamson surmised.

"No, sir. A heart attack refers to the death of a heart muscle because of a blood supply loss," Ward answered. "A cardiac arrest is caused by an arrhythmia—in this case, an abnormally slow heartbeat."

"Do the hospital records show the cause of Judge Micco's cardiac arrest?"

"Yes. Hypokalemia—a low potassium level that was fatal."

"Excuse me, Mr. Williamson," Judge Lyon scolded sternly, finally interrupting Williamson's questioning. "I didn't realize Mr. Ward was also a physician. Are you offering him as an expert witness?"

It was a question I had anticipated Judge Lyon asking much earlier in the hearing. He was overly tolerable, I'm sure, out of deference to Judge Giovanni Micco. But

Williamson had ventured out too far and Judge Lyon was about to reel him in.

"I apologize, Your Honor. I do have a learned treatise and a medical report connecting low levels of potassium with life-threatening arrhythmia."

Judge Lyon nodded, inviting Williamson to continue.

"Mr. Ward, did you obtain a search warrant for Judge Micco's apartment at the Watergate?"

"Yes."

"Did you file an inventory of the items seized during the search?"

"I did."

"Did the inventory include a medication bottle?"

"Yes."

"Where was the bottle?"

"In a kitchen cabinet."

"Why did you confiscate a bottle of medicine?"

"It's common practice whenever we're searching the residence of a decedent."

Ward's answer made sense, but I thought it to be contrived. A medicine bottle and its contents were unrelated to the purpose of his search. From what information I had gathered, in all likelihood, Ward's agent-in-charge probably ordered him to seize the Judge's computer and to search for the manuscript of a novel he was writing.

"What medication was in the bottle?" Williamson asked.

"The label read: 'Potassium—20mg.'"

"Did that cause you to be suspicious?"

"Not until I had later reviewed Judge Micco's medical records. His diagnosis roused my curiosity."

"Why?"

"Because the cause of his cardiac arrest was listed as Hypokalemia—yet he was taking a rather large dosage of Potassium."

Although I questioned Ward's motive, he was connecting dots, tracing clues that fed his suspicion, a first step, one link at a time, showing that Judge Giovanni Micco didn't die from natural causes.

"What did you do?" Williamson inquired.

"I took them to our lab for an analysis."

"Did you get a report back?"

"Yes. The following day."

Williamson walked back to counsel table, retrieved a document, handed it to the clerk, and asked that it be marked as Government's Exhibit B. Williamson approached the bench.

"I offer into evidence Government's Exhibit B, Your Honor. Please note that it's been authenticated."

Judge Lyon scanned through the exhibit.

"Offer admitted," he said.

Williamson continued.

"What does the report indicate, Mr. Ward?"

"The capsules were placebos."

Williamson paused and then slowly approached Judge Lyon. I leaned forward and digested the government's discovery. Ward's suspicion had paid a dividend. Someone had switched my father's medication.

"I have no further questions to ask Mr. Ward. Does the court wish to make any inquiry?"

Judge Lyon declined.

Williamson addressed his witness.

"You may step down from the witness stand, Mr. Ward."

Returning to counsel table, Williamson retrieved a document that he had marked as Government's Exhibit C. He approached the bench.

"Your Honor, as I informed the court earlier, I have a medical report from a distinguished cardiologist, Dr. Gregory Smyth, who has concluded that a low potassium level can cause life-threatening arrhythmia. I will ask the court to take judicial notice of Dr. Smyth's report."

"Were any blood samples taken at the Washington Hospital Center?" Judge Lyon asked Williamson suspiciously, an obvious question that also confounded me.

"Yes," he answered hesitantly.

"I assume Giovanni's potassium level was measured?" Judge Lyon asked suspiciously.

"It was," Williamson answered, standing alone in the court's well, the stranded sailor adrift.

"Then why must you exhume Judge Micco's body?" Judge Lyon asked sharply, his stare drilled on Williamson, pondering, I'm sure, whether there was an ulterior motive behind the government's motion.

Williamson glanced at Ward.

"Unfortunately," Williamson answered, "the blood test results are missing from Judge Micco's hospital records."

Relieved, Judge Lyon's stare turned easy.

"So, you have no way to support the Hypokalemia diagnosis?" he asked.

"That's correct."

Judge Lyon rested his elbows on the bench and steepled his hands, the missing records adding suspense to an otherwise pedestrian hearing. He mused for a second or two.

"Can Judge Micco's potassium level be measured through an autopsy?" Judge Lyon asked.

"Yes, Your Honor," Williamson responded. "In his report, Dr. Smyth states that a bone marrow biopsy can measure potassium levels."

"Do you have any further statements to make, Mr. Williamson?"

"Only this, Your Honor. If the Court grants the government's motion, we can retain the services of a forensic pathologist who will conduct an appropriate autopsy."

Showing that someone had switched the Judge's medication was only one element of the government's burden. A much more difficult task would be to zero in on the culprits responsible for replacing my father's potassium pills with placebos.

"As you know, it's part of your burden to show that the exhumation will aid anticipated litigation," Judge Lyon pointed out.

"That's correct, Your Honor."

"Does the litigation go beyond a possible murder?" Judge Lyon asked, prodding Williamson

Williamson glanced at Ward.

"Perhaps we should proceed in camera, your Honor."

Paul Williamson had just suggested that Judge Lyon adjourn the public hearing and continue the proceedings in the Judge's chambers.

"Why, Mr. Williamson?" Judge Lyon asked.

Williamson eyed Ward again.

"My answer to your question will require me to reveal sensitive information," Williamson answered.

Judge Lyon noted on the record that the only two people in the courtroom were Gianna and me.

"You are the executor of your father's estate, Mr. Micco," the Judge observed, directing a question to me. "Do you have any objection if we continue in camera?"

"No, Your Honor."

We all proceeded back to the Judge's chamber— Roosevelt Ward, Paul Williamson, Gianna, and I, along with the court reporter. Still wearing his black robe, Judge

Lyon lumbered behind his desk, sat in his high-back brown leather chair, leaned back, reached for a partially smoked cigar resting in an ashtray, and then lit the short butt. Hiding from the curling stream of smoke swirling into the air, he turned his head off to the side, extinguished the match, and then apologized for the stack of papers piled on his desk.

"All right, Mr. Williamson, tell me. Can you identify the litigation you intend to pursue?"

There was a short pause. Williamson turned to Ward.

"Your Honor, as you now know, the FBI is investigating the possible murder of Giovanni Micco," Ward answered. "We've also moved forward with our inquiry into the murders of Judge Micco's wife, Rosalina, and a third party—Saul Rosen."

"That's all well and good, gentlemen," Judge Lyon responded, "but we're dealing only with the death of Giovanni Micco."

Williamson glanced at Ward, who nodded.

"The FBI's inquiry extends far beyond the murder investigations, Your Honor," Williamson said, continuing. "It involves matters of national security. How Judge Micco died represents only a piece of the puzzle. Other than that, there's nothing more I can say."

Judge Lyon appeared reluctant to pry further.

"It's a close call, Mr. Williamson."

"I understand, Your Honor. And I apologize for not being able to provide the court with more details of the government's investigation."

Contemplating his decision, Judge Lyon turned retrospective. I suspected he'd salute the law, pay passing homage to the government's burden of proof, and then rest his decision on a more practical basis.

"You should know, gentlemen, that when the President appointed Judge Micco to the Court of Appeals, I replaced him here on the bench. He's been a friend for years."

I sensed the troubling question swirling in Judge Lyon's mind. What would Giovanni want me to do? He fixed his eyes on me.

"Do you have any objection to the Government's motion, Francesco?"

Unlike Judge Lyon, I had a personal stake in his decision. Why should I buck Roosevelt Ward?

"I have no objection, Your Honor."

Judge Lyon eyed the court reporter and placed his decision on the record.

"The court grants your motion, Mr. Williamson."

CHAPTER 54

ALEXANDRIA ARNOLD

"Take a bus up Georgia Avenue. Get off at Jefferson Street. I live in the first block. You have the address. Come at eleven tonight. Knock four times."

It was the message left with the concierge by Alexandria Arnold at the Four Seasons. I unsuccessfully tried to contact her the day after returning from my visit to New Castle following the exhumation hearing. However, the telephone number of Alexandria Arnold, described by my father as the "Antidote," was not published in the directory. Once again, I turned to Mendici Melrose for help. Through their influential contacts, Elisha provided me with her number.

While riding to Arnold's house, I sat in the rear of the Metro bus and studied the other passengers. Besides me, only three riders remained on the bus by the time it approached Jefferson Street. In front of me was a teenager dressed in baggy jeans, a bulky Washington Redskins jersey, and a ball cap fixed cockeyed on his head. The muffled clatter of rap music escaping from his headset entertained me. An older woman with a bag of groceries propped between her legs sat slumped in a seat facing the aisle. A man dressed in a gray security-guard uniform stood near the driver. He steadied himself by grasping a pole as the bus chugged up Georgia Avenue, ignoring a prominently displayed sign that read: "DO NOT TALK TO DRIVER WHILE BUS IS IN MOTION."

At the Jefferson Street stop, the other passengers remained on board. I got off. Alexandria Arnold lived in the first block of houses. Four dim lights, two on either side of the street, hung from telephone poles. One was flickering on and then off, and the other three did little to illuminate the area. Row houses that set back evenly from the sidewalk lined the narrow street. Because of the darkness, it was challenging to locate Alexandria Arnold's home. Hoping not to be seen, I walked up a brick walk and approached the corner house's porch. I'd find the number and get a bead on my destination.

Tacked onto a porch pillar was the house's street number—101. Alexandria Arnold lived at 107 Jefferson Street. I retraced my steps and made my way toward Arnold's home. There was a pole lamp shedding a glimmer of light on the walkway that led to her house. I looked at my watch. It was two minutes past eleven. I proceeded up the walkway and onto the porch. I knocked four times. The door opened—but only an inch or two. The safety latch remained fastened.

"Hand me your driver's license."

It was a female's voice. I reached into my wallet, removed the license, and passed it on to Alexandria Arnold. Satisfied I was her guest, she opened the door, and I entered a narrow hallway.

"Thanks for seeing me, Alexandria."

"Call me Alex," she said, handing me back my license.

She closed the door and attached the safety latch.

"Come into the kitchen. We can talk there."

I followed her through a hallway that led into a small galley kitchen. A rectangular table was shoved against a wall; two chairs were placed at opposite ends. A small lamp sat on the table. A fixture above the sink provided the only light. A window claimed most of the back wall.

"Sit here, Francesco."

She pulled out a chair and walked to the opposite side of the table. Alexandria Arnold was a middle-aged woman of medium height and slight build. She wore jeans, a gray sweatshirt, and white ankle socks. Her brown hair was pulled straight back and tied in a long ponytail secured by a black bow. She sat on the edge of her chair, crossed her legs, leaned forward, and clasped her hands, resting them on her legs. Our eyes met. The meeting began.

"Let me say this first, Francesco," she said stoically. "I recently learned that your sister had been kidnapped, and I also know you're searching for a disc. Perhaps I can help you."

"You know Grazia's been kidnapped?" I asked surprisingly, wide-eyed as my jaw dropped, jolted by her revelation, but more perplexed by the source of her information. A questing stare punctuated my curiosity.

"How do you know?" I asked, astounded.

"Claudio Armondi told me," she answered calmly.

"You knew him?" I asked curiously.

She sat back, arms folded, her stare resolute.

"Yes. Through your father. Let's leave it at that."

I nodded, her firm stare telling me that Alexandria Arnold wouldn't budge.

"How did you meet my father?" I asked, testing the boundaries of our conversation.

"We met at a cocktail party sponsored by the National Enterprise Federation a short time after your mother was murdered," she explained. "We talked for a while. I told him I was a senior military officer at the Pentagon and worked for the Near East South Asia Office. For some reason, he was intrigued."

Because of the ransom demanded by Grazia's kidnappers, I was mostly interested in the disc the Judge referred to in the message he sent to Guido Borgese. But Alex was connected to the Administration's new policy in the Middle East, a valuable source, a possible ally that could help me piece together Grazia's kidnapping, the murders, and the 'draconian plot' my father had discovered.

"What aroused my father's curiosity?" I asked, comfortable asking questions if she was open to answering them.

"My position."

"As an officer dealing with Middle Eastern affairs?"

"Yes," she answered, leaning forward, her eyes fixed on mine. "Your father began to quiz me about the Administration's new policy in the Middle East. I told him I was upset about certain events that were occurring at the Pentagon. I specifically worked on the Iran desk, and we were now operating under a new rubric: 'The Office of Strategic Plans.'"

According to my father, Alexandria Arnold was an antidote, a contact who could somehow counteract whatever ruse he had discovered. But I was more intrigued by Alex's relationship with Claudio Armondi and his possible connection to the Iran desk.

"Who runs the Office of Strategic Plans?" I asked.

"Richard Stone. He's the Director. Stone has worked on intelligence and foreign policy matters for years."

The puzzle's loose pieces were falling in place. It was Stone's conversation with a mole at another NEF seminar that spiked the curiosity of Professor Sabino, causing him to eavesdrop on their conversation while they enjoyed their favorite inebriant. I recalled General Ash's comment: *'When Stone drinks too much, he talks too much.'*

"Any other principals in the Office of Strategic Plans?" I asked, prying for details.

"Two others," Alex related. "One is Lester LaRouche. He's the adjunct foreign policy expert. He's also a senior policy advisor at the National Enterprise Federation. The other is Luca Botti."

"What does Botti do?" I asked, recalling his name and the number I had dialed on Anna Angilisanti's iPhone after she had left my father's Watergate condominium.

"Nobody knows," she answered, shrugging. "But sometime after Stone expanded the Iran desk, he was named the Deputy Under Secretary of Defense for Policy."

"Why the rubric change?"

"We were now responsible for implementing the Administration's new foreign policy for Iran."

"Which was?" I asked, testing the bounds of our conversation.

"A much more aggressive approach," she answered, smirking. "Like an 'in your face' policy. Threaten us, and we'll blow you to smithereens and take over your country."

I wasn't a student of politics, nor did I follow the machinations of government closely. But I sensed that I was about to become acquainted with the yields of deception—manufactured truths fed by demagogues to an unsuspecting public.

"Stone intended to start releasing the Administration's new Middle East policy on a well-plotted schedule," Alex revealed. "There was, however, one glitch—the new policy was leaked to Saul Rosen, but he didn't follow directions. He released the information to AIPAC prematurely."

"And that resulted in his indictment?"

"It did," she answered as a forlorn stare crossed her face. "Unfortunately for Rosen, our Attorney General—Luther Ash—was unaware that Stone *purposely* leaked the Administration's new Middle East policy to Rosen."

"The AG's office thought Rosen was intentionally passing on classified information to Israel," I surmised.

"Yes," Alex answered sadly, nodding, fingers clasped as her eyes dropped to the table.

It was nothing more than the 'back channeling' practice that Roosevelt Ward explained to me when we met at Ash's office—the leak of classified information to either the media or unidentified sources, in this case, Saul Rosen. As Ward said then, it's nothing more than a 'preview of coming attractions.'

"Rosen was murdered, and that ended the Government's case?" I asked rhetorically.

"Yes. And all because of a disc," she said, her words drawled, pausing as a grin slowly crossed her face.

"And, it was the second disc your father ordered the government to surrender to Saul Rosen's lawyers in their discovery request," she revealed slyly, tying Grazia's ransom to our discussion.

"How do you know it was the same disc that the government withheld in the Rosen case?" I asked eagerly.

"Because I read and listen—and I know what intel is stored on the disc," she bragged.

As a senior military officer, it wasn't surprising that Alex had access to classified information, her clearance level high, secret or top-secret, nothing less. The government had classified the data stored on the Rosen disc as sensitive, and Alex wouldn't expose herself to an indictment by sharing it with me, unless she was a zealot with a fanatical agenda. I decided to tread softly, listening while she talked.

"All high-level personnel meetings are recorded, reduced to a transcript, and then stored on a disc," she explained. "It's the same system that got Nixon in trouble in the Watergate scandal."

Alex leaned back, smirking as our eyes met.

"In much the same way," she continued, "by refusing to comply with your father's order, Stone and his gang of renegades were playing with fire."

Her pause left me an opening to ask a question.

"If the information was so incriminating, they could have easily destroyed the disc," I suggested.

Alex chuckled as she stared at me, my eyes squinted, lips pursed, my brow creased.

"Easier said than done," she chuckled.

A mischievous smile lit her face.

"I secretly recorded their meeting," she announced casually.

Once again, I was stunned, astonished by her grit, a blow that would have buckled my knees had I been standing. Alexandria Arnold was indeed a zealot, and in all likelihood, she had a plan—and I was part of it. Why else would she be passing classified information on to me?

"How were you able to do that?" I asked suspiciously.

"Let's just say I have friends at the Pentagon who shared my concerns. It was a black-bag job."

"A black-bag job?"

"Yeah," she answered smugly. "We covertly planted surveillance equipment in the Office of Strategic Plans meeting room."

"You bugged the room?"

"It was the right thing to do," she said smartly.

I applauded her daring game but questioned her judgment, even her sanity. Alex's gamble was an invitation to a treason indictment. But then again, the cabal who planned the scheme wouldn't want a revealing prosecution to stop the plots clock from ticking.

"We bugged the room," she added. "But we also scrubbed it clean."

"So, there are two discs of the same conversation—one in possession of Stone and friends and one in your possession?" I asked.

"Exactly."

"Whose voices appear on the disc?" I asked.

"Stone, Botti, and LaRouche."

"What were they discussing?"

"A burglary that would produce bogus intelligence."

"What's the bogus intelligence?"

"That's all I can tell you."

Her words cut deep.

"Why?"

"Because my father wants it that way."

"Who's your father?" I asked puzzled.

"Victor VonBronstrup. He and his wife adopted me when I was ten."

I wasn't shocked. The strange twists in this strange story had already immunized me. Thankfully, Nino had dug deep into the background of Dr. VonBronstrup. His request that Alex keep secret the bogus intelligence inched me closer to Nino's suspicion that H. Victor VonBronstrup and Judge Giovanni Micco had indeed formed a 'secret brotherhood.' And somewhere entangled in the mess was Claudio Armondi.

"You gave the disc to Dr. VonBronstrup?" I surmised.

"Yes."

"Why?"

"To use his words, he needed it to 'fulfill a prophecy.'"

I let her biblical response drop. Alex's answer was an apparent reference to The Rosecross and Dr. VonBronstrup's paranormal powers as a Rosicrucian. I didn't want to get mired down in a mystical conversation. That's Nino's bailiwick.

"Did Dr. VonBronstrup tell my father that he had the disc?"

"He did. But not until after your mother was murdered."

"Why did he wait until then?"

"Because he didn't know the Rosen case was pending before him."

"How did he find out?"

"His neighbor told him two days after your mother was murdered."

"His neighbor?"

"Yes. Giuseppe Sabino. He lives at 2115 K Street, next door to my father, and close to GW's campus where he teaches at the law school. They're close friends."

Once again, Sabino entered my father's story. It was clear to me that the elusive Professor was hiding a clue that connected Rosalina Micco's murder with the ruse discovered by Giovanni Micco.

"Sabino was out of sort," Alex explained. "As you know, two nights earlier, he had attended a NEF seminar with your mother."

"Why was he upset?"

"Earlier that day, two Virginia homicide detectives interviewed him," she said. "Other than the assassin, he was the last person to see her alive."

She paused, pondering for a moment.

"My father said that he reeled on and on about a written statement he had just given the police," Alex said haltingly, giving more thought to her father's disclosure. "That's when he mentioned the Rosen case."

"What did he say?"

"That he was in a 'fix' because he had helped your father decide the discovery issue in Rosen."

"Did your father ask Sabino why he was troubled by the written statement?"

"He tried, but Sabino kept mumbling gibberish my father could hardly understand. He finally returned to his apartment. My father hasn't seen him since then."

Alex shoved her chair back and stood.

"It's getting late," she said.

I thanked her and walked through the hallway to the door. One question remained unanswered.

"Why didn't Dr. VonBronstrup give the disc to my father?" I asked.

"Let's say they were in negotiations."

"They were bartering?"

"You could say that."

"Will he give it to me?"

Alex shrugged.

"Ask him."

CHAPTER 55

COMPETING INTERESTS

Following my visit with Alexandria Arnold, I returned to New Castle for a week to breathe life into my ailing law practice and, more importantly, to spend some much-needed quality time with Gianna and Michele. It was an uneventful seven days that stretched into an additional three after Michele came down with a case of early summer flu. The ER doctor hospitalized Michele overnight because he was dehydrated. I remained with him, watching throughout the night as bags hanging from an IV pole delivered him fluids. At about eight o'clock the following morning, he was examined by an attending doctor who said the lab tests were normal and that Michele "was good to go." After signing the release papers, I walked behind an aide as she wheeled Michele to the hospital entrance. Gianna was waiting at the curb. I strapped Michele into his car seat, opened the front door, and sat beside Gianna. She gave me a quick stare.

"Don't even think about it," she said sternly, staring through the car's windshield.

"About what?"

"About driving to Washington today. "You need to pal around with Michele—and then get eight hours sleep."

Gianna was right. It was a good suggestion, or should I say order, her voice resolute, leaving me with no option. A day together, just father and son. It was the kind of time I yearned for as a child, alone with my father, just us two, but he was too busy, always hurrying off to his jealous mistress—the law. As Gianna appropriately recognized, I was headed down the same road. She parked the car in the driveway, smiling as she walked through the garage and into the house.

Michele and I stayed outside, playing in the yard, his chubby legs churning as I chased him, his voice screeching as he slid down the sliding board at the school playground, his eyes skyward, watching breathlessly as a kite took flight. Chili dogs and french fries at Coney Island for lunch, ice cream at Forbush's before the merry-go-round, and Ferris wheel at Cascade Park. Six hours later, we returned home, exhausted and just in time for dinner.

"Did you guys have a good time?" Gianna asked. Michele ran toward her and wrapped his arms around his mother's legs as her hands mussed his sweaty hair.

"Thanks," I said to Gianna as we all hugged.

After dinner, I bathed Michele, helped him into his pajamas, and then tucked him in bed. His eyes were closed before I left the room. I turned, doused the light, leaving only the dim glare of the night lamp. I eased the door shut before giving him one last peek. At eight in the morning,

I was headed east on the Pennsylvania Turnpike—on my way back to Washington.

When I returned to the Four Seasons, I found Nino still poring over the Rosicrucian materials. As I dropped my luggage to the floor and threw my coat over a chair, he turned his attention to me.

"FedEx delivered an envelope for you today."

"When?"

"A few hours ago."

Nino slid his chair back and nodded to the edge of his desk. I placed my hand on his back as I reached for the envelope and held it in my hands. My name and address were written in script:

Francesco Micco, Esq.

Four Seasons Hotel

2701 Pennsylvania Ave.

Washington, D.C. 66702

I removed a note from the envelope. Nino stood and peeked over my shoulder. Anxiously, I opened the folded stationery. The message was handwritten on white parchment paper—a heavy stock. It was monogrammed with a gold cross. A red rose was etched in the center of the cross where the bars intersected. The message was penned

with broad strokes in bold, red ink. Together we read the
letter:

> *Dear Francesco,*
>
> *Through this writing, I am inviting you to a
> meeting of The Rosecross. Our gathering will
> begin at 10:00 p.m. Tuesday. The assembly
> room is located at 2113 K. St., N.W. The
> invitation is also extended to your friend,
> Nino Viola. Hudson D'Priest, who will escort
> you into our chambers, will greet you at the
> door of his apartment.*
>
> *H. Victor VonBronstrup*

I turned and stared at Nino.

"What day is it?"

"Tuesday."

Tonight, Nino and I will attend a meeting of The
Rosecross.

CHAPTER 56

THE MEETING

S uspecting that a gumshoe might shadow us, Nino and I left the Four Seasons by exiting through a back door that led to an alley. We then made our way onto Pennsylvania Avenue. A cab delivered us to 2113 K Street NW promptly at 10 p.m., the home of H. Victor VonBronstrup, the home of Hudson D'Priest, and the chambers of The Rosecross. Hudson D'Priest was waiting for us at the top of the stairs leading to his basement apartment. On this visit, he recognized us as guests.

Forcing a smile, he extended his hand, led us down the stairs and through his cluttered apartment. The disarray remained neatly in place. Dodging cut newspaper strips strewn over the floor, we approached the door leading to the assembly room. Hudson opened the first door and politely stood back as we entered the vestibule. He then approached the red door and tapped the brass knocker three times—most likely a ritual. After waiting a few moments, he opened that door and ushered us into the meeting room. We walked in. Our host had not arrived.

My eyes focused on the cross painted on the wall behind the altar. Two votive candles, both lit, were placed on each side of the cross. I stared at the body of Christ etched into the intersecting bars. Just as Nino had described, his arms were not nailed to the cross. Instead, he was holding a red rose. Fascination drew me to the marks painted on the wall above the Rose Cross:

$$X + \Delta = O$$

Through his Rosicrucian research, Nino had decoded the alchemical equation—silver plus copper equals gold. A Roman Missal and two cruets, one filled with water and the other with wine, remained placed on the altar beside a tabernacle with seven sides. A high-backed chair upholstered in red velvet, obviously reserved for the Grand Imperator, was placed next to the altar facing the three ornate velvet chairs. It was probably the royal seat of H. Victor VonBronstrup. It wouldn't surprise me if he walked into the meeting, pastoral staff in hand, wearing a gold miter and red cassock.

After inviting us to sit in the velvet chairs, Hudson removed a chalice from a small round table tucked in a corner and placed it on the altar directly in front of the tabernacle. He then rested a purificator on top of the chalice—a white linen cloth with a small red cross etched into the center. Like an altar server preparing for Mass, Hudson placed a large host on a paten and gently laid it on top of the purificator. Next, he set a pall on the paten and then draped the chalice with a red veil and a burse—a folding case covered in red cloth generally used to store a second purificator.

"Please remain silent until I return," D'Priest whispered, leaving the room.

After a short wait, there was a soft tap on the door. Hudson D'Priest entered. He announced that the meeting of The Rosecross would begin. Moments later, H. Victor VonBronstrup entered the meeting chamber. Nino and I respectfully stood. As I had suspected, Dr. VonBronstrup claimed the red leather chair facing the three ornate velvet chairs we sat in. I focused my eyes on H. Victor VonBronstrup. He was wearing his traditional garb— pajamas. There was, however, one difference. An inverted triangular apron, with The Rosecross stitched in the center, hung from his waist. We sat in unison, and the meeting of The Rosecross was off to a ceremonial start.

"Thank you both for accepting my invitation," Dr. VonBronstrup said, his voice raspy but welcoming.

We nodded. I suspected the first order of business would be Giovanni Micco. After clearing phlegm from his throat, Dr. VonBronstrup turned toward me.

"Your father was an old friend, Francesco. We go back to law school," he said, grinning. "Through the years, I religiously followed his career. Did you know that Rosalina and Giovanni invited me to their wedding?"

"I assume you went?" I asked, my question igniting his smile.

"Of course," he responded shrugging, thinking, I'm sure, that the answer to my question was glaringly obvious.

"I wouldn't think of missing the wedding of Rosalina Bartolacci and Giovanni Micco."

"So, you knew him while he was courting my mother?"

"Very well."

His smile broadened. Dr. VonBronstrup was reminiscing—or so his blind stare indicated—recalling less challenging times, he, an assistant U.S. Attorney devoting his life to public service; Giovanni, a general practitioner setting out to build a law practice.

"Your parents were true soul mates, coupled together by a mystical force," he said, his eyes glittering. "I listened to Giovanni's stories about his beloved Rosalina day and night. I knew their stars had crossed in a previous life. After dancing around the heavens without each other for five centuries, fate finally reunited them."

I passed over his celestial comment and moved on to a more earthly question.

"Did you maintain your friendship with him throughout the years?" I asked, prodding Dr. VonBronstrup, intrigued by his role in the secret brotherhood.

"To some extent," he said, pausing, his tone now somewhat somber. "Occasionally, we picked each other's minds. You know, sharing views about arcane legal questions that interested only your father and me."

I was surprised but pleased by our exchange of dialogue. The trappings suggested a more formal service. The accessories of a Roman Catholic Mass were all in place— the missal, cruets, chalice, votive candles, and burse, albeit a priest was missing. But Victor VonBronstrup was willing to talk, and I was ready to listen—and ask questions.

"Did you talk to my father after my mother's funeral?" I inquired.

"I tried," he answered, wheezing after he covered a wet cough with his fist. "Three days later, I left a message on Giovanni's answering machine."

"Did he return your call?" I asked.

"He did. I told him that it was important that we meet."

Strange bedfellows, I thought. A federal appeals court judge was huddling with a convicted felon. Was it a prophecy fulfilled, a precursor to the secret brotherhood that Nino suspected—a holy alliance between H. Victor VonBronstrup and Giovanni Micco?

"Did he visit you?" I inquired.

"Yes, the day following his call. We met upstairs in my apartment and then here in our chambers."

There was an easy flow in our dialogue, a rhythm that suggested he welcomed my questions, allowing me to collect evidence. At the same time, Dr. VonBronstrup waited patiently to complete *his* mission, whatever it was, my inquiries perhaps merging with the reason behind his invitation to visit The Rosecross Chambers.

"I assume you talked about Professor Sabino's visit with you—and the Rosen case?" I asked curiously, thinking that Alexandria Arnold had already told Dr. VonBronstrup about our meeting at her Jefferson Street home.

"Of course," he answered quickly. "That's one reason I suggested Giovanni and I meet."

"What did you tell my father?"

"First, Francesco, it's best that you understand the background."

Dr. VonBronstrup gasped, covered his mouth with yellow-stained fingers and coughed three, maybe four times. After clearing the phlegm, he continued, his voice scratchy.

"Giovanni already knew that he would affirm the trial court's decision and order the government to surrender the second disc," he recounted, sighing, now more comfortable. "But he wanted an academic's view on a procedural question."

"Why did my father ask Professor Sabino for counsel?" I inquired suspiciously.

"It was Sabino's area of expertise," Dr. VonBronstrup explained. "As I recall, Sabino wrote a treatise on the subject, mentioning your father in the acknowledgment page."

"What was the procedural question?" I asked, somewhat bewildered by Sabino"s involvement in the Rosen case, given that Giovanni could have sought the able guidance of his three law clerks, including Nino.

"Whether he or the trial court judge should listen to the second disc and determine if the national security interest outweighed the prejudice to Rosen," Dr. VonBronstrup answered—focusing in on the issue before his friend, Judge Micco.

"What did Sabino recommend?" I asked.

"He suggested that your father should review the information stored on the disc."

"Why?"

"Because if the trial judge reviewed the contents of the disc *en camera* and then granted the defense motion, an appeal to the circuit court would be inevitable. Valuable time would be lost."

"Did my father take Sabino's advice?"

"He did. To save time, Giovanni ordered the government to give *him* the second disc," he said scowling— then pausing, perhaps questioning the wisdom of my father's decision. "*Giovanni* would then decide whether the government's interest outweighed the prejudice to Rosen. But the issue became moot when Rosen was murdered."

Another twist of fate. The misfortunes visited upon the Micco family would have never happened if my father would have followed precedent—affirming the trial court's decision and referring the case back to the district court judge. Instead, he followed the recommendation of Professor Giuseppe Sabino who has mysteriously disappeared.

"So, Sabino was acutely aware of the Rosen case?" I concluded.

"Every minute detail," Dr. VonBronstrup answered, shrugging.

Although I was collecting facts, the puzzle's scattered pieces told me little, like the backside of an embroidered fabric, the dangling cross-stitches making little sense. Nevertheless, I plodded along, the beleaguered attorney trying desperately to extract evidence from his cooperating witness.

"Why was Sabino upset when he met with you?" I asked, confused by the Professor's bizarre behavior.

"I don't know," Dr. VonBronstrup answered as another round of coughs interrupted his response. After a sip of water, he continued. "But his demeanor told me that it had something to do with what Sabino overheard Richard Stone say at the NEF seminar."

"Did Sabino tell you what Stone said?"

"He did."

Another pause. More phlegm coughed up, another sip of water.

"Stone said, 'Someone has a copy of the disc,'" Dr. VonBronstrup recalled, the mucus cleared, his words drawled.

"Was Stone referring to the disc the Government refused to surrender?"

"He was, according to Professor Sabino."

"Did Sabino overhear anything else?" I asked, prodding.

"Yes. Stone and his friend were discussing a burglary that would jump-start the Administration's new Middle East policy."

Nino and I exchanged glances. Stone was discussing the ruse orchestrated by the Office of Strategic Plans—the machination captured by Alexandria Arnold during her black bag job.

"Do you know who Stone was talking to?" I asked, continuing to prod.

"Alex thinks it was Luca Botti."

Professor Sabino's strange behavior was a bewildering puzzle. Perhaps survival caught him between a crossfire, his loyalty with the Judge compromised, the conversation he overheard while eavesdropping an albatross—like the ancient mariner, a curse hanging from his neck.

"Did you see Sabino again after he met with you?"

"No," he answered, widening his eyes, another shrug, his lips pursed. "I knocked on the Professor's door twice. There was no answer."

VonBronstrup hesitated, his smile curious.

"Just yesterday, something strange happened," he said haltingly.

"Strange?" I commented curiously.

"Yes. A van pulled up in front of his house, and movers carried his furniture into the truck."

"He's no longer your neighbor?"

"Sure looks that way."

It was time to raise a delicate subject—my chance to acquire the disc that Grazia's captors had demanded as her ransom. I proceeded cautiously, assuming that Alex had told him that my sister had been kidnapped.

"When you met with Judge Micco after my mother's funeral, did you tell him about the conversation Sabino overheard?" I asked, choosing my words carefully.

"I did."

I glanced at Nino. He nodded. It was time for the Rosicrucian expert to examine Dr. VonBronstrup.

"Did you tell Judge Micco that you had a copy of the disc the Government wouldn't give him in the Rosen case?" Nino inquired.

"No," he answered sternly, quickly shaking his head. "But I did tell Giovanni that The Rosecross possessed the disc. I was only a conduit," he said, shrugging.

"Did he ask you for the disc?"

"He did."

"Your response?"

"I told him that The Rosecross would allow the change of possession only if he complied with a strict condition."

"Which was?" Nino asked, his head cocked, his eyes squinted.

"That he become a member of The Rosecross."

"Wasn't that an unreasonable request, Dr. VonBronstrup, considering Rosicrucian doctrine and Judge Micco's Catholic faith?" Nino asked sternly.

"Yes, it was Nino," Dr. VonBronstrup answered indifferently. "I knew that Giovanni was a Fourth Degree

Knight of Columbus, that he attended daily Mass, that he was an Opus Dei member, and that he taught classes at the Catholic Information Center on K Street."

Their differences clashed. The Rosicrucians taught that the world must sleep away the intoxication of the Catholic Church's poisoned chalice. Church doctrine threatened Catholics with expulsion if they joined a Freemasonry lodge.

"I assume you had a plan reconciling your differences with Judge Micco?" Nino inquired, his pointed question bringing a frown to Dr. VonBronstrup's face.

"We began a process," Dr. VonBronstrup answered curtly. "As the Judge in the Rosen case, Giovanni had access to a disc that contained intelligence that would plunge us into a war."

"The first disc—the one the Government surrendered to him?"

"Yes."

"And you had a disc that showed the intelligence to be bogus?"

"I did. I planned to arrange for the merger of the two discs and expose the truth."

Listening to Nino's questions, I focused on his Rosicrucian research. Just like Brother C.R.C.'s mission in *The Chemical Wedding of Christian Rosencreutz*, Dr. VonBronstrup planned to reveal a truth 'hidden from the average man.'

"Why did you refuse to give the disc to Judge Micco unless he became a member of The Rosecross?" Nino asked politely, being careful not to again offend Dr. VonBronstrup.

"Because Rosicrucian dogma would *command* him to reveal the truth," he answered calmly.

"What was Judge Micco's decision?"

"He refused to join The Rosecross."

I glanced around the chambers, the setting reminiscent of a Mass about to be celebrated in a Roman Catholic church. I envisioned an acolyte, vested in a red cassock and surplice, lighting the candles. Perhaps there *was* a reconciliation.

"Did you resolve your differences?" Nino asked carefully through squinted eyes.

"We were on a path," Dr. VonBronstrup said, smiling broadly. "For six consecutive days, we met here in the Rosecross meeting room."

"Something akin to the seven-day wedding feast in *The Chemical Wedding of Christian Rosencreutz?*" Nino suggested.

"Exactly," he answered smiling broadly, obviously impressed with Nino's knowledge of Rosicrucian history. "In each of the six days, Giovanni and I took steps that led toward a reconciliation."

"A reconciliation?" Nino asked—perhaps the precursor to the secret brotherhood of Giovanni Micco and H. Victor VonBronstrup, just as Nino had predicted.

"Yes. We both had time constraints," Dr VonBronstrup explained slowly, carefully choosing his words. "The Rosecross wanted to stop a war, and Judge Micco wanted justice for his wife and Saul Rosen. But in the end, we had a meeting of the minds."

"Which was?" Nino asked curiously.

"I agreed to remove the impediments that would allow Judge Micco to become a Knight of the Rosecross."

"What impediments?" Nino inquired starkly.

Dr. VonBronstrup explained that he would strike Chapters 8, 9, and 13 of *Confessio Fraternitatis* from Rosicrucian dogma. For his part, my father assumed the responsibility of writing a novella exposing the conspiracy, throwing light on my mother's murder while giving Rosen his day in court.

"At the end of the meeting on the sixth day, we promised to seal our covenant in blood," Dr. VonBronstrup related. "The Rosecross would then transfer the disc to your father at a special ceremony on the seventh day."

Dr. VonBronstrup paused as his eyes met mine.

"Unfortunately, your father died before our final meeting," he said sadly.

A reality struck me hard. My father's passing before the seventh meeting was a barrier that ended any chance of a spiritual reconciliation between H. Victor VonBronstrup and Giovanni Micco.

"What do you want from me?" I asked suspiciously.

"Find your father's manuscript."

"Why?"

"Because the story Giovanni was telling could stop a war," he answered, ignoring my mother's murder and the killing of Saul Rosen.

"And if I find the manuscript?" I asked.

"Then The Rosecross will give you the second disc. You can then write the last chapters of your father's novella," he answered, with no mention of Grazia and the ransom demanded by her kidnappers. Unfortunately, it made little difference. Giovanni Micco's manuscript was fed to a fire in Taormina.

CHAPTER 57

A FRIEND

When Nino and I returned to the Four Seasons, the night clerk motioned toward a man slumped in a chair. He was sleeping. I walked closer and nudged him. It was Roosevelt Ward. He rubbed his eyes, leaned forward, and stood.

"Can we talk, Francesco? Somewhere private," he asked, groggy after an apparent long nap on a stiff leather couch.

"Of course."

I nodded for him to follow us. We passed through the lobby. As we entered the elevator, he said that the pathologist who had performed the autopsy on my father was preparing a report and that he would soon provide me with a copy. It was filler conversation. Ward had more he wanted to say. As he spoke, my curiosity ran wild—his long wait in the hotel lobby, a harbinger of news, obviously something urgent, a message that had to be delivered immediately. The elevator door swung open. We walked down the hallway. The lights were dimmed; an exit sign adjacent to our suite cast a red glare. We entered. I switched on the lights. Ward glanced at the surroundings.

"Fancy digs," he said, canvassing our suite, now more alert.

Nino invited Ward to sit on the couch. My apprehension grew; I sat on one of the occasional twin chairs. Nino stood. Ward's eyes turned to Nino and then settled on me.

"We have a lead in your sister's case," Ward began, hunching forward, hands clasped, his broad smile a hint that he had good news. "We may know where the kidnappers are holding Grazia."

I sat up, speechless, jolted by the FBI's involvement.

"The Bureau knew that my sister was kidnapped?" I asked, surprised.

"We did," Ward answered calmly.

"Do you know the ransom demand?"

"We suspect it to be your father's manuscript and the Rosen disc," he answered slyly, hedging his answer.

I pressed him.

"How did you learn about the kidnapping?"

"From related surveillance. Let's leave it at that."

Ward's stark response was a sign that he couldn't be prodded further.

"Can you at least tell me where the kidnappers are holding my sister?" I pressed.

Ward grinned, a question he welcomed.

"When I first learned Grazia was kidnapped, I called Pete Cann, our agent in New Castle, just to put him on notice of the abduction. I had a hunch."

I glanced at Nino, somewhat suspect of the FBI's sudden interest in Grazia's kidnapping while conveniently ignoring my mother's murder. While I mused, Ward continued.

"Early yesterday afternoon, I received a call from Pete. He said he had talked with a young Amish boy. His name is Jonathan Lee. The lad delivers fruits and vegetables to the Cann house every week."

I was familiar with the Lee name, like Byler, common in the Amish community. It was a strange coincidence. Before he was elected a state trial judge, my father argued a case before the United States Supreme Court involving an Amish man and his right to practice his religion. His name was Edwin Lee— Jonathan's grandfather, perhaps? I realized it was a stretch. In the Amish community, a similar surname among unrelated members is not uncommon.

"Did Cann know Jonathan well?" I asked, curious about the family connections.

"He did. The lad was amused at the stories Pete fed the boy, mostly embellished yarns of FBI cases. Pete and his family often visited the Lee home."

Was it the same family? I wondered—a strange twist of fate that reintroduced me to the Lee family. Because the Amish don't drive automobiles, my father conferred with Ed Lee at his home. Religiously, at least once a week for about three months, Giovanni packed us all in the car and off we went to Amish country, Rosalina, in the front seat, Grazia, Giancarlo, and me cramped in the back.

"What did Jonathan tell Pete?" I asked.

"He said his father—his name is also Jonathan—had rented a small hut on their farm to two men about three weeks ago. It's nestled at the rear of their land and is hidden by a cluster of trees."

It *was* the same Lee family. I remember it well. When Ed Lee's meeting with my father ended, Lee's wife Katie brewed coffee while a tantalizing aroma escaped from an outdoor wood-fired oven. Inside were cinnamon rolls, hot, sticky, and succulent. While the men talked, and the women baked, along with the five Lee children, we often strayed toward the hut until we were yanked back by Ed Lee's loud bark.

"Get back here, kids!" he always bellowed.

Ward continued.

"Yesterday, while he was removing some brush near the shanty, the lad told Pete that one of the men came out and abruptly shooed him away."

"What did Pete do?" I asked.

"He became suspicious," Ward answered. "Although it was a long shot, he followed his gut feeling. Along with another agent, they staked out the area all night. He maneuvered from behind one tree to another until he got close to the hut."

"How close?" Nino asked.

"Close enough to look through a window," Ward responded, eyes wide, impressed with Cann's findings and eager to report them. "Unfortunately, whoever was inside had drawn the curtains. But they were sheers. Pete was able to make out the figures of two people—probably men."

"Did he see anyone else?"

"There was a third person whose hands appeared to be tied behind a chair."

"Was it my sister?"

"We suspect it's her."

"What's next?"

"As we speak, a SWAT team is flying to New Castle. We'll meet there to formulate a plan."

"What about the Lee family? Will they cooperate with us?"

"The boy's father has given us complete access to his farm," Ward related nodding. "He says the Amish community owes a debt of gratitude to the Micco family. Something about your father representing his father before the Supreme Court years ago."

Roosevelt Ward's hunch and Pete Cann's fortuitous meeting with Jonathan Lee had ferried me back to our visits to Amish country—memories I will forever cherish. After enjoying Kate's cinnamon treats, our families often sat at a round picnic table that Ed Lee had built. I can still see the shimmering light of a kerosene lamp sitting in the center reflecting off my mother's face, its shine igniting a glitter in her eyes, watching as we licked our fingers after enjoying one of Katie's sticky buns. Rosalina was content to be near the people she loved most, willing for time to stand still, wanting these moments to endure forever. I again admonished Giovanni Micco for straying so far from home.

CHAPTER 58

THE SHANTY

I left the Four Seasons with Ward. Nino decided to remain in Washington and delve deeper into his Rosicrucian research. Our destination was the Ronald Reagan Washington National Airport. A Learjet was waiting there to fly us to the Municipal Airport in New Castle. The flight would be short. Once airborne, sandwiched between telephone conversations with the agents already there, Roosevelt explained the rescue operation's details.

"First, Francesco, we must agree on a strategy that has the best chance to rescue your sister safely," he said, seemingly confident that the third person in the shanty was Grazia. "Remember, we're dealing with professionals. These guys know what they're doing."

"What's your plan?" I asked.

"We've already reduced our options to two," he began. "We either storm the shanty or we attempt to negotiate Grazia's release."

"Who makes the final decision?"

"I do. But each agent will be given a chance to voice their opinion. Our lives are on the line here. We rely on each other. That's the only way."

Roosevelt's cell phone rang again. He had to iron out another wrinkle in the operation before we touched down at the New Castle airport. As our plane glided through a scattering of thin cirrus clouds, I looked through a small porthole and wondered why my sister's abductors kidnapped her in Washington and then held her hostage in New Castle? When his call ended, I posed the question to Roosevelt.

"The answer is simple, Francesco. Do you remember the place of your mother's murder?"

How could I forget it? *La cucina.* The kitchen of our home.

"Yes, I remember. What's the connection?"

"Her kidnappers arranged it for effect," he explained, hesitating, apparently searching for the right words. "Assuming you find the manuscript and satisfy their ransom demand, they'll kill your sister anyway. You'll then find her body close to home. It sours your taste for retaliation because someone else in your family could be exposed to retribution—your wife, your son."

"What are you saying, Roosevelt?"

"I'm saying this," he said bluntly. "Even if you give her abductors the manuscript and disc, they will kill Grazia anyway. Unless we get her back today, you'll never see her alive again. That's the brutal truth."

The imagery gripped me, like a vice tightening its hold. I recalled our trips to Amish country where Grazia played with the Lee children, frolicking in the fields with friends outside the shack that now jails her. I picture the hut we were not allowed near while we played on the farm, Ed Lee's command shooing us away still bellowing. I smell the aroma of Katie's sticky cinnamon rolls, now haunting Grazia as she stares through the hut's grimy windows.

"Then why didn't they kill her and be done with it?" I asked, frustrated, a thoughtless question.

"Think about it," he answered grimly. "If you do satisfy their ransom demand, surely you'll want to talk with her before you surrender the manuscript and disc. That's common sense."

The red light above the cockpit door flashed. We began our descent into the New Castle Municipal Airport. Roosevelt fastened his seatbelt; I kept mine latched throughout the smooth ride. After a one-hour flight, the Learjet touched down. The pilot used all but a few feet of the short runway before bringing the jet to a stop. We taxied back to the small airport terminal. Pete Cann met us there. He was driving a nondescript Chevy Impala.

During the short flight from Washington to New Castle, Roosevelt had explained that the agents would conduct the rescue operation from two bases—the FBI field office and Jonathan Lee's farmhouse. His family had graciously vacated the house and was staying with neighbors for a few days. Lee insisted, however, that he be allowed to remain in the home during the rescue operation.

"You'll be coming with me to the farmhouse, Francesco," Ward said. "But we're stopping at the field office first."

Most of the FBI agents, as well as the SWAT team, had slipped into the farmhouse under cover of night. It was a clear, dry day when we touched down at the municipal airport, and the same camouflage wouldn't protect us. Pete parked the car, and, together, we entered the small FBI field office.

"Do you have the clothes, Pete?" Roosevelt asked.

"Yeah, come with me."

I followed Roosevelt to the rear of the suite into Pete's office.

"We have to change clothes, Francesco," Ward explained. "The trick is to blend into the Amish landscape. We'll be traveling in broad daylight. We mustn't make our friends suspicious."

Scattered on Pete's desk was a pile of wrinkled Amish garb—dark blue broadfall trousers and matching solid colored shirts, one shade lighter. There were no belts. Black suspenders held up our pants. The work shoes with thick socks were also black. After we changed clothes, Pete reached into a closet and tossed me a broad-brimmed straw hat. It fell over my ears. Pete laughed, but Roosevelt found no humor. Finally, Pete removed three fake beards from his closet. After applying spirit gum, we applied the facial hair. Ward left nothing to chance.

"Ready to go," Roosevelt barked. "We're burning daylight."

Outside, our chariot awaited—a two-team horse and a buggy with a brown canvas canopy that would carry us to the Lee farmhouse. Pete handled the reins. Contrasted by the smooth LearJet trip from Washington to New Castle, it was a bumpy two-mile ride in the horse and buggy. When we reached our destination, Pete tied the horses to the hitching post and we casually walked toward the two-story Amish farmhouse. The wood frame was painted stark white and the front door was powder blue, signaling that an eligible young lady of the house was waiting for her suitor. Stretched sheer curtains cut the windows into matching triangles.

Once inside, the farm's owner, Jonathan Lee, introduced himself—one of the Lee children I played with while our fathers conferred many years ago. Reminiscing, the scene warmed me—the lawyer preparing his argument, the Amish man listening, the wives conversing, the children playing. At first, we didn't recognize each other, but a firm handshake and a gentle hug rekindled our relationship. His Bishop, Jakob Hostitler, stood beside him. Apologetically, Lee explained that it was necessary to secure the Bishop's permission before allowing the FBI to transform his farmhouse into a mission-control center—now adorned with an array of technical gadgets that were religiously censured by the unpretentious Amish community.

"Thank you for your cooperation, Jonathan," I said gratefully. "My family appreciates your help."

Before responding, he took a long draw on his pipe. Jonathan Lee spoke in the traditional Amish monotone.

"Say nothing more, Francesco," he drawled. "Years ago, your father helped our Amish family. Now it's our turn to help your English family."

Jakob Hostitler, also puffing on a pipe, nodded in agreement as billows of smoke slowly swirled into the air. Pete and Roosevelt were huddled together at the kitchen table. The SWAT team was stashed away in the basement. An agent was standing behind a high-powered telescope positioned in front of a window. He aimed it at the shanty—about four hundred feet away—that hopefully housed Grazia and her two captors. Another agent, with the letters "FBI" spread on the back of her blue field jacket in large yellow characters, sat at a table wearing a headset. She was talking to someone on a two-way radio.

"She seems rather intense, Pete," I noted.

Pete approached a window above the kitchen sink.

"Come over here. Do you see that truck?" he asked, pointing.

He handed me binoculars and told me to focus on a van parked on the highway's berm about a hundred feet from the shanty. The words "Penn Power" conspicuously appeared on the side panel of the truck. Another truck, with a cherry picker basket, was parked nearby. The bucket was fully extended, and a workman was ostensibly repairing an overhead electrical wire.

"She's talking to our two agents who are in the truck," Pete explained.

"About what?"

"We're trying to learn who is communicating with our two friends inside."

"How do you do that?" I asked, eyes wide, impressed by the technology.

"Inside the truck is a device called a cell-site simulator," Pete explained. "We use it to page any cell phones that may be in the hut without ringing them. It's a neat trick if the phones are turned on and not in use. Any phones that are in the shanty will act as transmitters."

"Quite a setup," I remarked.

"Sure is. But it's only part of the operation," Pete said, bragging. "Our tech team also equipped the van with a device called a Triggerfish."

"A Triggerfish?"

"Yeah. It works by analyzing cell phone data, including any numbers that our friends may dial."

Pete gazed out the window.

"If you look closely," he said, pointing again, "you'll see an antenna attached to the roof of the van."

The gadgetry showed me the folly of my decision to rescue Grazia without the FBI's help. A question crossed my mind. Why did Claudio Armondi advise against involving the FBI? It was counsel I should have ignored.

"Have they dialed any numbers yet?" I asked.

"Not since we've been here."

"Can the Triggerfish do anything else?"

"Sure. We can use information from cell phone towers to locate an incoming call."

"This is all legal?" I asked, the lawyer in me concerned about his constitutional right to privacy.

"The government can't do anything, Francesco, unless we get a court order."

"I assume you've done that?"

"Of course," Pete said. "Yesterday a federal judge in Pittsburgh authorized a 'pen register' and a 'trap-and-trace.'"

"What's the difference?"

"A pen register identifies a number dialed, and a trap and trace can identify an originating number."

"So, if someone calls in through the phone company, you can learn their identity. And, if our friends dial a number, you can trace the call," I remarked, impressed by the technology at the FBI's disposal.

"That's right, Francesco," Pete said, wallowing in the FBI's field operation. "Then we'll have a good chance of zeroing in on the circle of conspirators who kidnapped your sister."

Roosevelt, who had been in the basement talking to the SWAT team, was now sitting alone at the kitchen table. He motioned for Pete to join him. While they spoke privately, I stared out the window. My sight zeroed in on the shanty we tried to explore as frolicking children, always hampered by Ed Lee's strong command to stay away, never giving us a chance to take a sneak-peek inside. I heard the screech of wood-on-wood. I turned. Ward was pulling his chair back. He walked toward the window and stood next to me, his eyes, like mine, focused on the shanty.

"I've made the decision," Ward said soberly. "I'm going with the consensus. We'll use the SWAT team."

I was troubled by the possibility of Grazia being caught in the crossfire.

"Why can't you negotiate with them?"

"It's too risky."

"Why?"

"If we give them too much time, they'll destroy their cell phones," Ward explained. "Then we'll lose any opportunity to use the trap-and-trace device. But, more importantly, they may harm your sister."

The plan chosen by Roosevelt seemed to be the best option. I had no say in the decision process anyway. Grazia's captives were probably armed and ready to do battle, and Roosevelt had determined that there was merit in the element of surprise.

"Do you plan to wait for nightfall, or are you going in now?" I asked.

"There are mixed blessings, either way, Francesco," Ward said, pausing for a moment. "We've weighed the pros and cons and decided there are too many impediments if we wait for the cover of night."

Roosevelt explained the details of the plan. The area to the back of the shanty was densely wooded. Four agents would work their way as close as possible to a place in the back of the hut. They should be able to get within fifteen feet. Meanwhile, two other agents, dressed as Amish men, would act as if they were plowing the field. One would be pushing a hand plow, and the other would be lagging not too far behind.

"The trick is for them to get as close to the shanty as possible—without causing suspicion," Roosevelt said, as he stared out the window, visualizing his plan unfolding. "Then, the trailing agent will casually walk toward the hut, and, when he's close enough, he'll toss a stun grenade into the hut."

"What's a stun grenade?" I asked.

"It's referred to as a flash-bang device. It will daze the kidnappers with an explosion that produces a blinding flash of light, along with a loud blast."

"Is there any chance it will harm my sister?"

"Just a small one," Roosevelt said, easing my concern. "The device is nonlethal. It's designed to overwhelm the senses for five to six seconds."

"When do the games begin?"

"I'm giving the signal now."

At that precise moment, Pete, who had been continually monitoring a laptop computer, called out to Roosevelt.

"Hold up, Roosevelt. Come over here."

I followed him.

"Read this!" Pete shouted. "It's an e-mail message from the Bureau in Washington."

Roosevelt and I stared at the monitor screen. The message was styled in large, bold letters:

ABORT THE MISSION.
IMMEDIATELY DEACTIVATE
THE TRAP AND TRACE AND
PEN REGISTER DEVICES.

Someone from the higher echelons of government had decided to abort the operation. Roosevelt and Pete stared at each other. Stunned, I looked out the window toward the shanty.

"What's wrong, Francesco?" Jonathan Lee asked.

"The government is pulling up stakes," I answered.

Jonathan Lee looked toward Jakob Hostitler who took a long drag on his pipe and then slowly blew a plume of smoke into the air, watching it swirl toward the ceiling as he nodded his head.

"Come here, Francesco," Jonathan said, motioning.

Shrouded from view, Jonathan pointed to a myriad of sites on his farm. There were Amish men hidden in every imaginable spot. Some crouched low and scattered behind trees, others lay prone, flat on their stomachs in the open field, and others squatted behind a wooden silo, all armed with pitchforks. They lay in wait, apparently ready to charge the shanty and rescue my sister.

"Another hundred men are waiting in the woods, Mr. Micco," Jonathan advised. "Just give me the word. We're ready to go."

With raised pitchforks, the Blue Army was about to launch a ground attack. I was suddenly in control of the rescue operation. Jonathan Lee had provided me with an option, but it was much less sophisticated than the government's plan. Time was moving fast, and Grazia's chance of survival was fading away. I recalled Roosevelt's words, spoken to me earlier: "*Unless we get her back today, you'll never see her alive again. That's the brutal truth.*" It was a calculated risk, but I had no other option.

"Go ahead, Jonathan," I said without any thought.

"Wait!" Ward shouted. "Who gave the order? The Attorney General or the U.S. Attorney in Washington?"

Pete studied the message.

"It came from the U.S. Attorney—not Luther Ash."

Ward headed to the basement where the SWAT team was waiting.

"Let's get this thing moving," Ward commanded.

Along with Pete, I positioned myself at the kitchen window. I saw the two SWAT team members slowly make their way toward the hut. One was pushing the hand plow, ostensibly turning the soil, and the other, lagging a short distance behind, carried a small pouch. When they finally got within striking distance of the hut, they stopped, and each agent pulled a pipe from his pants pocket. It was time for a smoke break.

The larger, burly agent who was pushing the plow took a match from his pocket and lit the trailing agent's pipe. Puffing on the pipe, the smaller, more agile agent casually walked toward the shack, sat and propped his back against a tree trunk. He was about thirty feet from the hut. Then suddenly, in one seamless motion, he rose, and with the accuracy of a southpaw pitcher, slung the stun grenade with his left hand through a window and into the hut. Immediately, I saw a bright, blinding flash, and then there was a loud explosion.

Attacking from the rear, a cadre of FBI agents surrounded the shack. Through binoculars, I saw an agent force his way through the front door as he stormed into the shanty, followed by three other agents. Simultaneously, the army of Amish men, pitchforks in hand, scattered behind the trees, in the fields, in the woods, and behind the silo, formed a human circle around the hut. The rescue effort was now fully operational. And then, in an instant, it was over. Order replaced the commotion caused by the flash-bang grenade. Pete looked at me.

"Let's go," he shouted.

We raced toward the hut. Finding it difficult to gain traction, I stumbled on the turned soil as I struggled across the field. Only resolve kept me on my feet; hope pulled me toward Grazia. By the time I reached the hut, sweat was pouring down my face. Roosevelt was already there.

"Wait here for a second, Francesco," he suggested. "Rest a bit. Your sister seems fine. Just some minor smoke inhalation. Our medic is treating Grazia now."

"What about our two friends?" I asked.

"Fortunately, the grenade landed closer to them," he answered, relieved. "Your sister's captors suffered some superficial flash burns. Nothing more."

Roosevelt peeked into the hut and then approached me.

"Do you want to see your sister now?"

"Yes, of course."

Together we walked into the damp, dreary shanty. Grazia was lying on a stretcher. She was drowsy, almost sleeping. I was stifled for a moment by the shock of her disheveled appearance.

"After a couple of days in the hospital, she'll be fine," Roosevelt said.

I bent down, gently touched her shoulder, and kissed her cheek. She opened her eyes and managed a faint smile.

"Welcome home, Grazia," I whispered. "Didn't Mr. Lee tell you to stay away from the shanty?"

CHAPTER 59

A FRIEND'S GOOD-BYE

I remained in New Castle until the end of August, tending to my ailing law practice and following Grazia's progress. On a Sunday morning, Nino telephoned me after Gianna, Michele, and I returned from Mass at St. Vitus.

"Dr. VonBronstrup's in the hospital. Hudson just called me," he said, alarmed.

"What's the problem?"

"I don't know. Hudson was distressed."

"Should I come?"

"It's your call."

Grazia was now safe. Family love tempted me to remain home, practice law, be a husband to Gianna and a father to Michele. But I couldn't ignore my role in the plot my father had bequeathed to me. The stakes were too high. Returning to Washington was a calculated risk, one that I explained in minute detail to Gianna, relieved to some extent by Uncle Claudio's Italian Army, his soldiers now permanently stationed across the street from our Sumner Avenue home. At least he had the foresight to protect my family, I mused. Thankfully, Gianna supported my decision, or, more accurately, *our* decision, her input being crucial. Like me, she had no option. In the early afternoon, I packed my bags and headed back to Washington.

———————

Early Sunday evening, I met Nino in the lobby of the George Washington University Hospital. We took the elevator to the third floor and winded our way through a labyrinth of hospital corridors before we reached Dr. VonBronstrup's unit. Hudson D'Priest was pacing in the hallway outside his room.

"What happened, Mr. D'Priest?" I asked warmly.

"As you may have guessed, Vic was diagnosed with lung cancer about three years ago," D'Priest said, his voice quivering. "For the last couple of days, he's been struggling. I brought him to the ER this morning, and the doctor admitted him."

"Have you spoken to his doctor?" I asked.

"Yeah. It's just a matter of time—days, maybe just hours."

"Is he conscious?"

"He may know you're here. But he can't talk."

"Where's Alex?"

"Just talked to her. She was in Chicago. Her plane arrives in about four hours."

Nino walked into Dr. VonBronstrup's room. I put my arm around Hudson D'Priest's shoulder and we followed Nino. The eyes of my father's law school friend were closed. Overhead, the zigzagging lines of a cardiac monitor displayed the electrical impulses of Dr. VonBronstrup's heart. A bag hanging from an intravenous pole slowly dripped fluids into his limp body while a mask covering his face fed him oxygen. Hanging on the side of his bed was a bag collecting the yellow urine being drained from his failing kidneys by a Foley catheter. As we entered the room, a nurse was just leaving, syringe in hand. She explained the shot would help him endure the pain. He was being drugged into an abyss and then into infinity. An eerie reality consumed me. Death would once again pay a visit to H. Victor VonBronstrup.

Hudson moved closer to the bed and gently touched Dr. VonBronstrup's hand. These two men had been friends for a lifetime, and soon Hudson D'Priest would be alone. Slowly, pronouncing every syllable of every word, Hudson tried to arouse Dr. VonBronstrup.

"Your friends are here, Vic," he whispered in his ear.

Dr. VonBronstrup's eyes remained closed. There was no response. The only sound was the steady, staccato beat of the heart monitor. Clasping his friend's hand, Hudson moved closer, bent down, and then spoke into his ear.

"Vic, your friends are here," he repeated louder.

Again, there was no response. Huddling together, we waited, praying we'd have a chance to speak with Dr. VonBronstrup.

Back and forth, the pendulum swung.

Back and forth.

With each tick, a speck of time disintegrated into eternity. One moment was consumed by the next. No words were exchanged. It was a silent vigil. Suddenly, the short, staccato sound of the heart monitor merged into a continuous hum. The serpentine electrical wave had collapsed into a single impulse, and now it traveled in a straight line along the monitor screen until it disappeared like the lights of a train's caboose fading into the night. Slowly, Dr. VonBronstrup's eyes opened. He stared eerily into the endless depth of space. The nurse, chasing death, rushed into the room. She reached for his wrist and tried to find a pulse. There was none. Sadly, she looked at Hudson.

"He has passed on, Mr. D'Priest," she said softly, grasping his hand.

I hugged Hudson. Sobbing, he placed both arms around me. For a moment, he wouldn't let go. Finally, he broke away. Along with Nino, Hudson and I joined hands and bowed our heads as we looked at our friend. Silently, I said a short prayer. Johann Valentin Andreae had died once again.

CHAPTER 60

THE MEMORIAL MESSAGE

A white embroidered-linen cloth covered the altar. A ciborium with a dome-shaped canopy conspicuously rested in the middle. Two votive candles, both lit, were placed on each side of the ciborium. Rising above the ciborium's canopy was a sculptured cross with a red rose etched at the bars intersection. The ciborium held the cremated remains of H. Victor VonBronstrup.

Hudson D'Priest escorted Nino and me into the meeting chambers and then excused himself. He was waiting for the last guest to arrive before beginning the memorial service. I suspected it was Alexandria Arnold. In less than a minute, he returned. Alex was with him. At Hudson's request, we all sat and faced the altar. He was strikingly composed. Hudson had combed his gray hair straight back. He was wearing a tweed sports jacket and pressed khaki trousers. A black tie fit snugly around his neck. Standing in front of the altar, Hudson D'Priest began the service.

"Allow me to welcome you to the Chambers of The Rosecross," he said solemnly.

Reaching into his inside coat pocket, he removed a few folded sheets of paper fastened together with a paperclip. Hudson fingered his reading glasses, cleared his throat, unfastened the clip, and flattened the papers while placing them on the podium.

"Today, we meet to honor the memory of our friend, H. Victor VonBronstrup," he began.

Relying on his scribbles, Hudson rambled on incessantly about the accomplishments of Dr. VonBronstrup, centering mostly on his scholarly achievements. There was not too much more he could say. The eccentric habits that held sway over H. Victor VonBronstrup's lifestyle stymied any chance that Hudson D'Priest may have had to assemble a chronicle of collegial accolades. In the end, the journalist had spliced together a eulogy that captured the life of his departed friend. Before adjourning the service, he paused for a moment and stared at the ciborium.

"There is, my friends, a second purpose for this gathering," he announced calmly but surprisingly.

Hudson D'Priest captured my attention.

"Before he died, Victor prepared a statement and requested that I read it after his demise," Hudson said as he shuffled through the papers spread on the podium. After finding what he was looking for, Hudson focused his eyes only on me as he unfolded the note penned by Dr. VonBronstrup.

"Allow me to read the message," he said, sliding his eyeglasses to the tip of his nose. Peering through bifocals,

Hudson read the post-mortem message of H. Victor VonBronstrup:

> *Friends,*
>
> *Only you can solve the murder mystery.*
> *But I can guide you. Focus on the bonds of*
> *friendship, two severed, the other intact. Then*
> *find the first betrayer. Justice will surface.*
> *Follow its path.*

When he finished, Hudson folded the paper and handed it to Nino.

"If you need me, I'll be in my apartment," he said before leaving.

———————

I stared at Alex, trying to suppress a feeling, compelled to admonish a daughter for her father's sins.

"Why did Dr. VonBronstrup leave us a riddle?" I asked sarcastically. "If he had information about my mother's murder, he could have given it to me."

"It wasn't possible," she answered politely, ignoring my taunt.

"Why?" I asked,

"Because Rosicrucian dogma prohibits accusations without supporting testimony."

"That's right," Nino interjected. "Chapter 17 of *Confessio Fraternitatis* states that 'Thou shall not prosecute thy neighbor without either the testimony of two witnesses or two supporting documents.'"

Alex's wide smile acknowledged Nino's recitation of Rosicrucian dogma as well as his knack to quote chapter and verse—the fruits of his photographic memory. Nino smiled back, the gifted student wallowing in the applause. I interrupted his awards ceremony.

"Can *you* decipher the message?" I asked Nino cynically.

He frowned and with an inviting glance suggested we should decode the message together. Alex and I moved our chairs close to Nino. We sat in a circle.

"Your father's three closest friends were Claudio Armondi, Salvatore Sacco, and Leonardo Mendici," Nino began. "Now, let's read Dr. VonBronstrup's message," he continued, reading the note. "'Focus on the bonds of friendship, two severed, the other intact.'"

"So, what's the point of the message?" Alex asked.

"Of the three," I said, responding to Alex, "Claudio supposedly was his best friend. That relationship apparently remained intact."

"And the Judge severed his friendships with Mendici and Sacco?" Alex suggested.

"That's the implication," Nino responded.

Nino handed me the paper on which Dr. VonBronstrup had scribbled his message. I read it.

"Next, he says, 'Find the first betrayer. Justice will surface.' What does he mean by that?" I asked, baffled.

"He may be telling us that Justice Sacco is the first betrayer," Nino surmised.

"First or second betrayer—what's the difference?" Alex asked.

"Who knows?" Nino responded. "Maybe he's establishing a sequence of events."

I glanced at Dr. VonBronstrup's message again.

"Finally, he says, 'But follow its path.' Any ideas?"

Nino thought for a second while Alex shrugged.

"None whatsoever," Nino answered.

As we left the The Rosecross Chambers, Hudson D'Priest was standing in the vestibule. He handed each of us a sealed envelope. I opened mine. It was an invitation:

THE SEVENTH DAY
You are invited to attend
The celebration of the Holy Sacrifice of
THE MASS
In the meeting chambers of
THE ROSECROSS
2113 K Street NW
Washington D.C
Tomorrow at Twelve Noon

CHAPTER 61

THE SEVENTH DAY

Nino, Alex, and I arrived fifteen minutes early. Hudson D'Priest met us at the stoop of 2113 K street. He led us down the steps, through his apartment, and into The Rosecross Chambers. A man, probably in his mid-thirties, sat in a chair on the altar—the royal seat once occupied by H. Victor VonBronstrup. He was wearing a white Alb and red chasuble, embroidered with a gold crucifix. But Christ's arms were not nailed to the cross. Instead, His hands were holding a red rose. Nino nudged me.

"That's Father Gil," he whispered.

"Father Gil?"

"Your father attended daily Mass at the Catholic Information Center," Nino explained, his eyes fixed on the priest. "I went with him at least once a week. Father Gil celebrates Mass there. He was a good friend of your father."

"His spiritual advisor?"

"You could say that."

Odd, I thought. When we first met in The Rosecross Chambers with Dr. VonBronstrup, Hudson had prepared the altar for a celebration of the Mass—but there was no priest. As it was then, everything was now in place. The votive candles were lit. Two cruets were filled with water and wine. A chalice was placed in front of a seven-sided tabernacle, with a linen purificator on top. A small red cross was etched into its center. Just as he had done before our first meeting in The Rosecross Chambers, Hudson placed a large host on a paten and laid it on top of the purificator. Next, he set a pall on the paten and then draped the chalice with a red veil and a burse—a folding case covered in red cloth used to store a second purificator. For a moment, we sat in silence as I recalled the words spoken by Dr. VonBronstrup during our last meeting: "*Your father and I promised to seal our covenant in blood and exchange the discs at a special ceremony here in our meeting room.*"

It was now noon.

Mass began.

The Seventh Day Celebration?

Father Gil rushed through the Introductory Rite. He reached the Liturgy of the Word. There was no sermon. Next came the Liturgy of the Eucharist. Father Gil raised the host and said, "This is the Body of Christ." He then reached for a cruet and poured wine into his chalice. He then added a splash of water from another cruet. Nino and I exchanged glances. Father Gil then blessed his chalice and offered another prayer.

"Blessed are you, Lord, God of all creation. Through your goodness, we have this wine to offer, fruit of the vine and work of human hands. It will become our spiritual drink."

After genuflecting, he raised the chalice above his head and again offered a prayer.

"In like manner, when supper was done, taking the cup into His hands, Christ said, 'This is the chalice of my blood, the blood of the new and eternal covenant. It shall be shed for you and for many for the forgiveness of sins.'"

The Transubstantiation—the water and wine, seconds before just symbols, had become the blood of Christ. I raised my eyes to the alchemic equation painted on the wall above the cross:

$$X + \Delta = O$$

Silver, plus copper, equals gold. My thoughts drifted to the *Confessio Fraternitatis*, the gospel of the Rosicrucians. Chapter Eight: '*The world must sleep away the intoxication of the poisoned chalice.*' The Mass continued.

At the communion, Father Gil stood in front of the altar, chalice in hand. Nino and I approached, accepted the host in hand, placed it on our tongue, drank from the cup, and returned to our seats. Hudson D'Priest followed and likewise accepted the host and drank from the cup.

Finally, the Concluding Rite. Before the blessing, Father Gil placed the used purificator on the chalice. He then laid a paten on the purificator, set a pall on the paten, and draped the chalice with the red veil and burse—the folding case covered in red cloth used to store a second purificator. Facing his congregation, he asked Hudson D'Priest to approach the altar. Father Gil spoke.

"Perfect Prelate, the Chapter being open, what remains to be done?" Father Gil asked formally.

"The candidate for Perfection, Brother Francesco, is willing to take an obligation in the name of the Holy and Undivided Trinity," Hudson D'Priest announced in reply.

"Let the candidate approach," Father Gil said as he turned and sat in the high back chair upholstered in red velvet.

Hudson motioned me to step forward. I glanced first at Alex and then Nino. The symbolism astounded me. I'd just attended a Catholic Mass in a Freemason meeting room, and I was about to become a candidate for membership in The Rosecross. And the Sovereign was a conservative Roman Catholic Priest.

"It's ludicrous, Nino," I whispered, my eyes fixed in Father Gil. "I have none of the degrees that would qualify me to become a Knight of the Rosecross."

"You're correct, my friend," Nino responded softly, his eyes likewise focused on Father Gil. "You need fourteen degrees. But Victor VonBronstrup and Giovanni Micco apparently reached a compromise—and you're part of it," he surmised.

Sitting in the red leather chair, Father Gil waited patiently. Hudson D'Priest stood beside him, staring me down.

"What should I do?" I asked, still whispering.

"It might be our chance to get the discs," he said quietly, nudging me to approach the altar. I rose cautiously, walked forward, and stood before Father Gil.

"Brother Francesco, are you willing to preserve the secrets and mysteries of The Rosecross?" he asked after standing to face me.

"I am," I responded carefully as Hudson handed him a sword.

"Then you will kneel on both knees," he instructed, "place your right hand upon the Holy Bible, and, with your left hand, hold this sword upright by the blade with the crossbar level with your eyes."

I complied. Father Gil continued.

"In the presence of God, Creator of the Universe, do you most solemnly promise upon this sacred book that you will expose the truth in all matters that might come before you and that you will not reveal any of the secrets or mysteries of the Ancient and Accepted Rite of The Rosecross?"

"I do."

"Worthy candidate, I rejoice to confer upon you the reward you have earned, and I trust that by the practices of Faith, Hope, and Charity, you will be led to Him and the truth."

Father Gil placed his right hand on my shoulder.

"By the power vested in me, I now seal you as a Knight of the Rose Croix. Rise, Knight of the Rose Croix, and receive the emblem of our Order."

Hudson handed me a wooden cross with a rose etched into the intersecting bars.

"The cross," Hudson said, "is a symbol of the suffering Christ, our Redeemer."

Tears welled Hudson's eyes.

"And the rose is a symbol of truth," he said.

Father Gill blessed his flock of four, stepped down from the altar, walked toward me, reached into the sleeve of his Alb, pulled out an envelope, and handed it to me. After pausing for a moment, he opened the red door and entered the vestibule. After the door closed, Hudson D'Priest reached into his inside coat pocket, pulled out another sealed envelope, and gave it to me. He, too, approached the red door, opened it, hesitated, and turned toward me before joining Father Gil in the vestibule.

I broke the seal of the envelope Hudson D'Priest had handed to me, pulled out a sheet of paper folded in half, and stared at a numbered square with nine blocks and five numbers appearing below it:

3	2	2
1	4	2
3	1	3

2-3-9-1-5

Next, I opened the envelope handed to me by Father Gil. Once again, I removed a sheet of paper folded in half.

It was the same square, but there were no numbers below the square.

"It's all imagery, Francesco," Nino explained, the comforting words of a Rosicrucian scholar.

Imagery? I thought. A Catholic Mass celebrated in the chamber of the Freemasons?

"Think about it, my friend," he continued. "Your father realized he was not negotiating with his old law school buddy, Victor VonBronstrup. He had to broker a deal with Johann Valentin Andreae."

"That's why they didn't simply exchange the discs each other wanted?" I commented curiously.

"From Dr. VonBronstrup's perspective—yes. As the reincarnated Johann Valentin Andreae, H. Victor VonBronstrup needed assurance from your father."

"A guarantee?" I suggested.

"Much more than that," Nino said firmly. "Dr. VonBronstrup demanded a sacred promise that your father would not only seek retribution for your mother's murder and give Rosen justice—but, more importantly, he would expose the conspiracy brewing at the Pentagon."

"So, they agreed to seal their covenant in blood. That was the mutual assurance binding them to their compromise?" I surmised.

Nino nodded as my thoughts centered once again on Chapter Eight of *Confessio Fraternitatis*, '*The world must sleep away the intoxication of the Catholic Church's poisoned chalice.*'

"Why did Dr. VonBronstrup agree to drink from the poisoned cup?" I asked curiously.

"Think, Francesco," Nino chided. "The cup was no longer poisoned. Remember, Dr. VonBronstrup had removed the impediments keeping your father from becoming a Knight of the Rose Cross—and that included Chapter Eight of *Confessio*."

"Did Dr. VonBronstrup truly believe that the mixture of water and wine became the blood of Christ?"

"Of course, but he viewed the transformation from the perspective of a spiritual alchemist."

Nino scribbled the equation on a sheet of paper.

"Water + Wine = The Blood of Christ."

"And my father viewed the change through the perspective of Catholic dogma?"

"Precisely. Transubstantiation—the transformation of water and wine into the blood of Christ."

"So, if they had both drank from the cup at the seventh meeting, their covenant would have been sealed in Christ's blood?"

"That was the plan," Nino said. "Unfortunately, before Dr. VonBronstrup and your father reached a compromise, they both died."

I shrugged.

"All I have are two squares filled with numbers scattered in nine blocks."

Nino smiled.

"Finding the discs will be the easy part," Nino announced proudly, the Oxford scholar once again basking in his Rosicrucian research. "Allow me to introduce you to the Freemason's Magic Square."

CHAPTER 62

ANOTHER CONFESSION

"Wait," Alex said, her voice quivering. "Before Nino explains the Magic Square, there's something you both should know."

For some reason, Alex's request delayed Nino's lecture. Somewhat confused, he and I exchanged glances and then turned our attention to Alex, her somber stare the mortified look of a death-bed penitent. She continued.

"We had a rogue among the gang who engineered the black bag job—a traitor we never identified," she began contritely.

Alex paused while her eyes fixed on the ciborium which held the cremated remains of her father. The two votive candles flanked on each side flickered before being replaced by swirls of white smoke rising from the spent wick. In deference to her loss, I said nothing until the silence forced me to ask a question.

"How did you learn that someone had betrayed you?" I asked quietly.

"I was confronted by Luca Botti."

"Did he know that you were the instigator of the scheme?" I asked curiously, suspecting that Botti had learned of her role in the caper.

"He did," she answered, gazing blindly past Nino and me. "Botti confronted me the day after an NEF seminar—the one your mother attended with Professor Sabino."

It must have been a delicate choice for Botti, aware that Alex had recorded the ruse but hesitant to silence Alex, murder being the most obvious remedy. But somehow, she had purchased her safety while Botti muffled her role as a whistleblower.

"How did you survive Botti's wrath?" I inquired, impressed by her ingenuity, whatever it was.

She didn't answer and I didn't pry. Whatever arrangement she had made with Botti was her business, and I had no right to infringe on their agreement. Fortunately, Alex was alive, still working in the Office of Strategic Plans, but—I'm sure—given only meaningless tasks that were fathoms away from the Administration's new policy in the Middle East.

"I assume Botti asked you for the disc?" I asked, pressing Alex.

"Of course."

"And you told him that you had given it to your father?" Nino added.

Alex lowered her eyes and rubbed her forehead. Her pensive stare told me that Alex was about to confess a deed that somehow would add another layer of turmoil to the role bequeathed to me by Judge Giovanni Micco.

"No. I lied," she said, drawling her words, sighing, taking a deep breath, committed to a perfect confession, pausing as she gazed blindly at the tabernacle.

"I told Botti that I had given the disc to *your* father."

I pursed my lips while combing my hands through my hair. My eyes bulged. I gave Alex a darting gaze while my anger merged with frustration. She had lied to protect her father while placing my family in jeopardy— her thoughtless act the root of my mother's murder and a decoy that tied my father and me, then Grazia, to the disc demanded by her kidnappers. Alex gave me a grim smile before looking away. Once again, she gazed to the altar, her eyes fixed on the seven-sided tabernacle; her thoughts, I'm sure, centered on the ciborium and the cremated ashes resting inside.

"Why did you lie?" I asked starkly.

"To shield my father and me," Alex answered, sighing, then shrugging, her eyes wet. "I told Botti that if he harmed either my father or me—Judge Micco would reveal the secret stored on the disc."

She paused and again looked away.

"I knew that Botti would kill to get the disc," she added soberly.

And he did, I thought, as Alex swallowed hard, searching for words.

"Thinking back, I reacted too quickly," she said remorsefully. "I didn't consider the consequences."

My anger was tempered somewhat by empathy.

"Why did you bother to tell me now?" I asked curiously, confused by Alex's confession, realizing that she could have avoided my wrath by keeping her secret. Alex shifted in her chair and faced me.

"I'm telling you now because you deserve to know the truth," she answered, the remorseful penitent, lowering her eyes as she studied Nino and me. "And I also have some advice," Alex added after a pause. "The disc is in these chambers somewhere. With Nino's help, you'll find it."

She riveted her eyes to mine.

"Give it to Botti. End this ordeal."

I turned toward Nino.

"You were about to explain the Magic Square."

CHAPTER 63

PYTHAGOREAN'S CHART

Nino's loyalties were divided evenly, I'm sure. But I found it difficult to be forgiving given the Micco family's tragedies caused by the disc. Indeed, Alex's error in judgment wasn't the reason my father had sent me on this journey; the ruse he discovered was the real culprit. After all, Alex, too, was a victim. Eventually, my feelings would soften, time, as usual, being the healer, I reasoned as Nino held the paper given to me by Father Gil, the one with the Magic Square.

Shoving my anger aside, I silently applauded Nino for his Rosicrucian research. He had amazingly uncovered a series of clues while digging through *The Chemical Wedding of Christian Rosenkreutz*—the seven-day mystical romance, the secret brotherhood, the gift of prophecy, the truths hidden from the average man, the cylindrical vault, and now the Freemason's magic square.

"Keep in mind," Nino began, "that the Square and Compass is the symbol of Freemasonry."

He paused, studying the numerical combinations.

"As you see, the Magic Square is filled with nine blocks containing numbers that are set in place so that the sum of any row is equal to the sum of any column."

I glanced at each square. Nino continued.

"Now read the numbers in each row and column. The sum is always the same—seven."

I added the first row:

$$3 + 2 + 2 = 7$$

I added the first column:

$$3 + 1 + 3 = 7$$

After a quick exercise in arithmetic, I found the sum was the same for the remaining rows and columns—seven.

"What does this imagery mean?" I asked.

"Remember what my Rosicrucian research revealed," Nino lectured. "After Rosencreutz died, his disciples visited the mausoleum."

"Refresh my recollection," I asked. "Did they find anything inside?"

"A cylindrical vault," Nino answered sharply. "Recall what I told you at the Four Seasons a few days ago. When they opened the vault, Rosencreutz's disciples saw a fireball carved into the ceiling—something akin to the sun. It was like a beacon casting its light into eternity."

"Interesting, Nino," I commented, "but how does the Magical Square fit into all of this?"

"The cylindrical vault found in Christian Rosencreutz's mausoleum—how many sides did it have?" Nino inquired, testing me.

"Seven."

"The tabernacle on the altar, Francesco—how many sides does *it* have?"

"Seven."

"If you open the door, my friend, I'm certain you'll find the disc your father promised to give Dr. VonBronstrup."

I approached the altar and opened the tabernacle door. It was pitch dark inside, but suddenly, a fixture in the vault's ceiling lit and spread a narrow light. It shined on a five-by-five plastic case propped up against the ciborium holding the cremated remains of H. Victor VonBronstrup. I snapped the plastic case open. There it was, a disc, probably the one my father was given access to in the Rosen case—the disc that caused him to become a target in a federal investigation. I recalled the inscription carved into the wall sealing Christian Rosencreutz's crypt. 'Thou shall find the Hidden Treasure.'

"How did it get there?" I asked Nino.

"Your father probably gave it to Father Gil for safekeeping. He placed it in the Tabernacle during Mass."

"What about the other disc, Nino?" I asked, turning to a more crucial issue.

"You mean the fruits of Alexandria's black bag job?" he answered, smirking.

"Yes," I responded, offended somewhat by his smugness. "The one that has brought so much havoc in my life."

Nino grinned, wallowing in his role as my mentor.

"Remember what I already told you," he continued. "The Judge realized he was not dealing with his old law school buddy."

"My father was negotiating with Johann Valentin Andreae, reincarnated centuries later as H. Victor VonBronstrup?" I said, a piece of the puzzle I happily set in place.

A smile crossed Nino's face, acknowledging his student's recollection.

"Exactly," Nino explained, his stare resolute. "For six days, Dr. VonBronstrup and your father met sub rosa or under the rose. It was their secret meeting. Just like Johann Valentin Andreae invited Christian Rosencreutz to a wedding feast that lasted seven days, Dr. VonBronstrup invited your father to 'a wedding feast' that was *supposed* to span seven days."

"But didn't," I offered, the Judge's sudden passing thwarting his final induction ceremony. "Instead, the negotiations ended with *my* induction as a Knight of the Rose Croix on the Seventh Day," I added.

Nino chuckled.

"Appears that way."

Nino turned to the second disc.

"To keep his part of the agreement, Dr. VonBronstrup used the Freemason's Magic Square—it's called a Pythagorean Chart named after the Greek philosopher, Pythagoras."

"Why do the numbers 2, 3, 9, 1, and 5 appear below his square?" I asked.

"Because the Freemasons used the numbers to spell a word. Allow me to explain."

Nino asked Alex for a pencil and paper.

"First, as you can see, the Freemason's Magic Square has nine squares."

"What's the significance?" I asked.

"It's a clue. Dr. VonBronstrup is telling me that to decipher his code, I must write the numbers 1 to 9 in a row."

He scribbled them on a sheet of paper:

1 2 3 4 5 6 7 8 9

"Now, to create The Pythagorean Chart, below each number I will write the English Alphabet in rows of three, beginning with the letter A and ending with the letter Z."

<u>1 2 3 4 5 6 7 8 9</u>

a b c d e f g h i

j k l m n o p q r

s t u v w x y z

2-3-9-1-5

Alex and I hovered over Nino's shoulder.

"Observe closely," he said. "The letters a, j, and s are associated with the number one," he began. "And the same scheme is true for the other letters appearing under the numbers two through nine."

After glancing at both Alex and me, he continued.

"Now, let's take the numbers Dr. VonBronstrup placed below the chart and associate them with the corresponding letters."

I studied the five numbers—2 3 9 1 5.

"But I caution you," Nino warned, "it's necessary to play with different combinations because more than one letter is associated with each number. Let's start."

Alex began decoding the message.

"The first number, two, is associated with the letters b, k, and t—which letter do we choose?" she asked.

"I have a hunch. Let's start with b," Nino suggested.

I took a turn.

"The second number, three," Nino said, "is associated with c, l, and u."

I hesitated.

"Choose a letter, Francesco," Nino urged.

I thought for a moment.

"How about an l?"

Alex lined up the two letters.

"Now we have b and l," Alex said.

Nino kept the procedure moving.

"The third number is nine," he said.

"We only have two letters to choose from," Alex observed, "i and r."

"Seems either will work. Let's try r," I suggested.

Again, Alex lined up the letters.

"Now we have b, l, and r."

"We're headed in the wrong direction," Nino observed after a few moments of reflection. "The fourth number is one."

"And neither of the associated letters—a, j, or s— will serve as the fourth letter of a word, will they?" Alex questioned.

"None that I can think of," Nino said after pondering.

The process was stalled while the Oxford scholar gathered his thoughts.

"Let's go back to Dr. VonBronstrup's second number— three—and make a different choice," he suggested. "Instead of l, let's choose u."

"Now we have b plus u."

"For the third letter, let's use Francesco's suggestion— an r," Nino said. He tallied the letters.

"We now have b, u, and r."

"The fourth number?" Nino asked.

I glanced at the Magical Square.

"It's one," I said. "Our choices are a, j and s."

Nino was on a roll.

"Let's use s," he said.

Alex joined the letters.

"Now we have b, u, r, and s."

Nino's ponderous expression brightened to a wide smile.

"Go no further. I've decoded Dr. VonBronstrup's message."

He jotted it on a sheet of paper:

2- B

3- U

9- R

1- S

5- E

I approached the altar. I took the burse in my hand—the folding case used to store a second purificator. I opened the burse. There it was, the second disc—the fruits of Alexandria Arnold's black bag job.

CHAPTER 64

THE BLACK BAG JOB

After untangling Pythagorean's Chart, Alex, Nino, and I boarded a Metrobus at Pennsylvania Avenue and 21st Street and transferred to Georgia Avenue. It was full, so we stood and steadied ourselves by holding onto a pole as the bus chugged up the hill toward Alex's house on Jefferson Street. Alex and I exchanged glances along the way, saying little, my disdain readily apparent. Once there, we huddled around her kitchen table. Alex inserted the disc—an audio CD—into her computer's loading tray. As the tray closed, she revealed one of the perks of her black-bag job.

"We used equipment that will allow us to both listen to the conversation and read the words as they're spoken," Alex said.

She pushed the power button and the belly of the computer spit out a cadence of syncopated clicking sounds as it booted up. Nino, saying nothing, sat to my left, his eyes fixed on the screen. Alex sat to my right, arms folded, leaning back, her stare apologetic, I'm sure, for involving the Micco family in her caper. Empathy required me to give her a quick smile, which she returned, the first sign of a reconciliation that would take some time. I scrolled down through the pleasantries exchanged by the three principles—Richard Stone, the Director of the Office of Strategic Plans; Lester LaRouche, the adjunct foreign policy advisor to the Administration; and Luca Botti, a Deputy Undersecretary of Defense for Policy. We riveted our eyes to the computer screen as we began listening to and reading the fruits of Alexandria Arnold's black-bag job:

Stone: Let's get down to business, gentlemen. Tell me, Luca, what's the status of the burglary?

A burglary? I mused curiously. Why would a sophisticated cabal take on a dangerous risk that could spell their demise? Judging from Nino's staid expression, he shared my sentiment.

Botti: We made the arrangements. It will be a simple break-in of the Nigerian embassy in Rome. Our agents will take nothing valuable: just stationery and a seal. The Italian police will conduct a meaningless investigation. There will be little, if any, media attention.

A relatively simple caper, I thought. But why not just forge the stationary, and duplicate the seal?

Stone: No screw-ups, Luca. I don't want to deal with another Watergate.

Botti: Trust me, Richard. Our agents are professionals. Plus, they're joined at the hip with the Italian police.

Stone: What tribe did we hire?

A joint venture with the Mafia?

Botti: La Camorra—the Calabrian family.

Thankfully, Luca Botti avoided Uncle Claudio. According to Guerino, he was a member of the Sicilian family—La Cosa Nostra.

LaRouche: One question for you, Richard. Will the document be sufficient for the Administration to justify a preemptive strike?

Stone: Of course. It will state that Niger will sell Iran 500 tons of uranium.

LaRouche: Could a geek identify the document as a forgery?

Botti: None. Our source in Italy is the best. That's the reason we're using their stationery and an official seal.

I assumed their 'source' was the Italian agent charged with the task of preparing a forged document that would fool the scrutiny of any eyes given the job of passing on the contract's authenticity.

LaRouche: Is the Vice-President still on board?

Botti: Of course. We couldn't pull this off without him. He's our direct line to the President.

LaRouche: I'm satisfied. Hopefully, we can turn the Middle East into a cauldron—the faster, the better. If we wage war effectively, we'll bring down the terror regime in Iran.

Stone: Does Citgo have their deal with the government in Iran in place?

Citgo Petroleum—one of the world's largest oil producers. What is its interest in the heist? Another player in the plot my father discovered?

LaRouche: I spoke with their contact at Blackwell & Juliano yesterday.

Stone: Citgo's lobbyist?

LaRouche: Yes.

Stone: And?

LaRouche: Citgo has finalized its deal with Iran. It will be worth billions.

Stone: I'm hearing rumblings about the President signing a regulation voiding all deals with Iran.

LaRouche: Don't worry. We have Sacco in our back pocket.

Dr. VonBronstrup's clue was telling—a friendship severed. Somehow, Supreme Court Salvatore Sacco was connected to the Office of Strategic Plans.

Stone: I'm still concerned about the Mafia being in charge of the break-in. Frankly, I don't trust Claudio Armondi.

Nino and I exchanged startled glances. It was a Mafioso joint venture. The union of La Cosa Nostra and La Camorra tied Claudio Armondi to a plot that eventually led to my mother's murder?

Botti: Why don't you trust Armondi?

Stone: Because he's a close friend of Giovanni Micco.

Botti: You're paranoid, Lester. I'm sure that Armondi doesn't talk to his good friend about his Mafia dealings. And, as Armondi himself told me. 'What happens in the Family stays in the Family.' The burglary will be very discreet.

My suspicion broadened. Claudio Armondi had direct communication with Luca Botti about the burglary of the Niger Embassy in Rome—a fact that deepened his involvement with the conspirators who planned to dupe Congress.

Stone: What's your opinion, Lester? Do you trust Armondi?

LaRouche: I'm comfortable with him. But if Armondi strays and Judge Micco learns about our plan, I'll ask our man to hire the broker.

Perhaps it's the same broker who hired Carlton Fisk, the assassin who murdered my mother. But the 'our man' reference is more intriguing—the missing link between the broker and Lester LaRouche.

Stone: Murder's a dangerous game, Lester. I have no desire to spend the remainder of my life in a rat-infested jail.

Botti: Don't worry, Richard. There's a wall between the Broker and us.

CHAPTER 65

ANOTHER MURDER

"We received the report from the pathologist yesterday, Francesco. Officially, the cause of your father's death was an aneurysm brought on by a lack of potassium. Simply put, someone fed him placebos in place of his potassium pills. He was murdered."

Those were the words of Roosevelt Ward. At the request of Luther Ash, Ward had arranged a meeting with me at the J. Edgar Hoover FBI building on E Street ostensibly to review the pathologist's findings.

"My father's murder is no surprise, Roosevelt," I remarked calmly. "Will the case be assigned to the D.C. police?"

"No," he answered, pausing, his thoughts apparently elsewhere. "The U.S. Attorney in Washington prosecutes all murders that occur in the District," he added. "His office will use the FBI to do the investigation."

There was another lull in our conversation. Roosevelt propped his elbows on his desk and fidgeted with a pencil cradled in both hands. He had a message for me but seemed reluctant to deliver it.

"There's something else, Francesco," he said grimly, hesitating yet again. "The U.S. Attorney has decided to terminate its investigation into the murders of Saul Rosen and your mother."

Although the Government's vacillating interests in the two murders infuriated me, it wasn't a surprise. Its goal in preempting my mother's case was nothing more than a plot to bury the investigation. Saul Rosen? His murder was apparently collateral damage. The broker was still in business and the assassins he employed were free to kill again.

"Why did the investigations die on the vine?" I asked.

"An Administration oligarch made the decision."

"Ash himself?"

"No. Beyond Ash. The official reason will be a lack of evidence."

"That's preposterous."

"No. That's politics."

"What about my sister's kidnapping?"

"So far, the two men who held her in the shanty are tight-lipped," Ward said. "The U.S. Attorney is preparing a criminal complaint charging them with kidnapping. I expect they'll be indicted by a federal grand jury soon."

There was another pause in our conversation; this lull was eerily uncomfortable. Pushing against his desk, Roosevelt rolled his chair back and stood. I followed his lead. He then pressed his index finger against his lips, signaling that I should remain quiet. Roosevelt opened the middle desk drawer, removed an envelope, and handed it to me. Remaining silent, he moved from around his desk and pointed to a message scribbled on the face of the envelope:

Francesco,

Put this envelope in your inside coat pocket. Do not read the contents until you are far away from the Hoover Building. BE CAREFUL.

A cold rain was falling as I left the FBI Building. I walked down E street and turned onto Pennsylvania Avenue. I took a cab to the Starbucks Coffee Shop a couple blocks up from the Four Seasons Hotel in Georgetown. I ordered a tall cappuccino from the barista and sat in the rear of the shop. Except for an older gentleman sitting at a window table reading *The Washington Post*, the coffee shop was empty. The drizzling mist that followed me from the Hoover Building had intensified into a blinding rainstorm. It was time to read the note. Slowly, I removed the envelope from my inside coat pocket. I broke the seal and removed a small piece of folded paper. The message was concise but revealing:

Francesco,

Luther Ash will resign tomorrow as the Attorney General of the United States. He has been forced out. The U.S. Attorney

for the District of Columbia will be his
temporary replacement. After Ash leaves,
the Government will conduct no further
investigation into your sister's kidnapping. The
decision was made at the highest level. That
said, the U.S. Attorney will indict Grazia's two
abductors. He will offer them a plea bargain
they can't refuse. <u>Read this carefully</u>.

A thunderbolt startled me. I looked up from the note and gazed outside through the frosted window. The rain had intensified. It was now darker, and a swirling wind kicked up debris scattered on the street. Water splashed against the glass before dribbling down the front window of the coffee shop. Blasts of thunder rolled across the skies. Except for the occasional bright flashes provided by lightning bolts, nothing outside was discernible. A scary, dark pall shrouded Pennsylvania Avenue. I read the rest of Ward's message:

While in the shanty, Grazia's kidnappers
made one telephone call. Through the 'trap
and trace' and 'pen register,' the subscriber has
been identified. The government knows the
identity of the person who received the call.
That information will die on the vine. The
name of the subscriber is—

Pellets of rain pounded hard on the windowpane as bolts of lightning, complemented by sporadic blasts of thunder and swirling wind gusts, continued to illuminate the black afternoon. I read the name of the subscriber. It was another Armageddon. Grazia's kidnappers had placed a telephone call to the Judge's friend—Leonardo Mendici.

CHAPTER 66

A FEDERAL TARGET

The wind and rain continued to thrash against the window as I tore Ward's note into bits and pieces and threw it in the trash can, the weather still too nasty to venture outside. While I waited at the counter for my second cappuccino, I felt my cell phone vibrate. I looked at the screen. It was Elisha.

"Where are you?" she asked excitedly. "I've been trying to call you for twenty minutes."

"I'm at a Starbucks on Pennsylvania Avenue in Georgetown."

"Stay away from the Four Seasons, Francesco," she shouted frantically. "Take a cab to my apartment. Do it now."

"Why?"

"Because U.S. Marshals are crawling around the hotel looking for you."

"How do you know?"

"Nino called me and said he had to talk with you immediately," she explained. "When he was coming back from his apartment in Georgetown, he saw three men with U.S. Marshall stamped on their shirts gathered in the lobby of the hotel."

Roosevelt Ward's note was a precursor, cautioning me to heed Alex's advice and turn the disc over to Luca Botti and end the ordeal, just as she had suggested. The campaign against me was just beginning, the U.S. Marshal's occupation of the Four Seasons a warning shot across the bow. I was battling against an enemy that had much more firepower than Francesco Micco.

"How did Nino know they were looking for me?" I asked nervously.

"A bellman told him."

"Why didn't he call me?"

"Unfortunately, Francesco, you never gave him your cell phone number. Luckily, I had it."

"Do you know why the Marshals are looking for me?" I asked, suspecting that the Italian carabinieri wanted to whisk me back to Sicily.

"I do," she said. "The United States Attorney has filed a Complaint asking the district court here in Washington to extradite you to Italy."

As I suspected, the wheels of justice were now churning. The U.S. Attorney had issued a warrant for my arrest, the first step in a procedural maze that would eventually land me in a jail somewhere in Sicily.

"How did you learn about the extradition hearing?" I asked suspiciously.

"A friend here at the firm called Justice while I've been trying to reach you."

Once again, I applauded the calculating mind of Elisha Ford—gathering facts, working contacts, warning me.

"Extradited for what?" I asked, curious about whatever information her friend was able to drag out of Justice.

"For the murder of a Lucia Lazzerini," she said, obviously startled by my implication in a homicide. "What's this all about?" she asked excitedly.

"I'll explain later."

Elisha didn't prod me.

"Can the Italian government ask a federal court to ship me to Italy?" I asked.

"Probably," she answered. "I'd venture a guess that the United States and the Republic of Italy are parties to an extradition treaty."

I hesitated, reluctant to expose Elisha to an accessory charge.

"Don't become an accomplice, Elisha," I said, warning her. "We should end our conversation now. Thanks for telling me."

"Wait," she shouted. "I'll take that chance. You'll need some time to think."

"It's risky," I cautioned.

"Like I said, Francesco. I'll take that chance."

"Where can we meet?"

"My place."

"What's your address?"

"1301 U Street, N.W. The Ellington. Apartment 301."

Because of the weather, I was unable to grab a cab. While I stood in the rain getting soaked, a jitney driver recognized my plight and offered me a ride at a slightly elevated fee in his circa 1980 Lincoln Town Car. Shivering, I climbed into the back seat. My clothes were drenched. We rode past the Four Seasons. After rubbing fog from a grimy window, I saw at least four federal agents stationed around the hotel's circular front drive. Two nondescript cars were parked in an adjoining driveway. A white van with the words "United States Marshal" prominently marked on its side panel occupied a spot under the canopy immediately in front of the hotel's revolving front door. I asked my chauffeur to drive faster. It was time to put distance between the Four Seasons and Francesco Micco.

———————

The ride to Elisha's apartment on U Street took about fifteen minutes. The fare was steep—forty dollars. There was no reason to add a tip. I walked into the vestibule of the lobby. To the left was a bank of mailboxes. Beyond the mailboxes was a telephone. A sign instructed visitors to dial the tenant's apartment number for admission. I dialed apartment 301.

"Hello."

"Elisha, it's me, Francesco."

"I'll buzz you in."

I took the elevator to the third floor, found my way to her apartment, and rang the buzzer. She unlatched the safety lock and opened the door.

"My God, Francesco, your clothes are soaked. You look terrible."

She extended her hand and led me into her apartment while closing the door.

"Go into the bathroom and get out of those wet clothes before you catch pneumonia. I'll get you some sweats."

Her apartment was spacious and decorated impeccably. It was also toasty warm, cozy, and comfortable. At least for the moment, I felt safe and sound.

"Are you hungry?" she asked.

"Not really. Just scared and confused."

"I'll make you some tea. It'll warm you up a bit."

I couldn't get too comfortable here. Elisha's apartment would serve as a temporary sanctuary. As I relaxed on her couch, Elisha, balancing two steaming cups of water on saucers, walked into the living area and placed them on a table set against a wall near the kitchen. While the bags steeped, and as we drank tea, I related the events that unfolded in Taormina the night an assassin killed Anna Angelisanti.

"Tomorrow, I'll surrender," I said as I placed my empty teacup on its saucer.

She agreed. We both knew I couldn't evade the clutches of the U.S. Marshal forever.

"You have no other choice," she said as she gathered the cups and saucers and placed them in the sink. "But you'll need an attorney who's acquainted with extradition law. I'll call Mr. Mendici. I'm sure that someone in the firm will represent you."

Elisha innocently offered to help me, but she knew nothing about the secret life of Leonardo Mendici and his plan to forever erase all traces of the Micco family. Perhaps I should be candid with her. But why complicate her life? At least for the present, I decided to tell her little about Mendici Melrose.

"Please trust me on this one, Elisha. Nino will represent me."

"That's a big-time mistake, Francesco," she shot back. "Leonardo Mendici is well connected in Washington."

True enough, I thought, but his 'connections' are conspiring to ship me off to Italy where the Sicilian police will exile me forever in a rat-infested cell. Fatigue eventually set in. Elisha dozed off on the chair. I stretched out on the sofa and fell asleep. In a couple of hours, the siren and the blasting horn of a passing fire truck startled me. I looked at my watch. It was seven in the morning. Sometime during the night, Elisha had propped my head on a pillow and placed a blanket on me. I removed my clothes from the dryer, tossed Elisha's sweats in the washer and dressed. I quietly approached her bedroom, turned the knob on the door, opened it, and peeked inside. She was asleep. Whispering, I thanked her for harboring a suspected felon. She didn't hear me. Not wanting to wake her, I quietly closed the door, left her apartment, rode the elevator to the ground floor, stood on the sidewalk and hailed a passing cab. The clouds had passed, and a chilly September morning greeted me. It was time for me to engage the enemy. Later in the day, I planned to surrender to the U.S. Marshall.

CHAPTER 67

ANOTHER TRIP TO ITALY

After leaving Elisha's apartment, I met Nino at his Georgetown walk-up. I informed him that our relationship had taken on a new dimension. Besides being my Rosicrucian scholar, he now represented me in an extradition proceeding filed in Washington's federal district court. A U.S. Magistrate Judge detained me in a holding cell after I surrendered to the U.S. Marshal late in the morning. The Judge scheduled my initial court appearance and arraignment for later in the afternoon. Rather than being detained as a flight risk, as suggested by the assistant U.S Attorney, I was released on a $10,000 unsecured bond after the Judge agreed with the federal public defender's argument.

"All rise, please. Anyone having business before the United States District Court for the District of Columbia, come forward and you will be heard. God save this Honorable Court," the clerk bellowed.

Two days had passed since my initial appearance. I now stood before United States District Judge G. Hawthorne Henderson, a newly minted federal jurist. Probably a conservative Republican who had passed the litmus test subtly fashioned by his political sponsor. The assistant U.S. Attorney assigned to represent the Government was B. Stanley Puttmen. His aloof demeanor suggested he was an ambitious prosecutor. Puttmen wore a three-button navy-blue suit and a stark white shirt with a button-down collar complemented by a solid red tie. A pin parading the American flag was fastened to his lapel. His shiny hair was jet black and slicked straight back—probably held in place by a generous smothering of styling gel. I turned toward Nino and whispered.

"Hey, Nino. He resembles Don Corleone."

Nino stared at me, smirking.

"If you could only be so lucky."

There was a sparse gathering of people seated in the courtroom including a smattering of media types. The hearing had generated some public interest because the Italian government had charged Judge Giovanni Micco's son with murder, and Italy sought his extradition. Gianna was seated in the front row beside Elisha. I had told Gianna most everything about Elisha, centering on our relationship when we were law students. I added that she represented my father's estate and arranged for Nino and me to stay at the Four Seasons. I thought it best not to tell her that Elisha had sheltered me in her apartment the night before I was arrested. Gianna would only shrug.

She trusted me. Alexandria Arnold sat in the last row, hiding in a shadowy corner seat. Leonardo Mendici was conspicuously absent. Elisha said he had a meeting with a client somewhere out West. Now comfortably perched on the bench, Judge Henderson sat behind a stack of Federal Reporters and a laptop computer. He asked Puttmen if the Government was ready to proceed.

"Yes, Your Honor. We will have two witnesses," he announced. "One is from Italy. He will be first."

"Do you have a translator?"

"No, Your Honor. He speaks fluent English."

"And you, Mr. Viola? Are you ready to proceed?"

"Ready to proceed on behalf of Mr. Micco, Your Honor."

"Call your first witness, Mr. Puttmen."

A man of slight build and medium height with a squared jaw, a broad mustache, and flinty eyes walked briskly toward the witness stand. He was wearing a charcoal-gray suit, a blue shirt with a buttoned-down collar, and a red striped tie. A pair of fashionable titanium glasses complimented his gimlet eyes.

"State your name, please," Puttmen asked.

"Vittorio Lagnese."

"What's your occupation?"

"I'm a police officer."

"From where?"

"Catania, in Sicily."

He was an Italian policeman—a carabinieri. I expected him to be decorated in his full official regalia rather than garb that placed him in the same conservative mold as the Government's two players—G. Hawthorne Henderson and B. Stanley Puttmen. Tucked under his right arm was a thin manila folder. While sitting, he unbuttoned his suit coat, exposing a pair of wide, black suspenders.

"What department do you work in?" Puttmen asked.

"Here in the States, you would call it the homicide department. I investigate murders."

I glanced back at Gianna sitting on the edge of her seat, eyes teary, the anxious wife listening as Puttmen began to present the Government's evidence. Once again, I regretted not heeding Alex's advice. As she suggested, it wasn't a fair match-up. I had little resources to defend myself—except the disc given to me by H. Victor VonBronstrup.

"Were you assigned to investigate the murder of a victim initially known as Anna Angelisanti?" Puttmen asked.

"I was," Lagnese answered.

"How was she identified?"

"We checked all transporation records, rail, bus, air."

"Did you have any success?"

"Eventually. We identified the victim through a photograph. I showed it to a taxi driver who drove her to Taormina from the airport in Catania."

"How did you locate the taxi driver?"

"We didn't. The driver contacted us after reading about the murder in the newspaper."

"How did you learn her name?"

"Through a credit card. The victim gave it to the driver to pay for the ride."

Puttmen was beginning to unfold a well-orchestrated plot. Vittorio Lagnese's story was a fabrication, probably an innocent one, but testimony supported by manufactured facts. The cabal housed in the Pentagon had to find a way to place Anna Angelisanti in our Taormina home the night of the murder. Enhancing the bank account of a taxi driver was the most convenient way. When we spoke after my arrest, I had informed Nino that Anna had rented a car at the airport and parked it somewhere on the Corso Umberto because of the storm. I now surmise she wasn't alone, her companion using the pedestrian walkway up the steep mountainside showing her the way to our home—and then lingering outside looking for the right moment to pull the trigger before jumping into a waiting car that slowly wove down the steep mountainside.

"It's all a fabrication, Nino."

Nino wasn't an experienced litigator, but he was well acquainted with the law. He explained that Judge Henderson's role was to determine if a treaty exists and if the complaint was supported by probable cause—does the evidence show that I committed a crime. Credibility wasn't an issue for the judge to decide, so my testimony would be meaningless—my word against his. At this stage of the extradition process, the scales weighed heavily in favor of the Government.

"Was the cause of her death determined?" Puttmen asked.

"Yes. A bullet wound that severed an artery in the victim's neck."

"Where was the victim's body found, Mr. Lagnese?"

"In Taormina—near Mazzaro Bay."

"Was anything found on her person?"

"A piece of paper was in her blouse pocket."

"Was something written on the paper?"

"Yes. The name of Francesco Micco."

"Anything else?"

"His phone number and address in Italy."

The perfect ploy, well thought out. Francesco Micco shot Anna Angelisanti at his Taormina home and then dragged her body to Mazzaro Bay. The carabinieri then found my name, address, and telephone number on a note found in her blouse pocket—planted evidence, the handiwork of an assassin who was in the business of killing people, part of the deal struck with his employer.

"Does Mr. Micco maintain a residence in Taormina?" Puttmen asked.

"As I understand it, his grandfather purchased a home there many years ago. The family uses it as a retreat."

"Do you know whether Anna Angelisanti was at the Micco home the day she was murdered?"

"Yes, she was."

"How did you establish that fact?"

"Through the taxi driver."

Nino stood.

"Objection, Your Honor. This testimony is hearsay, and I move that it be stricken from the record."

"Allow me to remind Mr. Viola that this is a preliminary examination. Hearsay is permitted," Puttmen lectured.

His response was condescending as he shot a patronizing glance at Nino, the glib look of a teacher mentoring his student. Puttmen's lecture continued.

"The purpose of this hearing is to determine whether there is sufficient evidence to surrender Mr. Micco to the demanding country," Puttmen said, his stare still fixed on Nino before he approached the bench. "As Your Honor knows, in this instance, the demanding nation is the Republic of Italy."

Judge Henderson appeared unwilling to accept the bald testimony of Vittorio Lagnese.

"That may be so, Mr. Puttmen, but this is a serious matter. Mr. Micco's liberty is at stake here," Judge Henderson said somberly. "Does the Government have anything to bolster Mr. Lagnese's testimony?"

As Judge Henderson was speaking, Vittorio Lagnese unraveled the string securing the manila envelope he had carried to the witness stand and removed a sheet of paper.

"Yes, Your Honor," Puttmen responded. "Mr. Lagnese has a verified written statement from the taxi driver that will support his testimony."

"May I see it?"

"Yes, of course, Your Honor."

Lagnese gave the paper he had removed from the manila folder to Puttmen who passed it onto the Judge's deputy. She marked it as Government Exhibit A. Judge Henderson took a moment to read the affidavit before returning it.

"Show the exhibit to Mr. Viola and Mr. Micco."

"Yes, Your Honor."

Puttmen hovered behind us.

Nino fired a salvo at him.

"Your Honor, I can't confer privately with my client," he said roughly.

"Move away, Mr. Puttmen," Judge Henderson barked.

"Sorry, Your Honor."

Together, Nino and I read the affidavit of the taxi driver. A paid perjurer had based it on a lie we couldn't explore—and there was no one present to cross-examine. Nino returned the affidavit to Judge Henderson's clerk. Puttmen, now more contrite, stood and addressed the court.

"The Government offers Exhibit A into evidence."

"Any objections, Mr. Viola?"

"None, Your Honor," Nino said reluctantly.

Puttmen had just paid the first installment on my one-way ticket to Italy through a fake document—he had established that Anna Angelisanti was at our home in Taormina the night she was murdered.

"Mr. Lagnese, did you ever gain access to the Micco house in Taormina?"

"Yes. On the day a passer-by found the victim's body, we searched the house."

"What did you find?"

"We were able to lift microscopic samples of blood from the kitchen floor."

"Were the samples analyzed?"

"Yes. We compared the blood found at the Micco home with the blood of Anna Angelisanti. We used DNA identification technology."

"Was there a match?"

"Yes. Through a genetic pattern-matching process, we were able to identify the blood found on the floor in the Micco home as being the blood type of Anna Angelisanti."

Putnam had the court reporter mark the lab report as Exhibit B. Nino reviewed it and had no objection. It was admitted into evidence.

"Was Francesco Micco home when you lifted the blood samples?"

"No. On the day after the murder, he had fled Sicily."

"How do you know that?"

Again, Lagnese reached into his bag of evidence and pulled out another document. Puttmen had it marked as Government Exhibit C and offered it into evidence. Nino reviewed it and had no objection. It was the statement of Caporale Rossi, the Italian Polizia whom Guerino confronted at the Taormina-Giardini train station. Caporale Rossi detailed the events that had unfolded as the train rolled from Taormina toward the Messina Strait.

"Was Corporal Rossi able to identify the passenger he questioned on the train?" Puttmen asked.

"Yes. I showed Rossi a photograph of Francesco Micco," Lagnese answered.

"And he was able to identify Mr. Micco as the passenger?"

"Yes."

"After reviewing the same photograph, can you identify Mr. Micco?"

With a gauntlet stare, Lagnese's eyes pierced mine.

"Yes. Francesco Micco is sitting at counsel table with his attorney."

The Government had now paid the next installment. Puttmen had established that I traveled from Taormina the day after Anna Angelisanti had been murdered—the prime suspect fleeing the crime scene.

"The Government has no further questions of this witness, Your Honor."

Judge Henderson turned to Nino.

"Cross-examine, Mr. Viola?"

Nino asked some superfluous questions. It was difficult to effectively cross-examine Vittorio Lagnese because his testimony had been based on hearsay. When he completed his examination, Nino returned to counsel table, but before he surrendered the witness, he asked me whether there were any other questions he should ask Lagnese.

"None that I can think of, Nino."

Nino stood and addressed the court.

"No further questions, Your Honor."

Again, it was the Government's turn.

"Call your next witness, Mr. Puttmen."

As if marching to a drum's beat, a man sequestered outside the courtroom walked toward the witness stand. He was short and his neatly-cropped crew cut accentuated his muscular physique. His sunken eyes, set far back in their sockets, resembled a pair of twin rockets about to be launched—and he aimed them directly at me. This man was ready to do battle.

"State your name, please," Puttmen asked.

"Luca Botti."

His snug, ill-fitting blue blazer contrasted with his pressed and cuffed khaki trousers. A striped blue and brown tie, marginally matching his blazer, fell to his crotch. Fashion was not the forte of the Government's second witness. After the clerk had administered the oath, he sat erect in the witness chair and faced his audience. Luca Botti was one of the conspirators doing business in the Office of Strategic Plans. I applauded the Government's bold decision to put him on public display at my extradition hearing.

"Who is your employer, Mr. Botti?" Puttmen asked.

"I'm employed by the United States Government."

"In what capacity?"

"I'm a Deputy Under Secretary of State at the Defense Department."

"Do you work at the Pentagon?"

"Yes, sir."

"Where were you previously employed?"

"I'm a retired United States Army officer."

"What are your precise duties as a Deputy Under Secretary of Defense?"

"I'm the liaison between the Secretary of Defense and the Defense Intelligence Agency."

"Would it be fair to say you work in the area of intelligence as it relates to the Defense Department?"

"Yes, Sir. That would be a fair statement. I report directly to the Secretary of Defense."

"Did you know Anna Angelisanti?"

Nino bolted from his chair.

"I'm asking for an offer of proof, Your Honor. What evidence does the Government intend to introduce from this witness that's relevant to their case?" Nino asked firmly, standing, his eyes staring Puttmen down.

Judge Henderson glanced at Puttmen.

"Your Honor," Puttmen began, "the victim was using an assumed name at the time of her murder. We intend to establish her true identity before Mr. Micco is extradited to Italy."

"You may proceed, Mr. Puttmen," Judge Henderson ruled quickly.

"Once again, Mr. Botti, did you know Anna Angelisanti?"

"I knew her. But her real name was Lucia Lazzerini."

"Would you please explain your answer?"

"Ms. Lazzerini worked as an agent for the Defense Intelligence Agency," Botti explained. "There came a time when I suspected there might have been a security breach."

"A security breach?"

"Yes. Judge Giovanni Micco, who was on the Court of Appeals for the D.C. Circuit, was a constant guest at several social events that were attended by officials of the Defense Department."

Nino snapped to attention.

"I *strenuously* object to this testimony, Your Honor," Nino shouted. "You are presiding over an extradition hearing. Not a judicial inquiry into the conduct of a distinguished federal appeals court judge."

Judge Henderson's steely eyes fastened on Puttmen, ready to defend his colleague.

"What's the relevancy of all this, Mr. Puttmen?" Judge Henderson's question tinged with anger.

"No disrespect to Judge Micco, Your Honor, but the Government must explain the reason Ms. Lazzerini was in Italy."

"Why?" the Judge asked.

"It will establish a motive."

Nino stood, his eyes riveted on Puttmen.

"Motive may be relevant at his trial in Italy, but it's not relevant at a preliminary examination," he said indignantly.

"You're straying too far, Mr. Puttmen," Judge Henderson said, his tone firm, chastising Puttmen. "The court grants Mr. Viola's objection."

"Any further questions, Mr. Puttmen?"

"None, Your Honor. The Government rests."

"You may present your witnesses, Mr. Viola."

"We have none, Your Honor."

Puttmen had tightly packaged the Government's evidence. There was little Nino could do. In the end, Judge J. Hawthorne Henderson would have only one option—to grant the Government's motion to extradite me to Italy. Nino made a passionate closing statement based on the Government's flimsy evidence, an argument even he found to be meritless. Taking his turn, Puttmen summarized the case for Judge Henderson, arguing that the government had easily met its probable cause burden of proof. Judge Henderson agreed.

"I find that there is probable cause to support the complaint," he announced soberly. "I will therefore issue a certificate of extraditability authorizing Francesco Micco's return to the Republic of Italy pursuant to Article XII of the Italian-American extradition treaty."

Even though Judge Henderson had granted the Government's motion to extradite me to Italy, Nino told me that the Secretary of State had the final word. The reality, nevertheless, struck me hard. I was now a detained fugitive, and the Secretary of State would not interfere with my extradition to Italy. The contrary was more likely, I thought. He would probably encourage it.

CHAPTER 68

JUSTICE ITALIAN STYLE

O ur flight arrived at Fiumicino Airport in Rome at eight in the morning. We took a connecting flight to Catania and landed at Fontanarossa International in the early evening. Once again, I was in Sicily. This time, I was a guest of the Republic of Italy. Inspector Lagnese was mostly silent throughout our flight, but his still demeanor conveyed a quiet kindness that eased my anxiety. Nevertheless, I was apprehensive when our plane touched down in Catania. The paying passengers exited first. When the aircraft emptied, Lagnese escorted me off the plane in leg irons and handcuffs.

"Required procedure," he explained apologetically.

As I shuffled down the narrow aisle, sliding one foot in front of the other, a flight attendant sympathized with my plight and offered me luck. Nodding, I returned her smile but said nothing. An Italian prosecutor had safely extradited me to Italian soil. Since we were now in Italy, Inspector Lagnese opted to speak with me in his native tongue.

"Stasera sarai in un carcere a Catania."

Tonight, he said, the Government would house me in a Catania holding cell.

"Domani comparirai davanti a un giudice istruttore."

Tomorrow morning, I will appear before a judge of preliminary inquiries. Knowing little about the Italian judicial system, I asked Inspector Lagnese to explain the purpose of my initial court appearance. He told me that it was another probable cause hearing—Italian style. The judge would determine whether there is sufficient evidence to hold me for trial and, if so, whether he should jail me during the prosecution of my case. Tonight, I'd lay awake and ponder the possibility of living the remainder of my life warehoused in captivity. Three people would like nothing better—Richard Stone, Luca Botti, and Lester LaRouche, along with several other traitors, including Leonardo Mendici.

———

A clerk had scheduled my hearing before the Giudici Dellele Indagini Preliminari at ten in the morning. Once again, in leg irons and handcuffs, I was led into the courtroom by un poliziotto—an Italian policeman— who escorted me to the hearing. The judge's bench was a desk sitting on a platform, raised about twelve inches above the floor. A green, red, and white Italian flag was draped on the courtroom's back wall. Two tables, facing the judge, were shoved together, one for the prosecutor and one for my lawyer. Five rows of pews, probably confiscated by the Italian Government from a closed church, accommodated courtroom visitors. When I entered the courtroom, Giancarlo and Guerino met me. Both sat in a front pew. A third man, seated next to Giancarlo, jumped to his feet and approached me as we walked in.

"Sono il tuo avvocato. Mi chiamo Fernando X. Ramaciotti."

He introduced himself as Fernando X. Ramaciotti, my lawyer. Before speaking with me, he turned his attention to the policeman who had escorted me to the hearing.

"Sono l avvocato di Francesco Micco. Vorrei qualche minuto solo con lui."

He asked to speak with me privately while slipping something into un poliziotto's hands. While Ramaciotti conferred with my escort, I hugged Giancarlo. Before she left for Washington, Gianna had contacted my brother and made him aware of the extradition hearing as well as the murder charge. Giancarlo immediately retained an attorney from Rome to represent me in the Italian courts. I watched as Ramaciotti spoke with my escort. Un poliziotto stood passively, saying nothing, occasionally nodding, grateful for the gratuity Ramaciotti had slipped into his hands.

My avvocato—my Italian lawyer—wore a double-breasted black suit with a black shirt and black tie. His monochromatic furnishings accentuated his imposing continental flare. His long, black hair, lined with scattered strands of gray, was pushed straight back into a ponytail secured by a diamond-studded barrette.

"Siediti e sta zitto. Parlero io," Ramaciotti instructed.

He told me to sit and say nothing. This lawyer seemed out of his element, appearing before the Giudice Delle Indagini Preliminari—the judge of preliminary inquiries. From what I knew about Italian law, he should have appeared in the Corte d' Assizes—the Appeals Court of Assizes.

After his conversation with un poliziotto had ended, Ramaciotti led me to counsel table. We sat and patiently waited for the hearing to begin. With Inspector Lagnese lagging, the Chief Public Prosecutor entered the courtroom. Taking even, long strides, he walked briskly toward the counsel table and, ignoring me, muttered an introduction to Fernando X. Ramaciotti. His name was Luciano Iodice. Remaining in his seat, Fernando politely acknowledged Iodice and said nothing more.

For this judicial hearing, Inspector Lagnese appeared in full formal police attire. He wore a dark-blue jacket accentuated by a stark red collar. A red caplet with a black stitched design accentuated his broad shoulders. His matching blue trousers were decorated with wide red stripes. Carrying a manila folder, Lagnese followed the chief prosecutor and sat at the far end of the counsel table, away from me. Space was a premium commodity in this courtroom, but my attorney didn't appear uncomfortable working in cramped quarters.

Luciano Iodice's appearance and demeanor personified the prototypical prosecutor. He wore a gray tweed sport coat with black trousers and a muted solid red tie. A square jaw accentuated his burly physique. A barber had cropped his dark, wavy black hair short—a modified crew cut. Appearing smug and rigid, he would not allow a smile to touch his face.

Precisely at ten o'clock, il Giudice—the judge—entered the courtroom from a door off to the side. There was no deputy to announce his appearance. There was, however, immediate silence. Fernando jumped to attention as if the Prime Minister himself had just entered the room. Luciano Iodice lagged. He was slow to acknowledge il Giudice's appearance. He was also far less flashy than Fernando X. Ramaciotti. The name of the Judge was printed on a placard sitting on the edge of the bench. It read in script: '*The Honorable Lido Pugliano*.' Judge Pugliano sat, adjusted his robe, and announced the case:

"Questa e l'udienza della Repubblica Italiana contro Francesco Micco."

His words stung me: "*The Republic of Italy against Francesco Micco.*"

"Puo chiamare i suoi testimoni," Judge Pugliano said starkly, his eyes fixed on Iodice—directing the Chief Prosecutor to present his evidence.

Because there was no witness chair, Inspector Vittorio Lagnese remained seated next to Iodice. He was the prosecution's first witness. Facing Lagnese, his back to Ramaciotti, Iodice began by asking questions that told the same story presented in the courtroom of Judge J. Hawthorne Henderson. Chief Prosecutor Luciano Iodice apparently borrowed the hearing transcript developed by Assistant U.S. Attorney J. Stanley Puttmen.

"Sai se Anna Angelisanti era a casa del Micco il giorno in cui e stata assassinata?"

"Si."

"Come?"

"Ha assunto un taxi per portarlo qui."

Iodice's final two questions related to the taxi cab driver who supposedly drove Anna Angelisanti from the Catania Airport to the Micco home in Taormina. Ramaciotti slid to the edge of his chair, his eyes riveted to Lagnese like two six-shooters, their chambers about to be emptied. Through Lagnese, Iodice had established that Anna Angelisanti had hired a taxi cab driver to bring her from the Catania Airport to the Micco home in Taormina. It was a fabrication Nino was unable to challenge during my hearing before the Honorable G. Hawthorne Henderson in the federal district court.

"Non ho ulteriori domande da porre a questo testimone," Iodice said.

Having no further questions, Iodice had concluded his examination of Lagnese and surrendered the witness for cross-examination. Like a vulture about to swoop down on his prey, Fernando X. Ramaciotti stood tall over Lagnese, who was seated next to Iodice.

"Sei sicuro che Anna Angelisanti abbia preso un taxi da Catania alla casa di Micco a Taormina?" Ramaciotti asked calmly.

"Si. Leggi l'affidavit del tassista," Lagnese answered.

After asking if he was sure that Anna Angelisanti had hired a taxi at the airport in Catania, Lagnese had responded 'yes' and referred Ramaciotti to the driver's affidavit. Ramaciotti grinned, backed away from Lagnese, gave a quick smile to Judge Pugliano, reached into his Oleg Cassini briefcase, and pulled out a paper embossed with a notaio—an Italian notary public seal. He approached the bench, clutching the document, eyes bulging, arms whirling, plea impassioned as he handed the document to Judge Pugliano. The affidavit from a rental agent at the Catania Fontanarossa International Airport established that Anna Angelisanti had leased a car from Hertz International the night before she was murdered.

"L 'agente della Hertz e in aula, pronto per essere interrogato," Ramaciotti shouted.

Like a boxer delivering his knockout punch, Ramaciotti then punctuated his statement by saying that if Judge Pugliano questioned the validity of his document, the rental agent, who was seated in the back of the courtroom, was available for the court's examination.

"Non sara necessario."

Judge Pugliano said it wasn't necessary. Iodice slouched, caught in a lie, probably unaware that the taxi cab driver's affidavit was a fabrication, the work of renegades far beyond his reach. But he had additional evidence he knew to be credible—the affidavit of Caporale Rossi, the railroad agent who tried to apprehend me when I fled Taormina the day after an assassin murdered Anna

Angelisanti. It was a link in the chain of evidence that pointed to me as the main suspect.

"Chiamo il caporale Rossi come testimone," Iodice said, summoning Rossi who was seated in the last row of pews. When he heard that Iodice had called Rossi as a witness, Ramaciotti jumped from his chair and stood erect as his steely stare shifted from Iodice to Judge Pugliano, his arms stretched high, his voice reaching a high crescendo.

"La testimonianza di Rossi non e rilevante senza un corpo nella casa di Micco," Ramaciotti shouted firmly, the calculating words of an experienced trial litigator—pleading passionately that Rossi's testimony was irrelevant because Iodice could not place Anna Angelisanti in the Micco home on the night of the murder.

His sharp stare drilling through the Italian prosecutor, Judge Pugliano agreed with Ramaciotti's argument and denied Iodice's attempt to call Caporale Rossi as a witness. But Iodice had more ammunition in his arsenal—the lab report that matched the blood found on the floor in the Micco home with the blood of the decedent. He marked the report as an exhibit, gave it to Judge Pugliano and a copy to Ramaciotti.

"Offro in evidenza il rapporto di laboratorio che corrisponde al sangue trovato nella casa di Micco con il sangue del defunto."

Iodice then offered the report into evidence. He labeled it: 'Analisi del sangue di Lucia Lazzerini'—Blood Analysis of Lucia Lazzerini. Ramaciotti reviewed the report. A smirk crossed his face. After pondering for a moment, he jumped to his feet with even more vigor.

"Questro e un rapporto di sangue di Lucia Lazzerini, non di Anna Angelisanti," he argued vehemently. The lab report identified the victim as Lucia Lazzerini. Iodice had failed to obtain the affidavit of Luca Botti—showing that Lucia Lazzerini was masquerading as Anna Angelisanti while she was duping my father.

"Lucia Lazzerini e estranea a questo caso," Ramaciotti said calmly, arguing that Lucia Lazzerini was a stranger to this case—and that the lab report had no relevance to the murder of a victim named Anna Angelisanti.

"E un alta frode in campo," Ramaciotti said slyly, adding to his argument, his eyes fixed on the judge. He labeled the report as a hoax, another fraud on the court, citing once again the taxi driver's false affidavit. In response, Iodice vainly attempted to show that Angelisanti and Lazzerini were the same person. Still, he had no evidence to support his argument—other than his bald hearsay claim, and that wasn't enough.

When Iodice finished, Judge Pugliano's gimlet eyes once again pierced the prosecutor like an arrow zeroing in on its bullseye. Without further argument from Fernando X. Ramaciotti and any plea from Chief Prosecutor Iodice, Judge Pugliano dismissed the case. Disgruntled, Iodice gathered his papers, hurriedly stuffed them in his briefcase, and bristled from the courtroom with Vittorio Lagnese lagging behind.

I stood and eyed my attorney.

"Grazie, Signor Ramaciotti," I said.

"Non deve ringraziare me, ma suo fratello Giancarlo," Ramaciotti answered, acknowledging my gratitude, but suggesting that I speak with Giancarlo who had retained his services early the previous morning. Muttering a good-bye as he grabbed his Oleg Cassini briefcase, Fernando X. Ramaciotti disappeared through a door at the rear of the courtroom, vanishing from my life as fast as he had appeared in it.

As a lawyer, I was surprised that el Guidice had dismissed my case with little argument or emotion from the prosecutor, Luciano Iodice. I turned to Giancarlo for answers, but he quickly excused himself, saying that he was due back in Lampedusa later in the day. Sanita per la Famiglia's project on that island, designed initially only as an outpatient clinic, had suddenly ballooned into the construction of a new hundred-bed hospital. Apologizing, he promised to call me in Taormina in the morning. Guerino, who was prepared to testify if it became necessary, had retired just ten days before my hearing. He agreed to drive me home. I would remain in Taormina until my host, the Republic of Italy, made flight arrangements for my return trip to the United States.

Perhaps I should have left my curiosity unsatisfied, but I pried for an answer to a question I wanted to be answered by Guerino during the ride to Taormina. Although the Judge struck the taxi driver's affidavit from the record, there remained sufficient evidence to detain me for trial. There was the note found in Anna Angelisanti's blouse pocket, the matching blood samples, Caporale Rossi's testimony showing that I had fled from Taormina—evidence that Judge Pugliano could have easily considered.

"Be candid with me, Guerino. Why was my case dismissed?" I asked.

First, there was a silence as we made our way along a narrow road toward Taormina. Somewhere along the way, Guerino decided to satisfy my curiosity.

"I will say this only once. Never tell anyone, not even yourself."

I nodded.

"The order came from the very top," he began. "Through Fernando Ramaciotti, Giancarlo informed the Prime Minister that he would abandon the Lampedusa project unless the court dismissed the charges. Because of his threat, Ramaciotti assured Giancarlo you would be protected, and overnight the project in Lampedusa was expanded from a clinic to a hundred-bed hospital."

It was nearly midnight as Guerino drove up the winding road that led to our Taormina home. When we arrived, he nodded to the back seat as I opened the car door.

"There's a bag on the floor. Take it."

"What's in it?"

"A gift from me to you."

I reached into the back seat, grabbed the bag, closed the door, and watched the taillights of his car disappear down the twisting road. As I walked toward the front door, I opened the bag. Inside was the blood-stained shirt I had discarded in the clothes hamper before I reported Anna Angelisanti's murder to my friend, Guerino Regantini.

CHAPTER 69

THE JUDGE'S MANUSCRIPT

―――――――

Finally, home in Taormina, I unlocked the door, turned the knob, and walked inside our Sicilian home. I stood in the darkness, smelling the stagnant air suffocating the empty house as memories ferried me back to our Easter celebrations. It was Holy Saturday, and Rosalina was roasting a ham as the wedding soup simmered in her big pan. The sweet aroma of the brown sugar bubbling around the ham drew me into la cucina— the kitchen. Lent would end soon, and, at noon, Giovanni and Rosalina, along with their three children, Francesco, Grazia, and Giancarlo, would kneel in la cucina and kiss the floor. We would then sit together as a family at the dining room table and feast on the wedding soup and ham after forty days of Lenten sacrifice.

My musings strayed to a different time. I remain trapped in la cucina. The silence was interrupted by the crack of a gunshot. Anna Angelisanti fell into my arms. Even as I stand here now, the warm blood oozing from her neck trickles down my arms, her face grimacing with pain. Anna's sad eyes are making a silent plea. She wants to say something but can manage only three words.

"Francesco, look under…"

I revisited my dinner engagement with Elisha at Primi Piatti, perplexed as she edged an envelope toward me. I slid it into my hands. Her words still echo. "There is something more, Francesco. Before your father left my office, he gave me an envelope and told me to deliver it to you, but only if he died." I focused on the Judge's message, spoken through a limerick:

> *Look to the past, and you will find*
> *an answer dwelling in your mind.*
> *The feast suspended,*
> *her time now ended,*
> *the alchemist's equation,*
> *the key to the rhyme.*

Musing introspectively, I visited 2113 K Street and the chambers of The Rosecross. My eyes rose to the alchemic equation painted above the altar:

$$X + \Delta = O$$

Copper + Silver = Gold

Like an epiphany, the clues merged. The past—Taormina; the feast suspended—our Easter celebrations; her time now ended—Rosalina's murder; the alchemist equation—copper, the kettle; silver, the silver-plated wooden spoon; and gold, obviously, the big pan. Holding Anna's lifeless body in my arms, I finished her sentence.

"Francesco, look under…the sink."

Dropping to my knees, I opened the door of the cabinet under the sink. I reached inside. The smaller pans clung as I shoved them aside. It was still there. I pulled it out—the copper kettle, the big pan. The silver-plated wooden spoon rested inside.

Kneeling on the floor, I slid open the drawer above the cabinet. Fortunately, someone had stored a flashlight there. Like a child amused with a toy, I sat on the floor and cradled the pan between my legs. Shining the light into the large caldron, I saw a package about one inch thick wrapped in brown paper and secured by twine. I untied the string and ripped off the wrapping paper.

It was the Judge's manuscript.

Inside, I found a stack of pages bound together by three strands of red string. Tucked underneath was a computer disc. A message from my father, I thought. In the morning, I would contact Guerino, confident he would locate a computer for me. Then I'd listen to the disc.

I traded the flashlight for a kerosene lamp. Recalling my fatal encounter with Anna Angelisanti in the kitchen, I opted to read the manuscript secluded in the privacy of the attic. I walked up the stairs to the second floor and pulled down the portable staircase. With the manuscript tucked under my arm, I managed to climb the staircase one step at a time. Once in the attic, I heard soft pellets of water falling gently on the tile roof. It was beginning to rain. I saw flashes of lightning casting volleys of light far off in the distance through the small windows at each end of the attic. The storm appeared to be heading in my direction.

Stowed in a corner, I recognized a chair that had served as a decorative piece in the Judge's study. Rosalina didn't like it, and she exiled it to the attic. I rested the kerosene lamp on a sturdy box and placed it next to the chair. Oblivious to the gathering storm, I settled in for my marathon reading session, determined to spend the remainder of the night, the early morning hours, or however long it would take, reading the novel authored by Giovanni Micco.

With the kerosene lamp providing the light, I began to read—first the prologue, and then the first few chapters, ending on page seventy. I turned to page seventy-one. It was blank. I flipped through the rest of the manuscript. The remaining pages were more blank sheets of paper. Amusingly, it struck me hard. The Judge's novel was a red herring. The manuscript sought so vigilantly by the cabal chasing after me was nothing more than an unfinished novella—with little detail exposing their machination.

The remnants of the storm passed just as the sun began to peek through the attic window. I had fallen asleep there. After climbing down the portable stairs, I called Guerino. He made arrangements for me to use a computer at la Questura—the police station in Taormina. Wasting little time, I zigzagged down the pedestrian pathway to the main street, the Corso Umberto. Once there, I walked in the direction of la Questura in the Piazza S. Domenico.

When I arrived, I was greeted by a young poliziotto who escorted me to a small, private room with no windows. It was sparsely furnished. A wooden chair was tucked under a table that had been shoved against a wall to conserve space. My eyes focused on the computer sitting on the tabletop. As il poliziotto left the room, he offered me a cappuccino.

"Prende un cappuccino?"

"No, Grazie."

Alone in the room, I inserted the disc into the loading tray, sat back, clicked on the CD icon, closed my eyes, and listened. I realized it would be eerie—hearing the Judge speak to me from his grave:

> *Dear Francesco,*
>
> *If you are listening to this message, it means that you have found the manuscript of my novel. By this time, you know that the purpose of The Rosecross is to expose the secret plan of a cabal of ideologues who are planning a war. To uncover their ploy, I joined the cause of The Rosecross. But since Rosalina's murder, I have also been chasing clues, trying to identify the persons responsible for that dastardly act. Since her death, that mission has consumed my life. But my time ran out, and I couldn't continue. As you now see, the novel I planned to write says little. I am asking that you take*

up the search, unravel the conspiracy behind Rosalina's murder, and write the story. May the force of God be with you.

CHAPTER 70

GIACOMO

It was early afternoon. Alitalia scheduled my flight to leave Rome at eight in the evening. Guerino drove me to the Catania International Airport but returned immediately to Taormina. Tonight, he'd be the honored guest at a lavish retirement dinner held at A Zammara, and I'd be stranded at the airport for about four hours, munching on a stale sandwich. While waiting, I was engaged by a young man, probably in his mid-twenties, sitting across from me in the cramped lounge. Sensing he was staring at me, I glanced from behind the magazine I was reading and snuck a look in his direction. Our eyes met. He left his seat and moved toward me.

"Francesco Micco?" he inquired.

He wore jeans, a gray monogrammed sweatshirt, and white sneakers. Earphones dangled from his iPod touch. He was probably listening to a cacophony of downloaded rap noise. His long, black hair touching his shoulders was partially hidden by a white sweatband wrapped around his forehead.

"Si. Sono Francesco Micco," I answered.

He handed me an envelope marked with my name, turned, walked away, merged into the crowd, and quickly disappeared. Somewhat stunned, I held the envelope for a second or two before I broke the seal and read the message. It was from Guido Borgese:

> *Francesco,*
>
> *Some time ago, through his family connections, Claudio became involved with a burglary without knowing that it someday would be the lynchpin to your mother's murder. That burglary now has become part of the story your father planned to write. He died, and that task now rests with you. It may sound strange, but I am asking that you participate in a burglary of the Niger embassy in Rome and then write. When your flight arrives in Rome, Giacomo will meet you. He will lead you safely through the burglary. Please commit this combination to memory— L74, R15, L30, R20. God be with you, Guido.*

A mechanical malfunction delayed my flight to Rome from Catania. The Alitalia plane finally touched down at Fiumicino in Rome shortly before ten at night. I wheeled my carry-on bag down the ramp and walked into a nearly-deserted airport terminal. A glance at the flight information display screen informed me that my connecting flight to New York was scheduled to depart from Fiumicino at nine-ten in the morning. I suspected, however, that my participation in the Niger embassy burglary would delay me in Rome. A duty placed me in a dilemma. Either join in the heist or board my flight home. Curiosity—mostly about Uncle Claudio's loyalty— prompted me to stay.

Small gatherings of people mingled in the lounge area, waiting to greet the exhausted passengers as they plodded through the tunnel, funneling them from the plane into the terminal. Off in a corner, I noticed a middle-aged man leaning against a wall holding a Styrofoam cup, probably filled with stale black coffee that had kept him awake while he waited for the delayed Alitalia flight to arrive from Catania. A wrinkled tan raincoat was flung over his arm. As I walked from the ramp, his eyes latched onto me. Before I reached the pedestrian corridor leading to the main terminal, he cut me off and quietly issued a command.

"Vieni con me, Francesco."

He had asked me to follow him. I assumed he was Giacomo, the man who would 'lead me safely through the burglary' as promised by Guido Borgese. While we walked together down the corridor of Terminal B, Giacomo said we'd take the Leonardo Express train to Rome's Termini Station. He stopped at an information kiosk and asked for a train schedule. Because it was a thirty-five-minute ride, Giacomo would explain the nature of our mission during the short trip to Rome. He didn't tell me his last name, and I didn't ask. Our strides widened and then expanded into a jog as we approached the Fiumicino station of the

Leonardo Express. The last departure was at ten-thirty, and the next train for Rome departed at seven-fifty in the morning. Giacomo was determined not to spend a long and sleepless night at Fiumicino.

Our sprint ended and we boarded the slick, shiny express train. For the first time, I was able to study Giacomo. He was wearing a black blazer with silver buttons, a black crew-neck sweater, probably cashmere, contrasted by a gold neck chain, tan, cuffed trousers, and buffed Italian boots. His jet-black hair, parted to the right and neatly combed, complimented his fashionable appearance. Before he slid into the window seat, he folded his raincoat and stuffed it in the overhead bin.

"Il viaggio in treno per Roma sarà breve," he said.

Giacomo explained that the ride into Rome would be short. I stowed my luggage under the aisle seat and sat beside him as the train began to roll toward Rome. Exhausted by the car ride from Taormina, the extended wait in the Catania airport while mechanics resuscitated the Alitalia plane, and the late flight to Rome, I dozed off. Before I fell into a deep slumber, Giacomo nudged me. It was time to talk. He began with his curriculum vitae.

Before returning to Italy five years ago, Giacomo had graduated from NYU. Recruited by Claudio Armondi, he worked for Marymount HealthCare in New York before becoming the Sanita per la Famiglia clinic manager in Puglia. Not surprisingly, Giacomo was a Mafioso, and his membership in the LaCorona family was a fact he unabashedly admitted. His Mafia boss had assigned him to assist me as a party to a burglary that would occur at the Niger embassy in Rome. Recognizing that the carriage was mostly full, and, choosing to be discreet, he mingled Italian with English.

"Ci troviamo su questo treno per Roma causa di Guido Borgese."

I already knew that Guido had asked me to participate in the burglary through the note delivered to me at the Catania Airport. Borgese apparently thought it would add reality to the story both my father and he had asked me to write—the protagonist, brushing away risk, exposing a ruse while solving his mother's murder. Giacomo continued, speaking English to better disguise our conversation.

"Guido Borgese told me that during a meeting of the bosses in Palermo, Mr. Armondi was approached by a man—Antonio LeDonne—who in the past has peddled information to a variety of spy organizations throughout Europe. He occasionally worked for the Italian SISMI."

"The SISMI?" I asked curiously.

"It's Italy's version of the CIA."

"What did LeDonne want?"

"Not much," Giacomo answered, shrugging. "Just five blank Niger government letterheads and five official seals."

"That's an odd request," I remarked, befuddled.

"Not really," he said curtly, his words drawled as he stared through the carriage's window into the dark night. "First, you must connect LeDonne with Niger's prized natural resource."

I recalled Lester LaRouche's question as we listened to the conversation that Alex had captured on the disc, the fruits of her black-bag job—*Any way to identify the document as a forgery?* and Botti's response, *None. Our source in Italy is the best.* It made sense. LeDonne is the player charged with the task of preparing the forged documents. He'll then sell them to his customer. At least that's what I anticipated his role to be in this caper, the former spy peddling his wares.

"Niger is a former French colony in the Sahara Desert," Giacomo explained. "Uranium dominates its economy. For the most part, Cogema Resources, a gigantic French company, controls Niger's mining industry."

I was becoming overwhelmed by the heist's consequences. A simple burglary of the Niger Embassy had implications that stretched far beyond a routine international buy-and-sale agreement.

"How does LeDonne fit into this picture?" I inquired to confirm my suspicion.

"He was recently fired by SISMI because he was convicted of a felony—receiving stolen checks of all things. He needed money," Giacomo answered.

"What did he do?" I asked, prodding Giacomo.

"What do you think?" he answered smugly. "LeDonne set out to replenish his bank account."

"How?" I asked, continuing to pry.

"Someone in the Niger embassy, probably an Italian functionary employed there, provided him with a letter

Francis X. Caiazza

showing that Iran was planning to expand its trade relations with Niger."

"Wasn't that enough to startle the international community?" I asked innocently, the guile of a naive plebe being asked to commit a crime.

"Hardly," Giacomo explained, chuckling. "The letter was written in French and purportedly sent to Iran's President, Mohammad Khatamt. It set out the terms of a proposed agreement that was nothing more than the typical relationship Arab oil states usually enter into with third-world countries."

It was a strange coincidence, I thought. A meaningless letter, probably discovered fortuitously, was the catalyst that sparked the Administration's new policy in the Middle East, a bonanza for the culprits who ran the Office of Strategic Plans and its benefactor— Citgo Petroleum. Their plan was straightforward. Attack Iran, put a friendly government in place, and give Citgo free rein to Iranian oil. Once again, I recalled the dialogue between Stone and LaRouche captured on the disc that has brought untold havoc to the Micco family:

Stone: "Does Citgo have their deal with the Iranian government in place?"

LaRouche: "Yes."

Stone: "And?"

LaRouche: "The deal has been signed. It will be worth billions."

"What did LeDonne do with the letter?" I asked.

"That's where the story *really* begins," Giacomo said as a wide smile lightened his face. "LeDonne sold the letter to his friends at SIMSI, who then informed the Defense Intelligence Agency in Washington that they had a letter disclosing Niger's agreement to sell uranium to Iran."

Giacomo smirked.

"Both SISMI and the DIA jumped to a hasty conclusion," he added smartly.

"Which was?" I asked.

"That the letter revealed an Iranian interest to purchase huge quantities of uranium from Niger that Iran would use in its nuclear program."

According to Giacomo, it was a gargantuan leap to a hasty conclusion, mainly because Iran was in the process of building a nuclear reactor to produce electricity, a fact ignored by Lester LaRouche and friends. But then again, the deception was far too appetizing to pass up, mostly because it justified a preemptive strike on a foreign sovereign blessed with an abundance of oil deposits.

"LeDonne latched on to a scheme that could make him piles of money?" I surmised.

"Precisely," Giacomo answered, shaking his head, lips pursed. "LeDonne knew that SISMI wanted to curry favor with the DIA. He also knew the Americans wanted a reason to launch an attack on Iran. But there was one glitch."

"The Americans want a forged document that will set out more detailed information?" I asked slyly—an assumption that was easy to foretell.

"Exactly," Giacomo answered starkly. "And that's where you and I enter the picture."

His stare settled on me as his cunning smile broadened.

"Unfortunately," he said, his mood swinging somber, "Niger's ambassador to Italy fired LeDonne's contact. He turned to the Mafia for help."

"So, you and I burglarize the Niger embassy, pilfer five letterheads and paper seals, and then pass them off to LeDonne?" I guessed, summing up my role in the caper. "LeDonne then forges the documents, showing that Iran is purchasing uranium from Niger?"

Giacomo glanced in my direction. A wide, mischievous grin crossed his face.

"Precisely," Giacomo answered, nodding. "LaDonne sells the document to the Italians who then pass the document off to the Americans, and he's paid his rather substantial fee."

With its horn bellowing and its steel wheels rolling melodiously on the steel tracks, the Leonardo Express raced toward Rome. As it approached the Termini Station, Giacomo and I walked down the narrow aisle. While waiting to exit, he turned toward me and offered more information.

"There's one more thing you should know, Francesco," he said, sending me a veiled message I found hard to understand. "LaDonne will allow us to be present when he passes the forgeries on to his customers."

CHAPTER 71

THE BURGLARY

The Leonardo Express arrived at the Roma Termini Railway Station at eleven-fifteen. We took a bus to the Piazzale Claudio Terminus from the Termini Station and walked two blocks down Viale Mazzini. In less than five minutes, we reached Viale Angelico where Giacomo had made reservations at a bed and breakfast owned by his cousin. It was close to the Niger Embassy in Rome's Mazzini district. We deposited our belongings and headed out about midnight.

The Embassy was located on the sixth floor at 10 Via Antonio Baiamonti. Giacomo punched in a series of numbers on a keypad to gain access to the building. A buzzer sounded. Giacomo opened the door. We walked into a small vestibule. There was no one at the reception desk.

"Where's the security guard?" I asked, surprised.

"He has the night off," Giacomo said, grinning.

We took a lift to the sixth floor and approached the entrance to the Niger embassy. The hallway was dimly lit. An armored door resembling a bank vault protected the offices. I asked Giacomo if he intended to blast his way into the embassy. Smiling, he stared at me.

"Guido said you have the combination."

I recalled Guido Borgese's message passed to me at the Catania airport 'Commit this combination to memory— L75, R15, L3, R20.' I turned the hand wheel according to Guido's instructions. Next, I pulled down on the handle. The door opened.

"This, my good friend," Giacomo said, "is why Antonio LeDonne sought the services of Claudio Armondi and the Mafia. We had easy access to the building."

The embassy was small. There were only three rooms. One was for the ambassador and another for the political adviser. We entered the space used by the secretary for administrative affairs, or so the signage said. Rummaging through the desk drawers, Giacomo found the official letterhead of the Niger government. He peeled off five letterheads and slid them into a manila envelope. Reaching in another drawer, Giacomo found the other items. He tore off five official seals of the Niger government and placed them in the same manila envelope. Our mission finished, we left the embassy and returned to the bed and breakfast.

CHAPTER 72

A RENDEZVOUS

It was noon the next day. Giacomo and I walked to an intimate restaurant nestled between the Piazza Mazzini and the Tiber—Cacio e Pepe. The restaurant was empty except for an older gentleman sitting at a corner table, sipping a glass of red wine. Strands of gray hair brushed his ears. A trimmed mustache and black, bushy eyebrows sprinkled with salt and pepper shades, complemented his silvery hair. Sunken, beady eyes accentuated the sullen expression fixed on his pale face; a wrinkled, off-white tropical suit and white shirt blended with his ashen complexion. A solid navy-blue tie offered the only color contrast. A wooden cane hung on the back of an adjacent chair. I followed Giacomo as he walked toward the table.

"Tu sei Antonio LeDonne?" Giacomo asked softly.

"Si. E tu sei Giacomo?"

"Si."

Shanking hands, Giacomo and Antonio LeDonne greeted each other. After introducing me as his associate, we sat. Just then, another couple entered the restaurant. The maitre d' seated them at a nearby table.

"Ti posso offrire un bicchiere di vino?"

LeDonne spoke first, offering us a glass of wine. Giacomo glanced at me and then returned his attention to LeDonne. Nodding, he accepted his offer.

"Si, un bicchiere di vino fa bene," Giacomo added.

Our host motioned for the waiter. He wore a black tuxedo with a crooked bow tie. The Cacio e Pepe was obviously one of LeDonne's regular haunts in Rome.

"Ti suggerisco il Cabernet Sauvignon. C` e anche un po di Merlot."

LeDonne recommended the house Cabernet Sauvignon, saying Cacio e Pepe's sommelier had mixed it with a hint of a Merlot. We nodded our approval. When the server returned with the wine, LeDonne suggested we order because time was of the essence. Eyeing the couple seated at the nearby table, he opted to speak in English.

"May I make another recommendation? The spaghetti alla Carbonara—it's delicious."

We nodded our approval. LeDonne collected the menus, returned them to the server, and placed our order.

"Noi prendiamo lo stesso...spaghetti alla Carbonara."

"Ottima scelta," the server responded—an excellent choice.

Staring at the yellow manila envelope Giacomo had placed on the tablecloth, LeDonne cradled a glass in his hand and swirled the wine, no doubt sensing that the prize it held would replenish his barren bank account. After swirling the wine and sniffing its bouquet, he took a sip.

"I assume your business venture was successful, Giacomo?" LeDonne asked quietly.

Glancing at me and then returning his attention to our dinner host, Giacomo slid the manila envelope toward LeDonne.

"Inside, you will find five official letterheads of the Niger government," Giacomo responded, his assuring stare fixed on LeDonne. "I also have five official seals. But I'll keep the seals until you have provided me with copies of the forgeries."

LeDonne took the envelope, reached for his worn, brown briefcase he had propped against his chair, unfastened the tarnished buckle, placed his bounty inside, and then fixed his eyes on Giacomo.

"That's agreeable," he said, nodding.

Giacomo glanced at me and then returned his attention to LeDonne.

"There's one more thing, Antonio," he said slowly, his eyes wide, gesturing toward LeDonne. Alarmed, LeDonne grimaced as he caressed his worn briefcase.

"I will need two copies of the final documents, one translation in English and the other in Italian," Giacomo said firmly.

"Why?" LeDonne asked, apparently reluctant to share his bounty.

"For our records—just in case we don't get paid."

"That will not be a problem," LeDonne responded after pondering for a moment.

"When and where do we make the final transfers?" Giacomo asked.

"Tomorrow morning in the Piazza del Popolo," LeDonne answered. "I'll be in the Santa Maria del Popolo— the church of Our Lady of the People."

A church was the venue of our meeting. It was also a parody—an exchange of forged documents, the fruits of a burglary, in the sanctity of Santa Maria. LeDonne continued.

"As you enter the vestibule to the left, you'll find the tomb of G.B. Gisleni," he explained. "We'll meet there, exchange the seals for the forged documents, and then enter the church. There's a Mass celebrated at seven."

Another parody. The priest's blessing after Mass an imprimatur guaranteeing the authenticity of the forged documents.

"During Mass, you'll inspect the agreement," LeDonne instructed, "and I'll inspect the seals—just to make sure that everything's in proper order."

There was a consensus. We agreed with the procedure recommended by Antonio LeDonne. Our business concluded, we adjourned our meeting and enjoyed the Cacio e Pepe, the Cabernet Sauvignon, and the spaghetti alla Carbonara.

CHAPTER 73

THE FINAL BLESSING

Giacomo and I arrived at Santa Maria del Popolo promptly at seven in the morning. We walked up the worn stone steps, pulled open the Gothic door, and entered the church's vestibule. Glancing to my left, I saw Antonio LeDonne standing beside the baptistery in front of the Tomb of Gisleni. Wearing the same wrinkled suit he had worn yesterday, he appeared haggard. LeDonne had probably spent the entire night supervising the forgery of the Niger documents.

As we approached LeDonne, he opened his briefcase, removed a yellow manila envelope, and passed it to Giacomo. LeDonne's sachet remained unfastened as Giacomo passed the manila envelope to me. Giacomo then unbuttoned his coat jacket, removed an envelope from an inside pocket, and offered it to LeDonne. Like a vulture sweeping down on its prey, LeDonne grabbed the envelope, slipped it into his briefcase, fastened the buckle, and walked into the church. Giacomo and I followed.

The church is a Renaissance Basilica with a wide aisle that leads to the main altar. I was impressed by a few pieces of Baroque artifacts: six wooden confessionals and two almost identical holy water stoups made of colored marbel. I dipped by finger in one and crossed myself.

We genuflected before entering the last row of pews. Giacomo and I sat to the left of the aisle; LeDonne sat to the right. Each party to this clandestine meeting had set up a separate shop in the Santa Maria del Popolo. There would be more than just a cursory inspection of the respective documents by my Mafioso friend Giacomo and the Italian spy, Antonio LeDonne.

I glanced at the altar. A Franciscan monk was celebrating Mass. It was the Offertory. On our side of the aisle, Giacomo broke the envelope's seal and removed the contents. Thoroughly inspecting each piece of paper, he placed the documents onto the seats and slid to me the one translated into English. I glanced at the sheet. To my naked eye, it appeared to be authentic. The blank letterheads we had removed from the embassy yesterday, each embossed with the Niger government's official emblem, were soon-to-be sealed documents that would memorialize an international agreement entered into by the Republic of Niger and the government of Iran. Once again, I glanced at the altar. The Mass continued. It was the Consecration. The priest was raising the Host. I knelt, made the Sign of the Cross, and read the first page of the document:

Niamey, July 27, 2002,

Mr. President,

I write in reference to Accord N 3B1-NI 2000, concerning the supply of uranium made at Niamey on July 6, 2002, between the Republic of Niger and Iran's government by their respective designated representatives.

This delivery, consisting of 500 tons of pure uranium per year, will be delivered in two installments.

Having examined this Accord, I approve it in whole and in part by the authority conferred upon me by the Constitution of May 12, 1966.

Accordingly, I pray you to consider this letter as the formal tool of approval of this agreement by the Republic of Niger's government that becomes by this rightfully engaged.

Please accept, Mr. President, the certainty of my highest regards.

Seal of the President of the Republic of Niger.

Giacomo leaned forward, caught LeDonne's attention, and nodded his approval. Antonio LeDonne returned the gesture. My attention returned to the altar. It was now the Communion of the Mass. LeDonne left his seat and, his hands folded, approached the rail to receive Communion.

Giacomo and I followed. I returned to my seat as Giacomo passed the forged documents to LeDonne. With LeDonne lagging for a minute or two, Giacomo and I quietly walked toward the vestibule. I glanced back, watching LeDonne place the official seals on the documents. As the Franciscan monk gave his final blessing to the congregation, LeDonne knelt and made the sign of the cross.

Now blessed by the Father, the Son, and the Holy Spirit, LeDonne walked into the vestibule, past the baptistery, and headed toward Gisleni's tomb. He motioned for Giacomo to join him. I followed close behind. With his briefcase tucked securely under his arm—now holding the forged documents he had just sealed—LeDonne surveyed the vestibule, assuring himself that we were cloistered before he made his final comment.

"Meet me tomorrow night at the Hotel De Russie at ten-thirty," he whispered. "It's located in the center of Rome, between the Spanish Steps and the Piazza del Popolo. I'll be in suite 703."

LeDonne began to walk away.

"Aren't you forgetting something, Antonio?" Giacomo asked with squinted eyes.

"Oh, I'm sorry," LeDonne apologized as he reached into his briefcase and gave Giacomo two copies of the forged documents, one in English, the other in Italian. Antonio LeDonne then turned away, opened the church door, walked down the worn stone steps, and disappeared into the crowd assembling in the Piazza del Popolo.

CHAPTER 74

A COVERT MEETING

Having some spare time before we met with LeDonne and his clients, I explored the Hotel De Russie. Just as LeDonne said, it was situated within Rome's heart, tucked between the Spanish Steps and the Piazza del Popolo on the fashionable Via del Babuino. As I walked through the hotel lobby, a stunning terraced garden complemented by white balustrades greeted me. It was an oasis in the middle of a bustling city. Later in the day, the Hotel De Russie would host our meeting with Antonio Le Donne and his undisclosed clients. Just as I was about to leave, my cell phone vibrated. It was Giacomo returning a call I had placed to him earlier.

"Can you give me the agreement that LeDonne translated into English?" I asked, realizing that it would be helpful when I wrote the chapter about our meeting with LaDonne at the Santa Maria del Popolo.

"That's not possible," Giacomo answered sharply.

"Why?"

"It's for Mr. Borgese."

"And the copy of the agreement translated into Italian?"

"It's also for Mr. Borgese."

I thought it odd that Guido needed copies of the agreement. The Mafia's part in the ruse was to steal the letterheads and seals, get paid its fee, then walk away, its role finished. It baffled me. Did the Mafia add another layer to the juggernaut, I wondered, blackmail their endgame, holding both SISMI and the DIA hostage— profiteers feeding off a machination that nearly destroyed the Micco family. Or was there another ulterior motive?

"Can you at least make a copy of the document?" I asked, puzzled.

"I will. But mums the word."

———————

At precisely ten-thirty, Giacomo and I rode the lift to the seventh floor and found suite 703. I used the gold knocker to tap on the door. LeDonne opened it. He was alone. His clients had not arrived. He said they were due at eleven o'clock. The suite was elegant. Floral photographs decorated the walls, painted in soft pastel hues. The pale, contrasting colors of the minimalist furniture spread a unique charm throughout the suite. Tied-back drapes, colored in complementary pastel tones, lined three louver-shuttered windows. Two glass doors led to a veranda that overlooked the terraced garden. A table with six high-backed chairs, three on each side, was placed in the suite's conference room.

"This should be a short meeting, gentleman," LeDonne said softly. "I'll show the documents to my clients. They'll review them and decide if there's any interest in purchasing them."

"How many visitors do you expect?" I asked.

"Three. Our clients will sit on one side of the table, and we'll sit on the other. I'll do the talking."

"How will you introduce us to your contacts?" Giacomo asked.

"There will be no introductions," LeDonne explained. "It's a covert gathering between international intelligence operatives. I'll set the rules for our side of the table. They'll do likewise for their side."

Preciously at eleven o'clock, there was a light, double tap on the door. LeDonne fixed his eyes first on Giacomo and then on me.

"Please, take your seats," he said, pointing to the outside chairs.

Our covert operation was moving toward its final act. We took the two end chairs at the conference table, leaving the middle seat for our spokesman, Antonio LeDonne. He walked toward the door and opened it as far as the secured latch allowed. I heard a muted voice in the hallway.

"Ciao, Antonio."

Le Donne unfastened the latch.

"Ciao, Nicolo. Sei solo?" LeDonne knew the visitor—Nicolo— and asked if he was alone.

"No. Ma prima che il collega venga devo fare un controllo."

Nicolo's colleagues were lagging in the hallway while he performed his due diligence. After frisking Antonio, Giacomo, and me, Nicolo swept thoroughly through the room. In about ten minutes, he completed his task. Nicolo then walked to the door, opened it, and motioned his comrades into the room.

"La stanza e pulita. Puoi entrare."

Nicolo stood back and two men entered. LeDonne invited them to sit. Nicolo was seated across from Giacomo. Although Nicolo was speaking to LeDonne, he fixed his eyes on me.

"Chi sono i tuoi due amici?"

Suspicious, Nicolo asked LeDonne to identify his two friends. LeDonne brushed Nicolo's question aside.

"Sono i Mafiosi che hanno fornito i documenti."

After saying that we were the two Mafiosi who provided the Nigerian stationery and seals for the documents, LeDonne reached for his briefcase, unfastened the buckle, and removed three copies of the forged memorandum of agreement between Iran and Niger. He slid them across the table, one for each of his diplomatic counterparts. Nicolo wasn't satisfied with LeDonne's answer. He pressed to explain our presence, inquiring if we had been paid.

"Perche sono qui? Non sono stati pagati?"

Disturbed by Nicolo's suspicion, LeDonne curtly said that we insisted on attending the meeting because his client's fee had not been paid. The man sitting across the table from me folded his arms, rested them on the table, and calmly spoke as he eyed LeDonne.

"I have their money—one million Euros," he said quietly.

I stared at him. He had combed thin strands of hair over his head's crown, trying to hide a bald spot. Above each ear, his hair thickened, the long, brown mane slicked to the back of his neck. Brown, bushy eyebrows with gray streaks matched his trimmed goatee. Swelled bags sat under his bulging eyes. A pockmarked face and a handlebar mustache partially hid his sullen expression.

"Where's the money?" LeDonne asked.

"In our briefcase," Nicolo responded.

A euphoric moment came as Nicolo answered LeDonne's question. I recognized this man from a photo Alex had shown me the day we heard the fruits of her black bag job. The bagman sitting across the table prepared to pay the Mafia's fee was Lester LaRouche, the adjunct foreign policy advisor to the White House—and a senior policy expert at NEF. He was also the chief architect of the Office of Strategic Plans and the author of the Administration's new Middle East bully policy. Signaling he was now satisfied that the Mafia fee would be paid, Giacomo turned toward me and nodded. Meanwhile, Nicolo glanced at the papers Giacomo had given him.

"Dobbiamo discutere la cosa privatamente fuori la veranda, Antonio," Nicolo said.

Saying his partners would privately inspect the documents on the suite's veranda, Nicolo shoved his chair back and stood. With the forged documents tucked under his arm, he walked toward the double-glass doors, opened them, and motioned for his colleagues to join him on the veranda.

"You know Nicolo, Antonio. Who is he?" Giacomo asked curiously.

"Nicolo D'Avanzo. He heads the SISMI."

"And the other guy?" I inquired.

"That's Enrico Baldino. He's Italy's Minister of Defense."

Giacomo had another concern.

"Why are the heavy hitters here, Antonio?" he asked.

"It's not my concern," LeDonne answered, shrugging. "But if I had to guess, I'd say there was a conspiracy brewing between the Italians and the Americans."

About fifteen minutes later, the double doors swung open, and Nicolo, followed by his comrades, entered the room.

"We'll take the documents, Antonio," Nicolo said as he slyly motioned with his head to a briefcase that was placed on a couch. Along with LaRouche, Enrico Baldino and Nicolo D'Avanzo left the room.

CHAPTER 75

A TELEPHONE CALL

—————

My Air Alitalia flight back to the United States was more pleasant. During this trip, I was not burdened by shackles and handcuffs, my extradition to Italy a chapter in my life I'd rather forget. Sitting in first-class accommodations, I clutched my briefcase, confident that the bounty in it would be part payment for my family's safety. Although the Judge's manuscript was worthless, it remained the prize sought by the traitors responsible for my parent's murders. The other half—the disc—was secure in a safety deposit box I had rented at United Bank in Washington. While the aircraft glided over the Atlantic headed to Kennedy International, I mulled over two options. Either surrender the manuscript and disc or stay true to The Roseross's mission. The price was steep, but the blackjack player in me was willing to honor the last wishes of Giovanni Micco and H. Victor VonBronstrup.

I arrived in New York on time to board my connecting flight. It landed at Pittsburgh International in the early afternoon. Carrying my briefcase, I hustled from the gate, jumped on the tram to the main terminal, and rode the escalator to the concourse level. As I approached the luggage carousel, I saw Gianna waiting for me. I hesitated, reveling in her elegance, my eyes drawn to the pendant pinned to her lapel, the one she wore when we first met after Mass in the St. Vitus Church parking lot. Just as the carousel began turning, Gianna turned and spotted me in the crowd rushing to claim their baggage. I hastened my pace as she ran to greet me. We embraced, then a gentle kiss, a broad, welcoming smile—her eyes, glassy but radiant, her words soft but reassuring.

"We missed you. Welcome home."

When we arrived in New Castle, Michele was napping. Gianna brewed a pot of coffee and cut two slices of lemon ricotta cake. Together we enjoyed our traditional afternoon repast, talking mostly about my Italian lawyer, Fernando X. Ramaciotti, the dismissal of my case, and the clues that finally led me to the Judge's manuscript. It was a pleasant conversation until she cleared the table and stood at the sink, glancing out the window, her voice soft.

"Before I left for the airport, you received a telephone call," she said.

"From whom?" I asked cautiously.

"Elisha Scott," she answered, her back toward me, still gazing into the side yard, her voice tinged with a suspicion she couldn't hide.

"What did she want?" I asked hesitantly after taking a deep breath.

"I didn't inquire," Gianna answered casually while scrubbing away crumbs from a dish. "She tried to call your cell, but apparently there was no service."

"Did she ask that I return her call?" I asked cautiously.

"Yes. She wants to talk with you…today."

Gianna turned and faced me.

"I tacked her number on the fridge."

"Please understand…"

Gianna stopped me in mid-sentence.

"Francesco, I trust you," she answered, her eyes teary, brushing away suspicion like lint from a garment.

She handed me the phone.

"Call her. She sounded distressed."

I dialed the number as I stretched the phone's long, twisting chord and sat at the table. Gianna leaned into the sink, still rinsing the dishes. I didn't move from the kitchen, reassuring Gianna, wanting her to hear every word of our conversation. Elisha answered after one ring.

"Thanks for returning my call," she said, relieved. "I didn't mean to alarm Gianna, but something happened at the firm today that you should know."

She paused, just long enough to collect her thoughts, I reasoned. Elisha Ford, the pinnacle of order, the trusted associate not easily aroused by petty office chatter.

"Where are you?" I asked.

"In my apartment," she answered, sighing. "I'm exhausted. It was a hectic day at Mendici Melrose."

"What happened?"

"When I arrived in the office at six this morning, Mendici was already there. He usually moseys in at about noon. He called me into his suite."

"Why you?"

"I was the only associate there."

"What did he want?"

"He gave me the job of researching a section of the Foreign Commerce Clause."

"Right up your alley," I said curtly. "As I recall, because of my tutoring, you got an A in constitutional law," a stray comment I quickly regretted.

"You remembered," she said softly.

While I spoke with Elisha, Gianna stacked the dishes in the kitchen cabinet, placed the ricotta cake in the fridge, careful not to make noise, listening to my words, wondering, I'm sure, what Elisha was saying. I motioned for her to sit with me at the table.

"What section did Mendici ask you to research?" I asked, wondering why a research project prompted her call to me.

"An arcane provision that deals with the government's power to regulate trade with foreign countries," she responded.

The assignment Mendici had just dumped on Elisha was the reason I had declined the offers of employment made to me by law firms in Washington and New York. Ironically, the avalanche of legal research Leonardo Mendici dumped on Elisha today was the culprit that ended our relationship, a strange coincidence.

"I started my research," she explained, "and then corralled two other associates later in the morning. We finished in the early afternoon."

"Why was the research so important?" I asked curiously, still wondering what urgency prompted her call to me.

As Elisha and I spoke, Gianna shoved her chair back and walked into the dining room, not wanting to appear as if she was eavesdropping. But she was still listening to my every word as she stared out the window, her eyes focused on the twin Japanese Red Maples in our front yard, questioning, I'm sure, if Elisha was enticing me back to Washington—a magnet that wouldn't release its hold.

"I didn't know at first," Elisha answered, "but I soon learned after I began to research the legal issue. Just yesterday, the Supreme Court had agreed to an expedited review of a case that was recently decided by the Court of Appeals for the D.C. Circuit."

"What's the name of the case?"

"*Citgo Petroleum v The United States.*"

Suddenly, Elisha had captured my full attention.

"What was the finding of the court?" I asked curiously.

"A three judge panel affirmed the trial judge's opinion," Elisha explained. "Essentially, the court found that that the executive branch of government has the power to regulate a domestic corporation's right to contract with a foreign country."

"What was the effect of the case?" I asked, suspecting that the courts had thrown a wrench into the nefarious plot authored by the Office of Strategic Plans.

"The court's decision essentially voided a contract between Citgo and Iran," Elisha answered, confirming my suspicion. I recalled Alexandria's Arnold's black-bag job and Lester LaRouche's statement, '*the deal between Citgo and Iran will be worth billions.*' The reason for the clamor at Mendici Melrose was abundantly clear. Unless the Supreme Court reversed the circuit court, the Administration's new Middle East policy would lose its purpose—putting an abrupt end to a well-planned machination.

"I assume you and your staff of indentured servants found sufficient authority to limit Congress' power to stick its nose into the business affairs of domestic corporations?" I asked cynically, stretching the phone's curled line as I walked into the vestibule.

"This is no time to vent your sarcasm, Mr. Micco," Elisha said sarcastically.

Michele's shout muffled her words, then a smile, surprised to see me as he carefully walked down the stairs after his afternoon nap, his hands touching the wall, balancing his chubby legs.

"Sorry, Elisha," I said as I reached down and bundled Michele in my arm, balancing the phone against my shoulder. Michele was still groggy as he rubbed his eyes with clenched fists.

"Did you finish your research?" I asked while smiling at Michele.

"Yes. We prepared a memo," she answered. "It wasn't a work of art, but it was thorough. After I grabbed a sandwich in the cafeteria, I printed the memorandum and brought it to his office."

"Did you give it to him personally?" I asked.

"Eventually," Elisha answered. "Mendici's secretary said that he was in a meeting and I should wait and give it to him myself. She seemed distressed and asked if I would cover the phone for a few minutes. It was mid-afternoon, and she hadn't had lunch."

"You agreed?"

"I did. But before leaving, she told me that Mendici was meeting with a Mr. Botti."

"Luca Botti?" I asked loudly, surprised to hear his name. My raised voice drew Gianna into the vestibule. She reached for Michele, cuddling him as she walked into the kitchen and sat him in his highchair.

"That's the man. Your good friend," she said smartly.

I glanced into the kitchen. Gianna was strapping Michele into his highchair. I watched as she opened the refrigerator door and reached for a jar of applesauce.

"Are you still there?" Elisha asked, distracted by the short pause. The lull lingered as I watched Gianna feed our son. I balanced their well-being not only against the retribution I sought for my parent's murders but, most notably, against the task bequeathed to me by H. Victor VonBronstrup and Giovanni Micco.

"Anyone else in the meeting?" I finally asked, turning my attention back to Elisha.

"According to Mendici's secretary, someone from Blackwell & Juliano," Elisha answered. "I did a quick google search on my iPhone when she left for lunch. Blackwell & Juliano is registered to lobby for Citgo Petroleum Corporation."

"And Mendici Melrose is their Washington contact?" I surmised. It was the same Dallas-based law firm that Lester LaRouche mentioned in his conversation with Luca Botti and Richard Stone—an alliance captured by Alexandria Arnold in her black bag job.

"Seems that way," Elisha answered, confirming my suspicion.

"Did you wait for Mendici's secretary to return?"

"Yes, I did. But soon after she left, all hell broke out in the meeting. I recognized Botti's voice from your extradition hearing. He was shouting. I moved closer to the door and eavesdropped."

"What did Botti say?"

"He was yelling about money. He said, '100 G's for Rosalina Micco, 100 G's for Lucia Lazzerini, and 100 G's for Carlton Fisk. Our asses had better be covered.'"

"What else did you hear?" I asked as I walked back into the kitchen, the phone's long cord dangling behind me, my loyalties divided while I gazed at Gianna. She was feeding Michele, her hand unsteady as she placed the spoon in his mouth—the lengthy conversation, my somber stare, signs that The Rosecross's mission was once again pulling me away from my family.

"I heard nothing for a while," Elisha answered. "Botti's voice softened a little, so I moved closer and placed my ear to the door. He asked a question about the Citgo Petroleum case."

"Were you able to hear it?"

"Just one question. Botti asked, 'Is Sacco on board?'"

"Any answer?"

"None that I could hear. But I did hear the third gentleman in the room make a comment."

"The guy from Blackwell & Juliano?"

"I assume."

Gianna removed the tray and lifted Michele from the highchair, caressing him as she stared out the kitchen window into the side yard, still listening intently, I'm sure, to my every word.

"What did he say?" I asked.

"'Citro Petroleum is depending upon on Mendici Melrose to protect its rights.'"

"That's it?"

"I couldn't hear anything else."

Gianna carried Michele into the living room and placed him on the floor. She watched as he crawled back into the kitchen and stared up at me. Again, I balanced the phone against my shoulder, stooped down, and lifted him into my arms; my attention was divided equally between Elisha's words and Michele's smile.

"The $300,000 seems like petty cash to me, considering what we're paying for a gallon of gas," I offered, a meaningless comment, Elisha's words now only muted sounds, my attention focused entirely on Gianna and Michele.

"There's more Francesco," Elisha said, the spark in her voice drawing me back into our conversation.

"What's that?" I asked.

"After their friend from Texas spoke, Botti said, 'You have Citgo's ten million dollars for Munson, Leonardo. I hope your trip out West convinced him to do business with you.'"

"Who's Munson?" I asked.

"I don't know," Elisha answered.

"Do you know where Mendici went out West?"

"No. But I do know that he keeps his calendar stashed away in his office safe."

Gianna and I talked well into the early morning hours after I had spoken with Elisha. After tucking Michele in bed, we opened a bottle of Sangiovese, trading thoughts as we sipped wine and munched on Fontina cheese. She encouraged me to follow my best judgment, a subtle endorsement of both my attempt to expose the ruse brewing at the Pentagon and to unravel the mystery surrounding my parent's murders, both plots having a common denominator. Although she was supportive, I suspected it was the alcohol talking.

"If you allow the past to rest, you'll regret it for the rest of your life," she advised.

I didn't answer, but she knew I'd be leaving soon. When our talk waned, Gianna snuggled close. I wrapped my arm around her, listening as she drew even breaths, finally falling asleep.

It was past two in the morning when I kissed Michele as he slept soundly in his bed. Gianna and I then spent the remainder of the early morning hours slumped on the living room couch. At seven o'clock, I woke, covered Gianna with a blanket, and brewed a pot of coffee before booking an early afternoon flight for Washington. Elisha had agreed to meet me at Reagan National. Gianna and I avoided any talk about the Pentagon ruse, mostly because it was a fragile subject steeped in danger. It was a meaningless topic anyway. Most of the jigsaw puzzle pieces remained scattered on the table. But there was one redeeming value. Although the facts were sketchy, I had begun to write my novel.

CHAPTER 76

A NOCTURNAL VISIT

I was waiting at the curb when Elisha arrived at Reagan International, driving the same shift-stick red Mercedes convertible she had when we were students at Georgetown. After tossing my luggage in the back seat, we inched through the congestion around the airport terminal and then headed toward Nino's apartment on M Street. Our stay at the Four Seasons ended when I learned that Leonardo Mendici was connected to Grazia's kidnapping.

Because of Gianna, I was reluctant to involve Elisha in the plot bequeathed to me by Dr. VonBronstrup and my father, but I had little choice. As I began writing the novel, I realized that Elisha's part in the story had taken on more than a supporting role. She had become a main character, mostly because of her employment at Mendici Melrose, an agent embedded with the enemy, willing to take chances. Although the information gathered by Elisha while she eavesdropped was enlightening, I was mostly intrigued by the ten million dollars that Blackwell & Juliano had given Mendici for someone 'out west' named Munson.

"Is there some way to track down Munson?" I asked.

Elisha smiled, her eyes staring through the car's windshield as she drove down Pennsylvania Avenue, headed toward Georgetown.

"As I said, Mendici keeps his schedule in an office safe," Elisha said shyly. "And *I* have a key to his suite."

"Are you offering to be my chaperone on a private visit to his office?" I asked.

"I am," she said, shifting gears down as we reached a red light before turning onto 28th Street.

Elisha was taking chances, first harboring a suspected felon, then eavesdropping, and now offering to break into the office of her boss, risks not too many people would be willing to take. As we turned onto M street, I asked her a question, anxious to satisfy my curiosity.

"Why are you helping me?"

She edged the Mercedes close to the curb in front of Nino's apartment and pushed a button as the convertible's canvas top raised high before tucking itself into the car's trunk. Lowering the visor, she reached for her sunglasses, turned, and stared at me for a moment, her blond hair brushed back by a soft wind, searching, I suspect, for words to answer my question.

"Let's just say that I'm helping an old friend and leave it at that."

Nodding, I reached for my luggage in the back seat, opened the door, and stood on the sidewalk while glancing at Elisha, keeping my distance but warmed by the same radiant smile that captured me when we were law students.

"Thanks," I said as the door clicked shut.

"Meet me here tomorrow night at eleven-thirty," Elisha said.

She slid her sunglasses on, shifted to first gear, revved the engine, and drove away.

———————

Elisha and I arrived at the main entrance of Mendici Melrose at midnight. We entered the vestibule and approached the officer sitting at the security desk.

"Good evening, Mrs. Scott," he said as Elisha signed the logbook, listing Brandon D'Leone as her guest.

"Good evening, Charles. We'll be in the building for about one hour."

I assumed that D'Leone was her current suitor. She didn't want Leonardo Mendici to know that she was hosting my nocturnal visit to the offices of Mendici Melrose. Elisha pushed the elevator button, and the door opened. It was empty. According to Elisha, except for a few strays trying to impress their supervisors, most of the associates usually were out of the office no later than ten at night. I felt a surge of adrenaline as the elevator door swung open on the third floor. Dimmed ceiling lights lit the shadowed hallway. Exit signs posted above the fire exits at each end of the long corridor added a red glare to the subdued light. We entered her office without being noticed. I closed the door and again assured Elisha that she remained free to abort our mission.

"Trust me, Francesco," she said. "I'm numbering my days here. Too many sinister things are going on. Let's get this over with."

Leonardo Mendici's office was on the tenth floor. We walked down the hall to the elevator. I pushed the illuminated up arrow. The door swung open immediately. Startled, I recoiled, surprised to see Charles—the security officer—standing in the glare of the elevator's lights. I smiled at him as he walked out of the elevator into the hallway. He nodded and then approached Elisha.

"Just making my rounds, Mrs. Scott. Are you leaving?"

"No, Charles," she said. "I'm going to show Mr. D'Leone the roof-top garden. It's so beautiful at night."

"Sure is, Mrs. Scott. Now you two be very careful," he cautioned. "It's dark up there."

"We will, Charles," Elisha said as he began to make his third-floor rounds. The door closed and the elevator began lifting us to the tenth floor. I asked Elisha if we should cancel our visit to Mendici's office.

"No," she said. "He probably suspects that we plan an exotic rendezvous in the garden upstairs. Besides, he's my good friend. I've treated him very well at Christmas— much better than Mendici Melrose."

The elevator opened; we were on the tenth floor. Directly across the hall was the private office suite of Leonardo Mendici. Elisha reached into her shoulder purse and pulled out a key.

"You must be a privileged associate, Elisha," I noted.

"No, not really," she answered, smirking. "Mr. Mendici's secretary gave me a key to his suite about a year ago. I can't even remember the reason. Fortunately for you, I forgot to give it back to her."

She unlocked the door. I glanced down the hallway in both directions as she slowly turned the knob. Quietly, Elisha opened the door, and we entered Mendici's suite.

"Any motion detectors?" I asked.

"None that I know of," she answered. "But we'll know in a few seconds."

The anteroom, Leonardo Mendici's secretary's office, was dark except for a bulkhead wall lamp that lit a corner of the room. Adjacent to the lamp was a set of double doors leading into the office of Leonardo Mendici. Before entering the hallowed sanctuary of Mendici Melrose's managing partner, Elisha again reached into her shoulder purse and pulled out a small flashlight.

"We'll need this. It's probably pitch-black inside."

For the most part, she was right. A small recessed fixture above the credenza spread a glimmer of light down onto the wall area behind Mendici's oversized mahogany desk. Elisha canvassed the flashlight along the wall span behind the credenza.

"What are you looking for?" I asked.

"The painting that's covering the safe."

"Why does he hide his schedule?"

"Think about it," she said, shrugging. "Considering Mendici's political connections, he has built his practice on conflicting interests. For the most part, where he goes and who he sees is a well-protected office secret."

"So, only his secretary knows his precise schedule?"

"That's about it."

Finding the painting, Elisha handed me the flashlight and moved toward a portrait of the founding partner of Mendici Melrose—Leonardo Mendici. With his eyes staring me down, I placed the flashlight in my pocket and helped Elisha lift the portrait from its hook. Together, we leaned it against the desk. Mendici's safe was now exposed. Being a skeptic, I addressed an obvious problem.

"As I see it, Elisha, our only option is to blow open the safe door with a stick of dynamite."

Ignoring my remark, Elisha opened the middle drawer of Mendici's desk, reached far into the back, and removed a narrow strip of laminated paper.

"Forget the dynamite. Here's the combination."

I was awestruck.

"How did you know to look in the drawer?"

"I watched Mendici's secretary open the safe a couple of times," Elisha explained calmly. "She didn't memorize the numbers, so she jotted the combination on a strip of paper, had it laminated, and then stored it in the middle drawer of Mendici's desk."

Together we approached the safe. Elisha read the combination as I turned the knob.

"Right 36, left 10, right 43," she instructed.

Slowly, I pulled down on the safe's handle and opened the door. I removed the flashlight from my pocket and shined it into the deep, dark cavity of the safe. Inside were various items, but my eyes focused on an appointment book wedged between the wall and a large box. It was a Day-Timer. I removed it and flipped to the day of my extradition hearing before Judge Henderson. Teasing Elisha, I said nothing, but the wide smile brightening my face signaled that our search had been productive.

"Don't keep me in suspense, Francesco," Elisha urged. "Where was Mendici on the day of your hearing?"

"Leavenworth, Kansas."

"Who did he see there?"

"Floyd Munson."

"The beneficiary of Blackwell & Juliano's ten-million-dollar gift?" Elisha asked.

"I assume."

After handing the Day-Timer to Elisha, I once again turned my attention to the safe. Reaching into its cavity, I grasped a large box, slid it out, removed the lid, and looked inside. I was astounded. Tightly bound with rubber bands were stacks of new one-hundred dollar bills. After counting the stacks, I estimated the cache to be about fifty thousand dollars.

"Don't get any ideas, Francesco. Return the box to the safe. Leave nothing out of place. His secretary is very observant."

"Does the firm have a larger safe?" I asked.

"Yes. A walk-end in the basement."

Elisha, fascinated by another discovery, smugly waved Mendici's Day-Timer in my face.

"There's something in here you missed, Mr. Attorney," she said melodiously.

"What's that?" I asked.

"Did you notice who Mendici visited the day before your extradition hearing?"

I looked at the entry. The day before my extradition hearing, Leonardo Mendici had visited Luca Botti at the Pentagon. Having gathered the information I needed, we carefully retraced our steps and removed any evidence that would reveal our nocturnal visit to the office suite of Leonardo Mendici. After quietly closing the outer door, we walked into the hallway, and then into the elevator. The door opened at the lobby level. Charles wasn't seated at the security desk. He was still making his rounds.

CHAPTER 77

THE PRODIGAL SON

I called Roosevelt Ward the day following my nocturnal visit to the office of Mendici Melrose. The Federal Bureau of Prisons operates the United States Penitentiary at Leavenworth, Kansas, and I had a hunch that Floyd Munson was an inmate there. My instinct paid a dividend. Ward learned that Munson was currently serving two consecutive life sentences at Leavenworth. Juries had convicted him twice for violations of the federal murder-for-hire statute.

Cutting through a morass of red tape, Roosevelt was also able to schedule a visit for me with Munson. I booked a direct flight from Reagan into Kansas City International and rented a car at the airport. Within fifteen minutes, I arrived at the prison. As I walked from the parking lot to the administrative offices, I focused on the shiny dome capping the rectangular building's rotunda. The inmates affectionately refer to Leavenworth as "The Big Top." When I entered, I passed through a metal detector before a guard escorted me to the visitors room. The duty officer asked for my identification and then logged in my name, arrival time, and date.

"Please have a seat, Mr. Micco. I'll get Floyd. It will take a few minutes."

Roosevelt had arranged for us to meet in a private room, realizing that Floyd Munson would be more apt to speak candidly in an unmonitored setting. Accompanied by a security officer, Munson entered through a door in the far corner of the room, unencumbered by either leg irons or handcuffs. As he approached me, I was impressed by my host's appearance. I had expected a round, rough, burly man with a ruddy complexion and pockmarks embedded in his face, partially camouflaged by days of stubble and an unkempt goatee. In all likelihood, his graying hair would be swept straight back in a long, braided ponytail.

"Hello, Mr. Micco. I'm Floyd Munson."

Instead, I was greeted politely by a tall, trim, man. Munson was at least six feet with short grizzled hair. A wide smile exposed his stark white teeth. I tried to return his gesture but couldn't. Reality had struck me hard. I was about to confer with a villain connected to my mother's murder. When Munson reached me, he clutched my hand with a firm grip.

At his invitation, we sat in wooden chairs opposite each other at a small round table. Munson sat erect. His attire was traditional prison garb—an orange jumpsuit with the word 'INMATE' prominently stamped on his jersey's back. I envisioned Floyd Munson dressed in a silk San Remo designer suit, a matching Gucci tie, and Louis

Vuitton boots. Although the visiting room was otherwise empty, except for the security guard who sat passively in a corner, Floyd Munson was in complete control of the universe surrounding him—given the limitations imposed on him because of his incarceration in a maximum-security prison.

"Thank you for seeing me, Mr. Munson," I said graciously.

After I expressed my gratitude, his smile closed fast. He quickly charted the course of our conversation.

"I believe in getting straight to the point, Mr. Micco," he said starkly. "First, I'm sure you understand I could have refused to have your name added to my approved visitor's list."

"Yes, I know, Mr. Munson, and I appreciate the opportunity to speak with you."

Munson glanced at the security guard who had nodded off and then returned his attention to me, relieved that what he was about to reveal would not be overheard.

"Before we begin, Mr. Micco, allow me to clarify something."

Pausing, he welded his eyes to mine, leaned back in his chair, his arms folded.

"Most people, Mr. Micco, think the Feds convicted me of violating the murder-for-hire statute. If you look closely, however, that's inaccurate."

"In what way?" I asked.

"The jury convicted me of conspiracy to violate the murder-for-hire statute. That's what separates me from the triggerman."

"Exactly what are you saying, Mr. Munson?"

"I'm saying that I was only a broker," he explained. "Whenever a client wanted someone murdered, I hired the hitman. It was only a business. Nothing more," Munson said, purging himself.

I sat back in my chair, saying nothing, wondering why Munson had agreed to meet with me and why he spoke so openly about his career as a murder broker. Placing both hands on the table, one on top of the other, Munson leaned forward and locked his steely eyes on mine.

"Mr. Micco. . ."

His cold stare numbed me.

". . . I recruited the man who killed your mother."

Frozen by his blunt admission, I suppressed my impulse to leap across the table and strangle the man sitting on the other side. I was here to squeeze information from Floyd Munson, and I wouldn't allow my thirst for retribution to distract me from my mission.

"Will you tell me the name of the assassin?"

"The names of my agents are confidential."

"Who hired you, Mr. Munson?"

"That information is also off-limits, Mr. Micco," he said, chiding me. "Let's just refer to him as my employer."

Thanks to Elisha and our midnight raid on the offices of Mendici Melrose, I knew that Leonardo Mendici had visited Munson at Leavenworth on the day of my extradition hearing. Continuing to play his chess game, I sensed that Munson was about to move one of his rooks, spoon-feeding me more information.

"I will tell you this, Mr. Micco," he said slyly. "By special invitation, my employer visited me here at Leavenworth."

"When?"

"A few months after your mother was murdered."

"And the purpose of your invitation?"

"Extortion," he admitted. "I told my employer that unless he came up with five million dollars, I would tell your father that he hired me to find a hitman to kill your mother."

"Did your employer meet your demand?" I asked.

"He said he couldn't come up with the money," he answered smugly. "Then he offered me something far less than I wanted. A measly fifty thousand."

"Your answer?"

"I told him the amount was non-negotiable."

"What did you do next?"

"I wrote a letter to your father and told him that I had information about his wife's murder."

"You invited him to visit you?" I asked, stunned.

"I did," Munson responded. "We met here about a month before he died."

I sat back, the prodigal son who never returned, regretting now, even more, my hollow relationship with Giovanni Micco—forcing my father to deal alone with the broker who hired my mother's assassin. As my eyes rested on Munson, I grappled with my conscience, realizing that if our relationship hadn't been so frayed, my father would have perhaps invited me on his trip to Leavenworth rather than face Munson alone.

"Did you reveal the identity of your employer to my father?"

"Of course not. It was my bargaining tool."

"Did you tell him you hired the assassin?"

"I did. It gave me credibility."

Feeling the pain of my mother's death, I could empathize with my father, fantasizing what he would have done to both the assassin and broker, vigilante justice being my first guess, something even I would consider.

"What did my father do?" I asked curiously.

"He wanted to strangle me," he said, mimicking, his hands raised, fingers curled. "But, like you, he maintained his composure. Giovanni Micco was after the real culprit, not me. Remember, I was only the broker."

Once again, remorse set in, a distaste I couldn't swallow. My father, a respected federal appeals court judge, forced to deal with a thug who was using him as a lure.

"I assume my father pressed you for more information?" I surmised.

"Yeah, but I didn't budge," Munson bragged, smirking. "I told him if my employer didn't honor my request, I would contact him."

"Did you tell my father that you had demanded five million dollars from your employer?"

"I did."

"What did my father say?"

"He gave me another option."

"Another option?"

"Yes. He offered me six million dollars."

It was a calculated move by my father—the implications ignored. He was playing in a game, the chips well beyond his means, banking on Uncle Claudio to finance his offer to Munson.

"So, you were now the beneficiary of a bidding war— my father versus your employer?"

"Precisely."

"What did you do?"

"What do you think?" he said, shrugging. "I called my employer and upped my demand to eight million dollars."

"His response?"

"He was outraged."

"Did he meet your demand?"

"No. He eliminated it."

It was a direct reference to my father's murder.

"My extortion plan died with Giovanni Micco," Munson added smugly.

Leaning back, my stare drilled through Munson. The reason he had agreed to see me was becoming starkly clear. I was a pawn in his plan.

"You strike me as a man of determination, Mr. Munson. I assume you had another option."

"Yes," he said, sneering. "It was a simple change. Your mother was murdered. I figured you would have the same uncompromising taste for Mosaic justice as your father. You know, 'An eye for an eye.'"

The chess game continued. Munson had just moved his second rook.

"So, you contacted your employer and substituted me in place of my father?" I surmised.

"Exactly. But the bidding war died with your father."

"Is that when your employer tried to kill me?" I asked.

"That's a reasonable assumption, Mr. Micco—but somehow, you were able to survive."

"And when that didn't work, they tried to extradite me to Italy?"

"Right again," he said. "Just think about it. I couldn't contact you if you were rotting away in a jail somewhere in Italy."

"So, I'm here now—in place of my father?"

His bulging eyes became fixed on the uninvited guest sitting across the table.

"Thanks for your visit, Francesco," he said, feigning gratitude. "It will give my employer more incentive to expedite the delivery of my money."

"Why do you need money?" I asked curiously. "You're serving two life sentences."

"The money isn't for me, Mr. Micco. I have five grandchildren. I see them only three times a year. The money is for them. One million dollars each."

Next came advice from a man in the pernicious business of killing people.

"So that you know. Be extremely careful," he advised. "Your father's death should be a sufficient warning to you."

As I pushed my chair back, its legs scratched the floor. The sound of wood sliding on wood woke the security guard. When we stood, Floyd Munson extended his right hand. I refused to acknowledge his gesture, my hatred for the man festering like an unbreakable fever. For Munson, it was an awkward moment. For me, it was a cleansing. If I'd had access to a knife, I would have satisfied my thirst for Mosaic justice by slashing a two-inch cut across his neck with exacting precision.

"I understand, Mr. Micco," he said, shaking his head. Before leaving The Big Top, I asked one last question.

"Tell me, Mr. Munson, why do you want to implicate yourself in another murder-for-hire scheme? This time you might be facing a death sentence."

"I'm seventy-five years old, Mr. Micco. By the time the government convicts me, I'll be a dead man."

I walked toward the door.

"One parting piece of information, Mr. Micco," he said, my back to him. "I do owe you something."

I faced the door; my hand was fixed on the knob.

"Remember this, Mr. Micco…"

He paused.

"… The hitman who killed your mother suffered a similar fate. That should tell you something."

"What's that?"

"If you're offered money in return for your silence— take it. You can't fight the power mongers."

CHAPTER 78

An Invitation

It was a mild October morning. Gianna and I sat on the front porch, chatting about Michele as we sipped our cappuccinos. A week had passed since I returned from Leavenworth. I'd been in New Castle tending to my law practice by day and writing by night. Sleep was a luxury. Parsing my words carefully as I spoke with Gianna, I segued into my meeting with Floyd Munson, making her aware of the dangers we faced as a family. Guido Borgese had purchased a house across the street for a sum that far exceeded its market value, and three Mafiosi were living there, providing surveillance around the clock. Gianna felt secure; at least that's what she told me—realizing that Dr. VonBronstrup and my father had immersed me in a ruse that would call me away again.

"Did you get any sleep last night?" Gianna asked.

"Just a couple of hours."

"Still writing?"

"Of course."

"Is Grazia editing for you."

"She is."

Gianna's questions relaxed me, but I assumed she was prodding. My wife was anxious for the story to end, for some normalcy to return in our lives. Unfortunately, I wasn't creating the chapters, using my imagination—just recounting events, waiting for the inevitable contact I knew was coming before I could write another chapter.

"Has Roosevelt called you?" she asked.

"Late last night."

"Did Mendici visit Munson yet?"

"Yesterday. I assume it's a done deal."

"Mendici arranged for the transfer of one million dollars for each of Munson's five grandchildren?" Gianna asked, amused, her eyes wide.

"That's my guess."

Gianna waved to a man sitting on the porch across the street, his feet propped on the railing. He waved back, giving me some comfort.

"One of your guardian angels?" I asked, grinning.

Gianna smiled, nodded, and then moved to the edge of her chair, facing me.

"Do you think it's time?" she asked, her eyes boring into mine.

"For what?"

"For you to finish the novel."

We sat, saying nothing, the silence chilling as Gianna and I surrendered to the inevitable.

———————

As my car wound through the mountains of central Pennsylvania, a kaleidoscope of exploding colors dazzled me. A soft, cool breeze signaled an early turn from a chilly autumn into a cold winter. Alone in the car, I reminisced. My thoughts drifted back to the Micco Candy Company and the time I spent with Grandpa Tony in the candy shop kitchen. I sat on a high stool, my feet dangling, watching as he filled the cavities of chocolate molds. And I listened as he encouraged me to follow my dream and become a writer. For a moment, my teary eyes drifted from the highway and onto the empty passenger seat. I glanced at a pile of papers lying there, secured by a rubber band—Chapters One through Seventy-Seven of my novel. A soft drizzle began to fall as I exited the Turnpike at the Breezewood Exchange. After a fuel stop at a Citgo station and a coffee at Starbucks, I headed south, back to Washington. I arrived in the early evening.

Struggling with my suitcase and a bag of food that Gianna had sent back with me, I climbed up three flights of stairs, turned the doorknob, and kicked open Nino's apartment door. He was sprawled out on the couch watching C-Span on his Daewoo television.

"Did your Citgo Petroleum research turn up anything?" I asked.

Nino eased himself off the couch, went to his desk, reached for his bifocals, opened the middle drawer, and slid out a stack of papers secured by a rubber band, and handed them to me.

"It's all here, Francesco," he said.

Nino had written 'Memorandum' atop the first page. The document resembled a research paper Nino prepared for my father. I was far too exhausted to suffer through the legal jargon.

"Just tell me what you found," I asked curtly.

Irritated by my shifting mood, Nino sat and swiveled his chair toward me.

"Citgo's problems began about a month ago when the President signed an executive order banning all U.S. investment and trade with Iran," he answered sharply.

"Tough new sanctions placed on Iran by the President?" I asked, mellowing, my quiet tone a veiled apology.

"They were more than tough. Essentially, the sanctions would halt any trading by American companies in Iran's oil," he answered, smiling, my contrition duly noted.

"A financial hit to domestic petroleum companies?" I asked.

"Citgo, especially."

"Why?"

Nino pointed to the memorandum, a nod to the details he had accumulated through his research, a silent suggestion that I should have taken the time to read it.

"Three months ago, Citgo signed a joint venture with the National Iranian Oil Company," he explained. "It was a deal that would dump billions into Citgo's coffers."

"The President's executive order essentially voided Citgo's deal with Iran?" I assumed.

"It did."

"And Citgo responded by filing a complaint in the federal district court in Washington?" I asked, my train of thought following the money.

"Yes—claiming an abuse of the Emergency Powers Act and a violation of the Foreign Commerce Clause of the Constitution."

"The district court denied Citgo's claim?"

"Correct. As did the D.C. Circuit."

"And the Supreme Court granted certiorari?"

"It did."

"So, Justice Sacco has the job of convincing the conservative wing of the court to reverse the district court's decision?" I asked rhetorically, my thoughts drifting back to Lester LaRouche's comment captured on the second disc by Alexandria Arnold during her black-bag-job : "*We have Sacco in our back pocket.*"

"That's an accurate assumption considering what we know," Nino answered, chuckling.

As I pondered about the President's executive order, it struck me that something had gone awry. His ban on doing business with Iran seemed to derail Lester LaRouche's plans, as well as his two co-conspirators, Luca Botti and Richard Stone. They had carefully mapped a chronology of events consisting of the burglary, manipulated intelligence, and a preemptive strike. The President's sanctions dismantled their ruse.

"What went wrong?" I asked Nino.

"I'd venture to say that the President relied on advice from the Secretary of State and didn't communicate with his foreign policy adviser."

"The President left LaRouche out of the loop?"

"Looks that way."

The sanctions were a blessing. Time was a commodity I didn't have. I planned to solve the murder mysteries, expose the ruse, write, and then deliver the disc and manuscript to someone I could trust. The President's action delayed their ploy—but the stay was only temporary.

"What will happen next?" I asked.

Nino smirked.

"Sacco will convince four other justices to reverse the district court," he surmised, "and LaRouche will give the President flawed intelligence showing that Iran is about to purchase 500 tons of uranium each year from Niger."

"And then the bombs will fall on Iran?"

"I'd say so."

"Do any other petroleum companies have deals with Iran."

"Not now or in the future." Nino answered. "That's what makes the deal worth billions. Citgo will have a monopoly on the oil market in Iran."

We sat in chairs facing each other, staring into space, contemplating our next move when my cell phone vibrated. I looked at the screen. It read: Caller Unknown. I answered it anyway.

"Hello."

"Is this Francesco Micco?"

"Yes, it is."

There was a pause.

"I will speak slowly. Meet me at 1400 Quincey Street tomorrow at 2 p.m. It's the Franciscan monastery. There will be a garden tour in progress. Join the tour, and I'll contact you."

It was the call I was waiting to receive.

CHAPTER 79

THE CATACOMBS

It was late the following morning. The apartment was stuffy, and I decided to walk down Pennsylvania Avenue and mingle with Georgetown's crowd. College students wearing their school's sweatshirts strolled the sidewalks, couples held hands, and leashed dogs were out for their morning walk. Diners sat at tables crammed on the sidewalks, munching sandwiches and sipping hot chocolates. Others, hoods slung over their heads, sat with fancy coffee drinks, their eyes glued to laptop computers as their fingers glided across the keyboards.

I walked closely behind a couple—probably tourists. Between them was a young child clinging tightly to the hands of his mother and father. For a moment, I lived vicariously. It was Gianna and me playfully walking along with Michele. On the count of three, we lifted him off the ground and high into the air, swinging him back and forth as his little legs kicked wildly in midair until he landed on his feet. The ritual repeated itself as we walked along the sidewalk. Michele's smile, along with his hearty laughter, begged us not to stop. We happily complied.

Exhausted, we finally reached an ice cream shop. It was now time to rest. The red and white candy-striped parlor pole and matching awning invited us in. Michele ordered his favorite treat—a vanilla milkshake crammed with Oreo bits and pieces. Gianna and I, less adventurous, settled for double scoops of chocolate ice cream that fell over the sides of our sugar cones. With our treats in hand, we walked outside, sat at a small table, and watched the symmetry of life unfolding around us. Like waking from a dream, my frolic into fantasy suddenly ended and I returned to reality.

"Am I on a fool's errand?" I asked myself.

Before my father had become consumed with political ambition, he would gather us weekly for a Bible study. When the lesson began, we recited the rosary. It was an experience that molded our family. For some reason, he focused on the Old Testament, especially the Book of Ecclesiastes. He said it taught a lesson "that controls our scramble for power and draws us closer to God." Reaching far back in time, I recalled the night he asked us to memorize Verse Three:

> *There is a time for everything,*
>
> *and a season for every activity under heaven:*
>
> *a time to be borne and a time to die,*
>
> *a time to plant and a time to uproot,*
>
> *a time to kill and a time to heal.*

But the last of Solomon's sage admonitions also counseled me—advice I chose to ignore:

There is a time to search,
and a time to give up.

It was one o'clock, and the time had come for me to visit 1400 Quincy Street, the Franciscan Monastery. It was about a fifteen-minute cab ride from Georgetown to the Brookland neighborhood in Washington. The Catholic University of America was on Michigan Avenue, close to the monastery. I was a half-hour early for my meeting with the anonymous caller so I decided to take a walk around the campus. As I strode along the same fieldstone pathways my parents walked when my mother was a student there, I recalled the passage Giovanni had written in his unfinished novella the night he met Rosalina:

> The room was crowded and I
> could only see the silhouette
> of a girl standing on the the
> fringe of a dimly lit room. I
> began to work my way to her.
> What was a mirage became
> real. I wanted to ask her to
> dance and I wanted the dance
> to last the rest of my life.

Not too many years later, they both lay peacefully together, side by side, in their final resting place—each the victim of a sinister murder plot. With the reality of their fate haunting me, I turned once again to the Book of Ecclesiastes, focusing this time on only one of Solomon's admonitions—*there is a time to uproot.* Now, more than ever, I was determined to weed out the culprits who murdered my parents. I vowed that retribution would be mine—no matter the means and no matter the cost.

Following the instructions given to me, I arrived at the Franciscan monastery promptly at two o'clock. Just as the anonymous caller promised, a monk was conducting a tour in the garden. I casually blended in with the crowd of people gathered before the replica of the grotto at Lourdes. After a few explanatory comments, we moved along. The young Franciscan monk conducting the tour, dressed in the traditional brown robe, secured by a white rope belt, pointed out that the Hail Mary etched into the entrance that covered the walkway "is translated into one hundred, eighty different languages." Other stops in the garden tour included the Manger at Bethlehem, the Garden of Gethsemane, and the Holy Sepulcher. Next, we moved into the chapel. As the monk entered the church, he explained that it was patterned after the Hagias Sophia, "Istanbul's renowned Byzantine Cathedral and its most famous landmark."

Once inside, we moved toward the replica of Christ's tomb. I lagged behind the group. Just as our guide began his comments, someone whispering over my shoulder asked that I walk toward the church's back row of pews, through the vestibule doors, and down a flight of stairs. I waited for the right opportunity. Separating myself from the tourists, I casually moved toward the church's rear and then into the vestibule. As promised, there was a circular staircase. I began the long walk down the steep flight of squeaky stairs when it dawned on me that I was entering the replica of the catacombs of ancient Rome—a fact I recollected because of an earlier visit to the Franciscan monastery when I was a law student at Georgetown.

I heard footsteps behind me as I walked down the stairs and descended onto the tunneled catacombs dirt floor. The same voice, now more demanding, ordered that I keep walking and not turn around. Having little choice, I complied with his demand. Adding to the ambiance was a maze of twisting tunnels dimly lit by kerosene lamps hanging from the sidewalls; empty subterranean vaults like those used by the early Christians lined the catacomb passageways. Once again, my faceless escort spoke.

"Stop when you see a chamber off to the left and go inside," he ordered softly.

I recalled my earlier tour of the catacombs. Some of the passageways had a series of private chambers set off from the low-pitched tunnel ceilings. The original underground mausoleums were privately owned vaults used by the early Christians to bury family members in stone coffins decorated with carvings and inscriptions. I took about five more steps and a chamber appeared on my left. As directed, I entered the room. It was dark. A kerosene lamp attached to an adjacent passageway wall shot a glimmer of light into the chamber. I was able to vaguely discern a silhouette—probably a man—standing in a corner. I walked closer. Separated now by only a few feet, he spoke.

"Hello, Francesco. I'm Luca Botti."

He was the host I had suspected. After instructing my escort to leave, he continued.

"Allow me first to say that I'm impressed with your perseverance—a quality many people your age lack," he began, patronizing me. "I assume you know who I am?"

"Yes, Sir, I do. I vividly recall the false testimony you gave in Judge Henderson's courtroom."

Botti ignored my sarcasm.

"I'll get directly to the point," he quickly said. "We don't have much time. There's no sense jousting back and forth. Another tour is due through here very shortly."

"I'm listening, Mr. Botti."

"You have something we want," he said starkly. "And we're willing to pay you handsomely."

"I assume you're referring to the manuscript of my father's novel," I responded, carefully omitting any mention of the disc—or *my* manuscript.

"Don't toy with me, Francesco," he cautioned. "We want the manuscript of the novel *you* are writing. But more importantly, we want the disc."

Somehow Botti knew that *I* was writing a story exposing their ruse, either through some form of secret surveillance used by the intelligence community—or perhaps from a Judas. The disc was somewhat different. Botti reasoned that I had the disc because of Alexandria Arnold's lie. He assumed that the Judge had passed it on to me.

"And if I agree to give you the manuscript and the disc…what will you give me?" I asked, my words drawled.

Botti's smile evidenced relief, but he was a cautious demagogue, carefully plotting the terms of surrender. Likewise, I was wary but determined to finalize a deal between a willing buyer and a willing seller.

"What will you get?" Botti responded, repeating my question. "Money, Francesco—lots of money. Enough to make you comfortable for a lifetime. You'll be a rich man," he announced, a lure aimed at closing the deal.

"And if I refuse your offer?" I said slyly.

"You'd be a fool," he responded sharply. "You're much too smart for that. Can't you see that even without the manuscript and disc, we're beginning to muscle our way into the Middle East?"

"Then, why are you willing to pay me money for something you don't need?" I asked casually, drawing Botti out.

"Let's just say it would be cleaner that way," he explained, shrugging. "You know—far less complicated. We wouldn't have to deal with any short-term political fallout."

Botti was hedging. And I was negotiating, assuring him that my only goal was to squeeze money from his clients.

"What about the legal repercussions the book and disc may cause if I refuse to deal with you, Mr. Botti?" I asked, continuing to negotiate, a strategy that seemed to please him.

"First, I highly doubt that a publisher will touch the book," he answered, smugly. "It would be far too risky. Our lawyers would make life miserable for them and you."

"What about the disc?" I asked, dangling my prime bargaining chip, the key to the deal.

"Same answer for the most part—only in a different context," Botti reasoned. "We'll explain to the people that our only purpose was to protect them from Middle East terrorists. That, my young friend, will be an effortless sale."

Botti looked away, staring at the carvings and inscriptions decorating the stone coffins, the glare of the kerosene lamp lighting his pale face.

"Unfortunately," he continued somberly, "you're part of the reality-based community."

"What does that mean?" I asked.

"It means this," Botti answered, musing philosophically. "People like you first take a long look at reality and then search for a solution to a problem. Face it. The world doesn't work that way anymore, Francesco."

Botti's comments were unsettling. Time was my enemy, and the need to move quickly was clear. Irrespective of the President's sanctions against Iran and the moratorium on oil deals, someone at the Pentagon was gearing up for a war. His homily continued.

"We're an empire," he said sternly, "and we must act like one. We create our reality."

"Regardless of the consequences?" I offered.

"There's always a price to pay but consider the benefits. They'll be everlasting" he envisioned before pausing. "Finally, democracy in the heart of the Middle East."

"Just what *is* your mission?" I asked.

"Let me answer your question this way," he answered briskly. "Do you consider it odd that I've asked you to meet me in a replica of the Roman catacombs?"

"Yeah, the thought crossed my mind. It's a dungeon down here."

"Well, son, there are two reasons. First, I often come to this church to pray. I meditate in these catacombs. I search for ways to bring everlasting peace to the world."

Before offering his second reason, Botti paused, a reflective moment, perhaps a short prayer asking for forgiveness before the bombs fall.

"The other reason?" I inquired.

He didn't answer my question. I remained silent, watching Botti as his eyes glistened in the dim glow of the kerosene lamps. Finally, waking from a trance, he spoke.

"I also come here, my friend, because these catacombs remind me of our mission," he mused. "In Rome, Julius Caesar outlawed the Christian religion because he considered it the enemy of Roman power. Caesar proclaimed Christianity to be *Astrana et illicita*—strange and unlawful."

He again paused his historical rant, creating a more somber mood, the willing buyer trying his best to entice a reluctant seller, relying on a passionate defense of Christianity to close the deal. He continued.

"It caused a battle, and the Romans splashed the early Christians blood on the walls of these catacombs," Botti ranted, his arms open wide. "We aim to remain faithful to that history. We, too, will do battle to save Christianity."

"What's the connection between then and now, Mr. Botti?" I asked.

"Consider the historical consequences of your visit here, Francesco," he answered, his eyes again roaming the room. "Just like these early Christians, we're on a mission from God. We're going to abolish persecution in the world and spread freedom. You, my good friend, can be part of it."

Luca Botti was playing an ideological rhapsody, and I assumed he based it on a preemptive invasion of Iran backed by scary rhetoric designed to inject fear into an unsuspecting public.

"Let me get this straight," I asked, summing up his deal. "I sell you the manuscript and disc so you can spread democracy in the Middle East, unencumbered by the truth—and in the end, we all satisfy the will of God by forcing the Muslims to become Christians?"

"You're being far too cynical, Francesco. Don't forget. There's a huge payday in this for you."

In the end, it was about money and power.

"How much do I get?"

Botti smiled.

"Ah, I'm pleased you're amenable to our solution to this little problem."

Time was short. I heard the rumblings of a crowd at the top of the staircase. Soon, the young Franciscan monk would be ushering tourists through the catacomb passageways.

"When will I hear your proposal?" I asked.

His smile widened.

"Be at Leonardo Mendici's office at eleven tomorrow morning."

CHAPTER 80

A Trusted Ally

I asked Roosevelt Ward to meet me in The Rosecross Chambers. Crowned a Knight of the Rose Croix, I enjoyed the amenities of membership, including the use of its facilities. Earlier in the day, I told Hudson D'Priest that I would be using the Chambers. Roosevelt arrived before me. I was caught in a traffic snarl. The delay gave Roosevelt time to study the mysticism shrouding the meeting room. He was mesmerized by what he saw.

"Quite an ornate place, Francesco. Friends of yours live here?"

I forced a smile.

"It's a long story, Roosevelt. Maybe someday I'll tell you. Thanks for meeting me on short notice. I'm pressed for time."

"I understand, Francesco. What's up?"

Other than Nino, Roosevelt had become my most trusted ally. I walked him through every detail that had devoured my life since the Judge's death, beginning with Lucia Lazzerini's appearance at my father's funeral and ending with my most recent meeting with Luca Botti in the catacombs of the Franciscan monastery. Lastly, I inserted the disc in the loading tray of my laptop computer. Together, we listened as Botti, Stone, and LaRouche conspire to forge a document sealing an agreement showing that the government of Niger had agreed to sell Iran 500 tons of pure uranium.

"That's some damaging stuff, Francesco," Roosevelt drawled grimly as his eyes circled The Rosecross Chambers, the disc, the ornate surroundings confounding him. As he spoke, I removed the disc from the computer's loading tray and slipped it in my coat pocket. Next, I opened my briefcase and pulled out a box secured by heavy brown twine.

"Take this, Roosevelt," I said, handing him the box. "It's a copy of an unfinished manuscript of a novel. The beginning through Chapter 79. Keep it in a safe place. If I don't survive, you'll have the only copy."

"Who's the author?" he asked curiously.

"I am."

"The plot?"

"Read it," I suggested.

"What will you do with the disc?" he asked.

"For now, I'll return it to a bank deposit box. My wife, Gianna, is listed as a co-depositor."

Roosevelt secured the package under his arm and began to stand, giving me a wary stare before sitting back in his chair.

"Something you want to tell me?' I asked suspiciously.

There was a lull as Roosevelt rested the package on his lap. A deep breath and long stare told me he was conflicted, weighing whether to tell me something that was best kept under wraps.

"What I'm about to say is classified," he said somberly, my suspicion validated. "Don't tell anyone—not even yourself."

Roosevelt leaned forward. His stare bore deeper into me.

"Our forensic lab was able to lift Leonardo Mendici's fingerprints from the medicine bottle I found in your father's cabinet," Roosevelt announced sharply.

Finally, some justice, I thought, sighing—but only if the Government prosecutes Mendici. How could the U.S. Attorney do otherwise? The fingerprint match was direct evidence that tied Leonardo Mendici to my father's murder.

"How did you make the comparison?"

"Through our database."

"What's next?" I asked.

"The Bureau is collecting evidence," Roosevelt answered. "Interviewing witnesses, asking a magistrate judge to issue a search warrant. After that, the U.S. Attorney most likely will prepare an arrest warrant charging him with murder."

"Where will the case be prosecuted?"

"In the Superior Court of the District of Columbia," Ward answered.

"When?"

"No sooner than a month from now."

Our business concluded, Roosevelt stood and cradled the box with my manuscript under his arm. We walked toward the red door, opened it, acknowledged Hudson D'Priest, and then left through his cluttered apartment. Roosevelt's car was parked at the curb. After opening the door and placing my manuscript on the passenger's seat, Ward stared at the next-door residence— Giuseppe Sabino's Brownstone.

"Is the Professor still missing?" Ward asked.

"Yes," I answered.

"Was Sabino ever a suspect?" I added.

"Not really. But I sense he's protecting someone," Ward said eerily, his eyes still riveted to Sabino's Brownstone.

"Any thoughts?" I asked.

There was a pause, the only sounds the hums of cars passing by on K Street.

"Odd," Ward mused. "Where did your mother live?" he asked curiously.

"On Days Farm Road in Northern Virginia."

Ward said nothing more, but his eyes widened as he moved his stare from Sabino's vacant Brownstone to me. We shook hands. Roosevelt closed the passenger door and walked around the car to the driver's side. I watched as his nondescript Chevrolet made its way through traffic down K Street.

CHAPTER 81

A CHOCOLATE ORDER

After an hour or so had passed, I left The Rosecross Chambers and returned to Nino's apartment on M Street. I had to finish the next chapters, even if my writing extended into the early morning hours. Because I was fascinated by a hunch, I called Grazia, recalling that the Judge had an animated telephone discussion with Salvatore Sacco while he was in Taormina. Giancarlo overheard the conversation. He described the Judge as being 'loud' and 'angry,' contrary to his mild-mannered demeanor. My father then ordered chocolates from Grazia—which Giancarlo assumed to be a peace offering for Salvatore Sacco.

"Do you recall the number of boxes he ordered, Grazia?" I asked.

"Yeah, just four."

"Did you send him the chocolates?"

"No, I didn't."

"Why?"

"First of all, he wanted a special box. It had to be bright red with a gold cross in the middle," she explained.

"And where the bars of the cross intersect, he wanted a red rose. The minimum order I could place was five hundred. The separation of colors was a real problem—and it was expensive."

"What did you do?"

"What do you think? I had my designer put something together, and then I placed the order."

"Do you remember the flavors?"

"Give me a moment to pull the file up on my computer. You seem intense about this."

I heard the clicks of Grazia's fingers sliding across the keyboard. While waiting for her answer, I recalled the riddle Dr. VonBronstrup left us: *Focus on the bonds of friendship, two severed the other intact.* While he was in Taormina, my father was immersed in the seven-day ceremonial process of becoming a Knight of the Rose Croix. Being a strict interpreter of rules, his search for a hidden truth was guided by Chapter 17 of *Confessio Fraternitatis: Thou shall not prosecute thy neighbor without the testimony of two witnesses, or two supporting documents.*

"Here it is," Grazia finally answered. "An odd order, but you know Dad. Let's see…two strawberry creams, two chocolate covered almonds, one lemon cream, one caramel, one coconut cream, and one orange cream."

"Do you know who the boxes were for?" I asked.

Again, I heard the sounds of her fingers tapping the keyboard. Soon she was back.

"Here are the names: One is H. Victor VonBronstrup, another is Uncle Claudio, and then there's a Guido Borgese."

She paused.

"There's one more name."

Another pause.

"Who?"

"You—his prodigal son."

The names intrigued me, all supposed allies, but each one with a personal agenda—Dr. VonBronstrup, his mission to reveal a hidden truth; Uncle Claudio, his connection to Luca Botti and friends still puzzling; and Guido Borgese, his strange insistence that I burglarize the Niger Embassy.

"You never shipped the chocolates?"

"No. After a short wait, I received the boxes from my vendor and packed the four he wanted. But before I shipped them, he died."

"Do you know where the boxes are now?"

"They're stored in the Phillips Mansion."

"Where in the mansion?"

"In the small room on the second floor. You know, the place where you always hid when you worked for Grandpa Tony."

I smiled as a memory ferried me back to my childhood. Reminiscing, I recalled the room in the Phillips Mansion where Grazia had stored the chocolate boxes. On the second floor, it was the smallest and most intimate room in the mansion. Three steps led down to the sunken oak-plank floor. A chandelier with tarnished brass branches hung from the ceiling. The late afternoon sun always poured a generous supply of light through twin-shuttered windows trimmed in solid oak. Decorative cornices crowned the top of each window. It was my secret asylum.

"Still editing?" I asked Grazia.

"Of course."

"What chapter are you on?"

"Seventy-Five. I'm not too far behind you."

CHAPTER 82

A Negotiated Deal

A t eleven in the morning, I was escorted into Leonardo Mendici's office by his secretary. His demeanor was pleasant but reserved—just as I had expected. He scribbled his signature on a few letters, looked up, and extended his hand as he sat behind his oversized mahogany desk. Mendici assumed a casual demeanor to neutralize my bargaining power, a tool I'm well acquainted with. No doubt, he planned to beat me down when we began to negotiate the consideration his clients would pay in return for the manuscript and disc. After exchanging salutations, Mendici started to shuffle through a neatly stacked pile of documents his secretary had carefully arranged on his desk.

"Never ends," he said, glancing over his bifocals. "Trees don't stand a chance."

I zeroed in on the charlatan who retained Floyd Munson to arrange my mother's murder. He was also the Judas who killed my father by substituting placebos in place of his potassium pills when he visited his Watergate apartment and the thug who plotted to kidnap my sister. Mendici had destroyed the Micco family, confident,

I'm sure, that the political capital he had accumulated through the years would safely escort him through any legal entanglements that he might encounter along the way. But I was determined to rip through his cocoon and quench my thirst for retribution by exposing his role in a cabal that would destroy his reign as Washington's most influential power broker.

"Glad you could come, Francesco," he said, a welcoming gesture. "I understand that you met yesterday with Luca Botti?"

I nodded while he continued to finger through the legal documents piled on his desk, observing the trappings that fed his ego—the timbered ceiling to the oriental rugs, the Pablo Picasso painting, the overstuffed black leather chairs, the gold floor lamps, and the marble-topped tables cluttered with family photographs. His greed duly noted, and the legal documents awaiting his signature having been examined and signed, Leonardo Mendici turned his attention to me.

"That's right, Mr. Mendici," I answered, grinning. "Botti and I met in the catacombs at the Franciscan Monastery. Hadn't seen him since he tried to whisk me off to a Sicilian jail for the rest of my life," I added sarcastically.

Mendici chuckled.

"Don't be too concerned about the meeting place," he said, ignoring my extradition to Italy. "Sometimes, Luca is eccentric. He says he goes to the monastery to contemplate."

"I just assumed he wanted our meeting to be private."

"Probably so, but there was no need for Luca to be so secretive," he said, shrugging. "Things, as he proposed to you, occur every day in this city. It's common."

Mendici reached for a humidor that sat on the credenza behind his desk. He unscrewed the lid and offered me a cigar.

"It's a Don Gabriel Esplendido," he bragged. "Smuggled in from Cuba. Would you like one?"

I refused politely.

"Do you mind if I light up?"

I nodded, offering no objection. Mendici snipped off the end of the cigar with a clipper, lit it, leaned back in his leather chair, and took a long drag. Whirling streams of smoke swirled high into the air before gently touching the timbered ceiling.

"Well, Francesco, allow me to tell you what I'm authorized to do on behalf of my clients," he said, resting his elbows on the desk, clenched fists propping his chin. "I understand you have a disc and a manuscript."

"I do."

Mendici would deny knowing that the disc stored incriminating statements made by his clients. He was only the broker negotiating a deal with a seller peddling an unpublished novel and a mysterious disc. I asked the question anyway.

"Do you know the reason your clients are willing to pay me for the manuscript and disc?"

"To be honest, Francesco, I don't know anything about the disc. I do know, however, that you must include it in the deal," he said firmly. "That's non-negotiable. Also, my clients want the manuscript with your promise, of course, that you will not publish the book."

"And if I agree to the terms, what do I get in return?"

He took a long drag on his Cuban cigar, leaned back in his chair, raised his head, and sent another swirl of smoke curling high into the air before answering my question.

"One million dollars. You'll soon be a rich man," he said stoically, expecting me to accept his offer without negotiation.

I knew that Mendici had stashed at least ten million dollars in the firm's office safe. Half of the money was committed to the grandchildren of Floyd Munson. He offered one million dollars to me. That left four million dollars unaccounted for—which I assumed was Mendici Melrose's fee for putting this deal together. I didn't respond to Mendici's offer. Uncomfortable, he leaned forward in his chair.

"It's a generous offer, Francesco," he said firmly, ruffled somewhat by my hesitation. "Even if you somehow get the novel published, which I seriously doubt, you'll never make that kind of money."

Leonardo Mendici knew he was not just purchasing the manuscript. Nor was he only buying the disc that linked his clients with the fictional characters in my novel. Instead, for a measly one million dollars, Mendici's clients were attempting to silence a voice that could easily thwart their Machiavellian plot.

"Well, Francesco. Is it a deal?" he asked gently, again resting his elbow on the desk, hands steepled, prodding me for an answer.

I fixed my eyes on his portrait before turning my attention back to Mendici. Again, he took a long, deep drag on his smuggled Cuban cigar. While patiently waiting for my answer, he slowly raised his head as swirls of smoke curled upward.

"I reject the offer," I said firmly, surprising Mendici.

I had made my first move. Mendici sat back in his chair as he balanced his cigar on the edge of the crystal ashtray sitting on his desk. His sharp stare slapped at my face. My rejection jarred Mendici, but the skilled negotiator, poker-faced, harnessed his anger. He had probably kept some bargaining money buried in his pocket—just in case he needed to sweeten the deal.

"Tell me what you want, Francesco," he said, trying to move the negotiations along, his voice turning soft, almost patronizing. "Everybody has a price. What's yours?"

Mendici flicked off an accumulation of white ashes dangling from his cigar, took another long drag, leaned forward, and waited for my answer.

"Yes, Mr. Mendici, I do have a price."

"Name it, Francesco."

I welded my eyes to his.

"Five million dollars."

Mendici's chin dropped. His gaping stare, mouth wide open, showed his anxiety. After resting his cigar on the crystal ashtray, he regained his composure.

"My clients will not even approach that figure," he said harshly. "They might go an extra hundred thousand or so but nothing more."

Floyd Munson taught me well.

"The figure, Mr. Mendici, is non-negotiable."

I had cornered Leonardo Mendici. His anger pushed him to adjourn our meeting. But he was reluctant to end our negotiations without consummating a deal. After investing ten million dollars, his clients expected their dilemma to disappear.

"I'm curious, Francesco," he said suspiciously, eyes squinted, folds in his brow. "Why have you placed such a ridiculous price on the manuscript and disc?"

"The price isn't high, Mr. Mendici—if you consider what your client is buying."

"My client is paying for the manuscript and disc—that's it."

"Wrong, sir, there's more. A lot more."

"What else is there?"

"You need to silence me."

"You want hush money?"

"Yes."

He squinted again, alarmed that our negotiations had taken on a cruel turn he didn't anticipate, my demand a veiled accusation suggesting that Leonardo Mendici had an interest in the deal that went well beyond his role as Botti's lawyer.

"Hush money for what?" he asked, a curious tone faking his innocence.

"For *your* part in my mother's murder."

Caught by surprise, his eyes widened like a deer caught in the glare of a car's headlights. Mendici jerked back. His complexion paled.

"You're making a wild accusation, young man," he said alarmingly, stunned by my accusation.

"I doubt that."

He reached for his cigar and took another drag, wanting, I'm sure, to call security and evict me from his office. But reason calmed his emotions, lecturing that he should hear me out, anxious as the blackjack player waiting for the next card to drop.

"Why do you think I played a part in your mother's murder?" he asked calmly.

I answered his question with one of my own.

"Do you recall our meeting with Luther Ash?"

"I do."

"Do you recall the name of the hitman his agents found murdered that day on 20th Street?"

"No, I don't."

"Allow me to refresh your recollection. The hitman's name was Carlton Frisk."

"Why is Frisk part of our conversation?" Mendici asked nervously, his pale face white as a ghost.

"Because he was the hit-man who slashed my mother's throat."

Mendici could see past the bend in the road, knowing that I had visited Floyd Munson at Leavenworth, the chain of command now readily apparent—Mendici, Munson, Frisk— the trifecta responsible for my mother's murder. Somehow, he reclaimed a calm demeanor, the tactic of a skilled negotiator, the poker player whose eyes are hard to read.

"How do you know that?" he asked.

"Something I learned at Leavenworth."

My trip to the federal prison was not a surprise to Mendici. It was the wedge Munson used to seal his deal, a meeting that seemingly didn't alarm Mendici, confident that his broker played by the rules and didn't identify him as the employer.

"Do you know Floyd Munson?" I asked calmly.

"No," he said, answering quickly, leaving no room to wiggle out of a lie.

"You're not being candid with me, Mr. Mendici— unless you visited another inmate at Leavenworth."

His mouth opened wide again, a reflex he couldn't control but quickly overcame by asking a question.

"How do you know that I visited Leavenworth?" Mendici asked.

"Funny how a C-note buys favors. A clerk there allowed me to glance at Munson's visitor log," I answered, garnishing the truth, not wanting to implicate Elisha. Mendici squirmed, reached for his Don Gabriel Espiendido, flicked off the ashes, placed it back on his crystal ashtray without taking a drag—caught in a lie that destroyed his bargaining position.

"What did Munson tell you?"

"Only that he was the broker who hired the assassin to kill my mother."

"Did he tell you anything else?"

"Just that he had asked someone—he referred to him as his employer—to pay him five million dollars of hush money."

"And *if* his employer didn't come up with the extortion money?" Mendici asked.

"Then, he would tell my father that *you* hired him to employ the assassin who killed my mother."

"You're saying I'm the employer who hired Munson?"

"I am."

"You're guessing."

"Not really. Why else would you travel to Leavenworth twice and meet with Floyd Munson?"

I wasn't 'guessing' as Mendici well knew, but still, I couldn't prove that he employed the broker. Cash silenced Munson, and Frisk was dead. I stared at Mendici. Something baffled me.

"Why were you so careless, Mr. Mendici?" I asked.

"What do you mean?"

"Traveling twice to Leavenworth. Signing the log-in book. Showing the whole world that you had visited a convicted felon."

Mendici leaned back in his chair and stared at his smuggled Don Gabriel Esplendidpos cigar. It had been reduced to a pile of smoldering ashes. He didn't respond to my question, but I knew the answer. The circle of conspirators was small, and his associates at Blackwell & Juliano were reluctant to expand it, forcing him to deal directly with Floyd Munson.

"Where can I contact you?" Mendici asked starkly.

"I'm returning home to New Castle, Mr. Mendici. I've been away from my family far too long."

After I left the offices of Mendici Melrose, I mailed a package at a post office on Pennsylvania Avenue in Georgetown. I had addressed it to Roosevelt Ward. It was Chapters Eighty and Eighty-One of my manuscript. I also mailed an invitation to the culprit who set in motion the chain of events that led to my mother's murder.

———

It was a beautiful autumn afternoon, so I decided to walk back to Nino's apartment on M Street. My pace was slow. I basked in the sun, cooled by the crisp fall air, marveling at the leaves, not long ago ablaze with color, now a musty brown, hanging tenaciously to their branches.

Soon even the stragglers would fall listlessly to the cold earth. The cycle of life, I thought.

Within an hour, I returned to Nino's apartment. I called Elisha to say good-bye. There was no answer. It's better that way, I thought. Alone, I sat my weary body down on Nino's couch and reflected on the convoluted events that had consumed my life over the past few months. Tomorrow I would outline Chapter 82, treat Nino to lasagna at Luigi's in the evening, and then gather my belongings. In mid-afternoon the following day, I'd return to New Castle—far from the person I was months ago when I had left home to begin the hunt for the assassins who murdered my mother.

As for Giovanni Micco, I now realized that he was a devoted father although he tempered love with a strict discipline that I sadly refused to accept. Selfishly, I thought that he should surrender his dream to become a Supreme Court Justice and cater to my whimsical demands. I wasn't fair with my father. Yet, ignoring Grazia and Giancarlo, he chose me to seek out the assassins who killed his soulmate. I would not disappoint him. In two days, I'd head home to New Castle. The chess pieces were in place. Let the game begin.

CHAPTER 83

THE PHILLIPS MANSION

It was seven o'clock in the evening. After dinner, Gianna and I cleared the table. Together we stacked the dishes in the sink. She rinsed, and I loaded the dishwasher. After tucking Michele in bed, we sat together in the living room. There was a nervous interlude before Gianna broke the silence.

"Will he come?" she asked.

"I sent him an invitation."

"But will he come?"

"I gave him a good reason."

It was now nearing nine o'clock, time for me to leave. We hugged. I backed the car out of the garage and headed down Albert Street, made a right onto Garfield and then to Mercer, Gianna's question echoing all the while—*Will he come*?

It was beginning to drizzle. I switched on the windshield wipers as I drove down Mercer toward Wallace, wondering whether the invitation engraved with The Rosecross would urge him to come—the courier charged with the task of delivering the blood money. From Wallace, I turned left and coasted down Jefferson Street Hill to Craig, hope my buoy, fear its partner. I was now close. From Craig, I made a left onto Beaver, and then a quick right onto Phillips Place.

Only one streetlight hung from a telephone pole. The brick street was narrow, and the string of vehicles parked bumper to bumper along one side allowed cars to pass through in only one direction. The Phillips Mansion sat on a steep hill above Phillips Place. I parked my car on the lower side of the street and walked up two steps to the elevated sidewalk in front of the mansion—the same two steps I scampered up when Rosalina drove me to work when I was in fifth grade.

I walked up the broad flight of stairs that led to the first landing and then up to the porch. The worn, black-slate blocks remained solidly fixed in place. Once on the porch, I unlocked the door and entered the spacious vestibule— the hub to the building's cavernous wings. Although the mansion was cold and dark, I felt the warmth of Grandpa and Grandma. After lighting the night lamp, I glimpsed down at Phillips Place and, through the darkness, saw my mother wave good-bye. She threw me a kiss, entered her car, and drove away.

Once inside the mansion, and guided by the glimmer of a flashlight, I walked up the long, steep flight of stairs that led to the hideaway that I had used as a sanctuary when I was a young employee of the Micco Candy Company. After carefully making my way down a narrow hallway, I stepped down three stairs into the sunken room. I shined a small circle of light around the walls. It was cluttered with piles of brown stock boxes tied together with heavy twine. Pushed against the windows was a small table and chair that captured my attention. As suggested by Grazia, I didn't use the room to hide from work. Insisting that I use my free moments to read, Rosalina had purchased the table and chair at a rummage sale. Alone—the Judge was always too busy devoting time to his law practice—she maneuvered the desk, step by step, up the long, steep flight of stairs, dragged it into the room, and placed it in front of two tall windows facing the room, leaving space for a chair. I followed her up the stairs, carrying the chair. I could still hear her soft voice:

"Now, you have a place to read and a place to study when you're not busy."

More than twenty years had logged their way into eternity, and the warmth of my mother's love remained alive in the Phillips Mansion. It was time, however, to shove sentimentality aside. Somewhere here, Grazia had stored the chocolates ordered by the Judge. With one hand, I held the flashlight, and, with the other, I tore open three, maybe four, containers packaged in brown wrapping paper. Scribbled on the outside of the containers in bold black letters was the word "ZAMBELLI." I ripped open the containers and found the private label boxes of an old customer—the Zambelli Fireworks Company, the First Family of Fireworks. Zambelli had changed its design years ago. Grazia had probably stowed them away as relics she'd resurrect whenever she decided to write a pictorial history of the Micco Candy Company.

Finally, tucked in a corner, I found the container that held the bright red boxes. I removed one. A gold cross with a red rose etched into the center of the intersecting bars decorated the lid. Rummaging through the paper container, I found four boxes wrapped in brown paper and ready for mailing. Grazia never shipped them because the Judge had died. She addressed the packages to H. Victor VonBronstrup, Claudio Armondi, Guido Borgese—and Francesco Micco.

Respecting the privacy of the others, I removed only the package addressed to me. My chair remained stored under the table. It hadn't been disturbed for years. Before sitting, I wiped off layers of dust. I set the flashlight down, unwrapped the package, and opened the box. It was rectangular, no more than ten by two inches. I stared at the lid. My eyes dwelled on the gold cross with the red rose etched into the intersecting bars. Packed inside were eight chocolate pieces lined-up in order. One-by-one, I removed first three pieces—a strawberry cream, then a chocolate-covered almond, and last, a lemon cream.

It was hauntingly quiet as I removed the five remaining pieces from the box. But the still of the Phillips Mansion was soon disturbed by the squeaky sounds of the Palladian door's hinges. I doused my flashlight, sat back in my chair, and listened to the night's sounds. The footsteps were barely audible. Disturbing the quiet slightly, my visitor, walking softly on the oak floor, moved with an even cadence across the vestibule and, finally, to the landing of the steep, long staircase. Hampered by darkness, my visitor's climb began.

Soon, the footsteps became louder. A flashlight's glare brightened the hallway. My visitor had reached the threshold at the top of the staircase. The footsteps became more pronounced. The light's long beam now shined into the room. A silhouette stood in the doorway as the flashlight was moved up and down, back and forth. Suddenly, the glare trapped me in a circle of light.

"Ah, Francesco. There you are."

The flashlight's beam moved from my face onto the table. I stared at the pieces of chocolates lined up before me. The strawberry cream—the 'S'; the chocolate covered almond —the 'A'; the lemon cream—the 'L.' The first name of my guest— SAL. The Judge used the same code—his Pythagorean Chart—to spell the last word. The other strawberry cream, the second almond nut; the caramel cream; the coconut cream, and finally, the orange cream— SACCO! Just as I had expected, my father became suspicious of Justice Sacco after they had spoken on the telephone when the Judge was in Taormina. *"I don't think you're truthful with me,"* and *"the professor won't return my calls,"* the words overhead by Giancarlo.

Recognizing that he might meet an early demise, my father devised his version of the Freemason's Magical Square. He then asked Grazia to mail the chocolates to his friends, giving them a clue to his suspicion. Not knowing their significance, Grazia stored them in the Phillips Mansion. Unfortunately, just as the Judge anticipated, he was murdered before he was able to expose Justice Salvatore Sacco.

"Welcome to the Phillips Mansion, Justice Sacco," I said.

"Thank you for hosting me tonight, Francesco," he responded. "And I thank you for leaving the Palladian door open. The night lamp in the vestibule helped. Luckily, I brought a flashlight."

He shined it around, canvassing the room.

"I haven't been here since Giovanni gave me a guided tour years ago," he continued. "It was kind of you to reciprocate."

He was referring to the note he had sent me:

> Meet me in the parking lot in front of the
> Klingle Mansion in Rock Creek Park at 3 a.m.
> I have information that may save your life.
> Come alone.

My invitation was similar:

> Meet me on the second floor of the
> Phillips Mansion on Phillips Place in
> New Castle at 10 p.m. next Tuesday. I
> have information connecting my mother's
> murder to a burglary and a disc.
> Come alone.

He stepped down the three stairs leading into the room, moving in closer. To get him here, I decided to dangle a lure—the disc. I knew that Mendici and Sacco would confer and that Mendici would suggest that he accept my invitation, the two traitors plotting a joint venture.

"Your invitation intrigued me, Francesco," he said calmly. "Why did you invite me?"

I stared at his silhouette. He held the flashlight in one hand. The other arm dangled in the shadow. He was holding something.

"Because you, sir, set in motion the wheels that led to my mother's murder," I answered bluntly.

Probably having been warned by Mendici, Sacco maintained his composure, as would most suspects, hiding his guilt but tempted by curiosity, the accused anxious to hear whatever evidence I was prepared to offer.

"Don't accuse me unless you can support a conviction, Francesco," he lectured briskly. "It's called the burden of proof."

Lawyer talk.

"I *can* meet my burden, Justice Sacco."

"Your burden is high, my friend," he said, inching closer, remarkably calm for a Supreme Court Justice doing the bidding for a den of crooks.

"Let's make it 'proof beyond a reasonable doubt,'" he suggested.

More legal jargon.

"That's an appropriate burden since we're dealing with a murder," I answered, needling Sacco.

He shined the flashlight in my face—the judge banging his gavel, directing that I present my evidence. First, he asked a question.

"So, you've solved the murder mystery?" he sneered.

"I did."

He raised his arm.

The flashlight blinded me.

I shadowed my eyes.

"How?" Sacco asked sharply.

I stood, leaned over my desk, the lawyer about to argue his case, a bench trial, no jury, Sacco the judge—and the accused.

"By building my case—piece by piece," I responded soberly.

"The first piece?" Sacco asked.

I realized that my burden was a hill too steep to climb—hearsay, speculation, relevancy, the objections made by a competent litigator that would exclude much of the evidence that I had gathered. In a court-room setting, a judge would dismiss my case, and he'd be right. Nevertheless, I began.

"I recalled my meeting with the Attorney General and your friend, Leonardo Mendici," I said, beginning my argument in an orderly fashion. "Luther Ash volunteered some telling information."

"Information that incriminates me?" Sacco asked, prodding.

"Not necessarily—but what he said led me to your role in the murder plot."

"What did he say?" Sacco asked anxiously.

"He told me that Professor Giuseppe Sabino was eavesdropping on a conversation at the NEF seminar he attended with my mother the night before she was murdered."

It was a fact I could prove, through Luther Ash or anyone else at the seminar who noticed Professor Sabino leaning into the conversation between Stone and Botti. Whatever they were saying was the lynchpin that tied Sacco to my mother's murder.

"Eavesdropping on whom?" he asked.

"On a conversation between Richard Stone and a mole standing at a bar during the NEF seminar. Evidentially, Stone drank too much—and talked too much."

"What did Stone say?" Sacco said, testing me.

I had pricked his curiosity. Sacco knew that a trial judge would exclude my account of the conversation between Professor Sabino and my mother as being either speculative or hearsay. The legal objections ignored by Justice Sacco, I satisfied his interest.

"Sabino told my mother what he overheard—that the disc the government refused to turn over to my father in the Rosen case was evidence of manipulated intelligence."

Through the darkness, I could almost feel Sacco cringe at the sheer mention of the disc. Just as I had expected, it was the magnet that drew him to the Phillips Mansion.

"Did Sabino tell your mother anything else?" Sacco asked nervously.

"Just that she should inform my father about the information stored on the disc when he returned from the Virgin Islands the following day."

Being embedded with Mendici, Sacco had heard of the disc, probably countless times, shocked at the exchange between Stone and LaRouche, afraid that it would tarnish his judicial career:

> *Stone: I hear ramblings about the President signing a regulation voiding all oil deals with Iran.*
>
> *LaRouche: Don't worry, we have Sacco in our back pocket.*

"Your mother knew about the disc the Government refused to turn over to your father in the Rosen case?" Sacco asked surprised.

"Yes."

"How?" he inquired.

I told Sacco about the note Nino and I had found when we visited the law library at George Washington University. My father's words were then confusing, but now crystal clear: *Unfortunately, I told your mother about a disc the government refused to give me in the Rosen case. Ask Professor Sabino about it. He has been on an extended sabbatical, and I have been unable to contact him.*

"Would you like to see the note?" I asked, reaching into my pocket.

"No," Sacco answered quickly, pondering before he continued. "Have you spoken to Professor Sabino?" he finally asked, a crucial inquiry, knowing that Professor Sabino was the lynchpin to his demise.

"Sabino fled somewhere, and he can't be found," I answered, playing Sacco's game, the Professor's disappearance no surprise to Sacco.

"Why did he flee?" Sacco asked, testing me.

"Probably because he lied to the agents who interviewed him the day following the murder."

"Lied about what?" Sacco asked, alarmed, realizing that I was on to something.

Being a lawyer, I knew that evidentiary rules riddled my mother's case with legal impediments caused mostly by Sabino's disappearance and the five million dollars that silenced Floyd Munson. Both Mendici and Sacco were beyond the reach of the law, their immunity from prosecution purchased by power, money, and greed. Nevertheless, I plotted along, conducting my kangaroo court, answering his question with one of my own.

"Where do you live, sir?" I asked.

It was a question prompted by my recent meeting with Roosevelt Ward in The Rosecross Chambers on K Street. At first, I was puzzled while Roosevelt stared incessantly at the Professor's Brownstone, but after some thought, I figured out the reason for his fascination with Giuseppe Sabino's residence and my mother's home.

"An odd question," Sacco commented. "But I'll play your silly game. I live in McLean."

"Where did my mother live?" I inquired.

"In Vienna."

"Near you?"

"As the crow flies."

"Do you know where Professor Sabino lived?"

"I have no idea," Sacco answered, still baffled.

"2111 K Street. Next door to Victor VonBronstrup."

"Frankly, I couldn't care less," Sacco commented flippantly. "If I were the trial judge, I would rule any evidence related to Sabino's address as irrelevant."

"Perhaps your ruling would be too impulsive," I suggested.

"Too impulsive? I doubt it," he chuckled arrogantly. "But I'll give you some leeway, counselor. Now, impress me. Establish the relevancy of Sabino's address to my involvement in your mother's murder."

"Do you recall our meeting at the Klingle Mansion?" I asked.

"I do."

"You told me that Roosevelt Ward had interviewed you about my mother's murder."

"I did."

"What did Ward ask you?"

"He asked if I spoke with either Sabino or your mother at the NEF seminar."

"Your answer?"

"I told him no."

"What else did you tell him?"

"That we left together, rode the elevator to the parking garage level, and said good-night. Professor Sabino and your mother went to their car. I went to mine."

I moved from the desk and took a step toward Sacco. He backed onto the first step leading into the room as he leaned down and retrieved a large briefcase he had laid on the floor adjacent to the doorway.

"Don't you think it odd that Professor Sabino would drive my mother to Vienna and then return to Washington when you could have easily driven her home and then make the short trip to McLean?" I asked, sneering, my words drawled as Sacco backed up the last step and into the hallway, briefcase in hand.

"You think *I* drove your mother home that night?" he surmised nervously.

"I do."

"That's absurd," Sacco said glibly, glossing over my tease. "Read the statement Sabino gave to the Virginia police. The Professor said *he* drove your mother to Vienna."

Without Sabino, I couldn't prove what I knew to be true. Luca Botti threatened the Professor, enticed him to lie, and then stowed him away somewhere—another murder being far too suspicious and much too risky.

"*You* drove my mother home," I said accusingly. "And on the way to Vienna, she told you about the conversation Professor Sabino had overheard."

"Your wild imagination fascinates me, Francesco," Sacco commented, quivering, eyes sprung wide. "What else did she tell me?" he asked, prodding anxiously, backing further down the hallway as I climbed up the short set of steps.

"That when my father returned from the Virgin Islands the following day, she planned to tell him that the disc the government refused to give him in the Rosen case was evidence of manipulated intelligence."

For Sacco, it was speculation, all conjecture, the fantasy of an amateur sleuth. But the twitch in his eyes, the hissing breadth, told me that I had caught him.

"How does that connect me to your mother's murder?" he asked uneasily, backing further down the hallway, stumbling, the briefcase hanging from his hand, the flashlight blinding as I moved in closer.

"When you returned home that night, you alerted Leonardo Mendici," I answered calmly.

"Why would I call Mendici?" he blurted quickly.

"For two reasons."

"Enlighten me," he asked smugly, trying to mask his anxiety.

"First, because you owe him."

"For what?"

"Consider this, Sir. You have an insatiable appetite for prestige," I answered, my sinister stare intimidating, backing Sacco further down the hallway as I moved closer to him. "When the President nominated my father, *your* chance of becoming a Supreme Court Justice came to an abrupt end."

"And so?"

"You had to do something—and fast. You took a look at the ages of the sitting Justices and concluded there would not be another vacancy for years," I continued, piecing together strands of evidence Sacco knew to be true. "You would be left stranded on the Court of Appeals while Giovanni Micco basked in the glare of the Supreme Court. That wasn't good enough for Salvatore Sacco."

He backed further down the hallway, listening as I supported speculation with facts and drew conclusions he knew to be true.

"You contacted Mendici. After all, he owed you a huge favor," I reasoned, moving even closer to Sacco. "Through your efforts, he corralled NEF as a client for Mendici Melrose when you were the EEOC chairman. The two of you then contrived a plan."

"A conspiracy?"

"You could say that."

"What did Mendici do?"

"He called one of his friends on the Senate Judiciary Committee and leaked my father's relationship with Claudio Armondi."

"And the President nominated me for a seat on the Supreme Court instead of your father?"

"Exactly."

We now stood almost face-to-face in the hallway, the darkness and silence intimidating. I said nothing, coaxing him to ask the next question.

"And the second reason I contacted Mendici?"

"You knew Mendici aligned himself with a cabal planning a preemptive strike of Iran."

"How can you prove that?"

"It's all on the disc."

"What did Mendici do?"

"He contacted the broker who hired Carlton Fisk. Fisk then paid a visit the following morning to my mother at our home on Days Farm Road."

Justice Sacco had reached the threshold of the staircase. He wanted out of the Phillips Mansion.

"Now that I've heard your theory, Francesco, let's consummate a deal," he suggested, his voice still quivering. "But remember one thing. What you have just told me is nothing more than conjecture." I offered no response, realizing regretfully that Sacco was beyond the reach of the law.

"This is for you, Francesco," Sacco said nervously, raising the briefcase.

I moved closer.

"Your demand has been met," he said, smirking. "There's fifty thousand dollars in this briefcase. More than four million is in the trunk of my car. Now, get me the disc and manuscript."

I shrugged.

"Here you stand, Salvatore Sacco, a Justice of the United States Supreme Court—the errand boy for Leonardo Mendici and his band of thugs."

He reached out.

"Here, Francesco, take the money," he said hurriedly, extending his arms, the briefcase almost touching my face. "Get me the disc and manuscript. I'll give you the rest of the money and be gone."

Standing at the top of the staircase, once again he offered me the money.

"Here, take it," he insisted.

Blinded by vengeance, I pushed on Justice Sacco's shoulders with the palms of my hands. His eyes spread wide open. Tightly clutching the briefcase close to his chest, he fell backward. With a deadly thud, his head struck squarely on a tread of the staircase. His legs somersaulted over his head as he began the long roll down the steep staircase. I heard the echoing shouts of excruciating pain as his head struck the balusters and the stair's treads. His twisted body finally reached the bottom. I tightly grabbed hold of the baluster that secured the spindled railing and watched as Sacco came to rest on the staircase's landing.

A still haunted the mansion. I slowly made my way down the flight of stairs, step by step. Finally, I reached Salvatore Sacco. Blood oozed from his mouth and nose. His open eyes looked eerily into mine. I took his pulse. There was none. Salvatore Sacco was dead. His arms remained wrapped around the money purse. Blood spilling from his mouth and nose saturated the money purse. I unfolded his arms and took possession of the fifty thousand dollars. I now had the manuscript, the disc, and the money. Before calling 911, I removed the car keys from his suit coat pocket, opened the Palladian door, walked down the steps, removed the money from the trunk, and stored my cache in the upstairs room. The following day the lead story in the *Washington Post* reported the untimely death of Salvatore Sacco:

> WASHINGTON: United States Supreme Court Justice Salvatore Sacco died yesterday following a fall down a flight of stairs while visiting family friends. Justice Sacco, rumored to be the next Chief Justice, was touring the storage facility of the Micco Candy Company in New Castle, Pa. The company is owned and operated by a daughter of Judge Giovanni Micco, an appeals court judge who, before his recent death, sat on the Court of Appeals for the District of Columbia. Justice Sacco and Judge Micco were close friends, and their relationship extended back many years. Francesco Micco, a son of Judge Micco, was with Justice Sacco when he fell down the flight of stairs. "It was dark, and Justice Sacco lost his footing on the first step. There was nothing I could do." Micco, an attorney, also said that the Justice's untimely death

"was a great loss to the federal judiciary."
He described Justice Sacco as a close family
friend "who will be missed by his family,
friends, and legal community."

One down.

CHAPTER 84

ENDINGS

B eing a family friend, the clerk of courts invited me to represent the Micco family at Justice Sacco's public viewing. At nine in the morning, I arrived at the Supreme Court building as six marine guards in full dress blues carried Justice Sacco's flag-draped coffin up the long, marble sweep of stairs in halting steps. The procession passed through the mammoth bronze doors and then into the columned room where the body of Supreme Court Justice Salvatore Sacco would lie in state for two hours. Once inside, the marine guards placed his coffin on the same catafalque hastily constructed for President Abraham Lincoln in 1865. It was draped in black velvet. The President had ordered that flags fly at half-staff.

His colleagues on the Court, staff members, and the full array of law clerks who served him during his tenure on the bench lined his coffin. A portrait of Justice Sacco rested on a tripod at the head of the casket. Public viewing would end at eleven o'clock. At noon, Cardinal Theodore McCarrick would celebrate a Mass of Christian Burial at St. Matthew's Cathedral; interment would follow in Arlington National Cemetery.

I sat in a section of the corridor reserved for guests. Soon I saw a familiar face in the line of public mourners approaching the bier. It was Giacomo—my partner in crime. Our eyes met. He motioned for me to join him and then slowly walked away. I excused myself, surprised to see him.

"Follow me, Francesco," he said when I had reached him.

We moved across the columned corridor, through the massive bronze doors, down the marble stairs, and into the back seat of a black Lincoln sedan. Giacomo motioned for the driver to leave. I thought it unusual that a mafioso, especially one who had participated in the Niger Embassy burglary in Rome, would be assigned a mission that involved me in the United States. As far as I knew, the Mafia's role in the ruse was only to provide Antonio LeDonne with official seals and stationery of the Nigerian government. Uneasy, his eyes focused on me.

"We must act fast," he said urgently. "LeDonne has provided sensitive information to my family's boss. He passed it on to La Cosa Nostra, and its boss sent it to Guido Borgese."

"Information about what?" I asked, wide-eyed, befuddled.

"A preemptive strike on Iran that must be stopped," Guido answered quickly.

"Why isn't Borgese here?" I asked, apprehensive about Giacomo's strange assignment, and thinking it odd that he knew I would be attending Sacco's funeral.

"He's in Lampedusa," Giacomo explained, "delivering money for Sanita per la Famiglia's hospital project on the island."

"Guido couldn't make it to Washington?" I repeated, still suspicious of Giacomo's sudden appearance at Sacco's public viewing.

"It was impossible for Guido to be here," Giacomo answered quickly. "Time is of the essence. It's a nine-hour ferry ride from Lampedusa to mainland Sicily."

Initially, the Mafia's role was to provide LeDonne the tools to forge a document, get paid its fee, and then move on to other nefarious affairs. But La Camorra apparently shifted gears and turned its attention to more honorable projects—perhaps because of Guido Borgese, his tie to Claudio Armondi, and the mission of The Rosecross. Nevertheless, the inconsistencies were piling up. Why would the Mafia provide the documents supporting a preemptive strike on a foreign sovereign—and then suddenly shift sides?

"What specific information did LeDonne pass on to La Camorra?" I asked.

"His sources say that the President will soon address Congress seeking authorization for a military strike on Iran," Giacomo responded. "He'll support his request for a joint resolution by using the forged document LeDonne sold to LaRouche during our meeting at the Hotel De Russie in Rome."

"When will the strike take place?" I asked, thinking that LeDonne had regretted his role in a plot that could cost countless lives. Painfully, I, too, thoughtlessly played a part in the ruse.

"I don't know when the bombs will fall," Giacomo answered, shrugging. "But Guido told me you had a disc that could stop the war. We have a way to get it into the hands of the President."

"How do we get the disc into The White House?" I asked, confused, conflicted, weighing my options, but reasoning it best to cooperate with Giacomo. The Mafia and LeDonne, for some unknown reason, were now trying to counteract the effect of the Niger embassy burglary. Perhaps it was the mystic powers of H. Victor VonBronstrup at work.

"According to Guido, your father met a man every Sunday at the Vietnam War Memorial," Giacomo explained. "His name is Alfonso Atkins. His son served with Claudio and your father in 'Nam. Unfortunately, the Atkins boy was killed in the war."

"How can Atkins help?"

"He works in the White House—on the service staff. He serves dinner to the First Family. Guido thinks that if we give him the disc, he can give it to the President."

"Putting the President on notice that LaRouche based the invasion of Iran on manufactured evidence?" I asked skeptically.

"Exactly."

"When do we meet Atkins?"

"Tomorrow."

"What time?"

"Ten in the morning."

"Where?"

"At the Vietnam Veterans Memorial Wall. I'll make contact with him and make arrangements."

My cell phone rang. I looked at my caller ID. It was Elisha. I had expected her to be at Justice Sacco's public viewing, but she wasn't there. More surprisedly, Leonardi Mendici's chair in the section reserved for guests was vacant. I tapped the 'answer' prompt.

"Hi, Elisha."

"Francesco, where are you?" she asked hastily, her voice frantic.

"On Constitution Avenue."

"Thank God you're in Washington, Francesco. I must see you—immediately. Please take a cab to my apartment."

"What's the problem?"

"All hell has broken out at the firm."

"Why"

"The FBI has just arrested Leonardo Mendici."

"Are you in any danger?"

"I am," she answered, quivering, an excited answer that alarmed me. "After the agents led Mendici out of the building in handcuffs, his secretary called and said she wanted to see me immediately."

"What did you do?"

"I was afraid. I hurried out of the building," she said frantically. "As I was leaving, Charles—the security officer—pulled me aside and told me that earlier in the day, Mendici had asked to see the security logs and video tapes on the dates I had checked into the building."

"Why?"

"Because when the agents searched his safe they probably found his cache of placebos."

"You were the main suspect?"

"Yes. He knew about our relationship."

"What's your plan?" I asked easily, trying to calm her.

"I'm going back to Boston—now."

I was surprised that Elisha called me; a cab ride would have been the fastest escape route to the airport. But she was leaving Washington, and I would return to New Castle. All she wanted was a final moment with me, I surmised. I shared her sentiment.

"Did Mendici suspect you helped me track down Floyd Munson?"

"He did."

"I assume Mendici reviewed the video tapes and saw you and I enter the building together?"

"Yes, Francesco. Please hurry," she urged. "He'll post bail later today."

"I'll be there in ten minutes."

I gave Giacomo Elisha's address. He moved to the front seat and asked the chauffeur to drive me there. It was a short ride to U Street. Leaving our relationship to his imagination, I explained to Giacomo that Elisha was a friend who worked for a large Washington law firm, Mendici Melrose. When we arrived at the Ellington Apartments, I raced into the lobby, dialed 301, and rode the elevator to the third floor. Hurriedly, I walked down the corridor toward Elisha's apartment, rang the buzzer, and identified myself. She opened the door, waved me inside, and quickly closed it. A travel bag sat in the hallway.

"Can you get me to Dulles? My flight leaves in two hours," she asked hurriedly.

"Of course."

I extended the handle of her travel bag and rolled it toward the elevator as she locked her apartment door. We rode down to the lobby, pushed through the revolving door, and walked toward the Lincoln sedan parked at the curb. The chauffeur lifted her travel bag into the trunk and then opened the door. She slid to the middle. I sat next to her and reached for her hand. Our eyes met, but we said nothing.

As the limousine slowly maneuvered through a typical Washington traffic snarl, Elisha and I stared out the same window and watched the city, abuzz with activity, pass by. It gave me time to think. Once again, Elisha would walk out of my life. I suspected she'd join her father's investment banking firm. A wise choice—provided Franklin Forde separated himself from his daughter's personal life. When we reached Dulles, the chauffeur hugged the curb in front of the USAir terminal and then brought the limousine to a gradual stop. He removed Elisha's travel bag from the trunk. I accompanied her into the airport. She had her boarding pass. We reached the security lane. It was short. Elisha turned toward me. Her eyes met mine as tears creased her blushed cheeks. I softly wiped them away and then reached for her hands. Her touch invited me to move closer. We caressed and gently kissed. She pushed me back but then embraced me, her head resting on my shoulders, her hair brushing against my cheek.

"I'll always love you," she whispered.

She broke our embrace. I moved toward her, but she backed away. Without turning, Elisha walked down the security aisle and passed through the metal detector. Rolling her travel bag, she moved down a ramp but stopped as a ray of sun burned through a window and touched her hair. She looked back, waved, and then walked out of my life. I never saw Elisha Ford again.

CHAPTER 85

THE VIETNAM WAR MEMORIAL

The names were endless, more than fifty-eight thousand, all carved into two V-shaped walls, sloping to the ground from a ten-foot apex. The soldiers whose names appeared on this monument were comrades, warriors—all brothers and sisters. I stood at the Vietnam Veterans Memorial with Giacomo. It was ten o'clock on Sunday morning. A cold November drizzle was falling, and water beads rolled down the polished black granite, most of the drizzles swallowed by the inscriptions. A tall, African-American man stood motionless about twenty feet away. Holding a long-stemmed red rose in both hands, he fixed his stare on the black granite wall. Then he moved forward, laid the rose at the foot of the memorial, stood back, and placed the palm of his hand on the wet wall.

"Is that Alfonso Atkins?" I quietly asked Giacomo.

"That's him," Giacomo responded, his eyes fixed on Atkins. "I drove him here about ten minutes ago. Thought he would appreciate a ride rather than taking the Metro."

We watched as Atkins slowly ran his gloved hand down the wall before placing it in the pockets of his trench coat, his other hand clutching an umbrella.

"On the way here, he told me that your father was Leonard's commanding officer," Giacomo explained. "He wrote a tribute letter to Alfonso after Leonard was killed."

"Did you inquire how Atkins met my father?"

"I did," Giacomo answered, nodding. "When the President appointed your father to the appeals court, he visited Alfonso in Washington. They remained in contact with each other and, when your father moved to the Watergate, they became friends."

"Did they agree to meet here each Sunday?"

"No. It happened fortuitously. Your father visited the Vietnam Memorial frequently. One Sunday, he saw Alfonso here—purely by chance. After that, they met every Sunday at ten in the morning."

"Did Atkins tell you why he chose to lay a red rose beneath his son's name?"

"No," Giacomo said, his eyes still on Atkins "Just that your father made arrangements for a long-stemmed red rose to be delivered to him every Saturday. He brings it here every Sunday."

I remained baffled by Guido Borgese's familiarity with Alfonso Atkins.

"How did Guido know that Atkins worked in the White House?" I asked skeptically.

"I assume through Claudio Armondi," Giacomo answered, shrugging, eyes widened, clearly annoyed by my reluctance to deal with Atkins, glancing woefully at me before returning his stare to a saddened parent standing before the wall. "They all served in the same Company in Vietnam. When he was in Washington, Claudio even joined your father and Alfonso when they paid their respects at the Memorial."

It was a bevy of information being fed to me, perhaps contrived, perhaps not. Unfortunately, I had little chance to measure his trust, giving me pause to deal with a stranger—Alfonso Atkins. Was I being duped, or was this my final chance to honor the mission bequeathed to me by Giovanni Micco and H. Victor VonBronstrup?

"Time is of the essence, Francesco," Giacomo warned. "Our sources say that the bombs will fall on Iran soon."

"That doesn't leave us much time," I said cautiously while fixing my eyes on Alfonso Atkins as he stepped back from the wall, watching intently as he managed a slow, calculating salute.

"The disc is all we need," Giacomo responded, cocking his head to one side, his eyes moving from me to Atkins. "If only Alfonso can get it past security and then to the President."

"Do you think Atkins can do that?" I asked, still dubious about the deal with Atkins and equally troubled by Giacomo's sudden and intense interest in stopping a war.

"There's a good chance," Giacomo said confidently, luring me, his words almost a plea. "Remember, Alfonso has a high-security clearance. He's been going in and out of the White House for the past thirty years."

His vigil over, Atkins began walking toward Giacomo and me. His trench coat was unbuttoned and he carried a closed umbrella. A gray peaked, flat cap kept the drizzle from whetting his head. A stark white shirt contrasted his black tie and black suit.

"I appreciate the ride to the Memorial," Atkins said, approaching Giacomo. "But I'd prefer to walk home."

"I understand," Giacomo said, nodding. He then smiled and introduced Atkins to me.

"It's an honor to meet you, too, Mr. Micco," Atkins said softly, extending his hand. "I'll always be in the debt of your father."

He stood back, his eyes sad, his voice toned with empathy.

"Please accept my belated sympathy for the loss of your dear mother and Judge Micco," Atkins said solemnly.

I offered him my condolences. Atkins nodded, acknowledging my expression of sympathy. A forced smile crossed his face.

"Every Sunday, I come to this sacred wall and touch the name of my son, Mr. Micco," he said, turning to face the Memorial. "And every Sunday, reality strikes. I will never know his wife. I will never know my grandchildren."

He paused.

"And I will never feel the comforting touch of a son while growing old—all because of a senseless war. Anything I can do to stop more killing will vindicate his death."

"Do you have the disc?" Giacomo asked me carefully, his squinted eyes and creased brow a sign. He was wondering whether his argument had won me over.

I reached into my pocket and, after sighing, gave the disc to Atkins, surrendering to Giacomo, the Mafia, and Guido Borgese—while hopefully honoring the mission of the Rosecross.

"I'll do my best, Mr. Micco," Atkins said, nodding as he forced a smile. I watched intently as he carefully secured the disc in the inner pocket of his suit coat.

Atkin's smile turned somber. He lowered his head and walked away. I watched through the drizzling rain as he passed the names engraved in the sloped monument—until he finally reached the haunting point where the polished black granite disappeared into the cold earth.

CHAPTER 86

A SURRENDER

The day following my meeting with Alfonso Atkins, I returned to New Castle to spend Thanksgiving with my family and write the novel's final chapters, a tiring effort that sent me to bed early in the evening. At midnight I was startled by a whirling wind pounding hard at the window. I jumped up. Aroused from her sleep, Gianna turned toward me.

"Another dream?"

"No. Just the wind. Get some rest."

I rolled from bed, splashed water on my face, and then sat at my desk in the spare bedroom. Rain pellets pounded hard against the windows, as zigzagging flashes of lightning, complemented by bursts of thunder and swirling winds, illuminated the night. My cell phone vibrated. It was Giacomo.

"Is the novel finished?" he asked.

"Just about. I finished Chapter 85 yesterday—our meeting with Alfonso Atkins."

"Where's the manuscript?"

"Locked in the trunk of my car."

"Any other copies?"

"None, that's it."

"You've described the burglary in the book—our frolic in Rome?" Giacomo asked briskly.

"Of course," I responded. "Every minute detail—including our rendezvous with LeDonne in the Piazza del Popolo. And you'll be happy to learn that I exposed the international operatives we met in the Hotel De Russie."

"Should make for interesting reading," Giacomo remarked. "But Alfonso is our only hope to stop the war."

"I agree. But be careful," I cautioned. "Remember, Alfonso has the only disc. There are no copies."

"Don't worry, Francesco. We made the right choice."

"Where are you?" I asked.

"In Lafayette Square—across from the White House."

"Where are you meeting Alfonso?"

"I rented a room for him at the Roger Smith. I talked to him a minute ago. Thought our leading man should bunk down in a historical landmark before he embarks on his journey into the history books."

"He remains on board?" I asked, curious to know if fear had taken its toll.

"Of course. Alfonso will be personally serving dinner to the President tomorrow evening."

"Is the war still on?"

"As far as I know."

"No heads-up to the President?"

"None."

"Do we have enough time?"

"Barely."

"Call me back when you get to the Roger Smith."

Our conversation ended.

I placed my cell phone on the nightstand and returned to bed. After tossing around, I got up, crept down the stairs, into the kitchen, and opened the refrigerator, searching for something to drink. I settled on cold milk. It was now four o'clock on a chilly November morning. Close to three hours had passed since I had spoken with Giacomo. I dialed his cell phone.

"Hello, Francesco."

Startled, I didn't respond for a moment. It was the chilled voice of Luca Botti.

"Where's Giacomo?" I asked starkly.

"Don't worry about him, Francesco," Botti drooled, his delight apparent. "Giacomo is the guest of the INS. Unfortunately, your friend was in this country illegally. I expect him to be deported back to Italy in a week or two."

"And Alfonso?"

There was a pause.

"He's still at the Roger Smith," he said vainly with a smirk I could easily sense. "But your errand boy won't be able to deliver the disc."

"Why?" I asked painfully, prodding Botti, knowing that the plan designed by Guido Borgese and carried out by Giacomo and me had gone awry.

"Because he's bound, gagged, blindfolded, and resting comfortably in a clothes closet at the Roger Smith. Housekeeping will find him."

"I assume you found the disc?"

"Yes," he answered briskly. "And I promptly burned it," he added brashly before pausing. "Fortunately," he continued, "I was able to cover the work of our bungling lawyer—Leonardo Mendici."

So ironic, I thought. Sacco dead, Mendici arrested, and a piece of plastic that destroyed the Micco family a pile of ashes, Luca Botti now taking great pride in the mission's end—two conspirators eliminated, and the voices of a conniving cabal silenced by a flame as the disc burned.

"But I'm surprised at you, Francesco," Botti mused melodiously, his words drawled.

"Why?" I asked.

"Because you have failed to respect the safety of your family," he said calmly, his tone menacing. "I'm sure you realize the pawns in our game are sleeping as we speak—snuggled in their beds safe and sound."

I hesitated, realizing that he was making more than a veiled threat.

"You surprise *me*, Mr. Botti," I countered, drawing him out.

"Why?" he bristled.

"Because you allowed Alfonso to live—my mother and father were not as fortunate. Neither was Saul Rosen."

"Your parents deaths were regrettable," he said shamelessly. "But Rosen—blame his death on your father. If he had denied the defense team's discovery request to produce to the disc, it would not have been necessary for us to eliminate him."

"Yes, I remember your reasoning. End Rosen's prosecution by killing him."

"The Jew's death was nothing more than collateral damage," Botti said smartly. "But we digress. I assume you know what we want from you."

Only one obstacle separated a ruse that would ignite a war from the mission of The Rosecross. The trail of carnage left by a cabal housed in the Pentagon was about to pay a considerable dividend, and Botti knew it. I could almost see the saliva dripping from his mouth, the junkyard dog feasting on its prey.

"You want my manuscript?" I remarked rhetorically.

"That's right, the manuscript you stowed away in the trunk of your car. And by the way—I applaud you."

"Why?"

"When you discovered that your father's novel was short on details—you authored one yourself."

Somehow Botti had been armed with an arsenal of information.

"You wired Giacomo's cell phone and mine—that's how you learned about Alfonso?"

Botti laughed arrogantly.

"And that's how you also learned that I stowed the manuscript in the trunk of my car?" I added.

"Yes, my friend," he scoffed. "As the Undersecretary of Defense for policy, I can do many things. For your future reference, we call our technology 'the cell spy.'"

While speaking with Botti, I recalled Floyd Munson's wise counsel: *If you're offered money in return for your silence—take it. You can't fight them. You'd be bucking too much power.*

"When do we meet?" I asked.

"For you to turn over the manuscript to me?"

"Yes.

"Be at the Hertz kiosk at the Pittsburgh airport in two hours. A car has already been reserved in my name, listing you as the principal driver. Directions will follow as you are driving back to New Castle."

Mendici was right. Botti *was* an eccentric character who had a flair for drama, a power freak whose fetish for control would dictate the terms of surrender.

CHAPTER 87

GATEWAY COMMERCE PARK

Following Botti's direction, I hired a cab and arrived at the Pittsburgh International Airport at about five o'clock in the morning. I rode the escalator down to the Hertz Rent-a-Car kiosk on the first level. After wading through a pile of documents cluttered with legal jargon, I declined the insurance option, scratched my name at the bottom of the last sheet, and hurried toward a set of sliding glass doors that hastily flung open. I passed through. The panels slammed shut behind me. I sat alone on a bench. In about five minutes, a vehicle approached the Hertz wait station. It was a black Lincoln four-door sedan. The driver brought the car to a stop, slid out, and walked toward me, dangling a set of keys.

"Mr. Micco?"

"Yes, that's me."

"Here are your keys, sir. The Lincoln's a complimentary upgrade. Enjoy. It's all we have left. Thanks for choosing Hertz."

With a nod of my head and managing a tired smile, I acknowledged his scripted remark. Saying nothing more, he headed toward the sliding glass doors and disappeared into the airport terminal's ground level. I walked around the front of the car, opened the door, slid in, fastened my seat belt, engaged the engine, and drove the vehicle from the terminal into a lane that funneled cars out of the airport onto Route 60. I headed north, waiting for directions from Luca Botti. Suddenly, a familiar voice coming from the shadows of the back seat roused me from my introspective musings.

"Good evening, Francesco."

Startled, I turned around and glanced at my passenger. Not surprisingly, it was Luca Botti.

"Just follow my directions, and you'll be fine," he said. "Take Route 60 to the Turnpike and then head east."

Following his directions, I peeled off Route 60 at the toll gate, drove down the east ramp, and circled onto the turnpike. After a few miles, I exited and drove north on Route 18, a dark two-lane road that was mostly void of traffic this early in the morning. Except to give directions, Botti said nothing. It was a quiet ride. After we traveled a short distance down Route 18, he finally broke the silence.

"Slow down, Francesco," he said. "Up ahead to the left, you'll see a sign. It says, 'Gateway Commerce Park.' Turn there."

As I approached the sign, I waited for an oncoming truck to pass. A two-lane asphalt road led into the park. As we approached the entrance, a large door, probably prompted by a remote opener held by Botti, slowly creaked open. I was about to drive into a cave carved into the side of a mountain. It struck me as a cruel anomaly. I was familiar with the catacombs when I met Luca Botti at the Franciscan Monastery in Washington. Because the Micco Candy Company used it as a storage facility, I was likewise acquainted with the Gateway Commerce Park. The door closed behind us. As it slammed shut, an eerie thought captured my attention. I was about to experience another subterranean rendezvous with Luca Botti.

The Gateway Commerce Park was a deep vault carved into the side of a mountain. It was a former limestone mine. When its resources dried up, an enterprising entrepreneur turned the empty seven million square feet of space into a storage facility. Closely spaced halogen lamps hanging on chains from the white limestone ceiling brightly illuminated the common entrance.

"You will soon come to a pillar that's painted a bright yellow, Francesco," Botti advised. "Turn left."

Solid yellow stripes painted on the black asphalt surface designated the lanes of vehicular travel. Red and white stop signs, placed at intersecting roads, controlled the traffic moving about within the cave. At least two hundred pillars of un-mined limestone supported the massive rock ceiling. As I drove deeper into the cave's cavity, the asphalt roads rolled into narrow dirt paths. The headlamps of my car provided the only light guiding me. I was now in the deepest recesses of the Gateway Commerce Park.

"Make a right here, Francesco, and park."

Again, I complied. As I turned, the headlamps illuminated a cement block wall. Immediately in front of the car was an industrial-gray steel door. No signs identified the tenant.

"Turn the engine off. Come with me."

The whine of the engine died. Along with Botti, I got out of the car and walked toward the steel door. A flashlight held by Botti provided only a glimmer of light. He focused the dim beam on the lock and handed me the key. I inserted it and pushed the door open.

At least a thousand square feet, the room was a sparsely-furnished oasis squirreled away in the cavity of a mountain. Set off at opposite ends of the room were two massive, off-white limestone support pillars. The concrete block walls, painted a stark white, matched the porcelain tile floor. Centered in the middle of the room was a boat-shaped conference table with beveled edges surrounded by at least twenty cushioned swivel chairs. A soft light gently fell from the recessed lighting carved into the limestone ceiling. Botti invited me to sit in one of the chairs. He sat opposite me. I surveyed my opulent surroundings and asked a question.

"Why have you brought me here?"

Botti ignored my inquiry.

"An interesting place, Mr. Botti. Are you the tenant?" I asked, trying to engage him in conversation.

"The Defense Logistics Agency leases this space," he finally remarked. "The government has rented six million square feet. At least for now, it's mostly empty."

"The Defense Logistics Agency?"

"Yes, the DLA is an agency within the Department of Defense. Its function is to provide worldwide logistics for our warfighters."

"Why do you need six million square feet of space?" I prodded.

Botti flashed a contrived smile.

"In case of war, we'll need a place to store munitions and supplies," he explained, an obvious reference to the preemptive strike on Iran.

"But enough about this place. Let's talk about Francesco Micco and his beautiful family," he said shrewdly, his smile contrived.

Botti began his scripted presentation with an event that I had stored away. I would have preferred to let it rest.

"I'm certain you recall Justice Sacco's visit to the Phillips Mansion and his *accidental* fall down the flight of stairs that cost him his life," he began slyly.

"Why do you ask?"

Botti welded his eyes to mine.

"Well, Francesco, he didn't travel to New Castle alone. I was with him."

Alarmed, I leaned back, startled by his disclosure. Is Botti testing me? I wondered.

"Why did you accompany him to New Castle?" I prodded calmly, hiding my anxiety, but curious to learn what he knew.

"Let's just say that Sacco and I had a mutual interest," he answered curtly. "For more than fifteen minutes, I sat in my car on Phillips Place."

"You drove separately?"

"We did," Botti answered. "After a while, I became concerned because of the bounty Justice Sacco carried. So, I climbed up the stairs that led onto the porch and quietly entered the mansion. The door wasn't locked, so I entered the vestibule."

Stunned, I realized Botti wasn't lying, his description of the Phillips Mansion hauntingly accurate. He *was* with Salvatore Sacco when he traveled to New Castle.

"After I entered the vestibule, I hid in the shadow of a dark corner," he continued, smirking. "You were standing on the top landing, facing Justice Sacco."

He flashed a sinister smile.

"Francesco, I saw you shove Sacco down the staircase."

His feral eyes bored into mine.

"I also watched you remove the cash from the trunk of his car."

Botti leaned back and sighed, wallowing in his work, confident that he had cleaned up Leonardo Mendici's mess.

"Enjoy your treasure, my friend," he said smugly. "You have our five million dollars. We'll now travel to New Castle. I'll be most happy to meet your beautiful family."

The menacing smile, the squinted eyes, his threat to victimize Gianna and Michele a veiled threat that pierced me like a dagger stuck in my back.

"I can watch as you destroy the manuscript," he said brightly, feigning the mood. "As far as I'm concerned, Francesco, that will be the final chapter of your story."

I expected a disclaimer to come next.

"But if you renege in any way..."

His sentence hung as an eerie pause slipped into a chilled warning.

"...after we dispose of Gianna and you, we'll bring your son, Michele, into the deepest recesses of this cave... and leave him blindfolded to find his way out."

He paused.

"Now, Francesco, shall we go to your home on Sumner Avenue?" he asked snidely. "I would like very much to meet your wife and son, Gianna and Michele. And I'm confident that you will assure their safety by keeping your part of the deal."

CHAPTER 88

A DANGEROUS DECISION

We arrived in New Castle by mid-afternoon. Not wanting to alarm Gianna, I introduced Botti only as Mario, a Random House agent working on the novel with me. She invited him to dinner, and he graciously accepted her invitation. Thankfully, she didn't recognize Botti. Her eyes were too teary as she listened to his testimony at my extradition hearing.

Accommodating Botti's request, it was an early dinner. Gianna placed the big pan on the stove and said she would make "a fast pot of marinara sauce." Saying nothing, Botti and I watched as she performed her magic. First, she heated olive oil and then sautéed a finely minced onion. Just then, Michele poked his head into the kitchen.

"This must be Michele," Botti remarked, looking down and offering his hand. I prompted Michele.

"Shake Mario's hand."

Saying nothing and looking up at Botti, Michele extended his arm and held his hand out. Bending low, Botti shook Michele's hand and reached into his coat pocket.

"Here, Michele, take this. It's a rare silver dollar," he said as he glanced at me, grinning. "By the time you graduate from high school, it will be worth thousands."

Gianna, who was sautéing slices of garlic I had peeled and chopped, looked over her shoulder at Michele.

"Tell Mario thanks," she said.

Michele looked up as Botti mussed his hair. Botti then walked toward the stove and stood next to Gianna, watching as she poured ripe plum tomatoes into the big pan. The mixture of olive oil, onions, and garlic sizzling on the stove generated a delicious aroma, teasing our appetites.

"You're a very fortunate young man, Francesco," he said, once again giving me a quick look, "having a wizard performing her magic in the kitchen."

Finally, she added a sprinkle of red wine, a touch of salt, and fresh basil. Stirring the sauce well, she brought it to a boil, lowered the heat, and simmered her creation for twenty-five minutes.

The meal was simple. Minestrone that Gianna had stored in the freezer, a mozzarella and pepper salad, and finally penne pasta with fresh marinara sauce. For dessert, Gianna served ricotta cake—a left-over from Sunday—and finally, we enjoyed a cup of espresso. Perversely, I enjoyed the meal. After dinner, I shoved my chair back and glanced at Botti.

"Michele and I have some yard work to do. Would you like to join us?"

"I'd love it."

A row of bushes in the back yard had trapped a pile of leaves blown in the thickets by the swirling force of a fall wind. It was time to rake them out. I started at the far end and worked my way toward the house. After a short while, I heard the patter of small feet carefully working their way down the wooden steps of the back porch. It was Michele. Behind him was Botti. Once off the porch, Michele ran as his outstretched hands reached out to me. Botti watched from the porch. With a broad smile gracing his face, Michele jumped into my arms. I raised him toward the sky. Gianna trailed behind, carrying his small rake.

"Here, Michele, help Daddy rake the leaves," she said.

Botti stood beside Gianna, waiting for my move, his steely eyes fixed on my wife, then Michele, and finally me. A sinister smile slowly swept across his face. Working together—father and son—Michele and I freed the leaves trapped in the bushes and raked them in piles. When we finished, and after the leaves were piled high, we playfully rolled in the stacks. Gianna stood near the trunk of a large maple tree, laughing as she watched us, content to be with the two people she loved the most.

When our frolic ended, we gathered the leaves and placed them in a large barrel. Carefully, I lit the leaves with a match, and the brown foliage Michele and I collected began to burn, discharging bellows of smoke that lazily rose in circles before the transparent vapors faded into the blue canopy. With Botti following me, I walked to my car and opened the trunk. Balancing a package in my arms, I carried it from the car and headed toward the barrel. I glanced at Gianna and Michele, folded the title page, placed it in my pocket, and then fed each sheet of manuscript to the fire—watching helplessly as the beryl sky swallowed my novel.

Before leaving with Botti, I slipped inside the house and called Roosevelt Ward on our land phone. The conversation was brief. I had little time.

"Did the wire on my phone work, Roosevelt?" I asked anxiously.

"The 'cell spy' performed very well," he chuckled. "Especially the part about Rosen—where Botti says that 'the Jew's death was nothing more than collateral damage.'"

"And it was heard by the Mafia's Jewish counterparts?"

"Loud and clear—they've been on your tail since you left the airport yesterday."

I went outside and saw Botti holding Michele, another sign meant to caution me. Gianna was standing nearby. Fear gripped me as I recalled Botti's warning: *"But if you renege in any way…"*

CHAPTER 89

THE JEWISH MAFIA

Botti spent most of the time during our ride to the Pittsburgh International Airport talking on his cell phone. Most of the conversations involved mundane matters that required his blessing. Having nothing to say to him, I welcomed his rude manners. Tame behavior, indeed, when considered within the context of his propensity to commit murder. It was better we ignored each other. Trapped within me was a pit bull waiting to devour his passenger. Be patient, I thought. Be true to the plan.

"How much longer?" Botti asked.

"Forty-five minutes," I answered.

"Good. I'll tell the captain to power the engines."

As the Undersecretary of Defense for Policy, the Government had given Botti many perks, including the private jet that awaited his arrival at Pittsburgh International. While he talked to the pilot about weather and wind conditions, a car whizzed by in the opposite direction as we traveled down Route 18. Suddenly a vehicle approached from behind. The reflection of its high beam lights off my rearview mirror blinded my view of the road. I slowed my vehicle as the trailing car began to pass, prompting a remark from Botti.

"Crazy son-of-a-bitch."

Suddenly, the passing car swerved into my lane, causing me to veer onto the shoulder of the road sharply. I slammed on the breaks. The tires squealed as the sliding wheels laid rubber on the dry asphalt. My grip on the steering wheel stiffened. My neck snapped back onto the headrest and propelled me forward. My seat belt tightened. The car stopped—a millisecond before slamming into the side of the vehicle blocking my access to the highway.

"What the hell is happening?" Botti barked.

I said nothing as three men jumped out of the car. One raised its trunk lid. The other two, weapons drawn, raced toward our vehicle. Again, I said nothing. Both men approached the passenger side, opened the door, pulled Botti out of the car, and wrestled him to the pavement. Struggling, they dragged him away as he shouted.

"Your whole family will pay for this," he yelled.

Walking briskly, the man who opened the trunk lid approached me.

"Just confirming the facts," he said calmly. "Is Luca Botti your passenger?"

"Yes."

"The man who said the Jew's death was only 'collateral damage'?" he inquired.

I nodded.

"Who are you?" I asked.

"Let's just say we have a score to settle with Mr. Botti."

Undoubtedly, the Mafioso's comrades—their Jewish counterparts, I thought.

"Where are you taking him?"

"To the Gateway Commerce Park. As you can see, he's bound and gagged," he said emotionless.

I watched as the other two hijackers dumped Botti into the trunk of their car and slammed the lid shut.

"We'll break both of his knees and then deposit him in the middle of the six million square feet he leases in the Gateway Commerce Park," he remarked calmly. "The rats can feed off him. It should be a succulent feast."

He started walking away but returned.

"Is Botti the guy who ordered your mother's murder?" he inquired.

"One of them."

He smiled.

"Glad we could help."

Hurriedly, he returned to his car and jumped in the back seat. Through my windshield, I watched as the red taillights of the vehicle carrying Luca Botti to his final resting place disappeared down Route 18.

Two down.

CHAPTER 90

A VISIT

Time passed quickly. Thanksgiving and the Christmas holidays were diversions from the mission of The Rosecross, but I had to write my novel's final chapters. It was now early January. Hopefully, it will be a better year. Gianna and I were awaiting the arrival of Roosevelt Ward. Perhaps we were masochists, but we planned to listen to the President's State of the Union address together.

Order was returning to my life. With a little persuasion, Nino had agreed to practice law with me in New Castle, a galactic distance away from the bustling confusion of a metropolitan law emporium. Emotionally drained after a year of walking through the maze bequeathed to us by the Judge, we craved our share of peace. Tiring of the cold weather and the trappings of The Rosecross, I awaited the new season and the spring foliage's perennial birth.

Gianna announced she was pregnant. We decided to name our child Rosalina, if the baby's a girl—and if a boy, Giovanni. Although it was a secret, Nino said he planned to surprise Gianna's twin sister with an engagement ring later in the summer. They'll be married the following spring if she'll accept his proposal. He suggested I pump Gianna for a clue. But because of the bond between siblings, I heard little. Somehow, I suspected her answer would be "yes."

———————

I watched through the dining room window as Roosevelt's car straddled the curb. After alerting Gianna, I rushed out the door and down the front walk to meet him.

"It's good to see you, my friend," I said as he opened the trunk lid and reached for his luggage.

"Thanks for the invitation. It's good to be here."

Roosevelt slammed the lid shut and opened the rear car door.

"I need some help," he said.

Roosevelt pulled out two boxes, one rather large, the other long and narrow, wrapped in white paper and tied with a red bow.

"Gifts for the lady of the house and the young gentleman."

"Where's mine?"

"FedEx will deliver it in two weeks."

We lingered for a moment on the porch. Roosevelt inquired about my family and law practice. I told him Gianna was pregnant and Michele was growing like a wild weed.

"Let's go inside. We can catch up later," I suggested.

As I hung Roosevelt's coat in the closet, Gianna, who was tucking Michele in bed, came down the stairs and greeted our guest.

"Roosevelt, welcome to our home," she said, her hands outstretched. "I'm so glad you're here," Gianna's radiant smile a welcoming gesture.

They hugged.

"Stand back," he said. "I heard the good news. Let me look at you."

Blushing, she moved away. Roosevelt then handed Gianna the rectangular package.

"A gift for you."

"May I open it now?"

"Please."

She untied the bow, removed the white wrapping paper, and opened the lid. Her face brightened. Her eyes bulged.

"Roosevelt, it's so thoughtful of you," she said warmly as they hugged.

Gianna showed Roosevelt's gift to me. It was a wooden stirring spoon with a gold placard attached that read: "To Gianna. You're a magical chef." She placed the lid back on the box and ushered us into the kitchen.

"Hope you're hungry," Gianna said briskly.

Roosevelt nodded, smiling broadly as we followed her into the kitchen.

"What's on the menu?" I asked.

"Margherita pizza."

Roosevelt and I watched as Gianna dusted a wood peel with flour. Next, she placed a pizza dough ball in the center, formed it into a disc shape, and then flattened it with a rolling pin. Finally, she spooned the sauce over the top and then sprinkled the dough with grated Pecorino Romano cheese.

"Here's where I need some help," she said.

Roosevelt volunteered.

She carried the wood peel to the stove, and together, Gianna and Roosevelt slipped the pie into the oven and onto a pizza stone resting on the middle rack.

"It's hot in there," Roosevelt said.

"Five hundred degrees," Gianna observed as she closed the oven door.

After several minutes, she removed the pizza. The crust was golden brown, and the cheese simmered. Gianna sprinkled basil leaves on top, along with a drizzle of olive oil. It was ready to eat.

"Now, for my husband's surprise."

I took a bottle from the wine cooler and placed it on the table.

"Made it myself, Roosevelt," I bragged. "A product of the Micco Family Winery."

I popped the cork and poured him a taste. He swirled the wine, smelled its aroma, and then took a sip.

"Outstanding," he said. "What is it?"

"It's our Sangiovese."

With raised glasses, I offered a toast.

"To our magical chef."

I stood and kissed Gianna.

"Tomorrow, you'll taste our Montepulciano d'Abruzzo," I announced.

Everything was outstanding, the pizza, the wine, the conversation, and the company. We talked, ate, and drank for an hour or more. Finally, Gianna stood and carried her dish to the sink.

"You two have a lot to talk about. Go into the living room."

Roosevelt and I stood, happy to oblige her.

"But tomorrow night," she cautioned, "you guys have kitchen duty."

Wine glasses in hand, Roosevelt and I moved into the living room.

CHAPTER 91

THE CONVERSATION CONTINUES

"Tell me about your practice," my friend said as he sat down. "Is business good?"

"We're keeping busy."

My house guest and I traded casual comments, but the idle talk waned, and the veneer covering our conversation was torn loose. After we exchanged pleasantries, he reached into his briefcase and removed a package wrapped in brown paper. It was the manuscript I gave him for safekeeping when we rendezvoused in the Rosecross chambers on K Street. Five days ago, I mailed him more pages. He now had all the chapters I had written.

"Does your publisher have the manuscript?" he asked somberly, "the copy you intend to send to Random House?"

"Not yet. My sister is still editing."

"Will you send me the final chapters?"

"I will."

He gave me an awkward stare that unsettled me.

"Something bothering you?" I asked curiously.

He sat on the edge of his chair, hands clasped, his eyes drilled on mine.

"You understand the novel implicates you in two murders," he warned bluntly.

"How can a fictional story incriminate me?" I asked, drawing him out, curious to learn if his theory aligned with mine—my story providing circumstantial evidence that would arouse the interest of a cunning prosecutor.

"You, my dear friend, have written a roman-a-clef novel, thinly disguising yourself as Francesco Micco—a character in your book who pushed a Supreme Court Justice down a flight of stairs and who was complicit in the murder of the Under Secretary of Defense for Policy."

"Salvatore Sacco and Luca Botti are fictional characters in my book, figments of my imagination—nothing more," I reminded him, testing his theory.

"You're a lawyer," he countered starkly, his eyes still riveted to mine. "Facts are facts. A real Supreme Court Justice died falling down a flight of stairs at the Phillips mansion while visiting New Castle. And the body of a real Under Secretary of Defense was found devoured in the Gateway Commerce Park—not too far from where you and I now sit."

"You consider my novel a confession," I suggested lightly, hiding my concern. "Or perhaps an admission that I murdered a Supreme Court justice and was complicit in the murder of an Under Secretary of Defense?"

He only nodded, his brash stare giving me pause.

"I don't think so," I answered, after pausing, casually dismissing his warning. "It would be a novel legal theory. But it won't work in a court of law."

"Trust me," he continued, not relenting, his plea now more intense, "there are too many similarities between your book and events that occurred in your life—your mother's murder, your father's murder, your sister's kidnapping, her rescue, your extradition to Italy—the list goes on and on. Need I elaborate?"

His warning made sense—my motive incriminating, my thirst for retribution, a recurring theme weaved throughout the story. I nodded and then glanced at my watch, anxious to change the subject.

"Hey, ten more minutes 'till the President's State of the Union Address."

Fresh from kitchen duty, my wife poked her head into the living room.

"I'm going to bed, guys," she said. "Thought you might like a drink before the President speaks."

She placed two glasses and a bottle of Romana Sambuca on the coffee table and then left.

"Quite a girl you have there, my friend."

I smiled. My house guest leaned back as I poured him a shot of Sambuca. It was time to listen to the President's State of the Union Address. As always, the beginning was a hollow salutation: "Good evening, my fellow Americans."

First, he rambled on about domestic affairs and then stumbled over the intricacies of foreign affairs. Endless rhetoric. Grand promises. Great expectations. As the words echoed throughout the chamber, the Republicans stood and cheered as the Democrats sat and sulked. Then, in the end, his eyes sad and his voice sober, the President spoke the sixteen-word hook that reeled in the Congress and struck fear in the hearts of his constituency.

"The Italian government has learned that Iran's government recently sought significant quantities of uranium from Niger."

Through a circuitous route, the handiwork of my character—Antonio LeDonne— had found its way into the President's State of the Union address. It will be the Administration's excuse for executing its new 'bully' policy in the Middle East. Mercifully, the end came sixty-seven minutes later:

"God bless every one of you. And God bless the United States of America."

We exchanged glances after listening to the President mislead a gullible Congress and an unsuspecting constituency. Based on a staged burglary, the President's sixteen words were destined to ignite a cauldron in the Middle East.

"What's the status of the investigation of Washington's most powerful lobbyist?" I asked.

"The Mendici character in your novel?"

"Yes."

"A grand jury indicted him yesterday on murder charges. A judge detained him until his preliminary examination," my guest answered, as his voice trailed off.

"Something else you want to tell me?" I asked, breaking a silence.

His stare turned somber.

"A guard found him in his cell last night. He hung himself."

With mixed emotions, I carried our glasses into the kitchen and returned to the vestibule. My friend hesitated before we walked up the stairs. I sensed something was on his mind. He turned toward me and placed his hand on my shoulder.

"Be careful," he cautioned.

"About what?"

"About the five million dollars."

CHAPTER 92

THE FIVE MILLION DOLLARS

Along with Grazia and Giancarlo, I attended a seven o'clock memorial Mass for our parents at St. Vitus the following Friday. After Mass, we had breakfast at the PO Lunch and then visited the cemetery. It was a cold, crisp January morning, and the sun had just burned through a passing cloud as I drove along the narrow lane that led to the Micco plot. White remnants of the last snowfall lay nestled against a sea of worn grave markers spread randomly throughout the cemetery. A gentle breeze rang the carillons of a wind chime dangling from the branches of a nearby tree just as I opened the car door.

Bundled in winter garb, hands tightly fastened, we gathered together as the Micco family at the foot of their graves. Our parents were cheated by the two murders that brought us to this quiet place on this brisk morning. Unable to share in their children's lives, Giovanni and Rosalina lay buried in the ground beneath our feet. As I stared at their gravestones, I realized I was not allowed even a shred of solace.

We each offered our prayers silently and then turned and walked away. Still clinging to the hands of my brother and sister, I hesitated, turned my head, and looked back one last time. As if I was waiting at a railroad crossing watching the carriages of a bullet train whizzing through the night, memories rushed through my mind while the blurred windows streaked by. I recalled the visits with our Amish friends, Ed and Katie Lee. Once again, we sat around the large rectangular oak table in the Lee kitchen. I visualized my mother, Rosalina, saying little as the oil lamp's muted light ignited a sparkle in her eyes. She wanted those moments to last forever. I recalled our home on Sumner Avenue and my mother's hope that it would serve us into the future by hosting the holidays, birthdays, graduations, and weddings destined to bless her family.

I, too, recalled the Judge's appointment to the Court of Appeals. I remembered our move to Washington. I visualized the lady-in-black removing the red veil from her face and draping it back over her head before she placed the red rose on the shroud covering the Judge's casket. But most of all, I relive the spring morning when I found Rosalina lying in a splatter of blood in our kitchen. Even now, as I walk away from my mother's grave, I feel her cold blood saturating my shirt, its chilling sensation still penetrating straight through to the inner sanctum of my soul.

Finally, after dutifully following the twisted path bequeathed to me by the Judge, I turned from the graves of my mother and father and walked away. I'm now free. May Giovanni Micco and Rosalina Bartolacci rest in peace and may their dance last forever—just as they wanted.

With her arm wrapped around mine, I escorted Grazia to our car. As I opened the passenger door, she turned toward me. Her moistened eyes were red. Removing a mitten, she reached into her coat pocket and found a tissue. She blotted away tears that slowly trickled down her blushed cheeks and then dabbed at her nose. Still struggling to control her emotions, Grazia turned away from me. After a moment, she gained her composure, but her words were interrupted by an occasional sob.

"We had good parents, Francesco."

I nodded as tears wetted my eyes. Closing the car door, I murmured to myself.

"You're right, Grazia—we did have good parents."

I glanced back. Giancarlo had returned to the grave, bent down on one knee, his head lowered. I placed my arm around his shoulder, waited for a second or two, and then walked away. As the youngest, he would be the last of the Micco children to leave the gravesite. Now, down on two knees, he made the sign of the cross, stood, turned, and stared at his parents' graves. As I waited for Giancarlo's vigil to end, I stood at the rear of the car. When he approached, I opened the trunk lid, and pointed to three large boxes that I had hidden under the cover of an old red blanket.

"In these boxes, Giancarlo, you'll find nearly five million dollars," I said softly. "Launder the cash through Marymount HealthCare and set up two trusts."

Stunned, Giancarlo stared into the trunk.

"Where did you get the money, Francesco?" he asked, eyes squinted, his suspicions running wild.

"Don't ask any questions, Giancarlo. Please just do as I ask."

"Two trusts?"

"Yes. Take three million and set up one trust for an endowed chair at Catholic University."

"For what course?"

"For a seminar entitled 'Ethics in Government.'"

"And the other?"

"Establish a trust in the name of Leonard Atkins."

"For what purpose?"

"To support the families of warriors killed in Vietnam."

"Who is Leonard Atkins?"

"I'll put you in touch with his father, Alfonso. He'll tell you all you need to know about Leonard."

Although I preferred to distance myself from the series of disquieting episodes that had invaded my life over the past year, I realized that now and again the present would visit the past. It was a rule of nature linked to the cycle of life. However, the Rosen case was not a casual visitor that would haunt me only from time to time. It stood alone. The vehicle used to drive the murders of my parents was indelibly connected to my life and would remain with me until the moment I die.

Following our visit to the cemetery, I returned Grazia to the Micco Candy Company. Soon, she'd be consumed by her work as an entrepreneur, and that was good. Giancarlo had decided to visit with Gianna and Michele before returning to finish the hospital project in Lampedusa. As for me, it was now time to face a gargantuan task. I must mend a broken law practice I'd abandoned for over a year. Before I walked into the office, I took a moment and dwelled on the newly painted sign decorating the glass entrance door.

Micco & Viola.

Being careful not to smudge the glass door with finger marks, I pushed it open and walked into Nino's small, cramped office, assuring him that one day we too would enjoy the comforts of an opulent suite. He was perched on the top rung of a ladder shelving volumes of United States Supreme Court Reporters. Nino stepped down from the ladder and surveyed the books filling the shelves behind his desk.

"Well, partner, how do they look?"

"Just fine," I responded, noting that he had devoted the top shelf to the Rosicrucians. We faced each other and, for a moment, said nothing. Then we embraced.

"Hey, enough of this," he said. "Gianna just called. She has dinner ready. You better hurry home."

"Do you care to join us?"

"Right behind you. Gianna already invited me."

CHAPTER 93

A Decision

It was the next day, a mild winter Saturday morning. Glancing out the kitchen window, I noticed that a small branch had been blown off the large oak tree in our side yard. After climbing a ladder and removing a saw from the garage rafter, I began to cut the branch into small pieces. Soon joined by Gianna and Michele, we raked some leaves that had been trapped in a thicket, collected the yard twigs, and placed the rubble on crumbled newspapers I had placed in a barrel. Together, we laid the cut branches atop the kindling. With my wife and son watching, I removed a match from my pocket, lit the paper, and watched for a second or two as the remains simmered and then began to burn.

Gianna, Michele, and I watched as red flames discharged black smoke high into a gray sky. I then went back into the house, into the vestibule, up and stairs, and into the spare bedroom. From the bottom drawer of my desk, I removed a wrapped stack of papers secured by a string. I carried the package from the house, into the yard, and headed toward the barrel. I untied the string, unfolded the wrapping paper, and stared at a stack of pages, more than 300, my novel, the manuscript I had stowed away in my upstairs office—the copy Grazia had been editing.

Heeding Roosevelt Ward's warning, I recalled a lesson my father taught me. He cautioned that I should jealously guard any jewels worth keeping, or else they'd be consumed by the pendulum of a clock and, one day, I'd wake and find that they had been stolen by time. Cherishing that thought, I decided to take Roosevelt's advice. Why publish the novel, and expose myself to the wrath of a cunning federal prosecutor?

With Gianna and Michele standing beside me, I crumbled the manuscript pages and, once again, fed my novel to a fire's flames, every word disappearing into the morning sky—except the last paragraph:

> It's Friday evening. I drove to my home on Sumner Avenue and found my wife and son playing in the backyard. After changing my clothes, I joined in their frolic, wishing that time would stand still and that this magical moment would somehow last forever. But I realize that as time slowly slips into eternity, our children will fly away. But my soulmate, Gianna, will walk hand-in-hand with me into eternity and back again. That's the beauty of life. That's the cycle of life. But for now, for this one, brief, beautiful moment, they belong to me. My family is secure. I'm home to stay.

CHAPTER 94

MY SECRET

I had made the decision alone. It was my secret, and I thought it best not to seek Gianna, Nino, or Roosevelt's counsel. In the end, my father rightfully admonished me, the sound judicious reasoning in his legal opinions my accuser, a lesson he taught from Ecclesiastes chastising me: *A time to search and a time to give up as lost.* My mother's assassins beyond the reach of the law, I regretfully reached for the only solace I could find—retribution. Justice by force is justice by tyranny would have been Judge Micco's mantra. Sadly, I couldn't reclaim the past. But I had been transparent, telling all, revealing even my most intimate thoughts, spread through page after page for anyone to read—even a skillful prosecutor.

Washington was the setting, the place where it all began, and where it would end. Nino offered to accompany me there, but I declined. I had to walk the final mile alone. I did, however, accept his offer to drive me to Amtrak's station in Pittsburgh. The Capital Limited was scheduled to depart at nine-thirty on Friday evening and arrive at Union Station in Washington at seven the next morning. I reclined in my seat and rested my head on a pillow given to me by the porter, but I couldn't sleep; a well-plotted series of events about to explode into a holocaust kept me awake. Congress had already passed a joint resolution authorizing a military strike on Iran. Manipulated intelligence justified the war, and the countless lives lost would be nothing more than collateral damage to a sinister plot. Judging from the President's State of the Union address and Congress's joint resolution, Iran's bombing was imminent.

―――――――――――

The Capital Limited arrived in Washington at eight o'clock on Saturday morning, an hour late. My cab headed out of Union Station Drive. It merged onto Massachusetts Avenue, its wipers flip-flopping back and forth, sweeping away the moisture left by a smattering of snowflakes sprinkled on the car's windshield. I began to reconsider my decision as the cab turned onto I Street, balancing family against duty, safety against the truth. The scales were evenly balanced. On Thirteenth Street, an ambulance whizzed by, its siren bellowing, my cab straddling the curb, a warning perhaps that I, too, should move aside and leave the future to fate. But by the time we turned onto K Street, my apprehension faded, convinced once again that I had made the right decision as the cab pulled to the curb. I had reached my destination—2113 K Street, NW. I paid the fare, grabbed my luggage, slid out, and slammed the door. Hudson D'Priest was waiting for me at the front stoop.

"Sorry, Mr. D'Priest. The train was an hour late."

His kind smile eased me.

"Good morning, Mr. Micco."

We walked down the stairs and into his basement apartment.

"How have you been?" I asked.

"Fine, Mr. Micco. But it's lonely here without Vic."

I opened my suitcase and removed a package wrapped in newspaper.

"Here, take this," I said. "There's $200,000 inside. Hide it somewhere safe and then open a bank account on Monday."

The money was part of the five million dollars Leonardo Mendici had stashed away in his firm's safe—the cash delivered to me by Salvatore Sacco.

"Thank you, Mr. Micco," he said, his eyes wide, astonished.

After I nodded toward the back door, he led me into the vestibule. I entered, wheeling my luggage.

"The Rosecross Chamber is open, Brother of the Rose Croix," he announced, as if a meeting was about to commence.

We entered. Hudson D'Priest closed the red door and sat in the rear of the Chamber. The two votive candles placed on each side of the seven-sided tabernacle spread a dim light on the altar. I opened the tabernacle door. Resting inside was the ciborium with a dome-shaped canopy holding the cremated remains of H. Victor VonBronstrup. My eyes turned to the red rose etched into the intersection of two gold bars. I stared at the ciborium, the charge bequeathed to me by Dr. VonBronstrup bellowing louder and louder—expose the truth. I then reached for the burse used by Father Gil when he celebrated Mass in The Rosecross Chambers and placed it in my coat pocket. I closed the tabernacle door, turned the lock, and handed the key to Hudson.

We left the chambers and walked through Hudson's apartment. At the entrance door, I stopped, turned, and offered him my hand. His eyes glassy, Hudson stood motionless. I set my luggage down and approached him. We hugged for a second or two. I then reached for my suitcase, opened the door, walked up the stairs and down the walkway. While standing at the curb hailing a cab, I called Roosevelt Ward. The call went immediately to his voice mail. As cars whizzed by in both directions, I thought for a moment and then left him a detailed message, revealing to Roosevelt the secret I had kept from Gianna and Nino. Horns honked, the traffic snarl thickened as I glanced at the Brownstone once occupied by Giuseppe Sabino. After a long wait a cab finally pulled to the curb.

"1150 15th Street, Northwest," I told the driver as I climbed into the back seat.

He grumbled. It was a short ride, but he'd take the fare. As we rode down K Street in bumper-to-bumper traffic, my thoughts strayed to my meeting with Alfonso Atkins at the Vietnam War Memorial. I recalled seeing a tall African-American man standing motionless before the monument. I watched him closely. His stare was fixed on the polished black granite wall. He balanced a red rose in both hands. Then he moved forward, laid the rose at the foot of the memorial, stood back, and placed the palm of his hand on the wet wall.

As the cab turned onto 22nd Street, I recalled the question I had asked Giacomo.

"Is that Alfonso Atkins?"

"That's him," Giacomo had responded. "I drove him here about ten minutes ago. I thought he would appreciate a ride rather than taking the Metro. It's a miserable day."

His vigil over, I recalled Alfonso approaching me.

His words resonated.

"It's an honor to meet you, Mr. Micco. Every Sunday, I come to this sacred place and touch the name of my son on the monument wall."

Do you? I thought.

The cab turned onto L Street. Before meeting Alfonso at the monument, I had consulted 'The Vietnam Veterans Memorial Directory' to locate the name of Leonard Atkins on the wall. The designer—Maya Lin—listed the 58,000 names according to the date of casualty. To verify Alfonso's identity, I arrived at the Memorial two hours before our meeting and found the name of his son, Leonard Atkins. Lin listed his name on Panel 18W, line 019.

I recalled standing with Giacomo. We fixed our eyes on Alfonso standing in front of the monument. Reality struck hard. There were a Judas and an imposter among us, I thought. I closed my eyes and relived the scene. I saw Alfonso touch the wall with the palm of his hand. He was ten feet from me, at Panel 20E—two panels away from the name of Leonard Atkins.

We turned onto 15th Street. The realities that struck me? Alfonso was an imposter. Giacomo was a Judas. Finally, I recalled Giacomo's last question as we stood at the Vietnam War Memorial.

"Do you have the disc?"

I had both hands in my coat pockets. In my left pocket, I stowed the fruits of Alexandria Arnold's black-bag job. In my right pocket was a blank disc. Did I have the disc, Giacomo? I thought as I approached my destination. Yes, I had it—but I gave the blank one to your imposter friend.

As my cab straddled the curb, with a loose fist, I touched my suit coat pocket. Tucked inside was the burse I removed from the tabernacle in The Rosecross Chambers. Inside the burse was the disc that memorialized the ruse planned by Lester LaRouche, Richard Stone, and Luca Botti. Then I boasted. Botti didn't have the good sense to listen to the disc before he burned it.

"Here we are, Sir," the cabbie said. "1150 15th Street— the *Washington Post* building."

I SHOULD HAVE KNOWN

Just as I reached into my wallet to pay the driver, a car stopped abruptly behind us—red lights flashed, a siren bellowed, doors swung open. I leaned sideways and glanced out the rear window. Two men rushed toward the cab; both were wearing ball caps monogrammed: U.S. Marshal. One, burly and expressionless, opened the door, dragged me out, and bent me over the cab's hood. The other frisked me, his hands patting my clothing from legs to chest. Finishing his search, he reached into my jacket and seized the burse from my inner coat pocket. Inside was the disc given to me by H. Victor VonBronstrup, the fruits of Alexandria Arnolds black-bag-job. I twisted my head to the side and saw another man dressed in a suit, observing closely as the two Marshalls conducted their search.

"Find it?" he asked.

"I think so," the deputy U.S. Marshal answered.

The burly Marshal released his hold, spun me around, tightly gripped my hands while the other cuffed me. I was disheveled; shackles weighed down my hands; my stare riveted through the third man. He flashed a badge, identifying himself as an FBI agent.

"What's going on?" I asked, startled.

He handed me what appeared to be an official document. I held it by my fingertips, unable to read it.

"What's this?" I inquired, struggling to grasp the moment's reality.

"It's a warrant for the arrest of Francesco Micco, issued this morning by a U.S. Magistrate Judge."

"For what crime?"

"For the assassination of Supreme Court Justice Salvatore Sacco."

Gripping my arm, he walked me to the car parked behind the taxi cab. Just as he was about to lower my head, leading me into the backseat, I observed a man sitting in the passenger's seat.

I gazed blankly into his eyes.

He gazed back.

Thoughts raced through my mind.

I should have known.

I was duped into doing their dirty work.

The clues were all there.

First, there was Leonardo Mendici and the bottle taken from my father's bathroom cabinet during the search of his Watergate condominium by two agents—one from the FBI and the other from the DIA who was conveniently allowed to be part of the search. The medicine bottle was an odd seizure of evidence I now realize, considering that the Government was supposedly only after the Judge's laptop computer. That said, Botti, Stone, and LaRouche knew that Mendici's fingerprints were plastered all over the bottle, a seamless way to dispose of their bungling lawyer, the employer who knew too much. And then there was Grazia's rescue and the sophisticated technology used to identify Leonardo Mendici as the culprit who arranged her kidnapping. Cleverly, that confidential information was slipped to me.

Oddly enough, I now recall the ease at which my meeting with Floyd Munson was arranged—a quick telephone call identifying Munson as an inmate at Leavenworth. And then there was the private meeting room and my revealing conversation with the broker, the antagonist certain that Munson would feed me just enough information tying Leonardo Mendici to my mother's untimely passing. He knew that somehow I would begin to quench my thirst for retribution by extracting from Mendici my pound of flesh—the five million dollars. I would be characterized as the victim whose avarice was blinding.

And then there was the untimely passing of Luca Botti. Conveniently, I had been given access to the Government's 'cell spy' technology, which eventually provided the Jewish Mafia their retribution for the murder of Saul Rosen. Luca Botti was the eccentric member of the cabal who had to be eliminated, and, with a little help, Francesco Micco was the likely candidate who would conspire with the Mafia's Jewish counterpart to deposit Botti in the deepest recesses of the Gateway Commerce Park.

One down.

And then there was Salvatore Sacco, a weak link in the chain who had to be eliminated, the Supreme Court Justice whose relationship with Leonardo Mendici was too troubling, too fragile. For the longest while, I couldn't tie Sacco to my mother's murder, but the chocolate order placed by the Judge told me that somehow he played a role in her demise. I remained stumped—until I stood in front of Giuseppe Sabino's residence on K Street with a good friend who stared incessantly at the Professor's vacant Brownstone, slyly planting a clue, a cunning ploy, allowing me to figure out what lie Sabino had told the two Virginia police officers investigating my mother's murder. It was only a matter of time, but he knew that somehow Francesco Micco would extract his revenge from Supreme Court Justice Salvatore Sacco. And I did.

Two down.

In the end, my naivety and a bottle of placebos would result in Leonardo Mendici's murder indictment. A judge's order would then jail him, his death by hanging ruled a suicide. But I knew the nefarious dealings of a broker were at work—a holding cell, a convenient place to arrange a murder.

Three down.

I gazed blankly at the onlooker in the front seat.

He gazed back.

The clues were all there.

But I missed them.

The passenger was Roosevelt Ward.

My arraignment was scheduled for later in the afternoon. Having little time to assure Nino's appearance, I was represented by a federal public defender. My old friend, B. Stanley Puttmen represented the Government. A magistrate judge asked if I had a copy of the indictment. I responded "Yes," and, on the advice of counsel, waived its reading. I then pled "Not Guilty." As expected, Puttmen objected to bail, and the judge scheduled a detention hearing for the next day. On my attorney's motion, it was continued until the following week, giving Nino a chance to confer with me before the hearing.

Nino arrived in Washington on a Friday, the day after my arrest, and met with me at the Central Detention Facility where I was jailed. On the following Monday, I appeared once again in the courtroom of Federal District Court Judge G. Hawthorne Henderson.

"All rise," his courtroom deputy announced. "This is the time set for the preliminary examination and detention hearing in the case of the United States of America versus Francesco Micco."

E. McWade Williams sat in a wheelchair next to Nino at counsel table. He had agreed to come out of retirement and act as Nino's co-counsel, the skilled trial lawyer offering sage advice, especially in cases involving Government deception—and corruption. As Judge Henderson sat, my eyes were drawn to a stack of papers secured by a thick rubber band placed on the Government's counsel table. It was a copy of my manuscript—the one I had given to Roosevelt Ward. It will be the main witness appearing against me. Laying conspicuously on top of my manuscript was the red burse confiscated by the FBI during my arrest in front of the Washington Post Building. Hopefully, Roosevelt Ward was using this occasion as the setting to reveal the manufactured intelligence stored on the disc. Judge Henderson placed his elbows on the bench and steepled his hands, surveying the crowded courtroom. Roosevelt Ward sat next to the prosecutor, B. Stanley Puttmen. Lester LaRouche and Richard Stone sat in the first row of the courtroom's gallery. Judge Henderson's deputy banged his gavel.

"This court is now in session," the deputy bellowed.

Williams nudged Nino.

I leaned in.

"Is that the burse that holds the disc?" Williams whispered.

"It is," Nino answered softly.

Williams wheeled his chair toward the bench.

"May I be heard, Your Honor?" he asked respectfully.

"Yes," Judge Henderson answered, smiling broadly as he nodded, the newly minted Judge acknowledging the esteemed trial lawyer.

"May we proceed in chambers for a brief moment?" Williams asked.

Judge Henderson turned toward Puttmen.

"Does the Government have any objection?" he asked.

"No, Your Honor," Puttmen answered, surprised.

The deputy banged his gavel again.

"This court is in recess."

I followed Williams and Nino into Judge Henderson's chambers, trailed by B.Stanley Puttmen and Roosevelt Ward. We all sat, circled in front of the Judge's desk. Judge Henderson removed his robe, slung it over a chair, sat, steepled his hands, and fixed his eyes on Williams.

"You asked to meet in chambers," Judge Henderson asked rhetorically.

"I did," Williams responded, staring at Ward who shuffled in his chair, seemingly uncomfortable.

"Why?" Puttmen asked, shrugging while he glanced at Williams.

"Because we believe the Government has a disc in its possession crucial to the defense that must be heard *before* the Government proceeds to prosecute Mr. Micco," Williams answered sternly.

Confused, Puttmen turned toward Ward.

"During Mr. Micco's arrest, our agents found a disc in his inside coat pocket," Ward explained. "As we were walking into the courtroom today, I gave it to Mr. Puttmen."

"With the Court's permission, we would like to listen to whatever information is stored on the disc," Williams said, his steely eyes fixed on Ward.

Ward shuffled nervously in his chair.

"May as well allow the Defense to listen to the disc now," Judge Henderson suggested. "In all likelihood, after a discovery request, they'll get it anyway."

The Rosen case revisited, I thought, as Puttmen eyed Ward and then turned toward Judge Henderson

"May I confer privately with Mr. Ward for a moment?' he asked.

"Of course," Judge Henderson replied.

Puttmen and Ward left Henderson's chambers while the Judge showered praise on E. McWade Williams, recognizing his career as an accomplished litigator. In about ten minutes, Ward and Puttmen returned. Ward was holding the disc, Puttmen a laptop computer.

"We'll honor Mr. Williams request," Puttmen announced.

Puttmen placed the laptop on Judge Henderson desk, facing it toward Williams, Nino, and me. The Judge circled from his desk and stood behind us. Ward placed the disc into the commuter's loading try. After a few syncopated sounds, we only saw a blank screen. And all we heard was a deafening silence.

"Just as I had expected," Williams whispered to Nino.

Wide-eyed, Judge Henderson shrugged while raising his hands. He then slid into his robes, watching as we all filed out of his chambers. In a minute or so he returned to the courtroom.

"This court is now in session," the deputy bellowed.

Puttmen stood, ready to prosecute the Government's case against me, the preliminary examination and the detention hearing the first step in a long journey I'll travel with Nino Viola and E. McWade Williams. I'm off to a new adventure— the story's end as foggy as the one I just told.

AUTHOR'S NOTE AND ACKNOWLEDGEMENTS.

Readers who have an addiction to politics may remember a 2002 letter which actually acknowledged the Republic of Niger's sale of uranium to a Middle Eastern country—Iraq. They may also recall the burglary of the Niger embassy in Rome during which letterheads and official seals were stolen. Also familiar to a political junkie should be the famous sixteen words that were spoken in the President's 2003 State of the Union Address. Reality ends there. The rest is fiction.

None of the characters in this tale are thinly disguised real people, although I do admit borrowing freely the family names and personalities of many acquaintances and friends, such as Professor Giuseppe Sabino. I hasten to say, however, that the real Professor Sabino who teaches at the Duquesne University School of Law—Joseph Sabino Mistick—would not be so easily intimidated as was the fictional character from the GW law School.

My background is the law—a lawyer, state judge, federal judge, and a professor at Duquesne University. So, I needed help—a lot— in writing this novel, and it came from my granddaughter, Grace, a Bard graduate. I'm certain she'll follow her dream and someday write a series of 'best sellers.' Finally, a huge thanks to my wife, Roselee—the girl I'll dance with into infinity and back again.

Made in the USA
Coppell, TX
28 February 2022

74228411R00332